W9-BJB-474

FANGIRL

A
NOVEL

FANGIRL

RAINBOW ROWELL

MACMILLAN

First published in the US 2013 by St. Martin's Press

This edition published in the UK 2014 by Macmillan Children's Books
a division of Macmillan Publishers Limited
20 New Wharf Road, London N1 9RR
Basingstoke and Oxford
Associated companies throughout the world
www.panmacmillan.com

ISBN 978-1-4472-8060-6

Copyright © Rainbow Rowell 2013

The right of Rainbow Rowell to be identified as the
author of this work has been asserted by her in accordance
with the Copyright, Designs and Patents Act 1988.

All rights reserved. No part of this publication may be
reproduced, stored in or introduced into a retrieval system, or
transmitted, in any form or by any means (electronic, mechanical,
photocopying, recording or otherwise), without the prior written
permission of the publisher. Any person who does any unauthorized
act in relation to this publication may be liable to criminal
prosecution and civil claims for damages.

1 3 5 7 9 8 6 4 2

A CIP catalogue record for this book is available from the British Library.

Designed by Anna Gorovoy
Printed and bound by CPI Group (UK) Ltd, Croydon CR0 4YY

This book is sold subject to the condition that it shall not,
by way of trade or otherwise, be lent, resold, hired out,
or otherwise circulated without the publisher's prior consent
in any form of binding or cover other than that in which
it is published and without a similar condition including this
condition being imposed on the subsequent purchaser.

For Jennifer, who always had an extra lightsaber

FALL SEMESTER, 2011

The Simon Snow Series

From Encyclowikia, the people's encyclopedia

> *This article is about the children's book series. For other uses, see* <u>*Simon Snow (disambiguation)*</u>*.*

Simon Snow is a series of seven fantasy books written by English philologist Gemma T. Leslie. The books tell the story of Simon Snow, an 11-year-old orphan from Lancashire who is recruited to attend the Watford School of Magicks to become a magician. As he grows older, Simon joins a group of magicians – the Mages – who are fighting the Insidious Humdrum, an evil being trying to rid the world of magic.

Since the publication of *Simon Snow and the Mage's Heir* in 2001, the books have been translated into 53 languages and, as of August 2011, have sold more than 380 million copies.

Leslie has been criticized for the violence in the series and for creating a hero who is sometimes selfish and bad tempered. An exorcism scene in the fourth book, *Simon Snow and the Selkies Four,* triggered boycotts among American Christian groups in 2008. But the books are widely considered modern classics, and in 2010, *Time* magazine called Simon "the greatest children's literary character since Huckleberry Finn."

An eighth book, the last in the series, is set to be released May 1, 2012.

Publishing history

Simon Snow and the Mage's Heir, 2001
Simon Snow and the Second Serpent, 2003
Simon Snow and the Third Gate, 2004
Simon Snow and the Selkies Four, 2007
Simon Snow and the Five Blades, 2008
Simon Snow and the Six White Hares, 2009
Simon Snow and the Seventh Oak, 2010
Simon Snow and the Eighth Dance, scheduled to be released May 1, 2012

ONE

There was a boy in her room.

Cath looked up at the number painted on the door, then down at the room assignment in her hand.

Pound Hall, 913.

This was definitely room 913, but maybe it wasn't Pound Hall — all these dormitories looked alike, like public housing towers for the elderly. Maybe Cath should try to catch her dad before he brought up the rest of her boxes.

"You must be Cather," the boy said, grinning and holding out his hand.

"Cath," she said, feeling a panicky jump in her stomach. She ignored his hand. (She was holding a box anyway, what did he expect from her?)

This was a mistake — this had to be a mistake. She knew that Pound was a co-ed dorm. . . . *Is there such a thing as co-ed rooms?*

The boy took the box out of her hands and set it on an empty bed. The bed on the other side of the room was already covered with clothes and boxes.

"Do you have more stuff downstairs?" he asked. "We just finished. I think we're going to get a burger now; do you want to get a burger? Have you been to Pear's yet? Burgers the size of your fist." He picked up her arm. She swallowed. "Make a fist," he said.

Cath did.

"*Bigger* than your fist," the boy said, dropping her hand and picking up the backpack she'd left outside the door. "Do you have more boxes? You've got to have more boxes. Are you hungry?"

He was tall and thin and tan, and he looked like he'd just taken off a stocking cap, dark blond hair flopping in every direction. Cath looked down at her room assignment again. Was this *Reagan*?

"Reagan!" the boy said happily. "Look, your roommate's here."

A girl stepped around Cath in the doorway and glanced back coolly. She had smooth, auburn hair and an unlit cigarette in her mouth. The boy grabbed it and put it in his own mouth. "Reagan, Cather. Cather, Reagan," he said.

"Cath," Cath said.

Reagan nodded and fished in her purse for another cigarette. "I took this side," she said, nodding to the pile of boxes on the right side of the room. "But it doesn't matter. If you've got feng shui issues, feel free to move my shit." She turned to the boy. "Ready?"

He turned to Cath. "Coming?"

Cath shook her head.

When the door shut behind them, she sat on the bare mattress that was apparently hers – feng shui was the least of her issues – and laid her head against the cinder block wall.

She just needed to settle her nerves.

To take the anxiety she felt like black static behind her eyes and an extra heart in her throat, and shove it all back down to her stomach where it belonged – where she could at least tie it into a nice knot and work around it.

Her dad and Wren would be up any minute, and Cath didn't want them to know she was about to melt down. If Cath melted down, her dad would melt down. And if *either* of them melted down, Wren would act like they were doing it on purpose, just to ruin her perfect first day on campus. Her beautiful new adventure.

You're going to thank me for this, Wren kept saying.

The first time she'd said it was back in June.

Cath had already sent in her university housing forms, and of course she'd put Wren down as her roommate — she hadn't thought twice about it. The two of them had shared a room for eighteen years, why stop now?

"We've shared a room for *eighteen years,*" Wren argued. She was sitting at the head of Cath's bed, wearing her infuriating I'm the Mature One face.

"And it's worked out great," Cath said, waving her arm around their bedroom — at the stacks of books and the Simon Snow posters, at the closet where they shoved all their clothes, not even worrying most of the time what belonged to whom.

Cath was sitting at the foot of the bed, trying not to look like the Pathetic One Who Always Cries.

"This is college," Wren persisted. "The whole point of college is meeting new people."

"The whole point of having a twin sister," Cath said, "is not having to worry about this sort of thing. Freaky strangers who steal your tampons and smell like salad dressing and take cell phone photos of you while you sleep . . ."

Wren sighed. "What are you even talking about? Why would anybody smell like salad dressing?"

"Like vinegar," Cath said. "Remember when we went on the freshman tour, and that one girl's room smelled like Italian dressing?"

"No."

"Well, it was gross."

"It's college," Wren said, exasperated, covering her face with her hands. "It's supposed to be an *adventure.*"

"It's already an adventure." Cath crawled up next to her sister and pulled Wren's hands away from her face. "The whole prospect is already terrifying."

"We're supposed to meet new people," Wren repeated.

"I don't need new people."

"That just shows how much you need new people. . . ." Wren squeezed Cath's hands. "Cath, think about it. If we do this together, people will treat us like we're the same person. It'll be four years before anyone can even tell us apart."

"All they have to do is pay attention." Cath touched the scar on Wren's chin, just below her lip. (Sledding accident. They were nine, and Wren was on the front of the sled when it hit the tree. Cath had fallen off the back into the snow.)

"You know I'm right," Wren said.

Cath shook her head. "I don't."

"Cath . . ."

"Please don't make me do this alone."

"You're never alone," Wren said, sighing again. "That's the whole fucking point of having a twin sister."

"This is really nice," their dad said, looking around Pound 913 and setting a laundry basket full of shoes and books on Cath's mattress.

"It's not nice, Dad," Cath said, standing stiffly by the door. "It's like a hospital room, but smaller. And without a TV."

"You've got a great view of campus," he said.

Wren wandered over to the window. "My room faces a parking lot."

"How do you know?" Cath asked.

"Google Earth."

Wren couldn't wait for all this college stuff to start. She and her roommate – *Courtney* – had been talking for weeks. Courtney was from Omaha, too. The two of them had already met and gone shopping for dorm-room stuff together. Cath had tagged along and tried not to pout while they picked out posters and matching desk lamps.

Cath's dad came back from the window and put an arm around her shoulders. "It's gonna be okay," he said.

She nodded. "I know."

"Okay," he said, clapping. "Next stop, Schramm Hall. Second stop, pizza buffet. Third stop, my sad and empty nest."

"No pizza," Wren said. "Sorry, Dad. Courtney and I are going to the freshman barbecue tonight." She shot her eyes at Cath. "Cath should go, too."

"*Yes* pizza," Cath said defiantly.

Her dad smiled. "Your sister's right, Cath. You should go. Meet new people."

"All I'm going to do for the next nine months is meet new people. Today I choose pizza buffet."

Wren rolled her eyes.

"All right," their dad said, patting Cath on the shoulder. "Next stop, Schramm Hall. Ladies?" He opened the door.

Cath didn't move. "You can come back for me after you drop her off," she said, watching her sister. "I want to start unpacking."

Wren didn't argue, just stepped out into the hall. "I'll talk to you tomorrow," she said, not quite turning to look at Cath.

"Sure," Cath said.

It did feel good, unpacking. Putting sheets on the bed and setting her new, ridiculously expensive textbooks out on the shelves over her new desk.

When her dad came back, they walked together to Valentino's. Everyone they saw along the way was about Cath's age. It was creepy.

"Why is everybody blond?" Cath asked. "And why are they all white?"

Her dad laughed. "You're just used to living in the least-white neighborhood in Nebraska."

Their house in South Omaha was in a Mexican neighborhood. Cath's was the only white family on the block.

"Oh, God," she said, "do you think this town has a taco truck?"

"I think I saw a Chipotle—"

She groaned.

"Come on," he said, "you like Chipotle."

"Not the point."

When they got to Valentino's, it was packed with students. A few, like Cath, had come with their parents, but not many. "It's like a science fiction story," she said, "No little kids . . . Nobody over thirty . . . Where are all the old people?"

Her dad held up his slice of pizza. "Soylent Green."

Cath laughed.

"I'm not old, you know." He was tapping the table with the two middle fingers of his left hand. "Forty-one. The other guys my age at work are just starting to have kids."

"That was good thinking," Cath said, "getting us out of the way early. You can start bringing home chicks now – the coast is clear."

"All my chicks . . . ," he said, looking down at his plate. "You guys are the only chicks I'm worried about."

"Ugh. Dad. Weird."

"You know what I mean. What's up with you and your sister? You've never fought like this before. . . ."

"We're not fighting *now*," Cath said, taking a bite of bacon-cheeseburger pizza. "Oh, geez." She spit it out.

"What's wrong, did you get an eyelid?"

"No. Pickle. It's okay. I just wasn't expecting it."

"You *seem* like you're fighting," he said.

Cath shrugged. She and Wren weren't even talking much, let alone fighting. "Wren just wants more . . . independence."

"Sounds reasonable," he said.

Of course it does, Cath thought, *that's Wren's specialty.* But she let it drop. She didn't want her dad to worry about this right now. She could tell by the way he kept tapping the table that he was already wearing thin. Way too many normal-dad hours in a row.

"Tired?" she asked.

He smiled at her, apologetically, and put his hand in his lap. "Big day. Big, hard day – I mean, I knew it would be." He raised an eyebrow. "Both of you, same day. *Whoosh.* I still can't believe you're not coming home with me. . . ."

"Don't get too comfortable. I'm not sure I can stick this out a whole semester." She was only slightly kidding, and he knew it.

"You'll be fine, Cath." He put his hand, his less twitchy hand, over hers and squeezed. "And so will I. You know?"

Cath let herself look in his eyes for a moment. He looked tired – and, yes, twitchy – but he was holding it together.

"I still wish you'd get a dog," she said.

"I'd never remember to feed it."

"Maybe we could train it to feed you."

When Cath got back to her room, her roommate – Reagan – was still gone. Or maybe she was gone again; her boxes looked untouched. Cath finished putting her own clothes away, then opened the box of personal things she'd brought from home.

She took out a photo of herself and Wren, and pinned it to the corkboard behind her desk. It was from graduation. Both of them were wearing red robes and smiling. It was before Wren cut her hair. . . .

Wren hadn't even told Cath she was going to do that. Just came home from work at the end of the summer with a pixie cut. It looked awesome – which probably meant it would look awesome on Cath, too. But Cath could never get that haircut now, even if she could work up the courage to cut off fifteen inches. She couldn't single-white-female her own twin sister.

Next Cath took out a framed photo of their dad, the one that had always sat on their dresser back home. It was an especially handsome photo, taken on his wedding day. He was young and smiling, and wearing a little sunflower on his lapel. Cath set it on the shelf above her desk.

Then she set out a picture from prom, of her and Abel. Cath was wearing a shimmering green dress, and Abel had a matching cummerbund. It was a good picture of Cath, even though her face looked naked and flat without her glasses. And it was a good picture of Abel, even though he looked bored.

He always looked kind of bored.

Cath probably should have texted Abel by now, just to tell him that she'd made it – but she wanted to wait until she felt more breezy and nonchalant. You can't take back texts. If you come off all moody and melancholy in a text, it just sits there in your phone, reminding you of what a drag you are.

At the bottom of the box were Cath's Simon and Baz posters. She laid these out on her bed carefully – a few were originals, drawn or painted just for Cath. She'd have to choose her favorites; there wasn't room for them all on the corkboard, and Cath had already decided not to hang any on the walls, out where God and everybody would notice them.

She picked out three. . . .

Simon raising the Sword of Mages. Baz lounging on a fanged black throne. The two of them walking together through whirling gold leaves, scarves whipping in the wind.

There were a few more things left in the box – a dried corsage, a ribbon Wren had given her that said CLEAN PLATE CLUB, commemorative busts of Simon and Baz that she'd ordered from the Noble Collection. . . .

Cath found a place for everything, then sat in the beat-up wooden desk chair. If she sat right here, with her back to Reagan's bare walls and boxes, it almost felt like home.

There was a boy in Simon's room.

A boy with slick, black hair and cold, grey eyes. He was spinning around, holding a cat high in the air while a girl jumped and clutched at it. "Give it *back*," the girl said. "You'll hurt him."

The boy laughed and held the cat higher – then noticed Simon standing in the doorway and stopped, his face sharpening.

"Hullo," the dark-haired boy said, letting the cat drop to the floor. It landed on all four feet and ran from the room. The girl ran after it.

The boy ignored them, tugging his school jacket neatly into place and smiling with the left side of his mouth. "I know you. You're Simon Snow . . . the Mage's Heir." He held out his hand smugly. "I'm Tyrannus Basilton Pitch. But you can call me Baz – we're going to be roommates."

Simon scowled and ignored the boy's pale hand. "What did you think you were doing with her cat?"

—from chapter 3, *Simon Snow and the Mage's Heir,*
copyright © 2001 by Gemma T. Leslie

TWO

In books, when people wake up in a strange place, they always have that disoriented moment when they don't know where they are.

That had never happened to Cath; she always remembered falling asleep.

But it still felt weird to hear her same-old alarm going off in this brand-new place. The light in the room was strange, too yellow for morning, and the dorm air had a detergenty twang she wasn't sure she'd get used to. Cath picked up her phone and turned off the alarm, remembering that she still hadn't texted Abel. She hadn't even checked her e-mail or her FanFixx account before she went to bed.

"first day," she texted Abel now. *"more later. x, o, etc."*

The bed on the other side of the room was still empty.

Cath could get used to this. Maybe Reagan would spend all her time in her boyfriend's room. Or at his apartment. Her boyfriend looked older – he probably lived off campus with twenty other guys, in some ramshackle house with a couch in the front yard.

Even with the room to herself, Cath didn't feel safe changing in here. Reagan could walk in at any minute, Reagan's boyfriend could walk in at any minute . . . And either one of them could be a cell- phone-camera pervert.

Cath took her clothes to the bathroom and changed in a stall. There was a girl at the sinks, desperately trying to make friendly eye contact. Cath pretended not to notice.

She finished getting ready with plenty of time to eat breakfast but didn't feel up to braving the dining hall; she still didn't know where it was, or how it worked. . . .

In new situations, all the trickiest rules are the ones nobody bothers to explain to you. (And the ones you can't google.) Like, where does the line start? What food can you take? Where are you supposed to stand, then where are you supposed to sit? Where do you go when you're done, why is everyone watching you? . . . *Bah.*

Cath broke open a box of protein bars. She had four more boxes and three giant jars of peanut butter shoved under her bed. If she paced herself, she might not have to face the dining hall until October.

She flipped open her laptop while she chewed on a carob-oat bar and clicked through to her FanFixx account. There were a bunch of new comments on her page, all people wringing their hands because Cath hadn't posted a new chapter of *Carry On* yesterday.

Hey, guys, she typed. *Sorry about yesterday. First day of school, family stuff, etc. Today might not happen either. But I promise you I'll be back in black on Tuesday, and that I have something especially wicked planned. Peace out, Magicath.*

Walking to class, Cath couldn't shake the feeling that she was pretending to be a college student in a coming-of-age movie. The setting was perfect – rolling green lawns, brick buildings, kids everywhere with backpacks. Cath shifted her bag uncomfortably on her back. *Look at me – I'm a stock photo of a college student.*

She made it to American History ten minutes early, which still wasn't early enough to get a desk at the back of the class. Everybody in the room looked awkward and nervous, like they'd spent way too much time deciding what to wear.

(*Start as you mean to go on,* Cath had thought when she laid out her clothes last night. Jeans. Simon T-shirt. Green cardigan.)

The boy sitting in the desk next to her was wearing earbuds and self-consciously bobbing his head. The girl on Cath's other side kept flipping her hair from one shoulder to the other.

Cath closed her eyes. She could feel their desks creaking. She could smell their deodorant. Just knowing they were there made her feel tight and cornered.

If Cath had slightly less pride, she could have taken this class with her sister – she and Wren both needed the history credits. Maybe she should be taking classes with Wren while they still had a few in common; they weren't interested in any of the same subjects. Wren wanted to study marketing – and maybe get a job in advertising like their dad.

Cath couldn't imagine having any sort of job or *career.* She'd majored in English, hoping that meant she could spend the next four years reading and writing. And maybe the next four years after that.

Anyway, she'd already tested out of Freshman Comp, and when she met with her adviser in the spring, Cath convinced him she could handle Intro to Fiction-Writing, a junior-level course. It was the only class – maybe the only thing about college – Cath was looking forward to. The professor who taught it was an actual novelist. Cath had read all three of her books (about decline and desolation in rural America) over the summer.

"Why are you reading that?" Wren had asked when she noticed.

"What?"

"Something without a dragon or an elf on the cover."

"I'm branching out."

"Shh," Wren said, covering the ears on the movie poster above her bed. "Baz will hear you."

"Baz is secure in our relationship," Cath had said, smiling despite herself.

Thinking about Wren now made Cath reach for her phone.

Wren had probably gone out last night.

It had sounded like the whole campus was up partying. Cath felt under siege in her empty dorm room. Shouting. Laughing. Music. All of it coming from every direction. Wren wouldn't have been able to resist the noise.

Cath dug her phone out of her backpack.

"you up?" Send.

A few seconds later, her phone chimed. *"isn't that my line?"*

"too tired to write last night," Cath typed, *"went to bed at 10."*

Chime. *"neglecting your fans already . . ."*

Cath smiled. *"always so jealous of my fans . . ."*

"have a good day"

"yeah - you too"

A middle-aged Indian man in a reassuring tweed jacket walked into the lecture hall. Cath turned down her phone and slid it into her bag.

When she got back to her dorm, she was starving. At this rate, her protein bars wouldn't last a week. . . .

There was a boy sitting outside her room. The same one. Reagan's boyfriend? Reagan's cigarette buddy?

"Cather!" he said with a smile. He started to stand up as soon as he saw her – which was more of a production than it should have been; his legs and arms were too long for his body.

"It's Cath," she said.

"Are you sure?" He ran a hand through his hair. Like he was confirming that it was still messy. "Because I really like Cather."

"I'm sure," she said flatly. "I've had a lot of time to think about it."

He stood there, waiting for her to open the door.

"Is Reagan here?" Cath asked.

"If Reagan were here" – he smiled – "I'd already be inside."

Cath pinched her key but didn't open the door. She wasn't up for this. She was already overdosing on *new* and *other* today. Right now she just wanted to curl up on her strange, squeaky bed and inhale three protein bars. She looked over the boy's shoulder. "When is she getting here?"

He shrugged.

Cath's stomach clenched. "Well, I can't just let you in," she blurted.

"Why not?"

"I don't even know you."

"Are you kidding?" He laughed. "We met yesterday. I was *in the room* when you met me."

"Yeah, but I don't know you. I don't even know Reagan."

"Are you going to make her wait outside, too?"

"Look . . ." Cath said. "I can't just let strange guys into my room. I don't even know your name. This whole situation is too rapey."

"Rapey?"

"You understand," she said, "right?"

He dropped an eyebrow and shook his head, still smiling. "Not really. But now I don't want to come in with you. The word 'rapey' makes me uncomfortable."

"Me, too," she said gratefully.

He leaned against the wall and slid back onto the floor, looking up at her. Then he held up his hand. "I'm Levi, by the way."

Cath frowned and took his hand lightly, still holding her keys. "Okay," she said, then opened the door and closed it as quickly as possible behind her.

She grabbed her laptop and her protein bars, and crawled into the corner of her bed.

Cath was trying to pace her side of the room, but there wasn't enough floor. It already felt like a prison in here, especially now that Reagan's boyfriend, Levi, was standing guard — or sitting guard, whatever — out in the hall. Cath would feel better if she could just talk to somebody. She wondered if it was too soon to call Wren. . . .

She called her dad instead. And left a voice mail.

She texted Abel. *"hey. one down. what up?"*

She opened her sociology book. Then opened her laptop. Then got up to open a window. It was warm out. People were chasing each other with Nerf guns outside a fraternity house across the street. Pi-Kappa-Weird-Looking O.

Cath pulled out her phone and dialed.

"Hey," Wren answered, "how was your first day?"

"Fine. How was yours?"

"Good," Wren said. Wren *always* managed to sound breezy and nonchalant. "I mean, nerve-racking, I guess. I went to the wrong building for Statistics."

"That sucks."

The door opened, and Reagan and Levi walked in. Reagan gave Cath an odd look, but Levi just smiled.

"Yeah," Wren said. "It only made me a few minutes late, but I still felt so stupid — Hey, Courtney and I are on our way to dinner, can I call you back? Or do you just want to meet us for lunch tomorrow? I think we're going to start meeting at Selleck Hall at noon. Do you know where that is?"

"I'll find it," Cath said.

"Okay, cool. See you then."

"Cool," Cath said, pressing End and putting her phone in her pocket.

Levi had already unfurled himself across Reagan's bed.

"Make yourself useful," Reagan said, throwing a crumpled-up sheet at him. "Hey," she said to Cath.

"Hey," Cath said. She stood there for a minute, waiting for some sort of conversation to happen, but Reagan didn't seem interested. She was going through all her boxes, like she was looking for something.

"How was your first day?" Levi asked.

It took a second for Cath to realize he was talking to her. "Fine," she said.

"You're a freshman, right?" He was making Reagan's bed. Cath wondered if he was planning to stay the night – that would *not* be on. At all.

He was still looking at her, smiling at her, so she nodded.

"Did you find all your classes?"

"Yeah . . ."

"Are you meeting people?"

Yeah, she thought, *you people.*

"Not intentionally," she said.

She heard Reagan snort.

"Where are your pillowcases?" Levi asked the closet.

"Boxes," Reagan said.

He started emptying a box, setting things on Reagan's desk as if he knew where they went. His head hung forward like it was only loosely connected to his neck and shoulders. Like he was one of those action figures that's held together inside by worn-out rubber bands. Levi looked a little wild. He and Reagan both did. *People tend to pair off that way,* Cath thought, *in matched sets.*

"So, what are you studying?" he asked Cath.

"English," she said, then waited too long to say, "What are you studying?"

He seemed delighted to be asked the question. Or any question. "Range management."

Cath didn't know what that meant, but she didn't want to ask.

"Please don't start talking about range management," Reagan groaned. "Let's just make that a rule, for the rest of the year. No talking about range management in my room."

"It's Cather's room, too," Levi said.

"Cath," Reagan corrected him.

"What about when you're not here?" he asked Reagan. "Can we talk about range management when you're not actually in the room?"

"When I'm not actually in the room . . . ," she said, "I think you're going to be waiting out in the hall."

Cath smiled at the back of Reagan's head. Then she saw Levi watching her and stopped.

Everyone in the classroom looked like *this* was what they'd been waiting for all week. It was like they were all waiting for a concert to start. Or a midnight movie premiere.

When Professor Piper walked in, a few minutes late, the first thing Cath noticed was that she was smaller than she looked in the photos on her book jackets.

Maybe that was stupid. They were just head shots, after all. But Professor Piper really filled them up – with her high cheekbones; her wide, watered-down blue eyes; and a spectacular head of long brown hair.

In person, the professor's hair was just as spectacular, but streaked with gray and a little bushier than in the pictures. She was so small, she had to do a little hop to sit on top of her desk.

"So," she said instead of "hello." "Welcome to Fiction-Writing. I recognize a few of you—" She smiled around the room at people who weren't Cath.

Cath was clearly the only freshman in the room. She was just starting to figure out what marked the freshmen. . . . The too-new backpacks. Makeup on the girls. Jokey Hot Topic T-shirts on the boys.

Everything on Cath, from her new red Vans to the dark purple eyeglasses she'd picked out at Target. All the upperclassmen wore heavy black Ray-Ban frames. All the professors, too. If Cath got a pair of black Ray-Bans, she could probably order a gin and tonic around here without getting carded.

"Well," Professor Piper said. "I'm glad you're all here." Her voice was warm and breathy – you could say "she purred" without reaching too far – and she talked just softly enough that everyone had to sit really still to hear her.

"We have a lot to do this semester," she said, "so let's not waste another minute of it. Let's dive right in." She leaned forward on the desk, holding on to the lip. "Are you ready? Will you dive with me?"

Most people nodded. Cath looked down at her notebook.

"Okay. Let's start with a question that doesn't really have an answer. . . . Why do we write fiction?"

One of the older students, a guy, decided he was game. "To express ourselves," he offered.

"Sure," Professor Piper said. "Is that why you write?"

The guy nodded.

"Okay . . . why else?"

"Because we like the sound of our own voices," a girl said. She had hair like Wren's, but maybe even cooler. She looked like Mia Farrow in *Rosemary's Baby* (wearing a pair of Ray-Bans).

"Yes," Professor Piper laughed. It was a fairy laugh, Cath thought. "That's why I write, definitely. That's why I *teach*." They all laughed with her. "Why else?"

Why do I write? Cath tried to come up with a profound answer – knowing she wouldn't speak up, even if she did.

"To explore new worlds," someone said.

"To explore old ones," someone else said. Professor Piper was nodding.

To be somewhere else, Cath thought.

"So . . . ," Professor Piper purred. "Maybe to make sense of ourselves?"

"To set ourselves free," a girl said.

To get free of ourselves.

"To show people what it's like inside our heads," said a boy in tight red jeans.

"Assuming they want to know," Professor Piper added. Everyone laughed.

"To make people laugh."

"To get attention."

"Because it's all we know how to do."

"Speak for yourself," the professor said. "I play the piano. But keep going – I love this. I love it."

"To *stop* hearing the voices in our head," said the boy in front of Cath. He had short dark hair that came to a dusky point at the back of his neck.

To stop, Cath thought.

To stop being anything or anywhere at all.

"To leave our mark," Mia Farrow said. "To create something that will outlive us."

The boy in front of Cath spoke up again: "Asexual reproduction."

Cath imagined herself at her laptop. She tried to put into words how it felt, what happened when it was good, when it was working, when the words were coming out of her before she knew what they were, bubbling up from her chest, like rhyming, like rapping, *like jump-roping,* she thought, jumping just before the rope hits your ankles.

"To share something true," another girl said. Another pair of Ray-Bans.

Cath shook her head.

"Why do we write fiction?" Professor Piper asked.

Cath looked down at her notebook.

To disappear.

He was so focused – and frustrated – he didn't even see the girl with the red hair sit down at his table. She had pigtails and old-fashioned pointy spectacles, the kind you'd wear to a fancy dress party if you were going as a witch.

"You're going to tire yourself out," the girl said.

"I'm just trying to do this right," Simon grunted, tapping the two-pence coin again with his wand and furrowing his brow painfully. Nothing happened.

"Here," she said, crisply waving her hand over the coin.

She didn't have a wand, but she wore a large purple ring. There was yarn wound round it to keep it on her finger. *"Fly away home."*

With a shiver, the coin grew six legs and a thorax and started to scuttle away. The girl swept it gently off the desk into a jar.

"How did you do that?" Simon asked. She was a first year, too, just like him; he could tell by the green shield on the front of her sweater.

"You don't *do* magic," she said, trying to smile modestly and mostly succeeding. "You *are* magic."

Simon stared at the 2p ladybird.

"I'm Penelope Bunce," the girl said, holding out her hand.

"I'm Simon Snow," he said, taking it.

"I know," Penelope said, and smiled.

—from chapter 8, *Simon Snow and the Mage's Heir,*
copyright © 2001 by Gemma T. Leslie

THREE

It was impossible to write like this.

First of all, their dorm room was way too small. A tiny little rectangle, just wide enough on each side of the door for their beds — when the door opened, it actually hit the end of Cath's mattress — and just deep enough to squeeze in a desk on each side between the beds and the windows. If either of them had brought a couch, it would take up all the available space in the middle of the room.

Neither of them had brought a couch. Or a TV. Or any cute Target lamps.

Reagan didn't seem to have brought anything personal, besides her clothes and a completely illegal toaster — and besides Levi, who was lying on her bed with his eyes closed, listening to music while Reagan banged at her computer. (A crappy PC, just like Cath's.)

Cath was used to sharing a room; she'd always shared a room with Wren. But their room at home was almost three times as big as this one. And Wren didn't take up nearly as much space as Reagan did. Figurative space. Head space. Wren didn't feel like company.

Cath still wasn't sure what to make of Reagan. . . .

On the one hand, Reagan didn't seem interested in staying up all night, braiding each other's hair, and becoming best friends forever. That was a relief.

On the other hand, Reagan didn't seem interested in Cath *at all*.

Actually, that was a bit of a relief, too – Reagan was scary.

She did everything so forcefully. She swung their door open; she slammed it shut. She was bigger than Cath, a little taller and a lot more buxom (seriously, *buxom*). She just *seemed* bigger. On the inside, too.

When Reagan was in the room, Cath tried to stay out of her way; she tried not to make eye contact. Reagan pretended Cath wasn't there, so Cath pretended that, too. Normally this seemed to work out for both of them.

But right at the moment, pretending not to exist was making it really hard for Cath to write.

She was working on a tricky scene – Simon and Baz arguing about whether vampires could ever truly be considered good and also whether the two of them should go to the graduation ball together. It was all supposed to be very funny and romantic and thoughtful, which were usually Cath's specialties. (She was pretty good with treachery, too. And talking dragons.)

But she couldn't get past, "Simon swept his honey brown hair out of his eyes and sighed." She couldn't even get Baz to *move*. She couldn't stop thinking about Reagan and Levi sitting behind her. Her brain was stuck on INTRUDER ALERT!

Plus she was starving. As soon as Reagan and Levi left the room for dinner, Cath was going to eat an entire jar of peanut butter. *If* they ever left for dinner – Reagan kept banging on like she was going to type right through the desk, and Levi kept *not leaving,* and Cath's stomach was starting to growl.

She grabbed a protein bar and walked out of the room, thinking she'd just take a quick walk down the hall to clear her head.

But the hallway was practically a meet-and-greet. Every door was propped open but theirs. Girls were milling around, talking and laughing. The whole floor smelled like burnt microwave popcorn. Cath slipped into the bathroom and sat in one of the stalls, unwrapping her protein bar and letting nervous tears dribble down her cheeks.

God, she thought. *God. Okay. This isn't that bad. There's actually nothing wrong, actually. What's wrong, Cath? Nothing.*

She felt tight everywhere. Snapping. And her stomach was on fire.

She took out her phone and wondered what Wren was doing. Probably choreographing dance sequences to Lady Gaga songs. Probably trying on her roommate's sweaters. Probably *not* sitting on a toilet, eating an almond-flaxseed bar.

Cath could call Abel . . . but she knew he was leaving for Missouri Tech tomorrow morning. His family was throwing him a huge party tonight with homemade tamales and his grandmother's coconut *yoyos* – which were so special, they didn't even sell them in the family bakery. Abel worked in the *panadería,* and his family lived above it. His hair always smelled like cinnamon and yeast. . . . Jesus, Cath was hungry.

She pushed her protein-bar wrapper into the feminine-hygiene box and rinsed off her face before she went back to her room.

Reagan and Levi were walking out, thank God. And *finally.*

"See ya," Reagan said.

"Rock on." Levi smiled.

Cath felt like collapsing when the door closed behind them.

She grabbed another protein bar, flopped onto the old wooden captain's chair – she was starting to like this chair – and opened a drawer to prop up her foot.

Simon swept his honey brown hair out of his eyes and sighed. "Just because I can't think of any heroic vampires doesn't mean they don't exist."

Baz stopped trying to levitate his steamer trunk and gave Simon a flash of gleaming fang. "Good guys wear white," Baz said. "Have you ever tried to get blood out of a white cape?"

Selleck Hall was a dormitory right in the middle of campus. You could eat there even if you didn't live there. Cath usually waited in the lobby for Wren and Courtney, so she wouldn't have to walk into the cafeteria alone.

"So what's your roommate like?" Courtney asked as they moved through the salad bar line. She asked it like she and Cath were old friends – like Cath had any idea what *Courtney* was like, outside of her taste for cottage cheese with peaches.

The salad bar at Selleck was completely wack. Cottage cheese with peaches, canned pears with shredded cheddar. "What is up with this?" Cath asked, lifting a scoop of cold kidney and green bean salad.

"Maybe it's another Western Nebraska thing," Wren said. "There are guys in our dorm who wear cowboy hats, like, all the time, even when they're just walking down the hall."

"I'm gonna get a table," Courtney said.

"Hey" – Cath watched Wren pile vegetables on her plate – "did we ever write any fic with Simon and Baz dancing?"

"I don't remember," Wren said. "Why? Are you writing a dance scene?"

"Waltzing. Up on the ramparts."

"Romantic." Wren looked around the room for Courtney.

"I'm worried that I'm making Simon too fluffy."

"Simon *is* fluffy."

"I wish you were reading it," Cath said, following her to the table.

"Isn't every ninth-grader in North America already reading it?" Wren sat down next to Courtney.

"And Japan," Cath said, sitting. "I'm weirdly huge in Japan."

Courtney leaned toward Cath, swooping in, like she was in on some big secret. "*Cath*, Wren told me that you write Simon Snow stories. That's so cool. I'm a *huge* Simon Snow fan.

I read all the books when I was a kid."

Cath unwrapped her sandwich skeptically. "They're not over," she said.

Courtney took a bite of her cottage cheese, not catching the correction.

"I mean," Cath said, "the books aren't *over*. Book eight doesn't come out until next year. . . ."

"Tell us about your roommate," Wren said, smiling flatly at Cath.

"There's nothing to tell."

"Then make something up."

Wren was irritated. Which irritated Cath. But then Cath thought about how glad she was to be eating food that required silverware and talking to someone who wasn't a stranger – and decided to make an effort with Wren's shiny new roommate.

"Her name is Reagan. And she has reddish brown hair. . . . And she smokes."

Courtney wrinkled her nose. "In your room?"

"She hasn't really been in the room much."

Wren looked suspicious. "You haven't talked?"

"We've said hello," Cath said. "I've talked to her boyfriend a little."

"What's her boyfriend like?" Wren asked.

"I don't know. Tall?"

"Well, it's only been a few days. I'm sure you'll get to know her." Then Wren changed the subject to something that happened at some party she and Courtney had gone to. They'd only been living together two weeks, and already they had a slew of inside jokes that went right over Cath's head.

Cath ate her turkey sandwich and two servings of french fries, and shoved a second sandwich into her bag when Wren wasn't paying attention.

Reagan finally stayed in their room that night. (Levi did not, thank God.) She went to bed while Cath was still typing.

"Is the light bothering you?" Cath asked, pointing at the lamp built into her desk. "I could turn it off."

"It's fine," Reagan said.

Cath put in earbuds so that she wouldn't hear Reagan's falling-asleep noises. Breathing. Sheets brushing. Bed creaking.

How can she just fall asleep like that with a stranger in the room? Cath wondered. Cath left the earbuds in when she finally crawled into her own bed and pulled the comforter up high over her head.

"You still haven't talked to her?" Wren asked at lunch the next week.

"We talk," Cath said. "She says, 'Would you mind closing the window?' And I say, 'That's fine.' Also, 'Hey.' We exchange 'heys' daily. Sometimes *twice* daily."

"It's getting weird," Wren said.

Cath poked at her mashed potatoes. "I'm getting used to it."

"It's still weird."

"Really?" Cath asked. "You're *really* going to start talking about how I got stuck with a weird roommate?"

Wren sighed. "What about her boyfriend?"

"Haven't seen him for a few days."

"What are you doing this weekend?"

"Homework, I guess. Writing Simon."

"Courtney and I are going to a party tonight."

"Where?"

"The Triangle House!" Courtney said. She said it the same way you'd say "the Playboy Mansion!" if you were a total D-bag.

"What's a Triangle House?" Cath asked.

"It's an engineering fraternity," Wren said.

"So they, like, get drunk and build bridges?"

"They get drunk and *design* bridges. Want to come?"

"Nah." Cath took a bite of roast beef and potatoes; it was always Sunday-night dinner in the Selleck dining room. "Drunk nerds. Not my thing."

"You like nerds."

"Not nerds who join fraternities," Cath said. "That's a whole subclass of nerds that I'm not interested in."

"Did you make Abel sign a sobriety pledge before he left for Missouri?"

"Is Abel your boyfriend?" Courtney asked. "Is he cute?"

Cath ignored her. "Abel isn't going to turn into a drunk. He can't even tolerate caffeine."

"That right there is some faulty logic."

"You know I don't like parties, Wren."

"And you know what Dad says — you have to try something before you can say you don't like it."

"Seriously? You're using Dad to get me to a frat party? I *have* tried parties. There was that one at Jesse's, with the tequila—"

"Did you try the tequila?"

"No, but you did, and I helped clean it up when you puked."

Wren smiled wistfully and smoothed her long bangs across her forehead. "Drinking tequila is more about the journey than the destination. . . ."

"You'll call me," Cath said, "right?"

"If I puke?"

"If you need help."

"I won't need help."

"But you'll call me?"

"God, Cath. Yes. Relax, okay?"

"But, sir," Simon pushed, "do I have to be his roommate *every* year, every year until we leave Watford?"

The Mage smiled indulgently and ruffled Simon's caramel brown hair. "Being matched with your roommate is a sacred tradition at Watford." His voice was gentle but firm. "The Crucible cast you together. You're to watch out for each other, to know each other as well as brothers."

"Yeah, but, sir . . ." Simon shuffled in his chair. "The Crucible must have made a mistake. My roommate's a complete git. He might even be evil. Last week, someone spelled my laptop closed, and I *know* it was him. He practically cackled."

The Mage gave his beard a few solemn strokes. It was short and pointed and just covered his chin.

"The Crucible cast you together, Simon. You're meant to watch out for him."

—from chapter 3, *Simon Snow and the Second Serpent,*
copyright © 2003 by Gemma T. Leslie

FOUR

The squirrels on campus were beyond domestic; they were practically domestically abusive. If you were eating anything at all, they'd come right up to you and *chit-chit-chit* in your space.

"Take it," Cath said, tossing a chunk of strawberry-soy bar to the fat red squirrel at her feet. She took a photo of it with her phone and sent it to Abel. *"bully squirrel,"* she typed.

Abel had sent her photos of his room – his *suite* – at MoTech, and of him standing with all five of his nerdy *Big Bang Theory* roommates. Cath tried to imagine asking Reagan to pose for a photo and laughed a little out loud. The squirrel froze but didn't run away.

On Wednesdays and Fridays, Cath had forty-five minutes between Biology and Fiction-Writing, and lately she'd been killing it right here, sitting in a shadowy patch of grass on the slow side of the English building. Nobody to deal with here. Nobody but the squirrels.

She checked her text messages, even though her phone hadn't chimed.

She and Abel hadn't actually talked since Cath left for school three weeks ago, but he *did* text her. And he e-mailed every once in a while. He said he was fine and that the competition at Missouri was already intense. *"Everybody here was the smartest kid in their graduating class."*

Cath had resisted the urge to reply, *"Except for you, right?"*

Just because Abel got a perfect score on the math section of the SATs didn't mean he was the smartest kid in their class. He was crap in American History, and he'd limped through Spanish. Through *Spanish*, for Christ's sake.

He'd already told Cath that he wasn't coming back to Omaha until Thanksgiving, and she hadn't tried to convince him to come home any sooner.

She didn't really miss him yet.

Wren would say that was because Abel wasn't really Cath's boyfriend. It was one of their recurring conversations:

"He's a perfectly good boyfriend," Cath would say.

"He's an end table," Wren would answer.

"He's always there for me."

". . . to set magazines on."

"Would you rather I dated someone like Jesse? So we can *both* stay up crying every weekend?"

"I would rather you dated someone you'd actually like to kiss."

"I've kissed Abel."

"Oh, Cath, stop. You're making my brain throw up."

"We've been dating for *three years*. He's my *boyfriend*."

"You have stronger feelings for Baz and Simon."

"Duh, they're Baz and Simon, like that's even fair – I like Abel. He's steady."

"You just *keep* describing an end table. . . ."

Wren had started going out with boys in the eighth grade (two years before Cath was even thinking about it). And until Jesse Sandoz, Wren hadn't stayed with the same guy for more than a few months. She kept Jesse around so long because she was never really sure that he liked her – at least that was Cath's theory.

Wren usually lost interest in a guy as soon as she'd won him over. The *conversion* was her favorite part. "That moment," she told Cath, "when you realize that a guy's looking at you differently – that you're taking up more space in his field of vision. That moment when you know he can't see past you anymore."

Cath had liked that last line so much, she gave it to Baz a few weeks later. Wren was annoyed when she read it.

Anyway, Jesse never really converted. He never had eyes *only* for Wren, not even after they had sex last fall. It threw off Wren's game.

Cath was relieved when Jesse got a football scholarship to Iowa State. He didn't have the attention span for a long-distance relationship, and there were at least ten thousand fresh guys at the University of Nebraska for Wren to convert.

Cath tossed another hunk of protein bar to the squirrel, but someone in a pair of periwinkle wingtips took a step too close to them, and the squirrel startled and lumbered away. *Fat campus squirrels,* Cath thought. *They lumber.*

The wingtips took another step toward her, then stopped. Cath looked up. There was a guy standing in front of her. From where she was sitting – and where he was standing, with the sun behind his head – he seemed eight feet tall. She squinted up but didn't recognize him.

"Cath," he said, "right?"

She recognized his voice; it was the boy with the dark hair who sat in front of her in Fiction-Writing – Nick.

"Right," she said.

"Did you finish your writing exercise?"

Professor Piper had asked them to write a hundred words from the perspective of an inanimate object. Cath nodded, still squinting up at him.

"Oh, sorry," Nick said, stepping out of the sun and sitting on the grass next to her. He dropped his bag between his knees. "So what'd you write about?"

"A lock," she said. "You?"

"Ballpoint pen." He grimaced. "I'm worried that everyone is going to do a pen."

"Don't be," she said. "A pen is a terrible idea."

Nick laughed, and Cath looked down at the grass.

"So," he asked, "do you think she'll make us read them out loud?"

Cath's head snapped up. "*No.* Why would she do that?"

"They always do that," he said, like it was something Cath should already know. She wasn't used to seeing Nick from the front; he had a boyish face with hooded blue eyes and blocky, black eyebrows that almost met in the middle. He looked like someone with a steerage ticket on the *Titanic*. Somebody who'd be standing in line at Ellis Island. Undiluted and old-blooded. Also, cute.

"But there wouldn't be time in class for all of us to read," she said.

"We'll probably break up into groups first," he said, again like she should know this.

"Oh . . . I'm kind of new around here."

"Are you a freshman?"

She nodded and rolled her eyes.

"How did a freshman get into Professor Piper's three-hundred-level class?"

"I asked."

Nick raised his furry eyebrows and pushed out his bottom lip, impressed. "Do you really think a pen is a terrible idea?"

"I'm not sure what you want me to say now," Cath answered.

"Do you have an eating disorder?" Reagan asked.

Cath was sitting on her bed, studying.

Reagan was holding on to her closet door, hopping, trying to pull on a black heeled boot. She was probably on her way to work – Reagan was always on her way somewhere. She treated their room like a way station, a place she stopped between class and the library, between her job at the Student Union and her job at the Olive Garden. A place to change clothes, dump books, and pick up Levi.

Sometimes there were other guys, too. Already in the last month, there'd been a Nathan and a Kyle. But none of them seemed to be a permanent part of Reagan's solar system like Levi was.

Which made Levi part of Cath's solar system, too. He'd seen her on campus today and walked with her all the way to Oldfather Hall, talking about some mittens he'd bought outside the Student Union. "Hand-knit. In Ecuador. Have you ever seen an alpaca, Cather? They're like the world's most adorable llamas. Like, imagine the cutest llama that you can, and then just keep going. And their wool – it's not really wool, it's fiber, and it's hypoallergenic. . . ."

Reagan was staring at Cath now, frowning. She was wearing tight black jeans and a black top. Maybe she was going out, not to work.

"Your trash can is full of energy bar wrappers," Reagan said.

"You were looking through my trash?" Cath felt a rush of anger.

"Levi was looking for a place to spit out his gum. . . . So? Do you have an eating disorder?"

"No," Cath said, pretty sure it was exactly what she'd say if she *did* have an eating disorder.

"Then why don't you eat real food?"

"I do." Cath clenched her fists. Her skin felt drawn and tight. "Just. Not here."

"Are you one of those freaky eaters?"

"No. I —" Cath looked up at the ceiling, deciding that this was one of those times when the truth would be simpler than a lie. "— I don't know where the dining hall is."

"You've been living here more than a month."

"I know."

"And you haven't found the dining hall?"

"I haven't actually looked."

"Why haven't you asked someone? You could have asked me."

Cath rolled her eyes and looked at Reagan. "Do you really want me asking you stupid questions?"

"If they're about food, water, air, or shelter — yes. Jesus, Cath, I'm your roommate."

"Okay," Cath said, turning back to her book, "so noted."

"So, do you want me to show you where the dining hall is?"

"No, that's okay."

"You can't keep living off diet bars. You're running out."

"I'm not running out. . . ."

Reagan sighed. "Levi *might* have eaten a few."

"You're letting your boyfriend steal my protein bars?" Cath leaned over her bed to check on her stash — all the boxes were open.

"He said he was doing you a favor," Reagan said. "Forcing the issue. And he's not my boyfriend. Exactly."

"This is a violation," Cath said angrily, forgetting for a moment that Reagan was probably the most intimidating person she'd ever met.

"Get your shoes," Reagan said. "I'm showing you where the dining hall is."

"No." Cath could already feel the anxiety starting to tear her stomach into nervous little pieces. "It's not just that. . . . I don't like new places. New situations. There'll be all those people, and I won't know where to sit — I don't want to go."

Reagan sat at the end of her own bed, folding her arms. "Have you been going to class?"

"Of course."

"How?"

"Class is different," Cath said. "There's something to focus on. It's still bad, but it's tolerable."

"Are you on drugs?"

"*No.*"

"Maybe you should be. . . ."

Cath pushed her fists into her bed. "This isn't any of your business. You don't even know me."

"*This,*" Reagan said. "This is why I didn't want a freshman roommate."

"Why do you even care? Am I bothering you?"

"We're going to dinner right now."

"No. We're not."

"Get your student ID."

"I'm not going to dinner with you. You don't even like me."

"I like you fine," Reagan said.

"This is ridiculous."

"Jesus Christ, aren't you hungry?"

Cath was squeezing her fists so hard, her knuckles were going white.

She thought about chicken-fried steak. And scalloped potatoes. And strawberry-rhubarb pie. And wondered whether the Pound dining hall had an ice cream machine like Selleck did.

And she thought about winning. About how she was letting *this* win, whatever this was – the crazy inside of her. Cath, zero. Crazy, one million.

She leaned over, compressing the knot in her stomach.

Then she stood up with as much dignity as she could scavenge and put on her Vans.

"I *have* been eating real food . . . ," she muttered. "I eat lunch at Selleck with my sister."

Reagan opened the door. "Then why don't you eat here?"

"Because I waited too long. I built up a block about it. It's hard to explain. . . ."

"Seriously, why aren't you on drugs?"

Cath walked past her out of the room. "Are you a licensed psychiatrist? Or do you just play one on TV?"

"I'm on drugs," Reagan said. "They're a beautiful thing."

There was no awkward moment in the dining hall, no standing at the doorway with a tray, trying to decide on the most innocuous place to sit.

Reagan sat at the first half-empty table she came across. She didn't even nod to the other people sitting there.

"Aren't you going to be late for work?" Cath asked.

"I'm going out. But I was gonna eat dinner here first anyway. We pay for all these meals; may as well eat them."

Cath's tray had a plate of baked macaroni and two bowls of Brussels sprouts. She was ravenous.

Reagan took a big bite of pasta salad. Her long hair fell over her shoulders. It was a dozen shades of red and gold, none of them quite natural. "Do you really think that I don't like you?" she asked with her mouth full.

Cath swallowed. She and Reagan had never had a conversation before today, never mind a serious one. "Um . . . I get the feeling that you don't want a roommate."

"I *don't* want a roommate." Reagan frowned. She frowned as much as Levi smiled. "But that has nothing to do with you."

"Why live in the dorms, then? You're not a freshman, right? I didn't think upperclassmen lived on campus."

"I have to," Reagan said. "It's part of my scholarship. I was supposed to get my own room this year — I was on the list — but all the residence halls are over capacity."

"Sorry," Cath said.

"It's not your fault."

"I didn't want a roommate either," Cath said. "I mean . . . I thought I was going to live with my sister."

"You have a sister who goes here?"

"Twin."

"Ew. Weird."

"Why is that weird?" Cath asked.

"It just is. It's creepy. Like having a doppelgänger. Are you identical?"

"Technically."

"Ew." Reagan shuddered melodramatically.

"It's not *creepy*," Cath said. "What is wrong with you?"

Reagan grimaced and shuddered again. "So why aren't you living with your sister?"

"She wanted to meet new people," Cath said.

"You make it sound like she broke up with you."

Cath speared another Brussels sprout. "She lives in Schramm," she said to her tray. When she looked up, Reagan was scowling at her.

"You're making me feel sorry for you again," Reagan said.

Cath turned her fork on Reagan. "Don't feel sorry for me. I don't want you to feel sorry for me."

"I can't help it," Reagan said. "You're really pathetic."

"I am not."

"You are. You don't have any friends, your sister dumped you, you're a freaky eater . . . And you've got some weird thing about Simon Snow."

"I object to every single thing you just said."

Reagan chewed. And frowned. She was wearing dark red lipstick.

"I have lots of friends," Cath said.

"I never see them."

"I just got here. Most of my friends went to other schools. Or they're online."

"Internet friends don't count."

"Why not?"

Reagan shrugged disdainfully.

"And I don't have a weird thing with Simon Snow," Cath said. "I'm just really active in the fandom."

"What the fuck is 'the fandom'?"

"You wouldn't understand," Cath sighed, wishing she hadn't used that word, knowing that if she tried to explain herself any further, it would just make it worse. Reagan wouldn't believe – or understand – that Cath wasn't just a Simon fan. She was one of *the* fans. A first-name-only fan with fans of her own.

If she told Reagan that her Simon fics regularly got twenty thousand hits . . . Reagan would just laugh at her.

Plus, saying all that out loud would make Cath feel like a complete asshole.

"You've got Simon Snow heads on your desk," Reagan said.

"Those are commemorative busts."

"I feel sorry for you, and I'm going to be your friend."

"I don't want to be your friend," Cath said as sternly as she could. "I *like* that we're not friends."

"Me, too," Reagan said. "I'm sorry you ruined it by being so pathetic."

Welcome to FanFixx.net – where the story never ends.

We are a volunteer-run archive and forum, accepting quality fiction from all fandoms. Volunteer or make a donation <u>here</u>. Set up a FanFixx.net author profile <u>here</u>. You must be 13 years old or older to submit or comment at FanFixx.net.

—FanFixx.net homepage welcome message,

retrieved July 1, 2011

FIVE

"Please don't make me sit in the hall," Levi said.

Cath stepped over his legs to get to her door. "I have to study."

"Reagan's running late, and I've already been sitting here half an hour." His voice dropped to a whisper: "Your neighbor with the pink Ugg boots keeps coming out to talk to me. Have mercy."

Cath frowned at him.

"I won't bother you," he said. "I'll just wait quietly for Reagan."

She rolled her eyes and walked in, leaving the door open behind her.

"I can see why you and Reagan hit it off." He got up to follow her. "You can both be extremely brusque sometimes."

"We didn't hit it off."

"That's not what I heard. . . . Hey, now that you're eating in the dining hall, can I eat your protein bars?"

"You were already eating my protein bars," Cath said indignantly, sitting at her desk and opening her laptop.

"I felt bad about doing it behind your back."

"Good."

"But aren't you happier now?" He sat at the end of her bed and leaned against the wall, crossing his long legs at the ankles. "You look better nourished already."

"Um, thank you?"

"So?"

"What?"

He grinned. "Can I have a protein bar?"

"You're unbelievable."

Levi leaned over and reached under the bed. "The Blueberry Bliss are my favorite. . . ."

Cath actually *was* happier now. (Not that she was going to admit that to Levi.) So far, being Reagan's charity case didn't require much – just going down to the dining hall together and helping Reagan ridicule everyone who walked by their table.

Reagan liked to sit next to the kitchen door, right where the buffet line dumped into the dining room. She called it parade seating, and no one was spared. "Look," she'd said last night, "it's Gimpy. How do you think he broke his leg?"

Cath looked up at the guy, a dangerously hip-looking character with shaggy hair and oversized glasses. "Probably tripped over his beard."

"Ha!" Reagan said. "His girlfriend is carrying his tray. Just look at her – that is one shiny unicorn. Do you think they actually met in an American Apparel ad?"

"I'm pretty sure they met in New York City, but it took them five years to get here."

"Oh, Wolf Girl at three o'clock," Reagan said excitedly.

"Is she wearing her clip-on tail?"

"I don't know, wait for it. . . . No. Damn."

"I kinda like her tail." Cath smiled fondly at the chubby girl with dyed black hair.

"If God put me into your life to keep you from wearing a fucking tail," Reagan said, "I accept the assignment."

As far as Reagan was concerned, Cath was already problematically weird. "It's bad enough that you have homemade Simon Snow posters," Reagan had said last night while she was getting ready for bed. "Do you have to have *gay* homemade Simon Snow posters?"

Cath had looked up at the drawing over her desk of Simon and Baz holding hands. "Leave them alone," she said. "They're in love."

"Pretty sure I don't remember that from the books."

"When I write them," Cath said, "they're in love."

"What do you mean when *you* write them?" Reagan stopped, pulling her T-shirt down over her head. "No, you know what? Never mind. I don't want to know. It's already hard enough to make eye contact with you."

Levi was right, they must be hitting it off, because now when Reagan said stuff like that, it made Cath want to laugh. If Reagan missed dinner, Cath would go down to the dining hall anyway and sit at their table. Then, when Reagan came back to the room later – *if* Reagan came back to the room later – Cath would tell her everything she'd missed.

"Soccer Sandals finally talked to Venezuelan Lindsay Lohan," Cath would say.

"Thank God," Reagan would answer, flopping down onto her bed. "The sexual tension was killing me."

Cath wasn't sure where Reagan went on the nights when she didn't come back to the dorms. Maybe to Levi's. Cath looked over at Levi now. . . .

Still sitting on Cath's bed, eating what must be his second Blueberry Bliss bar. He was wearing black jeans and a black T-shirt. Maybe Levi worked at the Olive Garden, too.

"Are you a waiter?" she asked.

"Presently? No."

"Do you work at the Lancôme counter?"

He laughed. "What?"

"I'm trying to figure out why you wear all black sometimes."

"Maybe I'm really gothy and dark" – he smiled – "but only on certain days." Cath couldn't imagine Levi ever being gothy and dark; he had the smilingest face she'd ever seen. He smiled all the way from his chin to his receding hairline. His forehead wrinkled up, his eyes twinkled. Even his ears got into the action – they twitched, like a dog's.

"Or maybe I work at Starbucks," he said.

She snorted. *"Really?"*

"Really," he said, still smiling. "Someday you'll need health insurance, and you won't think working at Starbucks is funny."

Levi and Reagan were always doing that to Cath – reminding her how young and naïve she was. Reagan was only two years older than Cath. She wasn't even old enough to drink yet. Not legally. (Not that it mattered on campus; there was booze everywhere. Wren already had a fake ID. "You can borrow it," she'd told Cath. "Say you got hair extensions.")

Cath wondered how old Levi was. He looked old enough to drink, but maybe that was just his hair. . . .

It's not that Levi was bald. Or anywhere near bald. (Yet.)

But his hairline came to a peak on his forehead, then retreated, dramatically, above his temples. And instead of letting his hair hang down or forward, to minimize it – or instead of giving up and wearing it really short, like most guys would – Levi swept it straight up and back in a sloppy blond wave. And he was always *messing* with it, drawing even more attention to his wide, lined forehead. He was doing it now.

"What are you working on?" he asked, pushing his fingers through his hair and scrubbing at the back of his head.

"Studying in silence," she said.

Cath had only posted one chapter of *Carry On, Simon* this week, and it was half as long as usual.

She usually posted something to her FanFixx page every night – if not a full chapter, at least a blog entry.

The comments on her page all week had been friendly. . . . *"How are you?" "Just checking in." "Can't wait for the next post!" "Gah! I need my daily Baz."* But to Cath, they felt like demands.

She used to read and respond to every comment on her stories – comments were like gold stars, like May Day bouquets – but ever since *Carry On, Simon* took off last year, it had all gotten too big for Cath to manage. She went from getting around five hundred hits per chapter to five thousand. Regularly.

Then one of the heavies on the biggest fansite, Fic-sation, called *Carry On "the* eighth-year fic" – and Cath's FanFixx page got thirty-five thousand hits in one day.

She still tried to keep up with comments and questions as much as she could. But it wasn't the same anymore.

She wasn't just writing for Wren and the friends they'd made in the old Snowflakes forums. It wasn't just a bunch of girls trading birthday fics and cheer-up fics and cracked-out "I wrote this to make you laugh" stories. . . .

Cath had an audience now, a following. All these people she didn't know, who expected things from her and questioned her decisions. Sometimes they even turned against her. They'd trash her on other fansites, saying that Cath used to be good, but she'd lost the magic – that her Baz was too canon or not canon enough, that her Simon was a prude, that she overwrote Penelope. . . .

"You don't owe them anything," Wren would say, crawling onto Cath's bed at three in the morning and pulling Cath's laptop away. "Go to sleep."

"I will. I'm just . . . I want to finish this scene. I think Baz is finally going to tell Simon he loves him."

"He'll still love him tomorrow."

"It's a big chapter."

"It's always a big chapter."

"It's different this time." Cath had been saying this for the last year. "It's the end."

Wren was right: Cath *had* written this story, Baz and Simon in love, dozens of times before. She'd written this scene, this line — "Snow . . . Simon, I love you" — fifty different ways.

But *Carry On* was different.

It was the longest fic she'd written so far; it was already longer than any of Gemma T. Leslie's books, and Cath was only two-thirds of the way through.

Carry On was written as if it *were* the eighth Simon Snow book, as if it were Cath's job to wrap up all the loose ends, to make sure that Simon ascended to Mage, to redeem Baz (something GTL would never do), to make both boys forget about Agatha . . . To write all the good-bye scenes and graduation scenes and last-minute revelations . . . And to stage the final battle between Simon and the Insidious Humdrum.

Everyone in fandom was writing eighth-year fics right now. Everyone wanted to take a crack at the big ending before the last Simon Snow book was released in May.

But for thousands of people, *Carry On* was already it.

People were always telling Cath that they couldn't look at canon the same way after reading her stuff. ("Why does Gemma hate Baz?")

Somebody had even started selling T-shirts on Etsy that said KEEP CALM AND CARRY ON with a photo of Baz and Simon glaring at each other. Wren bought Cath one for her eighteenth birthday.

Cath tried not to let it all go to her head. *These characters belong to Gemma T. Leslie,* she wrote at the beginning of every new chapter.

"You belong to Gemma," she'd say to the Baz poster over her bed at home. "I'm just borrowing you."

"You didn't borrow Baz," Wren would say. "You kidnapped him and raised him as your own."

If Cath stayed up too late writing, too many nights in a row — if she was obsessing over the comments or the criticism — Wren would climb into Cath's bed and steal her laptop, holding it like a teddy bear while she slept.

On nights like that, Cath could always go downstairs and keep writing on her dad's computer if she really wanted to — but she didn't like to cross Wren. They listened to each other when they wouldn't listen to anyone else.

Hey, guys, Cath started typing now into her FanFixx journal. She wished Wren were here, to read this before she posted it.

So I guess it's time for me to admit that college is hard — College is hard! Or, at least, time consuming! — *and I'm probably not going to be updating* Carry On *as much as I used to, as much as I'd like to. . . .*

But I'm not disappearing, I promise. And I'm not giving it up. I already know how this all ends, and I'm not going to rest 'til I get there.

Nick turned around in his desk as soon as class was dismissed. "You'll be my partner, right?"

"Right," Cath said, noticing a girl in the next aisle glance at them disappointedly. Probably because she wanted to work with Nick.

They were each supposed to find a partner and write a story together outside of class, trading paragraphs back and forth. The point of the exercise, Professor Piper said, was to make them extra-conscious of plot and voice — and to lead their brains down pathways they'd never find on their own.

Nick wanted to meet on campus at Love Library. (That was the actual name; thank you for your donation, Mayor Don Lathrop Love.) Nick worked there a few nights a week, shelving books down in the stacks.

Reagan looked suspicious when Cath started packing up her laptop after dinner. "You're leaving the dorm after dark? Do you have a *date*?" She said it like it was a joke. The idea of Cath on a date.

"I'm meeting someone to study."

"Don't walk home by yourself if it's late," Levi said. He and Reagan had class notes spread all over Reagan's side of the room.

"*I* walk home by myself all the time," Reagan snapped at him.

"That's different." Levi smiled at her warmly. "You don't rock that Little Red Riding Hood vibe. You're scary."

Reagan grinned like the Big Bad Wolf.

"I don't think rapists actually care about self-confidence," Cath said.

"You don't?" Levi looked over at her seriously. "I think they'd go for easy prey. The young and the lame."

Reagan snorted. Cath hung her scarf on her neck. "I'm not lame . . . ," she mumbled.

Levi heaved himself up off Reagan's bed and slid into a heavy, green canvas jacket. "Come on," he said.

"Why?"

"I'm walking you to the library."

"You don't have to," Cath argued.

"I haven't moved in two hours. I don't mind."

"No, really . . ."

"Just go, Cath," Reagan said. "It'll take five minutes, and if you get raped now, it'll be our fault. I haven't got time for the pain."

"You coming?" Levi asked Reagan.

"Fuck no. It's cold out."

It *was* cold out. Cath walked as quickly as she could. But Levi, long as his legs were, never broke an amble.

He was trying to talk to Cath about buffalo. As far as she could tell, Levi had a whole class that was just about buffalo. He seemed like he'd major in buffalo if that were an option. Maybe it *was* an option. . . .

This school was constantly reminding Cath how rural Nebraska was – something she'd never given any thought to before, growing up in Omaha, the state's only real city. Cath had driven through Nebraska a few times on the way to Colorado – she'd seen the grass and the cornfields – but she'd never thought much past the view. She'd never thought about the people who lived there.

Levi and Reagan were from some town called Arnold, which Reagan said smelled and looked "like manure."

"God's country," Levi called it. "All the gods. Brahma and Odin would love it there."

Levi was still talking about buffalo even though they were already at the library. Cath climbed the first stone step, hopping up and down to stay warm. Standing on the step, she was practically as tall as him.

"Do you see what I mean?" he asked.

She nodded. "Cows bad. Buffalo good."

"Cows good," he said. "Bison *better*." Then he gave her a lazy, lopsided grin. "This is all really important, you know – that's why I'm telling you."

"Vital," she said. "Ecosystems. Water tables. Shrews going extinct."

"Call me when you're done, Little Red."

No, Cath thought, *I don't even know your number.*

Levi was already walking away. "I'll be in your room," he said over his shoulder. "Call me there."

———

The library had six levels aboveground and two levels below.

The sublevels, where the stacks were, were shaped strangely and accessible only from certain staircases; it almost felt like the stacks were tucked under other buildings around campus.

Nick worked in the north stacks in a long white room – it was practically a missile silo with bookshelves. There was a constant hum no matter where you were standing, and even though Cath couldn't see any vents, parts of the room had their own wind. At the table where they were sitting, Nick had to set a pen on his open notebook to keep the pages from riffling.

Nick wrote in longhand.

Cath was trying to convince him that they'd be better off taking turns on her laptop.

"But then we won't see ourselves switching," he said. "We won't see the two different hands at work."

"I can't think on paper," she said.

"Perfect," Nick said. "This exercise is about stepping outside of yourself."

"Okay," she sighed. There was no use arguing anymore – he'd already pushed her computer away.

"Okay." Nick picked up his pen and pulled the cap off with his teeth. "I'll start."

"Wait," Cath said. "Let's talk about what kind of story we're writing."

"You'll see."

"That's not fair." She leaned forward, looking at the blank sheet of paper. "I don't want to write about, like, dead bodies or . . . naked bodies."

"So what I'm hearing is, no bodies."

Nick wrote in a scrawling half cursive. He was left-handed, so he smeared blue ink across the paper as he went. *You need a felt tip,* Cath thought, trying to read his handwriting upside down from across the table. When he handed her the notebook, she could hardly read it, even right side up.

"What's this word?" she asked, pointing.

"Retinas."

> *She's standing in a parking lot. And she's standing under a streetlight. And her hair's so blond, it's flashing at you. It's burning out your retinas one fucking cone at a time. She leans forward and grabs your T-shirt. And she's standing on tiptoe now. She's reaching for you. She smells like black tea and American Spirits — and when her mouth hits your ear, you wonder if she remembers your name.*

"So . . . ," Cath said, "we're doing this in present tense?"

"Second person," Nick confirmed.

Cath frowned at him.

"What's wrong?" he asked. "You don't like love stories?"

Cath could feel herself blushing and tried to stop. *Stay cool, Little Red.* She hunched over her bag to look for a pen.

It was hard for her to write without typing — and hard to write with Nick watching her like he'd just handed her a hot potato.

> *"Please don't tell Mom," she giggles.*
>
> *"Which part should I leave out?" you ask her. "The hair? Or the stupid hipster cigarettes?"*
>
> *She pulls meanly at your T-shirt, and you shove her back like she's twelve. And she practically is — she's so young. And you're so tired. And what is Dave going to think if you walk out on your first date to take care of your stupid, stupidly blond, little sister.*
>
> *"You suck, Nick," she says. And she's reeling. She's swaying again under the streetlight.*

Cath turned the notebook around and pushed it back at Nick.

He poked his tongue in his cheek and smiled.

"So our narrator is gay . . . ," he said. "And he's named after me. . . ."

"I love love stories," Cath said.

Nick nodded his head a few more times.

And then they both started laughing.

It was almost like writing with Wren – back when she and Wren would sit in front of the computer, pulling the keyboard back and forth and reading out loud as the other person typed.

Cath always wrote most of the dialogue. Wren was better at plot and mood. Sometimes Cath would write all the conversations, and Wren would write behind her, deciding where Baz and Simon were and where they were going. Once Cath had written what she thought was a love scene, and Wren had turned it into a sword fight.

Even after they'd stopped writing together, Cath would still follow Wren around the house, begging for help, whenever she couldn't get Simon and Baz to do anything but talk.

Nick wasn't Wren.

He was bossier and more of a showboat. And also, obviously, a boy. Up close, his eyes were bluer, and his eyebrows were practically sentient. He licked his lips when he wrote, tapping his tongue on his front teeth.

To his credit, he got over the gay thing pretty much immediately. Even when Cath gave gay-fictional Nick heavy black eyebrows and periwinkle blue wingtips.

Nonfiction Nick had trouble taking turns; he'd start to take the notebook out of Cath's hands before she was done writing, and her green pen would pull across the page.

"Wait," she'd say.

"No, I have an idea – and you're about to ruin it."

She tried hard to make her paragraphs sound like Nick's, but her own style kept leaking through. It was cool when she realized he was imitating her, too.

After a few hours, Cath was yawning, and their story was twice as long as it needed to be. "This is gonna take forever to type up," she said.

"Don't type it, then. We'll turn it in like this."

Cath looked down at the green-and-blue-smudged pages. "It's our only copy."

"So don't let your dog eat it." He zipped up a gray hoodie and reached for his ratty denim jacket. "It's midnight. I have to clock out."

The book cart next to their table was still heaped with books. "What about these?" Cath asked.

"The morning girl can do it. It'll remind her that she's alive."

Cath carefully tore their story out of Nick's notebook and tucked it into her backpack, then followed him up the winding staircase. They didn't see anyone else on their way to the first floor.

It was different being with him now. Different even from a few hours ago. *Fun.* Cath didn't feel like her real self was buried under eight layers of fear and diagnosable anxiety. Nick walked right next to her on the stairs, and they talked like they were still passing the notebook between them.

When they got outside, they stopped at the sidewalk.

Cath felt some of her nervousness creeping back. She fumbled with the buttons of her coat.

"All right," Nick said, putting his arms through his backpack. "See you in class?"

"Yeah," Cath said. "I'll try not to lose our novel."

"Our *first* novel," he said, taking the path that led off campus. "Good night."

"Good night." She watched him go, all dark hair and blue smudges in the moonlight. . . .

And then it was just Cath out on the quad. Cath and about a hundred trees that she never noticed during the daytime. The library lights switched off behind her; her shadow disappeared.

Cath sighed and got out her phone – she had two texts from Abel; she ignored them – then dialed her room, hoping her roommate wasn't asleep.

"Hello?" Reagan answered on the third ring. There was music in the background.

"It's Cath."

"Well, hello, Cath, how was your date?"

"It wasn't – Look, I'm just gonna walk home. I'll be fast. I'm already walking."

"Levi left as soon as the phone rang. You may as well wait for him."

"He doesn't have to—"

"It'll be a bigger hassle if he can't find you."

"Okay," Cath said, giving in. "Thanks, I guess."

Reagan hung up.

Cath stood next to a lamppost, so he'd see her, and tried to look like the huntsman, not the little girl with the basket. Levi showed up long before she expected him to, jogging down the pathway. Even his jogging looked laid-back.

She started walking toward him, thinking she'd save him at least a few steps.

"Catherine," he said, stopping when they met and turning to walk with her. "In one piece, even."

"That," she said, "isn't even my name."

"Just Cather, huh?"

"Just Cath."

"Did you get lost in the library?"

"No."

"I always get lost in the library," he said, "no matter how many times I go. In fact, I think I get lost there *more,* the more that I go. Like it's getting to know me and revealing new passages."

"You spend a lot of time in the library?"

"I do, actually."

"How is that possible when you're always in my room?"

"Where do you think I sleep?" he asked. And when she looked at him, he was grinning.

Simon curled on his bed like a wounded unicorn foal, holding the torn piece of green velvet to his tear-stained face.

"Are you okay?" Basil asked. You could tell he didn't want to ask. You could tell he found it quite distasteful to speak to his longtime enemy.

"Leave me alone," Simon spat, choking on his tears and hating Basil even more than usual. "She was my mother."

Basil frowned. He narrowed his smoky grey eyes and folded his arms, like he was forcing himself to keep standing there. Like what he really wanted to do was throw another sneezing spell at Simon.

"I know," Basil said almost angrily. "I know what you're going through. I lost my mother, too."

Simon wiped his snotty nose on the sleeve of his jacket and slowly sat up, his eyes as wide and blue as the Eighth Sea. *Was Basil lying? That would be just like him, the prat.*

—from "Friends for Life – and After," posted August 2006
by FanFixx.net authors *Magicath* and *Wrenegade*

SIX

"Dad? Call me."

———

"It's Cath again. Call me."

———

"Dad, stop ignoring my voice mail. Do you listen to your voice mail? Do you know how? Even if you don't, I know you can see my number in your missed calls. Call me back, okay?"

———

"Dad. Call me. Or call Wren. No, call *me*. I'm worried about you. I don't like worrying about you."

———

"Don't make me call the neighbors. They'll come check on you, and you don't speak any Spanish, and it'll be embarrassing."

———

"Dad?"

"Hey, Cath."

"*Dad*. Why haven't you called me? I left you a million messages."

"You left me too many messages. You shouldn't be calling me or even thinking about me. You're in college now. Move on."

"It's just school, Dad. It's not like we have irreconcilable differences."

"Honey, I've watched a lot of *90210*. The parents weren't even on the show once Brandon and Brenda went to college. This is your time – you're supposed to be going to frat parties and getting back together with Dylan."

"Why does everybody want me to go to frat parties?"

"Who wants you to go to frat parties? I was just kidding. Don't hang out with frat guys, Cath, they're terrible. All they do is get drunk and watch *90210*."

"Dad, how are you?"

"I'm fine, honey."

"Are you lonely?"

"Yes."

"Are you eating?"

"Yes."

"What are you eating?"

"Nutritious food."

"What did you eat today? *No lying.*"

"Something ingenious I discovered at QuikTrip: It's a sausage wrapped in a pancake, then cooked to perfection on a hot dog roller—"

"*Dad.*"

"Come on, Cath, you told me not to lie."

"Could you just go to the grocery store or something?"

"You know I hate the grocery store."

"They sell fruit at QuikTrip."

"They do?"

"Yes. Ask somebody."

"You know I hate to ask somebodies."

"You're making me worry about you."

"Don't worry about me, Cath. I'll look for the fruit."

"That is such a lame concession. . . ."

"Fine, I'll go the grocery store."

"*No lying* – promise?"

"I promise."

"I love you."

"I love you, too. Tell your sister I love her."

———

"Cath, it's your dad. I know it's late, and you're probably asleep. I hope you're asleep! But I had this idea. It's a great idea. Call me."

———

"Cath? It's your dad again. It's still late, but I couldn't wait to tell you this. You know how you guys want a bathroom upstairs? Your room is *right over* the bathroom. We could put in a trapdoor. And a ladder. It would be like a secret shortcut to the bathroom. Isn't this a great idea? Call me. It's your dad."

———

"Cath! Not a ladder – a fireman's pole! You'd still have to use the stairs to get up to your room – but, Cath, *a fireman's pole*. I think I can do this myself. I mean, I'll have to find a pole. . . ."

———

"Dad? Call me."

———

"Call me, okay?"

———

"Dad, it's Cath. Call me."

It was Friday night, and Cath had the dorm room to herself.

She was trying to work on *Carry On, Simon,* but her mind kept wandering. . . . Today in class, Professor Piper had handed back the story that she and Nick wrote together. The professor had filled the margins with *A*'s and drawn a little caricature of herself in the corner, shouting, *"AAAAAA!"*

She had a few of the writing teams – the people who had done really well – read their stories out loud in class. Cath and Nick went last, trading paragraphs so they were always reading what the other person had written. They got tons of laughs. Probably because Nick acted like he was doing Shakespeare in the park. Cath's cheeks and neck were burning by the time they sat down.

After class, Nick held up his pinkie to her. When she stared at it, he said, "Come on, we're making an oath."

She curled her finger around his, and he squeezed it. "Partners, automatically, any time we need one — deal?" His eyes were set so deep, it made everything he said more intense.

"Deal," Cath said, looking away.

"Goddamn," Nick said, his hand already gone. "We are so fucking good."

"I don't think she has any A's left after our paper," Cath said, following him out of the room. "People will be getting B-pluses for the next eight years because of us."

"We should do this again." He turned, suddenly, in the doorway.

Cath hip-checked him before she could stop herself. "We already swore an oath," she said, stepping back.

"Not what I mean. Not for an assignment. We should do it just because it was good. You know?"

It was good. It was the most fun Cath had had since . . . well, since she got here, for sure. "Yeah," she said. "All right."

"I work Tuesday and Thursday nights," Nick said. "You want to do this again Tuesday? Same time?"

"Sure," Cath said.

She hadn't stopped thinking about it since then. She wondered what they'd write. She wanted to talk to Wren about it. Cath had tried calling Wren earlier, but she hadn't picked up. It was almost eleven now. . . .

Cath picked up the phone and hit Wren's number.

Wren answered. "Yes, sister-sister?"

"Hey, can you talk?"

"Yes, sister-sister," Wren said, giggling.

"Are you out?"

"I am on the tenth floor of Schramm Hall. This is where . . . *all* the tourists come when they visit Schramm Hall. The observation deck. 'See the world from Tyler's room' — that's what it says on the postcards.' "

Wren's voice was warm and liquid. Their dad always said that Wren and Cath had the same voice, but Wren was 33 rpm and Cath was 45. . . . This was different.

"Are you drunk?"

"I *was* drunk," Wren said. "Now I think I'm something else."

"Are you alone? Where's Courtney?"

"She's here. I might be sitting on her leg."

"Wren, are you okay?"

"Yes-yes-yes, sister-sister. That's why I answered the phone. To tell you I'm okay. So you can leave me alone for a while. Okay-okay?"

Cath felt her face tense. More from hurt now than worry. "I was just calling to talk to you about Dad." Cath wished she didn't use the word "just" so much. It was her passive-aggressive tell, like someone who twitched when they were lying. "And other stuff. Boy . . . stuff."

Wren giggled. "Boy stuff? Is Simon coming out to Agatha again? Did Baz make him a vampire? Again? Are their fingers helplessly caught in each other's hair? Have you got to the part where Baz calls him 'Simon' for the first time, because that's always a tough one. . . . That's always a three-alarm fire."

Cath pulled the phone away so that it wasn't touching her ear. "Fuck off," she whispered. "I just wanted to make sure you were okay."

"Okay-okay," Wren said, her voice an edgy singsong. Then she hung up.

Cath set the phone on her desk and leaned back away from it. Like it was something that would bite.

Wren must be drunk. Or high.

Wren never . . . would never.

She never teased Cath about Simon and Baz. Simon and Baz were . . .

Cath got up to turn off the light. Her fingers felt cold. She kicked off her jeans and climbed into bed.

Then she got up again to check that the door was locked, and looked out the peephole into the empty hallway.

She sat back on her bed. She stood back up.

She opened her laptop, booted it up, closed it again.

Wren must be high. Wren would never.

She knew what Simon and Baz were. What they meant. Simon and Baz were . . .

Cath lay back down in bed and shook out her wrists over the comforter, then twisted her hands in the hair at her temples until she could feel the pull.

Simon and Baz were untouchable.

"This isn't any fun today," Reagan said, staring glumly at the dining hall door.

Reagan was always cranky on weekend mornings (when she was around). She drank too much and slept too little. She hadn't washed off last night's makeup yet this morning, and she still smelled like sweat and cigarette smoke. *Day-old Reagan,* Cath thought.

But Cath didn't worry about Reagan, not like she worried about Wren. Maybe because Reagan looked like the Big Bad Wolf – and Wren just looked like Cath with a better haircut.

A girl walked through the door wearing a red HUSKER FOOTBALL sweatshirt and skinny jeans. Reagan sighed.

"What's wrong?" Cath asked.

"They all look alike on game days," Reagan said. "I can't see their ugly, deformed true selves. . . ." She turned to Cath. "What are you doing today?"

"Hiding in our room."

"You look like you need some fresh air."

"Me?" Cath gagged on her pot roast sandwich. "You look like you need fresh DNA."

"I look like this because I'm alive," Reagan said. "Because I've had experiences. Do you understand?"

Cath looked back up at Reagan and couldn't help but smile.

Reagan wore eyeliner all the way around her eyes. Like a hard-ass Kate Middleton. And even though she was bigger than most girls – big hips, big chest, wide shoulders – she carried herself like she was exactly the size everyone else wanted to be. And everyone else went along with it – including Levi, and all the other guys who hung out in their room while Reagan finished getting ready.

"You don't get to look like this," Reagan said, pointing at her gray day-after face, "hiding in your room all weekend."

"So noted," Cath said.

"Let's do something today."

"Game day. The only smart thing to do is stay in our room and barricade the door."

"Do you have anything red?" Reagan asked. "If we put on some red, we could just walk around campus and get free drinks."

Cath's phone rang. She looked down at it. Wren. She pushed Ignore.

"I have to write today," she said.

———

When they got back to their room, Reagan took a shower and put on fresh makeup, sitting on her desk, holding a mirror.

She left and came back a few hours later with Target bags and a guy named Eric. Then she left again and didn't come back until the sun was setting. Alone, this time.

Cath was still sitting at her desk.

"Enough!" Reagan half shouted.

"Jesus," Cath said, turning toward her. It took a few seconds for Cath's eyes to focus on something that wasn't a computer screen.

"Get dressed," Reagan said. "And don't argue with me. I'm not playing this game with you."

"What game?"

"You're a sad little hermit, and it creeps me out. So get dressed. We're going bowling."

Cath laughed. "Bowling?"

"Oh, right," Reagan said. "Like bowling is more pathetic than everything else you do."

Cath pushed away from the desk. Her left leg had fallen asleep. She shook it out. "I've never been bowling. What should I wear?"

"You've never been bowling?" Reagan was incredulous. "Don't people bowl in Omaha?"

Cath shrugged. "Really old people? Maybe?"

"Wear whatever. Wear something that doesn't have Simon Snow on it, so that people won't assume your brain stopped developing when you were seven."

Cath put on her red CARRY ON T-shirt with jeans, and redid her ponytail.

Reagan frowned at her. "Do you have to wear your hair like that? Is it some kind of Mormon thing?"

"I'm not Mormon."

"I said *some kind*." There was a knock at the door, and Reagan opened it.

Levi was standing there, practically bouncing. He was wearing a white T-shirt, and he'd drawn on it with a Sharpie, adding a collar and buttons down the front, plus a chest pocket with *The Strike Out King* written above it in fancy script.

"Are we doing this?" he said.

Reagan and Levi were excellent bowlers. Apparently there was a bowling alley in Arnold. Not nearly as nice as this one, they said.

The three of them were the only people under forty bowling tonight, which didn't stop Levi from talking to absolutely every single person in the whole building. He talked to the guy who was spraying the shoes, the retired couples in the next lane, a whole group of moms in some league who sent him away with ruffled hair and a pitcher of beer. . . .

Reagan acted like she didn't notice.

"I think there's a baby in the corner you forgot to kiss," Cath said to him.

"Where's a baby?" His eyes perked up.

"No," she said. "I was just . . ." *Just*.

Levi set down the pitcher. He was balancing three glasses in his other hand; he let them drop on the table, and they landed without falling over.

"Why do you do that?"

"What?" He poured a beer and held it out to her. She took it without thinking, then set it down with distaste.

"Go so far out of your way to be nice to people?"

He smiled – but he was already smiling, so that just meant that he smiled more.

"Do you think I should be more like you?" he asked, then

looked fondly over at Reagan, who was scowling (somehow voluptuously) over the ball return. "Or her?"

Cath rolled her eyes. "There's got to be a happy medium."

"I'm happy," he said, "so this must be it."

Cath bought herself a Cherry Coke from the bar and ignored the beer. Reagan bought two plates of drippy orange nachos. Levi bought three giant dill pickles that were so sour, they made them all cry.

Reagan won the first game. Then Levi won the second. Then, for the third, he talked the guy behind the counter into turning on the kiddie bumpers for Cath. She still didn't pick up any strikes. Levi won again.

Cath had just enough money left to buy them all ice cream sandwiches from the vending machine.

"I really am the Strike Out King," Levi said. "Everything I write on my shirt comes true."

"It'll definitely come true tonight at Muggsy's," Reagan said. Levi laughed and crumpled up his ice cream wrapper to throw at her. The way they smiled at each other made Cath look away. They were so easy together. Like they knew each other inside and out. Reagan was sweeter – and meaner – with Levi than she ever was with Cath.

Someone pulled on Cath's ponytail, and her chin jerked up.

"You're coming with us," Levi asked, "right?"

"Where?"

"Out. To Muggsy's. The night is young."

"And so am I," Cath said. "I can't get into a bar."

"You'll be with us," he said. "Nobody'll stop you."

"He's right," Reagan said. "Muggsy's is for college dropouts and hopeless alcoholics. Freshmen never try to sneak in."

Reagan put a cigarette in her mouth, but didn't light it. Levi took it and put it between his lips.

Cath almost said yes.

Instead she shook her head.

When Cath got back up to her room, she thought about calling Wren.

She called her dad instead. He sounded tired, but he wasn't trying to replace the stairs with a water slide, so that was an improvement. And he'd eaten two Healthy Choice meals for dinner.

"That sounds like a healthy choice," Cath told him, trying to sound encouraging.

She did some reading for class. Then she stayed up working on *Carry On* until her eyes burned and she knew she'd fall asleep as soon as she climbed into bed.

"Words are very powerful," Miss Possibelf said, stepping lightly between the rows of desks. "And they take on more power the more that they're spoken. . . .

"The more that they're *said* and *read* and *written,* in specific, consistent combinations." She stopped in front of Simon's desk and tapped it with a short, jeweled staff. *"Up, up and away,"* she said clearly.

Simon watched the floor move away from his feet. He grabbed at the edges of his desk, knocking over a pile of books and loose papers. Across the room, Basilton laughed.

Miss Possibelf nudged Simon's trainer with her staff – *"Hold your horses"* – and his desk hovered three feet in the air.

"The key to casting a spell," she said, "is tapping into that power. Not just saying the words, but summoning their meaning. . . .

"Now," she said, "open your *Magic Words* books to page four. And *Settle down* there, Simon. *Please.*"

—from chapter 5, *Simon Snow and the Mage's Heir,*
copyright © 2001 by Gemma T. Leslie

SEVEN

When Cath saw Abel's name pop up on her phone, she thought at first that it was a text, even though the phone was obviously ringing.

Abel never called her.

They e-mailed. They texted – they'd texted just last night. But they never actually *talked* unless it was in person.

"Hello?" she answered. She was waiting in her spot outside Andrews Hall, the English building. It was really too cold to be standing outside, but sometimes Nick would show up here before class, and they'd look over each other's assignments or talk about the story they were writing together. (It was turning into another love story; Nick was the one turning it that way.)

"Cath?" Abel's voice was gravelly and familiar.

"Hey," she said, feeling warm suddenly. Surprisingly. Maybe she *had* missed Abel. She was still avoiding Wren – Cath hadn't even eaten lunch at Selleck since Wren drunked at her. Maybe Cath just missed home. "Hey. How are you?"

"I'm fine," he said. "I just told you last night that I was fine."

"Well. Yeah. I know. But it's different on the phone."

He sounded startled. "That's exactly what Katie said."

"Who's Katie?"

"Katie is the reason I'm calling you. She's, like, every reason I'm calling you."

Cath cocked her head. "What?"

"Cath, I've met someone," he said. Just like that. Like he was in some *telenovela*.

"Katie?"

"Yeah. And it's, um, she made me realize that . . . well, that what you and I have isn't real."

"What do you mean?"

"I mean our relationship, Cath – it isn't real." Why did he keep saying her name like that?

"Of course it's real. *Abel*. We've been together for three years."

"Well, sort of."

"Not sort of," Cath said.

"Well . . . at any rate" – his voice sounded firm – "I met somebody else."

Cath turned to face the building and rested the top of her head against the bricks. "Katie."

"And it's *more* real," he said. "We're just . . . right together, you know? We can talk about everything – she's a coder, too. And she got a thirty-four on the ACT."

Cath got a thirty-two.

"You're breaking up with me because I'm not smart enough?"

"This isn't a breakup. It's not like we're really together."

"Is that what you told Katie?"

"I told her we'd drifted apart."

"Yes," Cath spat out. "Because the only time you ever call is to break up with me." She kicked the bricks, then instantly regretted it.

"Right. Like you call me all the time."

"I would if you wanted me to," she said.

"Would you?"

Cath kicked the wall again. "Maybe."

Abel sighed. He sounded more exasperated than anything

else – more than sad or sorry. "We haven't really been together since junior year."

Cath wanted to argue with him, but she couldn't think of anything convincing. *But you took me to the military ball,* she thought. *But you taught me how to drive.* "But your grandma always makes *tres leches* cake for my birthday."

"She makes it anyway for the bakery."

"Fine." Cath turned and leaned back against the wall. She wished she could cry – just so that he'd have to deal with it. "So noted. Everything is noted. We're not broken up, but we're over."

"We're not over," Abel said. "We can still be friends. I'll still read your fic – Katie reads it, too. I mean, she always has. Isn't that a coincidence?"

Cath shook her head, speechless.

Then Nick rounded the corner of the building and acknowledged her the way he always did, looking her in the eye and quickly jerking up his head. Cath lifted her chin in answer.

"Yeah," she said into the phone. "Coincidence."

Nick had set his backpack on a stone planter, and he was digging through his books and notebooks. His jacket was unbuttoned, and when he leaned over like that, she could kind of see down his shirt. Sort of. A few inches of pale skin and sparse black hair.

"I've got to go," she said.

"Oh," Abel said. "Okay. Do you still want to hang out over Thanksgiving?"

"I've got to go," she said, and pressed End.

Cath took a slow breath. She felt lightheaded and strained, like something too big was hatching inside her ribs. She pushed her shoulders back into the bricks and looked down at the top of Nick's head.

He looked up at her and smiled crookedly, holding out a few

sheets of paper. "Will you read this? I think maybe it sucks. Or maybe it's awesome. It's probably awesome. Tell me it's awesome, okay? Unless it sucks."

Cath texted Wren just before Fiction-Writing started, hiding her phone behind Nick's broad shoulders.

"abel broke up with me."

"oh god. sorry. want me to come over?"

"yeah. at 5?"

"yeah. you OK?"

"think so. end tables end."

"Have you cried yet?"

They were sitting on Cath's bed, eating the last of the protein bars.

"No," Cath said, "I don't think I'm going to."

Wren bit her lip. Literally.

"Say it," Cath said.

"I don't feel like I have to. I never thought that *not* saying it would be this satisfying."

"Say it."

"He wasn't a real boyfriend! You never liked him like that!" Wren pushed Cath so hard, she fell over.

Cath laughed and sat back up, drawing her legs up into her arms. "I really thought I did, though."

"How could you think that?" Wren was laughing, too.

Cath shrugged.

It was Thursday night, and Wren was already dressed to go out. She was wearing pale green eyeshadow that made her eyes look more green than blue, and her lips were a shiny red. Her short hair was parted on one side and swept glamorously across her forehead.

"Seriously," Wren said, "you know what love feels like. I've read you describe it a thousand different ways."

Cath pulled a face. "That's different. That's fantasy. That's . . . *'Simon reached out for Baz, and his name felt like a magic word on his lips.'*"

"It's not all fantasy . . . ," Wren said.

Cath thought of Levi's eyes when Reagan teased him.

She thought of Nick tapping his short, even teeth with the tip of his tongue.

"I can't believe Abel told me this girl's ACT score," she said. "What am I supposed to do with that? Offer her a scholarship?"

"Are you sad at all?" Wren reached under the bed and shook an empty protein bar box.

"Yeah . . . I'm embarrassed that I held on for so long. That I really thought we could go on like we were. And I'm sad because it feels like now high school is finally over. Like Abel was this piece of a really happy time that I thought I could take with me."

"Do you remember when he bought you a laptop power cord for your birthday?"

"That was a good gift," Cath said, pointing at her sister.

Wren grabbed her finger and pulled it down. "Did you think of him every time you booted up?"

"I needed a new power cord." Cath leaned back against the wall again, facing Wren. "He kissed me that day, on our seventeenth birthday, for the first time. Or maybe I kissed him."

"Was it *charged* with passion?"

Cath giggled. "*No.* But I remember thinking . . . that he made me feel safe." She rubbed her head back against the painted cinder blocks. "I remember thinking that me and Abel would never be like Dad and Mom, that if Abel ever got tired of me, I'd survive it."

Wren was still holding on to Cath's hand. She squeezed it. Then she laid her head against the wall, mirroring Cath. Cath was crying now.

"Well, you did," Wren said. "Survive it."

Cath laughed and pushed her fingers up behind her glasses to wipe her eyes. Wren took hold of that hand, too. "You know my stand on this," she said.

"Fire and rain," Cath whispered. She felt Wren's fingers circle her wrists.

"We're unbreakable."

Cath looked at Wren's smooth brown hair and the glint of steel, the crown of gray, that circled the green in her eyes.

You are, she thought.

"Does this mean no more *tres leches* cake on our birthday?" Wren asked.

"There's something else I want to tell you," Cath said before she could think it through. "There's, I mean, I think there's . . . this guy."

Wren raised her eyebrows. But before Cath could say anything more, they heard voices and a key in the door. Wren let go of Cath's wrists, and the door swung open. Reagan barreled in and dropped her duffel bag on the floor. She rushed out again before Levi even made it into the room.

"Hey, Cath," he said, already smiling, "are you—?" He looked at the bed and stopped.

"Levi," Cath said, "this is my sister, Wren."

Wren held out her hand.

Levi's eyes were as wide as Cath'd ever seen them. He grinned at Wren and took her hand, shaking it. *"Wren,"* he said. "Such fascinating names in your family."

"Our mom didn't know she was having twins," Wren said. "And she didn't feel like coming up with another name."

"Cather, Wren . . ." Levi looked like he'd just now discovered sliced bread. *"Catherine."*

Cath rolled her eyes. Wren just smiled. "Clever, right?"

"Cath," Levi said, and tried to sit next to Wren on the bed, even though there wasn't enough room. Wren laughed and scooted toward Cath. Cath scooted, too. Reluctantly. *If you give Levi an inch . . .*

"I didn't know you had a mother," he said. "Or a sister. What else are you hiding?"

"Five cousins," Wren said. "And a string of ill-fated hamsters, all named Simon."

Levi opened his smile up completely.

"Oh, put that away," Cath said with distaste. "I don't want you to get charm all over my sister – what if we can't get it out?"

Reagan walked back through the open door and glanced over at Cath. She noticed Wren and shuddered. "Is this your twin?"

"You knew about the twin?" Levi asked.

"Wren, Reagan," Cath said.

"Hello," Reagan said, frowning.

"Don't take any of this personally," Cath said to Wren. "They're both like this with everyone."

"I have to go anyway." Wren slid cheerfully off the bed. She was wearing a pink dress and brown tights, and brown ankle boots with heels and little green buttons up the side. They were Cath's boots, but Cath was never brave enough to wear them.

"Nice meeting you, everybody," Wren said, smiling at Reagan and Levi. "See you at lunch tomorrow," she said to Cath.

Reagan ignored her. Levi waved.

As soon as the door closed, Levi popped his eyes again. Bluely. *"That's* your twin sister?"

"Identical," Reagan said, like she had a mouth full of hair.

Cath nodded and sat down at her desk.

"Wow." Levi scooted down the bed so he was sitting across from her.

"I'm not sure what you're getting at," Cath said, "but I think it's offensive."

"How can the fact that your identical twin sister is super hot be offensive to you?"

"Because," Cath said, still too encouraged by Wren and, weirdly, by Abel, and maybe even by Nick to let this get to her right now. "It makes me feel like the Ugly One."

"You're not the ugly one." Levi grinned. "You're just the Clark Kent."

Cath started checking her e-mail.

"Hey, Cath," Levi said, kicking her chair. She could hear the teasing in his voice. "Will you warn me when you take off your glasses?"

Agatha Wellbelove was the loveliest witch at Watford. Everyone knew it – every boy, every girl, all the teachers . . . The bats in the belfry, the snakes in the cellars . . .

Agatha herself knew it. Which you might think would detract from her charm and her beauty. But Agatha, at fourteen, never used this knowledge to harm or hold over others.

She knew she was lovely, and she shared it like a gift. Every smile from Agatha was like waking up to a perfect sunny day. Agatha knew it. And she smiled at everyone who crossed her path, as if it were the most generous thing she could offer.

—from chapter 15, *Simon Snow and the Selkies Four,*
copyright © 2007 Gemma T. Leslie

EIGHT

"Have you started your scene yet?"

They were in the subbasement of the library, the sub-subbasement, and it was even colder than usual – the wind was making Nick's bangs flutter over his forehead. *Do guys call them "bangs"?* Cath wondered.

"Why is it windy in here?" she asked.

"Why is it windy anywhere?" Nick answered.

That made her laugh. "I don't know. Tides?"

"Caves breathing?"

"It's not wind at all," Cath said. "It's what we feel when time suddenly jolts forward."

Nick smiled at her. His lips were thin but dark, the same color as the inside of his mouth. "English majors are useless," he said, twitching his eyebrows. Then he elbowed her – "*So.* Have you started your scene? You're probably done already. You're so fucking fast."

"I get lots of practice," she said.

"Writing practice?"

"Yeah." For a second, she thought about telling him the truth. About Simon and Baz. About a chapter a day and thirty-five thousand hits . . . "I write laps," she said. "Every morning, just to stay loose. Have you started *your* scene?"

"Yeah," Nick said. He was drawing swirls in the margin of the notebook. "Three times . . . I'm just not sure about this assignment."

Professor Piper wanted them to write a scene with an untrustworthy narrator. Cath had written hers from Baz's point of view. It was an idea she'd had for a while; she might turn it into a longer fic someday, someday when she was done with *Carry On*.

"This should be cake for you," Cath said, elbowing Nick back, more gently. "All your narrators are unreliable."

Nick had let her read some of his short stories and the first few chapters of a novel he'd started freshman year. All his stuff was dark — dirtier and grimier than anything Cath would ever write — but still funny. And bracing, somehow. Nick was *good*.

She liked to sit next to him and watch all that good come out of his hand. Watch the jokes spill out in real time. Watch the words click together.

"Exactly . . . ," he said, licking his top lip. He practically didn't have a top lip, just a smear of red. "That's why I feel like I need to do something special this time around."

"Come on." Cath pulled at the notebook. "My turn."

It was always hard to get Nick to give up the notebook.

The first night they'd worked on their extracurricular story, Nick had shown up with three pages already written.

"That's cheating," Cath had said.

"It's just the first push," he said, "to get us rolling."

She'd taken the notebook and written over and between his words, squeezing new dialogue into the margins and crossing out lines that went too far. (Sometimes Nick stretched his style too thin.) Then she'd added a few paragraphs of her own.

It had gotten easier to write on paper, though Cath still missed her keyboard. . . .

"I need to cut and paste," she'd say to Nick.

"Next time," he'd say, "bring scissors."

They sat next to each other now when they worked – the better to read, and write, during the other's turns. Cath had learned to sit on Nick's right side, so their writing hands didn't bump unintentionally.

It made Cath feel like part of a two-headed monster. A three-legged race.

It made her feel at home.

She wasn't sure what Nick was feeling. . . .

They talked, a lot, before class and during class – Nick would crank around in his chair completely. Sometimes after they got out, Cath would pretend she had to walk past Bessey Hall, where Nick's next class was, even though there was nothing past Bessey Hall but the football stadium. Thank God Nick never asked where she was going.

He never asked that when they left the library at night either. They always stopped for a minute on the steps while Nick put his backpack on and wound his blue paisley scarf around his neck. Then he'd say, "See you in class," and be gone.

If Cath knew Levi was in her room, she'd call and wait for him to come get her. But most nights she pressed 911 on her phone, then ran back to the dorm with her finger over the Call button.

Wren was on some weird diet.

"It's the *Skinny Bitch* diet," Courtney said.

"It's vegan," Wren clarified.

It was Fajita Friday at Selleck. Wren had a plate full of grilled green peppers and onions, and two oranges. She'd been eating like this for a few weeks.

Cath looked her over carefully. Wren was wearing clothes that

Cath had worn, too, so Cath knew how they usually fit. Wren's sweater was still tight over her chest; her jeans still rode too low over her ass. She and Wren were both bottom heavy – Cath liked to wear shirts and sweaters that she could pull down over her hips; Wren liked to wear things she could pull in at the waist.

"You look the same," Cath said. "You look like me, and look what I'm eating." Cath was eating beef fajitas with sour cream and three kinds of cheese.

"Yeah, but you're not drinking."

"Is that part of the *Skinny Bitch* diet?"

"We're skinny bitches on weekdays," Courtney said, "and drunk bitches on the weekend."

Cath tried to catch Wren's eye. "I don't think I'd want to aspire to be any kind of bitch."

"Too late," Wren said blandly, then changed the subject. "Did you hang out with Nick last night?"

"Yeah," Cath said, then smiled. She tried to turn it into a smirk, but that just made her nose twitch like a rabbit's.

"Oh! Cath!" Courtney said. "We were thinking we could *just happen* to come to the library some night, so we can see him. Tuesdays and Thursdays, right?"

"No. No way. No, no, no." Cath looked at Wren. "No, okay? Say *okay*."

"O*kay*." Wren stabbed her fork full of onions. "What's the big deal?"

"It's not a big deal," Cath said. "But if you came, it would *seem* like a big deal. You would destroy my *'Hey, whatever, you want to hang out? That's cool'* strategy."

"You have a strategy?" Wren asked. "Does it involve kissing him?"

Wren wouldn't leave the kissing thing alone. Ever since Abel had dumped Cath, Wren was on her about chasing her passions and letting loose the beast within.

"What about *him*?" she'd say, finding an attractive guy to point out while they were standing in the lunch line. "Do you want to kiss him?"

"I don't want to kiss a stranger," Cath would answer. "I'm not interested in lips out of context."

It was only partly true.

Ever since Abel had broken up with her . . . Ever since Nick had started sitting next to her . . . Cath kept noticing things.

Boys.

Guys.

Everywhere.

Seriously, *everywhere*. In her classes. In the Union. In the dormitory, on the floors above and below her. And she'd swear they didn't look anything like the boys in high school. *How can that one year make such a difference?* Cath found herself watching their necks and their hands. She noticed the heaviness in their jaws, the way their chests buttressed out from their shoulders, their hair. . . .

Nick's eyebrows trailed into his hairline, and his sideburns feinted onto his cheeks. When she sat behind him in class, she could see the muscles in his left shoulder sliding under his shirt.

Even Levi was a distraction. A near-constant distraction. With his long, tan neck. And his throat bobbing and cording when he laughed.

Cath felt different. Tuned in. Boy – even though none of these guys seemed like *boys* – crazy. And for once, Wren was the last person she wanted to talk to about it. Everyone was the last person Cath wanted to talk to about it.

"My strategy," she said to Wren now, "is to make sure he doesn't meet my prettier, skinnier twin."

"I don't think it would matter," Wren said. Cath noticed she wasn't arguing the "prettier, skinnier" point. "It sounds like he's into your brain. I don't have your brain."

She didn't. And Cath didn't understand that at all. They had the same DNA. The same nature, the same nurture. All the differences between them didn't make sense.

"Come home with me this weekend," Cath said abruptly. She'd found a ride back to Omaha that night. Wren had already said she didn't want to go.

"You know Dad misses us," Cath said. "Come on."

Wren looked down at her tray. "I told you. I've got to study."

"There's a home game this weekend," Courtney said. "We don't have to be sober until Monday at eleven."

"Have you even called Dad?" Cath asked.

"We've been e-mailing," Wren said. "He seems fine."

"He misses us."

"He's supposed to miss us – he's our father."

"Yeah," Cath said softly, "but he's different."

Wren's face lifted, and she glared at Cath, shaking her head just slightly.

Cath pushed away from the table. "I better go. I need to run back to my room before class."

When Professor Piper asked for their unreliable-narrator papers that afternoon, Nick grabbed Cath's out of her hand. She grabbed it back. He raised an eyebrow.

Cath tilted her chin and smiled at him. It was only later that she realized she was giving him one of Wren's smiles. One of her evangelical smiles.

Nick pushed his tongue into his cheek and studied Cath for a second before he turned around.

Professor Piper took the paper from her hand. "Thank you, Cath."

She smiled warmly and squeezed Cath's shoulder. "I can hardly wait."

Nick twisted his head back around at that. *Pet,* he mouthed.

Cath thought about reaching up to the back of his head and petting his hair down to the point at his neck.

It had been two hours since they watched the drawbridge lock into the fortress.

Two hours of squabbling about whose fault it had been.

Baz would pout and say, "We wouldn't have missed curfew if you hadn't gotten in my way."

And Simon would growl and say, "I wouldn't *have* to get in your way if you weren't wandering the grounds nefariously."

But the truth, Simon knew, was that they'd just gotten so caught up in their arguing that they'd lost track of time, and now they'd have to spend the night out here. There was no getting around the curfew – no matter how many times Baz clicked his heels and said, *"There's no place like home."* (That was a seventh-year spell anyway; there was no way Baz could pull it off.)

Simon sighed and dropped down onto the grass. Baz was still muttering and staring up at the fortress like he might yet spot a way in.

"Oi," Simon said, thumping Baz's knee.

"Ow. What."

"I've got an Aero bar," Simon said. "Want half?"

Baz peered down, his long face as grey as his eyes in the gloaming. He flicked his black hair back and frowned, settling down next to Simon on the hill. "What kind?"

"Mint." Simon dug the candy out from the pocket in his cape.

"That's my favorite," Baz admitted, grudgingly.

Simon flashed him a wide, white grin. "Mine, too."

—from "Secrets, Stars, and Aero Bars," posted January 2009
by FanFixx.net authors *Magicath* and *Wrenegade*

NINE

Cath had an hour or so to kill before she left for Omaha, and she didn't feel like sitting in her room. It was the best kind of November day. Cold and crisp, but not quite freezing, not icy. Just cold enough that she could justifiably wear all her favorite clothes – cardigans and tights and leg warmers.

She thought about going to the Union to study but decided to walk around downtown Lincoln instead. Cath almost never left campus; there wasn't much reason to. Leaving campus felt like crossing the border. What would she do if she lost her wallet or got lost? She'd have to call the embassy. . . .

Lincoln felt a lot more like a small town than Omaha. There were still movie theaters downtown and little shops. Cath walked by a Thai restaurant and the famous Chipotle. She stopped to walk through a gift shop and smell all the essential oils. There was a Starbucks across the street. She wondered if it was Levi's Starbucks, and a minute later, she was crossing over.

Inside it was exactly like every other Starbucks Cath had ever been to. Maybe with a few more professorial types . . . And with Levi briskly moving behind the espresso machine, smiling at something somebody was saying in his headset.

Levi was wearing a black sweater over a white T-shirt. He looked like he'd just gotten a haircut – shorter in the back but still sticking up and flopping all over his face. He called out someone's name and handed a drink to a guy who looked like a retired violin teacher. Levi stopped to talk to the guy. Because he was Levi, and this was a biological necessity.

"Are you in line?" a woman asked Cath.

"No, go ahead." But then Cath decided she may as well get in line. It's not like she'd come here to observe Levi in the wild. She didn't know what she was doing here.

"Can I help you?" the guy at the register asked.

"No, you cannot," Levi said, pushing the guy down the line. "I got this one." He grinned at her. "Cather."

"Hey," Cath said, rolling her eyes. She hadn't thought he'd seen her.

"Look at you. All sweatered up. What are those, leg sweaters?"

"They're leg warmers."

"You're wearing at least four different kinds of sweater."

"This is a scarf."

"You look tarred and sweatered."

"I get it," she said.

"Did you just stop by to say hi?"

"No," she said. He frowned. She rolled her eyes again. "I came for coffee."

"What kind?"

"Just coffee. Grande coffee."

"It's cold out. Let me make you something good."

Cath shrugged. Levi grabbed a cup and started pumping syrup into it. She waited on the other side of the espresso machine.

"What are you doing tonight?" he asked. "You should come over. I think we're gonna have a bonfire. Reagan's coming."

"I'm going home," Cath said. "Omaha."

"Yeah?" Levi smiled up at her. The machine made a hissing noise. "I bet your parents are happy about that."

Cath shrugged again. Levi heaped whipped cream onto her drink. His hands were long – and thicker than the rest of him, a little knobby, with short, square nails.

"Have a great weekend," he said, handing her the drink.

"I haven't paid yet."

Levi held up his hands. "Please. You insult me."

"What is this?" She leaned over the cup and took a breath.

"My own concoction – Pumpkin Mocha Breve, light on the mocha. Don't try to order it from anyone else; it'll never turn out the same."

"Thanks," Cath said.

He grinned at her again. And she took a step backwards into a shelf full of mugs. "Bye," she said.

Levi moved on to the next person, smiling as wide as ever.

Cath's ride was a girl named Erin who'd put a sign up in the floor bathroom about splitting gas back to Omaha. All she talked about was her boyfriend who still lived in Omaha and who was probably cheating on her. Cath couldn't wait to get home.

She felt a surge of optimism as she ran up the steps to her house. Somebody had raked the leaves – people who stayed up all night making mountains out of mashed potatoes rarely had the presence of mind for leaf raking.

Not that her dad would actually do that, the mashed potato thing. That wasn't his style at all.

A fireman's pole to the attic. Spur-of-the-moment road trips. Staying up for three nights because he discovered *Battlestar Galactica* on Netflix . . . That was the MO to his madness.

"Dad?"

The house was dark. He should be home by now – he said he would come home early.

"Cath!" He was in the kitchen. She ran forward to hug him. He hugged her back like he needed it. When she pulled away, he smiled at her. Sight-for-sore-eyes and everything.

"It's dark in here," she said.

Her dad looked around the room like he'd just got there. "You're right." He walked around the main floor, flipping on lights. When he started on the lamps, Cath switched them off behind him. "I was just working on something . . . ," he said.

"For work?"

"For work," he agreed, absentmindedly turning on a lamp she'd just switched off. "How do you feel about Gravioli?"

"I like it. Is that what we're having for dinner?"

"No, that's the client I'm on."

"You guys got Gravioli?"

"Not yet. It's a pitch. How do you feel about it?"

"About Gravioli."

"Yeah . . ." He tapped the middle fingers of his left hand against his palm.

"I like the gravy? And . . . the ravioli?"

"And it makes you feel . . ."

"Full."

"That's terrible, Cath."

"Um . . . happy? Indulgent? Comforted? Doubly comforted because I'm eating two comfort foods at once?"

"*Maybe . . . ,*" he said.

"It makes me wonder what else would be better with gravy."

"Ha!" he said. "*Possible.*"

He started walking away from her, and she knew he was looking for his sketchbook.

"What *are* we having for dinner?" Cath asked.

"Whatever you want," he said. Then he stopped and turned to her, like he was remembering something. "No. Taco truck. Taco truck?"

"*Yes.* I'm driving. I haven't driven in months. Which one should we go to? Let's go to them all."

"There are at least seven taco trucks, just in a two-mile radius."

"Bring it on," she said. "I want to eat burritos from now until Sunday morning."

They ate their burritos and watched TV. Her dad scribbled, and Cath got out her laptop. Wren should be here with her laptop, too, sending Cath instant messages instead of talking.

Cath decided to send Wren an e-mail.

I wish you were here. Dad looks good. I don't think he's done dishes since we left, or that he's used any dishes other than drinking glasses. But he's working. And nothing is in pieces. And his eyes are in his eyes, you know? Anyway. See you Monday.
Be safe. Try not to let anyone roofie you.

Cath went to bed at one o'clock. She came back down at three to make sure the front door was locked; she did that sometimes when she couldn't sleep, when things didn't feel quite right or settled.

Her dad had papered the living room with headlines and sketches. He was walking around them now, like he was looking for something.

"Bed?" she said.

It took a few seconds for his eyes to rest on her.

"Bed," he answered, smiling gently.

When she came back down at five, he was in his room. She could hear him snoring.

Her dad was gone when she came downstairs later that morning.

Cath decided to survey the damage. The papers in the living

room had been sorted into sections. "Buckets," he called them. They were taped to the walls and the windows. Some pieces had other papers taped around them, as if the ideas were exploding. Cath looked over all his ideas and found a green pen to star her favorites. (She was green; Wren was red.)

The sight of it – chaotic, but still sorted – made her feel better.

A little manic was okay. A little manic paid the bills and got him up in the morning, made him magic when he needed it most.

"I was magic today, girls," he'd say after a big presentation, and they'd both know that meant Red Lobster for dinner, with their own lobsters and their own candle-warmed dishes of drawn butter.

A little manic was what their house ran on. The goblin spinning gold in the basement.

Cath checked the kitchen. The fridge was empty. The freezer was full of Healthy Choice meals and Marie Callender's pot pies. She loaded the dishwasher with dirty glasses, spoons, and coffee cups.

The bathroom was fine. Cath peeked into her dad's bedroom and gathered up more glasses. There were papers everywhere in there, not even in piles. Stacks of mail, most of it unopened. She wondered if he'd just swept everything into his room before she got home. She didn't touch anything but the dishes.

Then she microwaved a Healthy Choice meal, ate it over the sink, and decided to go back to bed.

Her bed at home was so much softer than she'd ever appreciated. And her pillows smelled so good. And she'd missed all their Simon and Baz posters. There was a full-size cutout of Baz, baring his fangs and smirking, hanging from the rail of Cath's canopy bed. She wondered if Reagan would tolerate it in their dorm room. Maybe it would fit in Cath's closet.

———

She and her dad ate every meal that weekend at a different taco truck. Cath had *carnitas* and *barbacoa, al pastor* and even *lengua*. She ate everything drenched in green tomatillo sauce.

Her dad worked. So Cath worked with him, logging more words on *Carry On, Simon* than she'd written in weeks. On Saturday night, she was still wide awake at one o'clock, but she made a big show of going to bed, so that her dad would, too.

Then she stayed up an hour or two more, writing.

It felt good to be writing in her own room, in her own bed. To get lost in the World of Mages and stay lost. To not hear any voices in her head but Simon's and Baz's. Not even her own. This was why Cath wrote fic. For these hours when *their* world supplanted the real world. When she could just ride their feelings for each other like a wave, like something falling downhill.

By Sunday night, the whole house was covered in onionskin sketch paper and burrito foil. Cath started another load of drinking glasses and gathered up all the delicious-smelling trash.

She was supposed to meet her ride out in West Omaha. Her dad was waiting by the door to take her, rattling his car keys against his leg.

Cath tried to take a mental picture of him to reassure herself with later. He had light brown hair, just Cath and Wren's color. Just their texture, too – thick and straight. A round nose, just wider and longer than theirs. Every/no-color eyes, just like theirs. It was like he'd had them by himself all along. Like the three of them had just split their DNA evenly.

It would be a much more reassuring picture if he didn't look so sad. His keys were hitting his leg too hard.

"I'm ready," she said.

"Cath . . ." The way he said it made her heart sink. "Sit down, okay? There's something I need to tell you real quick."

"Why do I have to sit down? I don't want to have to sit down."

"Just" – he motioned toward the dining room table – "please."

Cath sat at the table, trying not to lean on his papers or breathe them into disorder.

"I didn't mean to save this . . . ," he said.

"Just say it," Cath said. "You're making me nervous." Worse than nervous; her stomach was twisted up to her trachea.

"I've been talking to your mom."

"What?" Cath would have been less shocked if he told her he'd been talking to a ghost. Or a yeti. "Why? *What?*"

"Not for me," he said quickly, like he knew that the two of them getting back together was a horrifying prospect. "About you."

"Me?"

"You and Wren."

"Stop," she said. "Don't talk to her about us."

"Cath . . . she's your mother."

"There is no evidence to support that."

"Just listen, Cath, you don't even know what I'm going to say."

Cath was starting to cry. "I don't care what you're going to say."

Her dad decided to just keep talking. "She'd like to see you. She'd like to know you a little better."

"*No.*"

"Honey, she's been through a lot."

"No," Cath said. "She's been through nothing." It was true. You name it, Cath's mom wasn't there for it. "Why are we talking about her?"

Cath could hear her dad's keys banging against his leg again, hitting the bottom of the table. They needed Wren here now. Wren didn't twitch. Or cry. Wren wouldn't let him keep talking about this.

"She's your mother," he said. "And I think you should give her a chance."

"We did. When we were born. I'm done talking about this." Cath stood up too quickly, and a pile of papers fluttered off the table.

"Maybe we can talk about it more at Thanksgiving," he said.

"Maybe we can *not* talk about it at Thanksgiving, so that we don't ruin Thanksgiving – are you going to tell Wren?"

"I already did. I sent her an e-mail."

"What did she say?"

"Not much. She said she'd think about it."

"Well, I'm not thinking about it," Cath said. "I can't even *think* about this."

She got up from the table and started gathering her things; she needed something to hang on to. He shouldn't have talked to them about this separately. He shouldn't have talked to them about it at all.

The drive to West Omaha with her dad was miserable. And the drive back to Lincoln without him was worse.

Nothing was going right.

They'd been attacked by a *venomous crested woodfoul.*

And then they'd hidden in the cave with the *spiders* and the whatever-that-thing-was that had bitten Simon's tennis shoe, *possibly a rat.*

And then Baz had taken Simon's hand. Or maybe Simon had taken Baz's hand. . . . Anyway, it was totally forgivable because *woodfoul* and *spiders* and *rats.*

And sometimes you held somebody's hand just to prove that you were still alive, and that another human being was there to testify to that fact.

They'd walked back to the fortress like that, hand in hand. And it would have been okay – *it would have been mostly okay* – if one of them had just let go.

If they hadn't stood there on the edge of the Great Lawn, holding this little bit of each other, long after the danger had passed.

—from "The Wrong Idea," posted January 2010
by FanFixx.net author *Magicath*

TEN

Professor Piper wasn't done grading their unreliable-narrator scenes (which made Nick crabby and paranoid), but the professor wanted them all to get started on their final project, a ten-thousand-word short story. "Don't save it till the night before," she said, sitting on her desk and swinging her legs. "It will *read* like you wrote it the night before. I'm not interested in stream of consciousness."

Cath wasn't sure how she was going to keep everything straight in her head. The final project, the weekly writing assignments — on top of all her other classwork, for every other class. All the reading, all the writing. The essays, the justifications, the reports. Plus Tuesdays and sometimes Thursdays writing with Nick. Plus *Carry On*. Plus e-mail and notes and comments . . .

Cath felt like she was swimming in words. Drowning in them, sometimes.

"Do you ever feel," she asked Nick Tuesday night, "like you're a black hole — a reverse black hole. . . ."

"Something that blows instead of sucks?"

"Something that sucks *out*," she tried to explain. She was sitting at their table in the stacks with her head resting on her backpack. She could feel the indoor wind on her neck. "A reverse black hole of words."

"So the world is sucking you dry," he said, "of language."

"Not dry. Not yet. But the words are flying out of me so fast, I don't know where they're coming from."

"And maybe you've run through your surplus," he said gravely, "and now they're made of bone and blood."

"Now they're made of breath," she said.

Nick looked down at her, his eyebrows pulled together in one thick stripe. His eyes were that color you can't see in the rainbow. Indigo.

"Nope," he said. "I never feel like that."

She laughed and shook her head.

"The words come out of me like Spider-Man's webbing." Nick held out his hands and touched his middle fingers to his palms. "Fffffssh."

Cath tried to laugh, but yawned instead.

"Come on," he said, "it's midnight."

She gathered up her books. Nick always took the notebook. It was his notebook after all, and he worked on the story between library dates. (Or meetings or whatever these were.)

When they got outside, it was much colder than Cath was expecting. "See you tomorrow," Nick said as he walked away. "Maybe Piper'll have our papers done."

Cath nodded and got out her phone to call her room.

"Hey," someone said softly.

She jumped back. It was just Levi — leaning against the lamppost like the archetypical "man leaning against lamppost."

"You're always done at midnight." He smiled. "I thought I'd beat you to the punch. Too cold out here to stand around waiting."

"Thanks," she said, walking past him toward the dorms.

Levi was uncharacteristically quiet. "So that's your study partner?" he asked once they were halfway back to Pound.

"Yeah," Cath said into her scarf. She felt her breath, wet and freezing in the wool. "Do you know him?"

"Seen him around."

Cath was quiet. It was too cold to talk, and she was more tired than usual.

"He ever offer to walk you home?"

"I've never asked," Cath said quickly. "I've never asked you either."

"That's true," Levi said.

More quiet. More cold.

The air stung Cath's throat when she finally spoke again. "So maybe you shouldn't."

"Don't be ridiculous," Levi said. "That wasn't my point."

The first time she saw Wren that week, at lunch with Courtney, all Cath could think was, *So this is what you look like when you're keeping a giant secret from me – exactly the same as usual.*

Cath wondered if Wren was ever planning to talk to her about . . . what their dad had brought up. She wondered how many other important things Wren wasn't telling her. And when had this started? When had Wren started filtering what she told Cath?

I can do that, too, Cath thought, *I can keep secrets.* But Cath didn't have any secrets, and she didn't want to keep anything from Wren. Not when it felt so good, so easy, to know that when she was with Wren, she didn't have to worry about a filter.

She kept waiting for a chance to talk to Wren without Courtney, but Courtney was always around. (And always talking about the most inane things possible. Like her life was an audition for an MTV reality show.)

Finally, after a few days, Cath decided to walk to class with Wren after lunch, even though it might make her late.

"What's up?" Wren asked as soon as Courtney was on her

merry way to Economics. It had started snowing — a wet snow.

"You know I went home last weekend . . . ," Cath said.

"Yeah. How's Dad?"

"Fine . . . *good,* actually. He's pitching Gravioli."

"Gravioli? That's huge."

"I know. And he seemed into it. And there was nothing else — I mean, everything seemed fine."

"I told you he didn't need us," Wren said.

Cath snorted. "He obviously needs us. If he had a cat, the man would be one bad day away from *Grey Gardens*. I think he eats all of his meals at QuikTrip, and he's sleeping on the couch."

"I thought you said he was doing good."

"Well. For Dad. You should come home with me next time."

"Next time is Thanksgiving. I think I'll be there."

Cath stopped. They were almost to Wren's next class, and Cath hadn't even gotten to the hard part yet. "Dad told me . . . that he'd already told you . . ."

Wren exhaled like she knew what was coming. "Yeah."

"He said you were thinking about it."

"I am."

"Why?" Cath tried really hard to say it without whining.

"Because." Wren hitched up her backpack. "Because she's our mom. And I'm thinking about it."

"But . . ." It wasn't that Cath couldn't think of an argument. It was that there were so many. The arguments in her brain were like a swarm of people running from a burning building and getting stuck in the door. "But she'll just mess everything up."

"She already messed everything up," Wren said. "It's not like she can leave us again."

"Yes. She can."

Wren shook her head. "I'm just thinking about it."

"Will you tell me if you decide anything?"

Wren frowned. "Not if it's going to make you this upset."

"I have a right to get upset about upsetting things."

"I just don't like it," Wren said, looking away from Cath, up at the door. "I'm gonna be late."

So was Cath.

"We're already roommates," Baz argued. "I shouldn't have to be his lab partner, as well. You're asking me to bear far more than my fair share of apple-cheeked protagonism."

Every girl in the laboratory sat on the edge of her stool, ready to take Baz's place.

"That's enough about my cheeks," Snow muttered, blushing heroically.

"Honestly, Professor," Baz said, waving his wand toward Snow in a *just look at him* gesture. Snow caught the end of the wand and pointed it at the floor.

Professor Chilblains was unmoved. "Sit *down,* Mr. Pitch. You're wasting precious lab time."

Baz slammed his books down at Snow's station. Snow put his safety goggles on and adjusted them; it did nothing to dim his blue eyes or blunt his glare.

"For the record," Snow grumbled. "I don't want to spend any more time with you either."

Stupid boy . . . Baz sighed to himself, taking in Snow's tense shoulders, the flush of anger in his neck, and the thick fall of bronze hair partially trapped in his goggles. . . . *What do you know about want?*

—from "Five Times Baz Went to Chemistry
and One Time He Didn't," posted August 2009
by FanFixx.net authors *Magicath* and *Wrenegade*

ELEVEN

The hallway was perfectly quiet. Everyone who lived in Pound Hall was somewhere else, having fun.

Cath stared at her computer screen and heard Professor Piper's voice again in her head. She kept forcing herself to remember the entire conversation, playing it back and playing it back, all the way through, forcing a finger down her memory's throat.

Today, at the beginning of class, Professor Piper had passed their unreliable-narrator scenes back. Everybody's but Cath's. "We'll talk after class, okay?" the professor said to Cath with that gentle, righteous smile she had.

Cath had thought this exception must be a good thing – that Professor Piper must have really liked her story. She really liked Cath, you could tell; Cath got more of those soft smiles than just about anybody else in the class. More than Nick, by far.

And this scene was the best thing Cath had written all semester; she knew it was. Maybe Professor Piper wanted to talk about the piece in more detail, or maybe she was going to talk to Cath about taking her advanced class next semester. (You had to have special permission to register.) Or maybe just . . . something good. *Something.*

"Cath," Professor Piper said when everybody else was gone and Cath had stepped up to her desk. "Sit down."

Professor Piper's smile was softer than ever, but it was all wrong. Her eyes were sad and sorry, and when she handed Cath her paper, there was a small, red *F* written in the corner.

Cath's head whipped up.

"Cath," Professor Piper said. "I don't know what to make of this. I really don't know what you were thinking—"

"But . . . ," Cath said, "was it *that* bad?" Could her scene really have been that much worse than everyone else's?

"Bad or good isn't the point." Professor Piper shook her head, and her long, wild hair swayed from side to side. "This is plagiarism."

"No," Cath said. "I wrote it myself."

"You wrote it yourself? You're the author of *Simon Snow and the Mage's Heir*?"

"Of course not." Why was Professor Piper saying this?

"These characters, this whole world belongs to someone else."

"But the story is mine."

"The characters and the world *make* the story," the older woman said, like she was pleading with Cath to understand.

"Not necessarily . . ." Cath could feel how red her face was. Her voice was breaking.

"Yes," Professor Piper said. "Necessarily. If you're asked to write something original, you can't just steal someone else's story and rearrange the characters."

"It's *not* stealing."

"What would you call it?"

"Borrowing," Cath said, hating that she was arguing with Professor Piper, not ever wanting to make Professor Piper's face look this cold and closed, but not able to stop. "Repurposing. Remixing. Sampling."

"*Stealing.*"

"It's not illegal." All the arguments came easily to Cath; they were the justification for all fanfiction. "I don't own the characters, but I'm not trying to sell them, either."

Professor Piper just kept shaking her head, more disappointed than she'd seemed even a few minutes ago. She ran her hands along her jeans. Her fingers were small, and she was wearing a large, narrow turquoise ring that jutted out over her knuckle. "Whether it's legal is hardly relevant. I asked you to write an original story, *you*, and there's nothing original here."

"I just don't think you understand," Cath said. It came out a sob. She looked down at her lap, ashamed, and saw the red *F* again.

"I don't think *you* understand, Cath," the professor said, her voice deliberately calm. "And I really want you to. This is college – what we do here is real. I've allowed you into an upper-level course, and so far, you've greatly impressed me. But this was an immature mistake, and the right thing for you to do now is to learn from it."

Cath locked her jaw closed. She still wanted to argue. She'd worked so hard on this assignment. Professor Piper was always telling them to write about something close to their hearts, and there was nothing closer to Cath's heart than Baz and Simon. . . .

But Cath just nodded and stood up. She even managed a meek thank you on the way out of the classroom.

Thinking about it now, again, made the skin on Cath's face feel scorched clean. She stared at the charcoal drawing of Baz pinned up behind her laptop. He was sitting on a carved black throne, one leg draped over its arm, his head tilted forward in languid challenge. The artist had written along the bottom of the page in perfect calligraphy: *"Who would you be without me, Snow? A blue-eyed virgin who'd never thrown a punch."* And below that, *The inimitable Magicath*.

Cath picked up her phone again. She'd called Wren at least six times since she left class. Every time, the call went straight to voice mail. Every time, Cath hung up.

If she could just talk to Wren, she would feel better. Wren would understand – probably. Wren *had* said all that mean stuff about Baz and Simon a few weeks ago. But she'd been drunk. If Wren knew how upset Cath was right now, she wouldn't be a bitch about it. She'd understand. She'd tug Cath back from the edge – Wren was really good at that.

If Wren were here . . . Cath laughed. It came out like a sob. (*What the eff*, she thought, *why is everything coming out like a sob?*)

If Wren were here, she'd call an Emergency Kanye Party.

First she'd stand on the bed. That was the protocol back home. When things were getting too intense – when Wren found out that Jesse Sandoz was cheating on her, when Cath got fired because her boss at the bookstore didn't think she smiled enough, when their dad was acting like a zombie and wouldn't stop – one of them would stand on her bed and pretend to pull an imaginary lever, a giant switch set in the air, and shout, "Emergency Kanye Party!"

And then it was the other person's job to run to the computer and start the Emergency Kanye playlist. And then they'd both jump around and dance and shout Kanye West lyrics until they felt better. Sometimes it would take a while. . . .

I'm authorized to call an Emergency Kanye Party, Cath thought to herself, laughing again. (This time it came out slightly more like a laugh.) *It's not like I need a quorum.*

She reached toward her laptop and opened her Kanye playlist. There were portable speakers in one of her drawers. She got them out and plugged them in.

Then she turned the volume all the way up. It was a Friday night; there was nobody in the building, maybe nobody on campus, to disturb.

Emergency Kanye Party. Cath climbed onto her bed to announce it, but she stepped right down. It felt silly. And pathetic. (Is there *any*thing more pathetic than a one-person dance party?)

She stood in front of the speakers instead and closed her eyes, not really dancing, just bouncing and whispering the lyrics. After the first verse, she was dancing. Kanye always crawled right under her skin. He was the perfect antidote to any serious frustration. Just enough angry, just enough indignant, just enough the-world-will-never-know-how-ridiculously-awesome-I-am. Just enough poet.

With her eyes closed, Cath could almost pretend that Wren was dancing on the other side of the room, holding a Simon Snow replica wand for a microphone.

After a few songs, Cath didn't need to pretend.

If any of her neighbors had been home, they would have heard her shouting the lyrics.

Cath danced. And rapped. And danced. And eventually there was knocking.

Damn. Maybe the neighbors are home.

She opened the door without looking and without turning down the music (Kanye-impaired thinking), but ready to apologize.

It was just Levi.

"Reagan isn't here!" Cath shouted.

He said something, but not loud enough.

"What?" she yelled.

"Then who is here?" Levi shouted, smiling. Levi. Always smiling. Wearing a plaid flannel shirt with the sleeves unbuttoned at the wrists. Couldn't even be trusted to dress himself. "Who's in there, listening to rap music?"

"Me," Cath said. She was panting. She tried not to pant.

He leaned toward her so he wouldn't have to shout. "This can't be Cather music. I'd always pegged you as the mopey, indie type." He was teasing her; only genuine emergencies were allowed to interrupt the Emergency Kanye Party.

"Go away." Cath started to shut the door.

Levi stopped it with his hand. "What are you doing?" he said, laughing, and pushing his head forward on the "doing."

She shook her head because she couldn't think of anything reasonable to say. And because it wouldn't matter anyway; Levi was never reasonable. "Emergency dance party – go away."

"Oh *no*," Levi said, pushing the door open and sliding in. Too skinny. Too tall.

Cath shut the door behind him. There was no protocol for this. She'd call Wren for a sidebar consultation if there was any chance Wren would answer the phone.

Levi stood in front of Cath, his face serious (for once) (seriously, *for once*) and his head deliberately bobbing up and down. "So," he said loudly. "Emergency dance party."

Cath nodded.

And nodded. And nodded.

Levi nodded back.

And then Cath started laughing and rolled her eyes away from him, moving her hips from side to side. Just barely.

And then her shoulders.

And then she was dancing again. Tighter than before – her knees and elbows almost locking – but dancing.

When she looked back at Levi, he was dancing, too. Exactly the way she would have imagined him dancing if she'd ever tried. Too long and too loose, running his fingers through his hair. (*Dude. We get it. Extreme widow's peak.*) His eyes were absolutely gleaming with mirth. Putting out light.

Cath couldn't stop laughing. Levi caught her eyes and laughed, too.

And then he was dancing with her. Not close or anything. Not any closer, actually – just looking at her face and moving with her.

And then she was dancing with him. Better than him, which was nice. She realized she was biting her bottom lip and stopped.

She started rapping instead. Cath could blow these songs backwards. Levi raised his eyebrows and grinned. He knew the chorus and rapped with her.

They danced into the next song and through it and into the next. Levi stepped toward her, maybe not even on purpose, and Cath whirled up onto her bed. He laughed and jumped up onto Reagan's, practically bumping his head on the ceiling.

They kept on dancing together, imitating each other's goofiest moves, bouncing at the end of the beds. . . . It was almost like dancing with Wren. (But not, of course. Really, really not.)

And then the door swung open.

Cath jumped back away from it and fell flat on her mattress, bouncing and rolling onto the floor.

Levi was laughing so hard, he had to lean against the wall with both hands.

Reagan walked in and said something, but Cath didn't catch it. She reached up to her desk and closed the laptop, stopping the music. Levi's laughter rang out in the sudden quiet. Cath was completely out of breath, and she'd landed wrong on her knee.

"What. The. Major. *Fuck*," Reagan said, more shocked than angry — at least Cath didn't think she seemed angry.

"Emergency dance party," Levi said, jumping off the bed and reaching out to help Cath. Cath held on to the desk and stood up.

"Okay?" he asked.

She smiled and nodded her head.

"Have you met Cather?" Levi said to Reagan, his face still shining with amusement. "She spits hot fire."

"This is exactly the sort of day I'm having," Reagan said, setting down her bag and kicking off her shoes. "Weird shit around every corner. I'm going out. You coming?"

"Sure." Levi turned to Cath. "You coming?"

Reagan looked at Cath and frowned. Cath felt something sticky blooming again in her stomach. Maybe the scene with Professor Piper was coming back to her. Or maybe she shouldn't have been dancing with her roommate's boyfriend. "You should come," Reagan said. She seemed sincere.

Cath tugged at the hem of her T-shirt. "Nah. It's already late. I'm just gonna write. . . ." She reached for her phone out of habit and checked it. She'd missed a text message – from Wren.

"at muggsy's. COME NOW. 911."

Cath checked the time – Wren had texted her twenty minutes ago, while she and Levi were dancing. She set her phone on the desk and started putting her boots on over her pajama pants.

"Is everything okay?" Levi asked.

"I don't know. . . ." Cath shook her head. She felt ashamed again. And scared. Her stomach seemed thrilled to have something new to twist about. "What's Muggsy's?"

"It's a bar," he said. "Near East Campus."

"What's East Campus?"

Levi reached around her and picked up her phone. He frowned at the screen. "I'll take you. I've got my car."

"Take her where?" Reagan asked. Levi tossed her Cath's phone and put on his coat. "I'm sure she's fine," Reagan said, looking at the text. "She probably just had too much to drink. Mandatory freshman behavior."

"I still have to go get her," Cath said, taking back the phone.

"Of course you do," Levi agreed. "Nine-one-one is nine-one-one." He looked at Reagan. "You coming?"

"Not if you don't need me. We're supposed to meet Anna and Matt—"

"I'll catch up with you later," he said.

Cath was already standing by the door. "Your sister's fine, Cath," Reagan said almost (but not quite) gently. "She's just being normal."

Levi's car was a truck. A big one. *How did he afford the gas?*

Cath didn't want any help getting in, but the running board was missing – it was an especially shitty truck, she noticed now that she was up close – and she would've had to climb in on all fours if he hadn't taken her elbow.

The cab smelled like gasoline and roasted coffee beans. The seat belt was stuck, but she still managed to get it buckled.

Levi swung into his seat smoothly and smiled at her. He was trying to be encouraging, Cath figured.

"What's East Campus?" she asked.

"Are you serious?"

"Why wouldn't I be serious right now?"

"It's the other part of campus," he said. "Where the Ag School is?"

Cath shrugged impatiently and looked out the window. It had been sleeting since this afternoon. The lights looked like wet smears on the streets. Fortunately, Levi was driving slow.

"And the law school," he said. "And there are dormitories and a perfectly adequate bowling alley. And a *dairy*. Seriously, none of this is ringing any bells?"

Cath let her head rest on the glass. The truck's heater was still blowing cold air. It had been a half hour now since the text. A half hour past 911. "How far is it?"

"A few miles. Ten minutes from here, maybe longer with the weather. East Campus is where most of my classes are. . . ."

Cath wondered if Wren was alone. Where was Courtney? Weren't they supposed to be skinny-bitching together?

"There's a tractor museum," Levi said. "And an international quilt education center. And the food in the residence halls is outstanding. . . ."

It wasn't right. Having a twin sister was supposed to be like having your own watcher. Your own guardian. BUILT-IN BEST

FRIEND — their dad had bought them shirts that said that for their thirteenth birthday. They still wore them sometimes (though never at once) just to be funny. Or ironic or whatever.

What's the point of having a twin sister if you won't let her look out for you? If you won't let her fight at your back?

"East Campus is just so much better than City Campus in every way. And you don't even know that it exists."

The light ahead turned red, and Cath felt the tires spin beneath them. Levi shifted gears, and the truck rolled to a perfect stop.

They had to park quite a ways from the bar. This whole street was bars, block after block of them.

"They're not going to let me in," Cath said, wishing Levi would walk faster. "I'm underage."

"Muggsy's never checks."

"I've never even been in a bar."

A dozen girls spilled out of the doorway ahead of them. Levi grabbed Cath's sleeve and pulled her out of the way. "I have," he said. "It's going to be fine."

"It's not fine," Cath said, more to herself than to Levi. "If it was fine, she wouldn't need me."

Levi pulled on her sleeve again and opened a heavy, black, windowless door. Cath glanced up at the neon sign over their heads. Only the UGGSY and a four-leaf clover lit up. There was a big guy sitting just inside on a stool, reading a *Daily Nebraskan* with a flashlight. He flipped the light up at Levi and smiled. "Hey, Levi."

Levi smiled back. "Hey, Yackle."

Yackle held a second door open with one hand — he didn't even look at Cath. Levi patted him on the arm as they walked past.

It was dark inside the bar and crowded, people pressed shoulder to shoulder. There was a band playing on a couch-sized stage near the door. Cath looked around, but she couldn't see past the crush of bodies.

She wondered where Wren was.

Where had Wren been forty-five minutes ago?

Hiding in the bathroom? Crouched against a wall?

Had she been sick, had she passed out? She did that some-times. . . . Who had been here to help her? Who had been here to hurt her?

Cath felt Levi's hand on her elbow. "Come on," he said.

They squeezed by a high-top table full of people doing shots. One of the guys fell back into Cath, and Levi propped him back up with a smile.

"You hang out here?" Cath asked when they were past the table.

"It's only douchey like this when there's a band playing."

She and Levi moved farther from the stage, closer to the bar. A movement near the wall caught Cath's eye – the way someone flipped back her hair. "Wren," Cath said, surging forward. Levi held her arm and pushed in front of her, trying to clear the way.

"Wren!" Cath shouted over the crowd, before she was even close enough for Wren to hear. Cath's heart was pounding. She was trying to make out the situation around Wren – a big guy was standing in front of her, his arms caging Wren against the carpeted wall.

"Wren!" Cath knocked one of the guy's arms away, and he pulled back, nonplussed. "Are you okay?"

"Cath?" Wren was holding a bottle of dark beer halfway up to her mouth like her arm was stuck there. "What are you doing here?"

"You told me to come."

Wren huffed. Her face was flushed, and she had drunk, droopy eyelids. "I didn't tell you anything."

"You sent me a text," Cath said, glowering up at the big guy until he took another step back. " 'Come to Muggsy's. Nine-one-one.' "

"Shit." Wren pulled her phone out of her jeans and looked down at it. She had to stare at it for a second before she could focus. "That was for Courtney. Wrong *C*."

"Wrong *C*?" Cath froze, then threw her hands into the air. "Are you kidding me?"

"Hey," somebody said.

They both turned. A fratty-looking guy was standing a foot away, nodding his head at them. He curled his lip and grinned. "Twins."

"Fuck off," Wren said, turning back to her sister. "Look, I'm sorry—"

"Are you in trouble?" Cath asked.

"No," Wren said. "No, no, no . . ."

"Pretty hot," the guy said.

"Then why the nine-one-one?" Cath demanded.

"Because I wanted Courtney to come quick." Wren waved her beer bottle toward the stage. "The guy she likes is here."

"Dude, check it out. Hot twins."

"Nine-one-one is for emergencies!" Cath shouted. It was so loud in here, you *had* to shout; it made it way too easy to lose your temper.

"Do you really think that's appropriate?" Cath heard Levi say in his smiling-for-strangers voice.

"Fucking twins, man. That's the fantasy, right?"

"Take a pill, Cath," Wren said, rubbing her eyes with the back of her hand. "It's not like I *actually* called nine-one-one."

"You realize that they're sisters, right?" Levi said, his voice getting tighter. "You're talking about incest."

The guy laughed. "No, I'm talking about buying them drinks until they start making out."

"Is that what happens with you and your sister?" Levi stepped away from Cath, toward the guy and his friend. "Who fucking raised you?"

"Levi, don't." Cath pulled on his jacket. "This happens all the time."

"This happens all the time?" His eyebrows jerked up in the middle, and he turned on the guy. . . .

"These two girls have *parents*. They have a *father*. And he should never have to worry that they're going to end up in a bar, debasing themselves for some pervert who still jerks off to *Girls Gone Wild* videos. That's not something a father should ever have to *think about*."

The pervy guy wasn't paying attention. He leered drunkenly over Levi's shoulder at Cath and Wren. Wren flipped him off, and he arched his lip again.

Levi stepped closer to the guy's table. "You don't get to look at them that way, just because they look alike. You fucking pervert."

Another fratty guy stepped up, carrying three beers, and glanced over. He grinned when he saw Cath and Wren. *"Twins."*

"Fucking fantasy," the first guy said.

Then, before anyone saw him coming, the guy standing next to Wren – the big one who had been caging her in – stepped past Levi and plowed the drunk pervert right in the chin.

Levi looked up at the big guy and grinned, clapping him on the shoulder. Wren grabbed his arm – "Jandro!"

The pervy guy's friends were already helping him off the floor.

Levi took Cath's sleeve and started pushing Jandro into the crowd. Jandro dragged Wren behind him. "Come on," Levi said, "out, out, out."

Cath could hear the perv shouting curses behind them.

"Oh, fuck you, *Flowers in the Attic*!" Levi shouted back.

They practically fell through the front door. The bouncer stood up. "Everything cool, Levi?"

"Drunks," Levi said, shaking his head. Yackle headed back into the bar.

Wren was already out on the sidewalk, shouting at the big guy. At Jandro. Was he her date, Cath wondered, or was he just somebody who threw a punch for her?

"I can't believe you did that," Wren said. "You could get arrested." She hit his arm, and he let her.

Levi hit Jandro's other arm in a kind of salute. They were about the same height, but Jandro was broader, a dark-haired guy – probably Mexican, Cath thought – wearing a red Western shirt.

"Who's going to get arrested?" someone asked. Cath spun around. *Courtney*. Clomping toward them in five-inch pink heels. "Why are you guys standing outside in this shit?"

"We're not," Cath said, "we're leaving."

"But I just got here," Courtney whined. She looked at Wren. "Is Noah in there?"

"We're leaving," Cath said to Wren. "You're drunk."

"Yes –" Wren held up her beer bottle. "– finally."

"Whoa, there," Levi said, snagging the bottle and dropping it into a trash can behind her. "Open container."

"That was my beer," Wren objected.

"A little louder there, jailbait. I don't think every cop on the street heard you." He was smiling.

Cath wasn't. "You're drunk," she said. "You're going home."

"No. Cath. I'm not. I'm drunk, and I'm staying out. That's the whole fucking point of *being* out." She swayed, and Courtney giggled and put her arm around her. Wren looked at her roommate and started giggling, too.

"Everything's 'the whole fucking point' with you," Cath said quietly. The sleet was hitting her cheeks like gravel. Wren had tiny pieces of ice in her hair. "I'm not leaving you alone like this," Cath said.

"I'm *not* alone," Wren replied.

"It's okay, Cath." Courtney's smile couldn't be more patronizing. Or more coated in pink lipstick. "I'm here, Han Solo's here —" She smiled up flirtily at Jandro. "— the night is young."

"The night is young!" Wren sang, laying her head against Courtney's arm.

"I can't just . . ." Cath shook her head.

"It's fucking freezing out here." Courtney hugged Wren again. "Come on."

"Not Muggsy's," Jandro said, starting to walk away. He glanced back at Cath, and for a second she thought he was going to say something, but he kept on walking. Wren and Courtney followed him. Courtney clomped. Wren didn't look back.

Cath watched them walk up the block and disappear under another broken neon sign. She wiped the ice off her cheeks.

"Hey," she heard someone say after a cold, wet minute. Levi. Still standing behind her.

"Let's go," Cath said, looking down at the sidewalk. On top of everything else that was going wrong right this minute, Levi must think she was an idiot. Cath's pajama pants were soaked, and the wind was blowing right through them. She shivered.

Levi walked past her, taking her hood and pulling it up over her head on his way. She followed him to his truck. Now that she realized how cold she was, her teeth were starting to chatter.

"I've got it," she said when Levi tried to help her in. She waited for him to walk away before heaving herself up onto the seat. Levi slid behind the wheel and started the truck, cranking up the heat and the windshield wipers, and holding his hands up to the vents. "Seat belt," he said after a minute.

"Oh, sorry . . ." Cath dug for the seat belt.

She buckled up. The truck still didn't move.

"You did the right thing, you know."

Levi.

"No," Cath said. "I don't know."

"You had to go check on her. Nine-one-one is nine-one-one."

"And then I left her — completely wasted — with a stranger and a moron."

"That guy didn't seem like a stranger," Levi said.

Cath almost laughed. Because he hadn't argued with the moron part. "I'm her sister. I'm supposed to look out for her."

"Not against her will."

"What if she passes out?"

"Does that happen a lot?"

Cath looked over at him. His hair was wet, and you could see the tracks where he'd pushed his fingers through it.

"I don't want to talk about this anymore," she said.

"Okay . . . Are you hungry?"

"No." She looked down at her lap.

The truck still didn't move.

"Because *I'm* hungry," he said.

"Aren't you supposed to meet up with Reagan?"

"Yep. Later."

Cath rubbed her face again. The ice in her hair was melting and dripping into her eyes. "I'm wearing pajamas."

Levi put the truck into reverse. "I know just the place."

The pajama pants weren't a problem.

Levi took her to a twenty-four-hour truck stop near the edge of town. (Nothing in Lincoln was too far from the edge of town.)

The place felt like it hadn't been redecorated ever, like maybe it had been built sixty years ago out of materials that were already worn and cracking. The waitress started pouring them coffee without even asking if they wanted any.

"Perfect," Levi said, smiling at the waitress and shuffling out of his coat. She set the cream on the table and brushed his shoulder fondly.

"Do you come here a lot?" Cath asked, when the waitress left.

"More than I go other places, I guess. If you order the corned beef hash, you don't have to eat for days. . . . Cream?"

Cath didn't usually order coffee, but she nodded anyway, and he topped off her cup. She pulled her saucer back and stared down at it. She heard Levi exhale.

"I know how you feel right now," he said. "I have two little sisters."

"You don't know how I feel." Cath dumped in three packs of sugar. "She's not just my sister."

"Do people really do that to you guys all the time?"

"Do what?" Cath looked up at him, and he looked away.

"The twin thing."

"Oh. That." She stirred her coffee, clacking the spoon too hard against her cup. "Not all the time. Only if we're around drunks or, like, walking down the street. . . ."

He made a face. "People are depraved."

The waitress came back, and Levi lit up for her. Predictably. He ordered corned beef hash. Cath stuck with coffee.

"She'll grow out of it," he said when the waitress walked away from their booth. "Reagan's right. It's a freshman thing."

"I'm a freshman. I'm not out getting wasted."

Levi laughed. "Right. Because you're too busy throwing dance parties. What was the emergency anyway?"

Cath watched him laugh and felt the sticky black pit yawn open in her stomach. *Professor Piper. Simon. Baz. Neat, red* F.

"Were you anticipating an emergency?" he asked, still smiling. "Or maybe summoning one? Like a rain dance?"

"You don't have to do this," Cath said.

"Do what?"

"Try to make me feel better." She felt the tears coming on, and her voice wobbled. "I'm not one of your little sisters."

Levi's smile fell completely. "I'm sorry," he said, all the teasing gone. "I . . . I thought maybe you'd want to talk about it."

Cath looked back at her coffee. She shook her head a few times, as much to tell him no as to shake away the stinging in her eyes.

His corned beef hash came. A whole mess of it. He moved Cath's coffee cup to the table and scooped hash onto her saucer.

Cath ate it — it was easier than arguing. She'd been arguing all day, and so far, no one had listened. And besides, the corned beef hash was really good, like they made it fresh with real corned beef, and there were two sunny-side-up eggs on top.

Levi piled more onto her plate.

"Something happened in class," Cath said. She didn't look up at him. Maybe she could use a big brother right now — she was currently down a twin sister. *Any port in a storm, and all that . . .*

"What class?" he asked.

"Fiction-Writing."

"You take Fiction-Writing? That's an actual class?"

"That's an actual question?"

"Does this have something to do with your Simon Snow thing?"

Cath looked up now and flushed. "Who told you about my Simon Snow thing?"

"Nobody had to tell me. You've got Simon Snow stuff everywhere. You're worse than my ten-year-old cousin." Levi grinned; he looked relieved to be smiling again. "Reagan told me you write stories about him."

"So *Reagan* told you."

"That's what you're always working on, right? Writing stories about Simon Snow?"

Cath didn't know what to say. It sounded absolutely ridiculous when Levi said it.

"They're not just stories . . . ," she said.

He took a giant bite of hash. His hair was still wet and falling (wetly, blondly) into his eyes. He pushed it back. "They're not?"

Cath shook her head. They *were* just stories, but stories weren't *just* anything. Simon wasn't *just*.

"What do you know about Simon Snow?" she asked.

He shrugged. "Everybody knows about Simon Snow."

"You've read the books?"

"I've seen the movies."

Cath rolled her eyes so hard, it hurt. (Actually.) (Maybe because she was still on the edge of tears. On the edge, period.) "So you haven't read the books."

"I'm not really a book person."

"That might be the most idiotic thing you've ever said to me."

"Don't change the subject," Levi said, grinning some more. *"You write stories about Simon Snow. . . ."*

"You think this is funny."

"Yes," Levi said. "But also sort of cool. Tell me about your stories."

Cath pressed the tines of her fork into her place mat. "They're just, like . . . I take the characters, and I put them in new situations."

"Like deleted scenes?"

"Sometimes. More like what-ifs. Like, what if Baz wasn't evil? What if Simon never found the five blades? What if Agatha found them instead? What if Agatha was evil?"

"Agatha couldn't be evil," Levi argued, leaning forward and

pointing at Cath with his fork. "She's 'pure of heart, a lion of dawn.'"

Cath narrowed her eyes. "How do you know that?"

"I told you, I've seen the movies."

"Well, in my world, if I want to make Agatha evil, I can. Or I can make her a vampire. Or I can make her an actual lion."

"Simon wouldn't like that."

"Simon doesn't care. He's in love with Baz."

Levi guffawed. (*You don't get many opportunities to use that word,* Cath thought, *but this is one of them.*)

"Simon isn't gay," he said.

"In my world, he is."

"But Baz is his *nemesis.*"

"I don't have to follow any of the rules. The original books already exist; it's not my job to rewrite them."

"Is it your job to make Simon gay?"

"You're getting distracted by the gay thing," Cath said. She was leaning forward now, too.

"It is distracting. . . ." Levi giggled. (Did guys "giggle" or "chuckle"? Cath hated the word "chuckle.")

"The whole point of fanfiction," she said, "is that you get to play inside somebody else's universe. Rewrite the rules. Or bend them. The story doesn't have to end when Gemma Leslie gets tired of it. You can stay in this world, this world you love, as long as you want, as long as you keep thinking of new stories—"

"Fanfiction," Levi said.

"*Yes.*" Cath was embarrassed by how sincere she sounded, how excited she felt whenever she actually talked about this. She was so used to keeping it a secret – used to assuming people would think she was a freak and a nerd and a pervert. . . .

Maybe Levi thought all those things. Maybe he just found freaks and perverts amusing.

"Emergency dance party?" he asked.

"Right." She sat back in the booth again. "Our professor asked us to write a scene with an untrustworthy narrator. I wrote something about Simon and Baz. . . . She didn't get it. She thought it was plagiarism." Cath forced herself to use that word, felt the tar wake up with a twist in her stomach.

"But it was *your* story," Levi said.

"*Yes.*"

"That's not exactly plagiarism. . . ." He smiled at her. She needed to come up with more words for Levi's smiles; he had too many of them. This one was a question. "They were your words, right?"

"Right."

"I mean, I can see why your professor wouldn't want you to write a Simon Snow story – the class isn't called *Fan*fiction-Writing – but I wouldn't call it plagiarism. Is it illegal?"

"No. As long as you don't try to sell it. GTL says she loves fanfiction – I mean, she loves the idea of it. She doesn't actually read it."

"Is your professor reporting you?"

"What do you mean?"

"Is she reporting you to the Judicial Board?"

"She didn't even mention that."

"She would have mentioned it," he said. "So . . . okay." He waved his fork in a straight line between them, holding it like a pencil. "This isn't a big deal. You just don't turn in any more fanfiction."

It still felt like a big deal. Cath's stomach still hurt.

"She just . . . she made me feel so stupid and . . . *deviant*."

Levi laughed again. "Do you really expect an elderly English professor to be down with gay Simon Snow fanfiction?"

"She didn't even mention the gay thing," Cath said.

"Deviant." He raised an eyebrow. Levi's eyebrows were much darker than his hair. Too dark, really. And arched. Like he'd drawn them on.

Cath felt herself smile, even though she was trying to hold her lips and face still. She shook her head, then looked down at her food and took a big bite.

Levi scraped more eggs and hash onto her plate.

Sneaking around the castle, staying out all night, coming home in the morning with leaves in his hair . . .

Baz was up to something; Simon was sure of it. But he needed proof – Penelope and Agatha weren't taking his suspicions seriously.

"He's *plotting*," Simon would say.

"He's always plotting," Penelope would answer.

"He's *looming*," Simon would say.

"He's always looming," Agatha would answer. "He is quite tall."

"No taller than me."

"Mmm . . . a bit."

It wasn't just the plotting and the looming; Baz was *up* to something. Something beyond his chronic gittishness. His pearl grey eyes were bloodshot and shadowed; his black hair had lost its luster. Usually cold and intimidating, lately Baz seemed chilled and cornered.

Simon had followed him around the catacombs last night for three hours, and still didn't have a clue.

—from chapter 3, *Simon Snow and the Five Blades,*
copyright © 2008 by Gemma T. Leslie

TWELVE

It was too cold to wait outside before Fiction-Writing, so Cath found a bench inside Andrews Hall and sat with one leg tucked beneath her, leaning back against the cream-colored wall.

She took out her phone and opened a fic she'd been reading. (She was too nervous to study.) Cath never read other people's Simon/Baz anymore – she didn't want to unconsciously mimic another author or steal someone's ideas – so when she did read fic, it was always about Penelope. Sometimes Penelope/Agatha. Sometimes Penelope/Micah (the American exchange student who only appeared in Book Three). Sometimes just Penelope, all on her own, having adventures.

It felt like an act of open rebellion to be reading fanfiction while she sat in the English building, waiting to see Professor Piper for the first time since their talk. Cath had actually considered skipping class today, but she figured that would just make it even more painful to face Professor Piper the next time. It's not like Cath could skip class for the rest of the semester – better to just get it over with.

Cath'd already faced Wren, and that hadn't gone nearly so badly as she'd expected. They'd eaten lunch together twice this week, and neither of them had brought up the scene at Muggsy's. Maybe Wren had been too drunk to remember the details.

Courtney didn't seem to get that they were avoiding the subject.

(That girl had the subtlety of a Spencer's Gifts shop.)

"Hey, Cath," Courtney said at lunch, "who was that cute blond boy you were with Friday night? Was that your hot librarian?"

"No," Cath said. "That's just Levi."

"Her roommate's boyfriend," Wren said, stirring her vegetable soup. Wren seemed tired; she wasn't wearing mascara, and her eyelashes looked pale and stubby.

"Oh." Courtney stuck out her bottom lip. "Too bad. He was super cute. Farm boy."

"How could you tell he's a farm boy?" Cath asked.

"Carhartt," they both said at once.

"What?"

"His coat," Wren explained. "All the farm boys wear Carhartt."

"Trust your sister on this." Courtney giggled. "She knows *all* the farm boys."

"He's not my hot librarian," Cath had said.

No one is my hot librarian, she thought now, losing her place in the fic she was reading. *No one is my hot anything.*

And besides, Cath still wasn't sure whether Nick was actually hot or whether he just projected hotness. Specifically in her direction.

Someone sat down next to her on the bench, and Cath glanced up from her phone. Nick tilted his chin up in greeting.

"Think of the devil," she said, then wished she hadn't.

"You thinking about me?"

"I was thinking . . . of the devil," Cath said stupidly.

"Idle brains," Nick said, grinning. He was wearing a thick, navy blue turtleneck sweater that made him look like he was serving on a Soviet battleship. Like, even more so than usual. "So, what did Piper want to talk to you about last week?"

"Nothing much." Cath's stomach was such a mess today, she hardly felt it wrench.

Nick unwrapped a piece of gum and set it on his tongue. "Was it about taking her advanced class?"

"No."

"You have to make an appointment to talk to her about it," he said, chewing. "It's like an interview. I'm meeting with her next week – I'm hoping she'll give me a teaching assistantship."

"Yeah?" Cath sat up a little straighter. "That'd be great. You'd be great at that."

Nick gave her a sheepish smile. "Yeah, well. I wish I would have talked to her about it before that last assignment. It was my worst grade of the semester."

"Really?" It was hard to make eye contact with Nick – his eyes were almost buried under his eyebrows; you had to dig into his face. "Mine, too," Cath said.

"She said that my writing was 'overly slick' and 'impenetrable.' " He sighed.

"She said worse about mine."

"Guess I've gotten used to writing with backup," Nick said, still smiling at her. Still sheepish.

"Codependent," Cath said.

Nick snapped his gum at her. "We writing tonight?"

Cath nodded and looked back at her phone.

"Reagan isn't here," Cath said, already closing the door.

Levi leaned into the door with his shoulder. "I think we're past that," he said, walking into the room. Cath shrugged and went back to her desk.

Levi flopped down on her bed. He was dressed in black – he must have just gotten off work. She frowned at him.

"I still can't believe you work at Starbucks," she said.

"What's wrong with Starbucks?"

"It's a big, faceless corporation."

He raised a good-natured brow. "So far, they've let me keep my face."

Cath went back to her laptop.

"I like my job," he said. "I see the same people every day. I remember their drinks, they like that I remember their drinks, I make them happy, and then they leave. It's like being a bartender, but you don't have to deal with drunks. *Speaking of* . . . How's your sister?"

Cath stopped typing and looked at him. "Fine. She's . . . fine. Back to normal, I guess. Thanks, you know, for driving me. And everything." Cath had told Levi thank you Friday night, but she felt like she owed him a few more.

"Forget about it. Did you guys have a big talk?"

"We don't have to have big talks," she said, holding two fingers to her temple. "We're twins. We have telepathy."

Levi grinned. "Really?"

Cath laughed. "No."

"Not even a little bit?"

"No." She went back to typing.

"What are you working on?"

"A biology essay."

"Not secret, dirty fanfiction?"

Cath stopped again. "My fanfiction is neither a secret, obviously, nor is it dirty."

He ran his fingers through his hair, making it stick up in the middle in sandy blond plumes. Shameless.

"What do you put in your hair to make it stick up like that?" she asked.

He laughed and did it again. "Nothing."

"Nothing? Something—"

"I think it does that because I don't wash it. . . ."

She grimaced. "Ever?"

"Every month or so, maybe."

Cath wrinkled her nose and shook her head. "That's disgusting."

"No, it isn't. I still rinse it."

"Still disgusting."

"It's perfectly clean," he said. He leaned toward her, and his hair touched her arm. This room was too small. "Smell it."

She sat back. "I'm not smelling your hair."

"Well, I'll smell it." He pulled a piece down his long forehead; it came to the bridge of his nose. "It smells like freshly mown clover."

"I don't think you mow clover."

"Can you imagine how sweet it would smell if you did?" Levi sat back, which was a relief – until he picked up her pillow and started rubbing his head into it.

"Oh, God," she said, "stop. That's such a violation."

Levi laughed, and she tried to grab her pillow from him. He held it to his chest with both hands. *"Cather . . ."*

"Don't call me that."

"Read me some of your secret, dirty fanfiction."

"It's *not* dirty."

"Read me some anyway."

She let go of the pillow; he'd probably already filthed it beyond redemption.

"Why?"

"Because I'm curious," he said. "And I like stories."

"You just want to make fun of me."

"I won't," he said. "I promise."

"That's what you and Reagan do when I'm not here, right? Make fun of me. Play with my commemorative busts. Do you have a stupid nickname for me?"

His eyes sparkled. "Cather."

"I don't exist to amuse you, you know."

"*One,* are you sure? Because you do. And, *two,* we don't make fun of you. Very much. Anymore. And, *three* . . ."

He was counting on his fingers, and his cheeks were twitching, and it was making Cath laugh.

"*Three,*" he said, "I won't make fun of you, to anyone but you, from now on, if you'll just once, right now, read me some of your fanfiction."

Cath gave him a level stare. A mostly level stare. She was still giggling a little. And blinking hard. And occasionally looking up at the ceiling. "You're curious," she said.

He nodded.

She rolled her eyes again and turned to her laptop. Why not. She didn't have anything to lose. *Yes, but that's not the point,* part of her argued. *What do you have to gain?*

It's not like Levi was going to be impressed by her fanfiction; entertained wasn't the same as impressed. He already thought she was a weirdo, and this was just going to make her seem that much weirder. Did the bearded lady get excited when cute guys came to her freak show?

Cath shouldn't want this kind of attention. And Levi wasn't even that cute. His forehead was lined even when he wasn't making a face. Sun damage, probably.

"Okay," she said.

He grinned and started to say something.

"Shut up." She held up her left hand. "Don't make me change my mind. Just . . . let me find something. . . ."

She opened the *Simon/Baz* folder on her desktop and scrolled through it, looking for something suitable. Nothing too romantic. Or dirty.

Maybe . . . yeah. This one'll do.

"All right," she said, "you know how, in the sixth book—"

"Which one is that?"

"Simon Snow and the Six White Hares."

"Right, I've seen that movie."

"Okay, so Simon stays at school during Christmas break because he's trying to find the fifth hare."

"And because his dad has been kidnapped by monsters in creepy costumes — so no happy Christmas dinner at the Snow house."

"They're called the Queen's Ogres," Cath said. "And Simon still doesn't know that the Mage is his dad."

"How can he *not* know?" Levi demanded. Cath was encouraged by how indignant he sounded. "It's so obvious. Why does the Mage show up every time something important happens and get all weepy, talking about how 'he knew a woman once with Simon's eyes—'"

"I know," Cath said, "it's lame, but I think Simon wants so badly for the Mage to be his dad that he won't let himself accept the overwhelming evidence. If he were wrong, it would ruin him."

"Basil knows," Levi said.

"Oh, Baz totally knows. I think Penelope knows, too."

"Penelope Bunce." Levi grinned. "If I were Simon, I'd be all-Penelope, all the time."

"Ech. She's like a sister to him."

"Not like any of my sisters."

"Anyway," Cath said. "This story takes place during that Christmas break."

"Okay," Levi said, "got it." He closed his eyes and leaned back against the wall, holding Cath's pillow. "All right. I'm ready."

Cath turned to the computer and cleared her throat. (Then felt stupid about clearing her throat.) Then glanced back at Levi one more time. She couldn't believe she was doing this. . . .

Was she really doing this?

"If you keep pacing like that," Baz said, "I'm going to curse your feet into the floorboards."

Simon ignored him. He was thinking about the clues he'd found so far, trying to see a pattern . . . the rabbit-shaped stone in the ritual tower, the stained glass hare in the cathedral, the sigil on the drawbridge –

"Snow!" Baz shouted. A spell book sailed past Simon's nose.

"What are you *thinking*?" Simon asked, genuinely surprised. Flying books and curses were fair game in the hallways and classrooms and, well, everywhere else. But if Baz tried to hurt him *inside* their room – "The Roommate's Anathema," Simon said. "You'll be expelled."

"Which is why I missed. I know the rules," Baz muttered, rubbing his eyes. "Did you know, Snow, that if your roommate dies during the school year, they give you top marks, just out of sympathy?"

"That's a myth," Simon said.

"Lucky for you I'm already getting top marks."

Simon stopped pacing to really look at his roommate. Normally he liked to pretend that Baz wasn't here. Normally, Baz *wasn't* here. Unless he was spying or plotting, Baz hated to be in their room. He said it smelled like good intentions.

But Baz had hardly left the room in the last two weeks. Simon hadn't seen him in the caf or at football, he'd seemed drawn and distracted in class, and his school shirts – usually pressed and bright white – were looking as manky as Simon's.

"Because he's a vampire, Simon!" Levi interjected.

"In this story," Cath said, "Simon doesn't know that yet."

"He's a vampire!" Levi shouted at her laptop. "And he's hunting you! He stays up all night, watching you sleep, trying to decide whether to eat you whole or one chunk at a time."

"Simon can't hear you," Cath said.

Levi sat back, hugging the pillow again. "They are kind of gay, aren't they? What with all the watching each other sleep . . . and the ignoring Penelope."

"They're obsessed with each other," Cath said, as if this were one of life's absolute givens. "Simon spends the entire fifth book following Baz around and describing his eyes. It's like a thesaurus entry for 'gray.'"

"I don't know," Levi said. "It's hard for me to get my head around. It's like hearing that Harry Potter is gay. Or Encyclopedia Brown."

That made Cath laugh out loud. "Big Encyclopedia Brown fan?"

"Shut up. My dad used to read them to me." He closed his eyes again. "Okay. Go on."

> "Is . . . something wrong?" Simon asked, then couldn't believe he'd asked it. It's not like he really cared. If Baz said yes, Simon would likely say *"Good!"* Still, it seemed cruel not to ask. Baz may have been the most despicable human being Simon had ever met . . . but he was still a human being.
>
> "I'm not the one pacing the room like a hyperactive madman," Baz mumbled, his elbows on his desk, his head resting in his hands.
>
> "You seem . . . down or something."
>
> "Yes, I'm down. I'm down, Snow." Baz raised his head and spun his chair toward Simon. He really did look terrible. His eyes were sunken and shot with blood. "I've spent the last six years living with the most self-centered, insufferable prat ever to carry a wand. And now, instead of celebrating Christmas Eve with my beloved family, drinking mulled cider and eating toasted cheese – instead of warming my hands at my ancestral hearth . . . I'm playing a tortured extra in the bloody *Simon Snow Show*."
>
> Simon stared at him. "It's Christmas Eve?"

"Yes . . . ," Baz groaned.

Simon walked around his bed glumly. He hadn't realized it was Christmas Eve. He'd have thought that Agatha would have called him. Or Penelope . . .

Levi sighed. *"Penelope."*
Cath read on.

Maybe his friends were waiting for Simon to call *them*. He hadn't even bought them gifts. Lately, nothing had seemed as important as finding the white hares. Simon clenched his square jaw. Nothing *was* as important; the whole school was in danger. There must be some pattern he wasn't seeing. He quickened his step. *The stone in the tower, the stained glass window, the sigil, the Mage's book . . .*

"I give up," Baz whined. "I'm going to go drown myself in the moat. Tell my mother I always knew she loved me best."

Simon stopped pacing at Baz's desk. "Do you know how to get down to the moat?"

"I'm not *actually* going to kill myself, Snow. Sorry to disappoint."

"No. It's just . . . you use the punts sometimes, don't you?"

"Everyone does."

"Not me," Simon said. "I can't swim."

"*Really* . . . ," Baz hissed with a hint of his old vigor. "Well, you wouldn't want to *swim* in the moat anyway. The merwolves would get you."

"Why don't they bother the boats?"

"Silver punt poles and braces."

"Will you take me out on one?" It was worth a try. The moat was one of the only places left in the school that Simon hadn't searched.

"You want to go *punting* with me?" Baz asked.

"Yes," Simon said, tilting his chin up. "Will you do it?"

"Why?"

"I . . . want to see what it's like. I've never done it – why does it matter? It's Christmas Eve, and you obviously don't have anything better to do. Apparently even your parents can't stand to be around you."

Baz stood suddenly, his grey eyes glinting dangerously in the shadow of his brow. "You know *nothing* about my parents."

Simon stepped back. Baz had a few inches on him (for now), and when Baz made an effort, he could seem dangerous.

"I'm . . . look, I'm sorry," Simon said. "Will you do it?"

"Fine," Baz said. The flare of anger and energy had already faded. "Get your cloak."

Cath glanced over at Levi. His eyes were still closed. After a second, he opened one. "Is it over?"

"No," she said. "I just didn't know if you wanted me to go on. I mean, you get the idea."

Levi closed his eyes and shook his head. "Don't be stupid. Keep going."

Cath looked at him for another second. At the lines in his forehead and the scruff of dark blond hair along his jaw. His mouth was small, but bowed. Like a doll's. She wondered if he had trouble opening it wide enough to eat apples.

"Your madness must be catching," Baz complained, untangling a rope.

The boats were stacked and tied off for the winter. Simon hadn't been thinking about the cold. . . . "Shut up," he said anyway. "It'll be fun."

"That's the point, Snow – since when do we have fun together?

I don't even know what you do for fun. Teeth-whitening, I assume. Unnecessary dragon-slaying—"

"We've had fun before," Simon argued. Because he didn't know how to do anything with Baz *but* argue – and because surely Baz was wrong. In six years, they must have shared *some* fun. "There was that time in third year when we fought the chimaera together."

"I was trying to lure you there," Baz said. "I thought I'd get away from the thing before it attacked."

"Still, it was fun."

"I was *trying to kill you*, Snow. And on that note, are you sure you want to do this? Alone with me? On a boat? What if I shove you over? I could let the merwolves solve all my problems. . . ."

Simon twisted his lips to one side. "I don't think you will."

"And whyever not?" Baz cast off the last of the ropes.

"If you really wanted to get rid of me," Simon said thoughtfully, "you would have by now. No one else has had as many opportunities. I don't think you'd hurt me unless it played into one of your grand plans."

"*This* could be my grand plan," Baz said, shoving one of the punts free with a grunt.

"No," Simon said. "This one is mine."

"Aleister Crowley, Snow, are you going to help me with this or what?"

They carried the boat down to the water, Baz swinging the punt pole lightly. Simon noticed for the first time the silver plating at one end.

"Snowball fights," he said, following Baz's lead as they settled the boat in the water.

"What?"

"We've had lots of snowball fights. Those are fun. And food fights. That time I spelled gravy up your nose . . ."

"And I put your wand in the microwave."

"You destroyed the kitchen," Simon laughed.

"I thought it would just swell up like a marshmallow Peep."

"There was no reason to think that. . . ."

Baz shrugged. "*Don't put a wand in the microwave* – lesson learned. Unless it's Snow's wand. And Snow's microwave."

Simon was standing on the dock now, shivering. He really hadn't considered how cold it would be out here. Or the fact that he'd actually have to get into a boat. He glanced down at the cold, black water of the moat and thought he saw something heavy and dark moving below the surface.

"Come on." Baz was already in the punt. He jabbed Simon's shoulder with the pole. "This is your grand plan, remember?"

Simon set his jaw and stepped in. The boat dipped beneath his weight, and he scrabbled forward.

Baz laughed. "Maybe this *will* be fun," he said, sinking the pole into the water and shoving off. Baz looked perfectly comfortable up there – a long, dark shadow at the end of the punt – as elegant and graceful as ever. He shifted into the moonlight, and Simon watched him take a slow, deep breath. He looked more alive than he had in weeks.

But Simon hadn't come out here to watch Baz – God knows he had plenty of other opportunities. Simon turned, looking around the moat, taking in the carvings along the stone walls and the tiles at the water's edge. "I should have brought a lantern . . . ," he said.

"Too bad you're not a magician," Baz replied, conjuring a ball of blue flame and tossing it at Simon's head. Simon ducked and caught it. Baz had always been better than he was at fire magic. *Show-off.*

The tiles glittered in the light. "Can we get closer to the wall?" Simon asked. Baz obliged smoothly.

Up close, Simon could see there was a mosaic that stretched beneath the water. Wizard battles. Unicorns. Symbols and glyphs. Who knew how far down it went. . . . Baz guided them slowly along the wall, and Simon held the light up, gradually leaning over the side of the boat to get a better look.

He forgot about Baz in a way he normally wouldn't allow himself to do outside the protection of their room. Simon didn't even notice at first when the boat drifted to a stop. When he looked back, Baz had stepped toward him in the punt. He was curled above Simon, washed blue by his own conjured fire, his teeth bared and his face thick with decision and disgust. . . .

The door flew open.

Reagan always kicked it as soon as she had it unlocked; there were dusty shoe prints all over the outside of their door. She swept in, dropping her bags on the floor. "Hey," she said, glancing over at them.

"Quiet," Levi whispered. "Cath's reading fanfiction."

"*Really?*" Reagan looked at them with more interest.

"Not really," Cath said, shutting her laptop. "Just finished."

"*No.*" Levi leaned over and opened it. "You can't stop in the middle of a vampire attack."

"Vampires, huh?" Reagan said. "Sounds pretty exciting."

"I've got to finish my biology essay," Cath said.

"Come on." Reagan turned to Levi. "Plant Phys. Are we doing this?"

"We're doing it," he grumbled, sliding off Cath's bed. "Can I use your phone?" he asked her.

Cath handed him her phone, and he punched a number in. His back pocket started playing a Led Zeppelin song. "To be continued," he said, handing it back to her. "Solid?"

"Sure," Cath said.

"Library?" Reagan asked.

"Hi-Way Diner." Levi picked up his backpack and opened the door. "Fanfiction makes me crave corned beef hash."

"See ya," Reagan said to Cath.

"See ya," Cath said.

Levi ducked his head back at the last minute to flash her a wide grin.

If you wanted to meet other *Star Trek* fans in 1983, you'd have to join fan clubs by mail or meet up with other Trekkies at conventions. . . .

When readers fell for Simon in 2001, the fan community was as close as the nearest keyboard.

Simon Snow fandom exploded on the Internet – and just keeps exploding. There are more sites and blogs devoted to Simon than to the Beatles and Lady Gaga combined. You'll find fan stories, fan art, fan videos, plus endless discussion and conjecture.

Loving Simon isn't something one does alone or once a year at a convention – for thousands of fans of all ages, loving Simon Snow is nothing less than a lifestyle.

—Jennifer Magnuson, "Tribe of Simon,"
Newsweek, October 28, 2009

THIRTEEN

Cath wasn't trying to make new friends here.

In some cases, she was actively trying *not* to make friends, though she usually stopped short of being rude. (Uptight, tense, and mildly misanthropic? Yes. Rude? No.)

But everyone around Cath – everybody in her classes and in the dorms – really *was* trying to make friends, and sometimes she'd have to be rude not to go along with it.

Campus life was just so predictable, one routine layered over another. You saw the same people while you were brushing your teeth and a different set of the same people in each class. The same people passing you every day in the halls . . . Pretty soon you were nodding. And then you were saying hello. And eventually someone would start a conversation, and you just had to go along with it.

What was Cath supposed to say, *Stop talking to me*? It's not like she was Reagan.

That's how she ended up hanging out with T.J. and Julian in American History, and Katie, a nontraditional student with two kids, in Political Science. There was a nice girl in her Fiction-Writing class named Kendra, and she and Cath both studied in the Union for an hour on Tuesday and Thursday mornings, so it made sense to sit at the same table.

None of these friendships spread into Cath's personal life. T.J. and Julian weren't inviting her to smoke weed with them, or to come over and play *Batman: Arkham City* on the PlayStation 3.

No one ever invited Cath to go out or to parties (except for Reagan and Levi, who felt more like sponsors than friends). Not even Nick, whom Cath was writing with regularly now, twice a week.

Meanwhile Wren's social calendar was so crowded, Cath felt like even calling her sister was an interruption. Cath had thought they were over the bar-tastrophe, but Wren was acting even more irritable and remote than she'd been at the start of the year. When Cath did try to call, Wren was always on her way out, and she wouldn't tell Cath where she was going. "I don't need you to show up with a stomach pump," Wren said.

In some ways, it had always been like this.

Wren had always been the Social One. The Friendly One. The one who got invited to *quinceañeras* and birthday parties. But before – in junior high and high school – everyone knew that if you invited Wren, you got Cath. They were a package deal, even at dances. There were three years' worth of photos, taken at every homecoming and prom, of Cath and Wren standing with their dates under an archway of balloons or in front of a glittery curtain.

They were a package deal, period. Since always.

They'd even gone to therapy together after their mom left. Which seemed weird, now that Cath thought about it. Especially considering how differently they'd reacted – Wren acting out, Cath acting in. (Violently, desperately in. *Journey to the Center of the Earth* in.)

Their third-grade teacher – they were always in the same class, all through elementary school – thought they must be upset about the terrorists. . . .

Because their mom left on September 11th.

The September 11th.

(Cath still found this incredibly embarrassing; it was like their mom was so self-centered, she couldn't be trusted not to desecrate a national tragedy with her own issues.)

Cath and Wren had been sent home from school early that day, and their parents were already fighting when they got there. Her dad was upset, and her mom was crying. . . . And Cath thought at first that it *was* because of the World Trade Center; their teacher had told them about the airplanes. But that wasn't it, not exactly. . . .

Her mom kept saying, "I'm done, Art. I'm just done. I'm living the wrong life."

Cath went out and sat on the back steps, and Wren sat beside her, holding her hand.

The fight went on and on. And when the president flew over their heads that afternoon on the way to the air force base, the only plane in the sky, Cath thought maybe the whole world was going to end.

Her mom left for good a week later, hugging both of the girls on the front porch, kissing their cheeks again and again, and promising that she'd see them both soon, that she just needed some time to feel better, to remember who she really was. Which didn't make any sense to Cath and Wren. *You're our mom.*

Cath couldn't remember everything that happened next.

She remembered crying a lot at school. Hiding with Wren in the bathroom during recess. Holding hands on the bus. Wren scratching a boy who said they were gay in the eye.

Wren didn't cry. She stole things and hid them under her pillow. When their dad changed their sheets for the first time – not until after Valentine's Day – he found Simon Snow pencils and Lip Smackers and a Britney Spears CD.

Then, in one week, Wren cut some other girl's dress with safety scissors, and Cath wet her pants during Social Studies because she was scared to raise her hand to ask for a bathroom pass; their teacher called their dad in and gave him a business card for a child psychologist.

Their dad didn't tell the therapist their mom was gone. He didn't even tell Grandma until summer break. He was so sure she was going to come back. . . . And he was such a disaster.

They were all three such a disaster.

It had taken years to put themselves back together, and so what if some things didn't get put back in the right place? At least they could hold themselves up.

Most of the time.

Cath closed her biology book and reached for her laptop. Reading was too quiet – she needed to write.

It startled her when the phone rang. She stared at it for a second before she answered, trying to recognize the number. "Hello?"

"Hey. It's Levi."

"Hi?"

"There's a party at my house tonight."

"There's always a party at your house."

"So you'll come? Reagan's coming."

"What would I do at your party, Levi?"

"Have fun," he said, and she could hear that he was smiling.

Cath tried not to. "Not drink. Not smoke. Not get high."

"You could talk to people."

"I don't like to talk to drunk people."

"Just because people will be drinking doesn't mean they'll be drunk. I won't be drunk."

"I don't need to go to a party to talk to you. Did Reagan tell you to invite me?"

"No. Not exactly. Not like that."

"Have fun at your party, Levi."

"Wait — Cath."

"What?" She said it like she was hassled, but she wasn't. Not really.

"What are you doing?"

"Trying to write. What are you doing?"

"Nothing," he said. "Just got off work. Maybe you should finish reading me that story. . . ."

"What story?" She knew what story.

"The Simon Snow story. Vampire Baz was just about to attack Simon."

"You want me to read to you over the phone?"

"Why not?"

"I'm not going to read to you over the phone."

There was a knock at the door. Cath eyed it suspiciously.

More knocking.

"I know that's you," she said into the phone. Levi laughed.

She got up and opened the door, ending the call. "You're ridiculous."

"I brought you coffee," he said. He was wearing all black — black jeans, black sweater, black leather work boots — and holding two Christmassy red cups.

"I don't really drink coffee." Their previous encounters notwithstanding.

"That's okay. These are more like melted candy bars. Which do you want, gingerbread latte or eggnog?"

"Eggnog reminds me of mucus," she said.

"Me, too. But in a good way." He held out his hand. "Gingerbread."

Cath took the cup and smiled in resignation.

"You're welcome," Levi said. He sat on her bed and smiled expectantly.

"You're serious?" She sat down at her desk.

"Come on, Cath, don't you write these stories so that people can enjoy them?"

"I write them so that people will read them. I'll send you a link."

"Don't send me a link. I'm not much of an Internet person."

Cath felt her eyes get big. She was about to take a sip of her coffee, but stopped. "How do you not like the Internet? That's like saying, 'I don't like things that are convenient. And easy. I don't like having access to all of mankind's recorded discoveries at my fingertips. I don't like light. And knowledge.'"

"I like knowledge," he said.

"You're not a book person. And now you're not an Internet person? What does that leave you?"

Levi laughed. "Life. Work. Class. The great outdoors. *Other people*."

"Other people," Cath repeated, shaking her head and taking a sip. "There are other people on the Internet. It's awesome. You get all the benefits of 'other people' without the body odor and the eye contact."

Levi kicked her chair. He could reach it without stretching. "*Cath*. Read me your fanfiction. I want to know what happens next."

She opened her computer slowly, as if she were still thinking about it. As if there were any way she was going to say no. Levi wanted to know *what happened next*. That question was Cath's Achilles' heel.

She opened the story she'd been reading to him. It was something she'd written last year for a Christmas-fic festival ("Deck the Hols with Baz and Simon"). Cath's fic had won two awards: "Tastes Like Canon" and "Best in Snow."

"Where did we leave off?" she said, mostly to herself.

"Baz's teeth were bared, and his face was filled with disgust and decision."

Cath found the spot in the story. "Wow," she said. "Good memory."

Levi was smiling. He kicked her chair again.

"Okay," she said, "so they're in the boat, and Simon is leaning over, looking at the tiles on the moat wall. . . ."

Levi closed his eyes.

Cath cleared her throat.

When he looked back, Baz had stepped toward him in the punt. He was curled above Simon, washed blue by his own conjured fire, his teeth bared and his face thick with decision and disgust. . . .

Baz held the pole just over Simon's face, and before Simon could reach his wand or whisper a spell, Baz was driving the pole forward over Simon's shoulder. The boat shook, and there was a gurgling howl – a frenzied splash – from the water. Baz raised the pole and drove it down again, his face as cold and cruel as Simon had ever seen it. His wide lips were shining, and he was practically growling.

Simon held himself still while the boat rocked. When Baz stepped back again, Simon slowly sat up. "Did you kill it?" he asked quietly.

"No," Baz said. "I should have. It should know better than to bother the boats – and *you* should know better than to lean into the moat."

"Why are there merwolves in the moat anyway?" Simon flushed. "This is a school."

"A school run by a madman. Something I've been trying to explain to you for six years."

"Don't talk that way about the Mage."

"Where's your Mage now, Simon?" Baz asked softly, looking up at the old fortress. He looked tired again, his face blue and shadowed in the moonlight, his eyes practically ringed in black. "And what are you looking for anyway?" he asked waspishly, rubbing his eyes. "Maybe if you told me, I could help you find it, and then we could both go inside and avoid death by drowning, freezing, or torn jugular."

"It's . . ." Simon weighed the risks.

Usually when Simon was this far along on a quest, Baz had already sniffed out his purpose and was setting a trap to foil him. But this time Simon hadn't told anyone what he was doing. Not even Agatha. Not even *Penelope.*

The anonymous letter had told Simon to seek out help; it said that the mission was too dangerous to carry out on his own – and that's exactly why Simon hadn't wanted to involve his friends.

But putting Baz at risk . . . Well, that wasn't so distasteful.

"It's dangerous," Simon said sternly.

"Oh, I'm sure – danger is your middle name, etc. Simon Oliver *Danger* Snow."

"How do you know my middle name?" Simon asked warily.

"Great Crimea, what part of 'six years' is lost on you? I know which shoe you put on first. I know that your shampoo smells like apples. My mind is fairly bursting with worthless Simon Snow trivia. . . . Don't you know mine?"

"Your what?"

"My middle name," Baz said.

Morgan's tooth, he was stroppy. "It's . . . it's Basilton, right?"

"Quite right, you great thumping idiot."

"That was a trick question." Simon turned back to the mosaic.

"What are you looking for?" Baz demanded again, snarling through his teeth like an animal.

This was something Simon *had* learned about Baz in six years:

he could turn from peevish to dangerous in half a heartbeat.

But Simon still hadn't learned not to rise to the bait. "Rabbits!" he blurted out. "I'm looking for rabbits."

"Rabbits?" Baz looked confused, caught mid-snarl.

"Six white hares."

"Why?"

"I don't know!" Simon shouted. "I just am. I got a letter. There are six white hares on school grounds, and they lead to something—"

"To what?"

"I. Don't. *Know.* Something dangerous."

"And I don't suppose," Baz said, leaning against the pole, resting his forehead on the wood, "that you know who sent it."

"No."

"It could be a trap."

"There's only one way to find out." Simon wished he could stand and face Baz without tipping the boat; he hated the way Baz was talking down to him.

"You really think that," Baz scoffed, "don't you? You really think that the *only way* to sort out whether something is dangerous is to barrel right into it."

"What else would you suggest?"

"You could ask your precious Mage, for starters. You could run it past your swotty friend. Her brain is so enormous, it pushes her ears out like a monkey's – maybe she could shed some light."

Simon yanked on Baz's cloak and made him lose his balance. "Don't talk about Penelope like that."

The punt wobbled, and Baz recovered his cool stance. "Have you talked to her? Have you talked to anyone?"

"No," Simon said.

"Six hares, is it?"

"Yes."

"How many have you found so far?"

"Four."

"So you've got the one in the cathedral and the one on the drawbridge—"

"You know about the hare on the drawbridge?" Simon sat back, startled. "That took me three weeks to find."

"That doesn't surprise me," Baz said. "You're not very observant. Do you even know my *first* name?" He started pushing them through the water again – pushing them toward the dock, Simon hoped.

"It's . . . it begins with a *T*."

"It's Tyrannus," Baz said. "Honestly. So the cathedral, the drawbridge, and the nursery—"

Simon clambered to his feet, pulling himself up by Baz's cloak. The punt bobbed. "The nursery?"

Baz lowered an eyebrow. "Of course."

This close, Simon could see the purple bruises under Baz's eyes, the web of dark blood vessels in his eyelids. "Show me."

Baz shrugged – practically shuddered – away from Simon and out of the boat. Simon jerked forward and grabbed a post on the dock to keep the boat from floating away.

"Come on," Baz said.

Cath realized that she'd started doing Simon and Baz's voices – at least doing the version of their voices that she heard in her head. She glanced over at Levi to see if he'd noticed. He was holding his cup with both hands against his chest and resting his chin on top, like it was keeping him warm. His eyes were open but unfocused. He looked like a little kid watching TV.

Cath turned back to her computer before he caught her watching him.

It took longer to put the boat away than it had to get it out, and by the time it was tied up, Simon's hands were wet and freezing.

They hurried back into the fortress, side by side, both of them pushing their fists into their pockets.

Baz was taller, but their strides matched exactly.

Simon wondered whether they'd ever walked like this before. In six years – six years of always walking in the same direction – had they ever once fallen into step?

"Here," Baz said, catching Simon's arm and stopping at a closed door. Simon would have walked right past this door. He must have a thousand times – it was on the main floor, near the professors' offices.

Baz tried the handle. It was locked. He pulled his wand out of his pocket and started murmuring. The door came open suddenly, almost as if the knob were reaching for Baz's pale hand.

"How did you do that?" Simon asked.

Baz just sneered and strode forward. Simon followed. The room was dark, but he could see that it was a place for children. There were toys and pillows, and train tracks that wound around the room in every direction.

"What is this place?"

"It's the nursery," Baz said in a hushed voice. As if children might be sleeping in the room right now.

"Why does Watford need a nursery?"

"It doesn't," Baz said. "Not anymore. It's too dangerous here now for children. But this used to be the place where the faculty brought their children while they worked. And other magical children could come, too, if they wanted to get an early start on their development."

"Did you come here?"

"Yes, from the time I was born."

"Your parents must have thought you needed a lot of extra help."

"My mother was the headmistress, you idiot."

Simon turned to look at Baz, but he couldn't quite see the other boy's face in the dark. "I didn't know that."

He could hear Baz roll his eyes. "Shocking."

"But I've met your mother."

"You've met my stepmother," Baz said. He stood very still.

Simon matched his stillness. "The last headmistress," he said, watching Baz's profile. "Before the Mage came, the one who was killed by vampires."

Baz's head fell forward like it was weighted with stones. "Come on. The hare is this way."

The next room was wide and round. Cribs lined the walls on each side, with small, low futons placed in a circle in the middle. At the far end was a huge fireplace – half as tall as the high, curved ceiling. Baz whispered into his hand and sent a ball of fire blazing through the grate. He whispered again, twisting his hand in the air, and the blue flames turned orange and hot. The room came to life a bit around them.

Baz walked toward the fireplace, holding his hands up to the heat. Simon followed.

"There it is," Baz said.

"Where?" Simon looked into the fire.

"Above you."

Simon looked up, then turned back to face the room. On the ceiling above him was a richly painted mural of the night sky. The sky was deep blue and dominated by the moon – a white rabbit curled tightly in on itself, eyes pressed closed, fat and full and fast asleep.

Simon walked out into the middle of the room, his chin raised high. "The fifth hare . . . ," he whispered. "The Moon Rabbit."

"Now what?" Baz asked, just behind him.

"What do you mean?"

"I mean, *now what*?"

"I don't know," Simon said.

"Well, what did you do when you found the others?"

"Nothing. I just found them. The letter just said to find them."

Baz brought his hands to his face and growled, dropping into a frustrated heap on the floor. "Is this how you and your dream team normally operate? It's no wonder it's always so easy to get in your way."

"But not so easy to stop us, I've noticed."

"Oh, shut up," Baz said, his face hidden in his knees. "Just – no more. No more of your drippy voice until you've got something worth saying. It's like a drill you're cranking between my eyes."

Simon sat down on the floor near Baz, near the fire, looking up at the sleeping rabbit. When his neck started to cramp, he leaned back on the rug.

"I slept in a room like this," Simon said. "In the orphanage. Nowhere near this nice. There was no fireplace. No Moon Rabbit. But we all slept together like this, in one room."

"Crowley, Snow, was that when you joined the cast of *Annie*?"

"There are still places like that. Orphanages. You wouldn't know."

"Quite right," Baz said. "My mother didn't *choose* to leave me."

"If your family is so grand, why are you celebrating Christmas with me?"

"I wouldn't call this a celebration."

Simon focused again on the rabbit. Maybe there was something hidden in it. Maybe if he squinted. Or if he looked at it in a mirror. Agatha had a magic mirror; it would tell you if something was amiss. Like if you had spinach in your teeth or something hanging from your nose. When Simon looked at it, it always asked him who he was kidding. "It's just jealous," Agatha would say. "It thinks I give you too much attention."

"It was my choice," Baz said, breaking the silence. "I didn't want to go home for Christmas." He leaned back onto the floor, an arm's length from Simon. When Simon glanced over, Baz was staring up at the painted stars.

"Were you here?" Simon asked, watching the light from the fire play across Baz's strong features. His nose was all wrong, Simon had always thought. It started too high, with a soft bump between Baz's eyebrows. If Simon looked at Baz's face for too long, he always wanted to reach up and tug his nose down. Not that that would work. It was just a feeling.

"Was I here *when*?" Baz asked.

"When they attacked your mother."

"They attacked the nursery," Baz said, as if he were explaining it to the moon. "Vampires can't have children, you know – they have to turn them. They thought if they turned magical children, they'd be twice as dangerous."

They would be, Simon thought, his stomach flopping fearfully. Vampires were already nearly invulnerable; a vampire who could do *magic* . . .

"My mother came to protect us."

"To protect *you*," Simon said.

"She threw fire at the vampires," Baz said. "They went up like flash paper."

"How did she die?"

"There were just too many of them." He was still talking to the sky, but his eyes were closed.

"Did the vampires turn any of the children?"

"Yes." It was like a puff of smoke escaping from Baz's lips.

Simon didn't know what to say. He thought it might be worse, in a way, to have had a mother, a powerful, loving mother, and then to lose her – than to grow up like Simon had. With nothing.

He knew what happened next in Baz's story: after the headmistress, Baz's mother, was killed, the Mage took over. The school changed; it had to. They weren't just students now. They were warriors. Of course the nursery had closed. When you came to Watford, you left your childhood behind.

All right for Simon. He had nothing to lose.

But for Baz . . .

He lost his mother, Simon thought, *and he got me instead.* In a hiccup of tenderness or perhaps pity, Simon reached for Baz's hand, fully expecting Baz to yank his arm from its socket.

But Baz's hand was cold and limp. When Simon looked closer, he realized that the other boy was asleep.

The door flew open then, and for once, Cath thought, Reagan's timing was perfect. Cath closed her laptop, to let Levi know she was done reading.

"Hey," Reagan said. "Oh, *hey*. Christmas cups. Did you bring me a gingerbread latte?"

Cath looked down guiltily at her cup.

"I brought you an eggnog latte," Levi said, holding it out. "And I've been keeping it warm in my mouth."

"Eggnog." Reagan wrinkled her nose, but she took it. "What are you doing here so early?"

"I thought we could study before the party," Levi said.

"*Jacob Have I Loved*?"

He nodded.

"You're reading *Jacob Have I Loved*?" Cath asked. "That's a kids' book."

"Young adult literature," he said. "It's a great class."

Reagan was shoving clothes in her bag. "I'm taking a shower at your place," she said. "I'm so goddamn sick of public showers."

Levi scooted forward on Cath's bed and leaned an elbow on her desk. "So is that how Baz became a vampire? When the nursery was attacked?"

Cath wished he wouldn't talk about this in front of Reagan. "You mean, for real?"

"I mean in the books."

"There is no nursery in the books," Cath said.

"But in your version, that's how it happens."

"Just in this story. Every story is a little different."

"And other people have their versions, too?"

"Oh yeah," she said. "There're all these fans, and we're all doing something different."

"Are you the only one who writes about Baz and Simon falling in love?"

Cath laughed. "Uh, no. The entire Internet writes about Baz and Simon. If you go to Google and type in 'Baz and Simon,' the first search it suggests is 'Baz and Simon in love.'"

"How many people do this?"

"Write Simon-slash-Baz? Or write Simon Snow fanfiction?"

"Write fanfiction."

"God, I don't know. Thousands and thousands."

"So, if you didn't want the books to be over, you could just keep reading Simon Snow stories forever online. . . ."

"Exactly," Cath said earnestly. She'd thought Levi must be judging her, but he got it. "If you fall in love with the World of Mages, you can just keep on living there."

"I wouldn't call that living," Reagan said.

"It was a metaphor," Levi said gently.

"I'm ready," Reagan said. "Are you coming, Cath?"

Cath smiled tightly and shook her head.

"Are you sure?" Levi asked, lifting himself off her bed. "We could come back for you later."

"Nah, that's okay. See you tomorrow."

As soon as they left, Cath headed down to eat dinner by herself.

"Maybe I'm not supposed to have a wand. Maybe I'm supposed to have a ring like you. Or a . . . a wrist thingy like mangy old Elspeth."

"Oh, Simon." Penelope frowned. "You shouldn't call her that. She can't help her fur – her father was the Witch King of Canus."

"No, I know, I just . . ."

"It's easier for the rest of us," she said, soothing. "Magicians' instruments stay in families. They're passed from generation to generation."

"Right," he said, "just like magic. It doesn't make sense, Penelope – my parents *must* have been magicians."

He'd tried to talk to her about this before, and that time it had made her look just as sad.

"Simon . . . they couldn't have been. Magicians would never abandon their own child. Never. Magic is too precious."

Simon looked away from her and flicked his wand again. It felt like something dead in his hands.

"I think Elspeth's fur is pretty," Penelope said. "She looks soft."

He shoved the wand into his pocket and stood up. "You just want a puppy."

—from chapter 21, *Simon Snow and the Third Gate,*
copyright © 2004 by Gemma T. Leslie

FOURTEEN

Their dad came to pick them up the day before Thanksgiving. When he pulled up in front of Pound Hall, Wren and Courtney were already sitting in the back of the Honda.

Wren and Cath usually sat in the backseat together. Their dad would complain that he felt like a cabdriver, and they'd say, "No, *limo* driver. Home, James."

"Wow, look at this . . . ," he said when Cath sat in the front seat next to him. "Company." She tried to smile.

Courtney and Wren were talking in the backseat – but with the radio up, Cath couldn't hear them. Once they were on the interstate, she leaned over to her dad. "How's Gravioli?" she asked.

"What?" He turned down the radio.

"Dad," Wren said, "that's our jam."

"Sorry," he said, shifting the volume to the backseat. "What's that?" he asked Cath.

"Gravioli," she said.

"Oh." He made a face. "To hell with Gravioli. Did you know that it's actually canned ravioli soaked in slimy brown gravy?"

"That sounds disgusting," Cath said.

"It's revolting," he said. "It's like dog food for people. Maybe that's what we should have pitched. . . . 'Do you secretly want to eat dog food? Does the smell of it make your mouth water?'"

Cath joined in, in her best announcer's voice: "Is the only thing keeping you from eating dog food the fear that your neighbors will notice all the cans – and realize that you don't have a dog?"

"Graaavioli," her dad said, rounding out every vowel sound. "It's dog food. *For people.*"

"You didn't get the business," Cath said. "I'm sorry."

He shook his head for a little too long. "We *did* get it. Sometimes getting it is infinitely worse than not getting it. It was a shoot-out— six agencies. They picked us, then they rejected every good idea we had. And *then,* out of desperation, Kelly says in a client meeting, 'Maybe there's a bear who comes out of hibernation really hungry, and all it can say is *Grrr.* And then the bear gets a big bowl of delicious *Grrr*avioli, and it turns into a human being. . . . ' And the client just loved the idea, just fucking flipped, started shouting, *'That's it!'*"

Cath glanced back to see if Courtney was listening. Their dad only cursed when he was talking about work. (And sometimes when he was manic.) He said that ad agencies were worse than submarines, all cussing and claustrophobia.

"So now we're doing cartoon bears and *Grrr*avioli," he said.

"That sounds terrible."

"It's torture. We're doing four TV spots. Four different bears turn into four different people – *four,* so we can cover our races. And then fucking Kelly asks if we should make the Asian guy a *panda* bear. And he was serious. Not only is that racist, *panda bears don't hibernate.*"

Cath giggled.

"That's what I have to say to my boss – 'It's an interesting idea, Kelly, but panda bears don't hibernate.' And do you know what he says?"

Cath laughed. "Uh-uh. Tell me."

"Don't be so literal, Arthur."

"No!"

"Yes!" Her dad laughed, shaking his head again, too fast, too long. "Working on this client is like making my brain dig its own grave."

"Its own *grrr*ave-ioli," Cath said.

He laughed again. "It's all right," he said, tapping the steering wheel. "It's money. Just money."

She knew that wasn't true. It was never about the money with him — it was about the work. It was about coming up with the perfect idea, the most elegant solution. Her dad didn't really care *what* he was selling. Tampons or tractors or dog food for people. He just wanted to find the perfect puzzle-piece idea that would be beautiful and right.

But when he found that idea, it almost always got killed. Either the client rejected it, or his boss rejected it. Or changed it. And then it was like someone had tapped straight into her dad's heart and was draining the sap from his soul.

After they dropped Courtney off in West O, Wren slid forward in her seat and turned down the radio.

"Seat belt," their dad said.

She sat back and buckled up again. "Is Grandma coming over tomorrow?"

"No," he said. "She went to stay in Chicago with Aunt Lynn for a month. She wants to spend the holidays with the kids."

"We're kids," Wren said.

"Not anymore. You're sophisticated young women. Nobody wants to watch you unwrap gift cards. Hey, what time is your mom coming to get you?"

Cath turned sharply to look at her sister.

Wren was already watching Cath. "Noon," she said guardedly. "They're having lunch at one."

"So we'll eat at six? Seven? Will you save some room?"

"She's coming to get you?" Cath asked. "She's coming to our house?"

Their dad looked strangely at Cath – then into the mirror at Wren. "I thought you guys were gonna talk about this."

Wren rolled her eyes and looked out the window. "I knew she'd just freak out—"

"I'm not freaking out," Cath said, feeling her eyes start to sting. "And if I am freaking out, it's because you're not telling me things."

"It's not a big deal," Wren said. "I've talked to Mom a few times on the phone, and I'm going to hang out with her for a couple hours tomorrow."

"You talk to her for the first time in ten years, and that's not a big deal? And you call her *Mom*?"

"What am I supposed to call her?"

"You're not." Cath turned almost completely to face the backseat, straining against the seat belt. "You're not *supposed* to call her."

She felt her dad's hand on her knee. "Cath—"

"No," Cath said. "Not you, too. Not after everything."

"She's your mother," he said.

"That's a technicality," Cath said. "Why is she even bothering us?"

"She wants to get to know us," Wren answered.

"Well, that's bloody convenient. Now that we don't need her anymore."

"'Bloody'?" Wren said. "Wotcher there, Cath, you're slipping into Snow speak."

Cath felt tears on her cheeks. "Why do you keep doing that?"

"What?"

"Making little comments about Simon and Baz."

"I wasn't."

"You were," Cath said. "You are."

"Whatever."

"She *left* us. She didn't love us."

"It isn't that simple," Wren said, watching the buildings go by.

"It is for me." Cath turned back around in her seat and folded her arms. Her dad's face was red, and he was tap-tap-tapping on the steering wheel.

When they got home, Cath didn't want to be the one to go upstairs. She knew that if she went upstairs, she'd just feel trapped and miserable, and like the Crazy One. Like the little kid who'd been sent to her room.

Instead she went to the kitchen. She stood next to the counter and looked out into the backyard. Their dad still hadn't taken down their swing set. She wished he would; it was a death trap now, and the neighbor kids liked to sneak into the yard and play on it.

"I thought you guys were talking about all this." He was standing behind her.

Cath shrugged.

He put his hand on her shoulder, but she didn't turn around. "Wren's right," he said. "It isn't that simple."

"Stop," Cath said. "Just stop, okay? I can't believe you're taking her side."

"I'm on both your sides."

"I don't mean *Wren's* side." Cath whipped around. She felt a new wave of tears. "*Hers*. Her side. She left you."

"We weren't good together, Cath."

"Is that why she left us, too? Because we weren't good together?"

"She needed some time. She couldn't handle being a parent—"

"And you could?"

Cath saw the hurt in his eyes and shook her head. "I didn't mean it that way, Dad."

He took a deep breath. "Look," he said, "to be honest? I don't love this either. It would be so much easier for me if I never had to think about Laura, ever again . . . but she's your mother."

"Everybody needs to stop saying that." Cath turned back to the window. "You don't get to be the mother if you show up after the kids are already grown up. She's like all those animals who show up at the end of the story to eat the Little Red Hen's bread. Back when we needed her, she wouldn't even return our phone calls. When we started our periods, we had to google the details. But now, after we've stopped missing her, after we've stopped crying for her – *after we've got shit figured out* – *now* she wants to get to know us? I don't need a mother now, thanks. I'm good."

Her dad laughed.

She glanced over her shoulder at him. "Why are you laughing?"

"I don't know," he said. "The bread thing, I think. Also . . . did you really google your period? You could have asked me about that – I know about periods."

Cath exhaled. "It's okay. We googled everything back then."

"You don't have to talk to her," he said softly. "Nobody's gonna make you."

"Yeah, but Wren has already – she's already let down the drawbridge."

"Wren must have some shit she still needs to figure out."

Cath clenched her fists and pushed them into her eyes. "I just . . . don't *like* this. . . . I don't like thinking about her, I don't want to see her. I don't want her in this house, thinking about how it used to be her house, about how we used to be hers, too. . . . I don't want her brain touching us."

Her dad pulled Cath into his arms. "I know."

"I feel like everything's upside down."

He took another deep breath. "Me, too."

"Did you freak out when she called?"

"I cried for three hours."

"Oh, Dad . . ."

"Your grandmother gave her my cell phone number."

"Have you seen her?"

"No."

Cath shuddered, and her dad squeezed her tight. "When I think about her coming here," she said, "it's like that scene in *Fellowship of the Ring* when the hobbits are hiding from the Nazgûl."

"Your mother isn't evil, Cath."

"That's just how I feel."

He was quiet for a few seconds. "Me, too."

Wren didn't get back in time for Thanksgiving dinner; she ended up staying the night.

"I feel like if we set the table and pretend everything's normal," Cath said to her dad, "it's just going to be worse."

"Agreed," he said.

They ate in the living room, turkey and mashed potatoes, and watched the History Channel. The green bean casserole sat in the kitchen and got cold because Wren was the only person who ever ate it.

Baz. "Have you ever done this before?"

Simon. "Yes. No."

"Yes or no?"

"Yes. Not like this."

Baz. "Not with a boy?"

Simon. "Not when I really wanted it."

—from "Shall We?" posted April 2010
by FanFixx.net author *Magicath*

FIFTEEN

When Cath saw it was Levi standing outside the door, she was so happy to see his always-friendly face, she just let him in. She didn't even bother telling him that Reagan wasn't there.

"Is Reagan here?" he asked as soon as he was in the room. Levi's face wasn't friendly. His forehead was furrowed, and his little bow lips were drawn tight.

"No," Cath said. "She went out hours ago." She didn't add: *With a giant guy named Chance who plays lots of intramural football and looks like he could play John Henry in the movie version of John Henry.*

"Fuck," Levi said, leaning back against the door. Even angry, he was a leaner.

"What's wrong?" Cath asked. Was he finally jealous? Didn't he know about the other guys? Cath always figured he and Reagan had an arrangement.

"She was supposed to study with me," he said.

"Oh . . . ," Cath said, not understanding. "Well, you can still study here if you want."

"No." Angry. "I need her help. We were supposed to study last night and she put me off, and the test is tomorrow and—" He hurled a book down on Reagan's bed, then sat at the end of Cath's, looking away from her but still hiding his face. "She said she'd study with me."

Cath walked over and picked up the book. "*The Outsiders*?"

"Yeah." He looked up. "Have you read it?"

"No. Have you?"

"No."

"So read it," she said. "Your test is tomorrow? You have time. It doesn't look very long."

Levi shook his head and looked at the floor again. "You don't understand. I have to pass this test."

"So read the book. Were you just gonna let Reagan read it for you?"

He shook his head again — not in answer, more like he was shaking his head at the very idea of reading the book.

"I told you," he said. "I'm not much of a book person."

Levi always said that. *I'm not a book person.* Like books were *rich desserts* or *scary movies.*

"Yeah, but this is school," she said. "Would you let Reagan take the test for you?"

"Maybe," he huffed. "If that was an option."

Cath dropped the book next to him on her bed and went to her desk. "You may as well watch the movie," she said distastefully.

"It's not available."

Cath made a noise like *hunh* in her throat.

"You don't understand," Levi said. "If I don't get a C in this class, I get kicked out my program."

"So read the book."

"It's not that simple."

"It's *exactly* that simple," Cath said. "You have a test tomorrow, your girlfriend isn't here to do your work — read the book."

"You don't understand . . . anything."

Levi was standing now; he'd walked to the door, but Cath wouldn't turn to face him. She was tired of fighting. This fight wasn't even hers.

"Okay," she said, "I don't understand. Whatever. Reagan isn't here, and I have a ton of reading to do – and nobody to do it for me – so . . ." She heard him jerk open the door.

"I tried to read it," he said roughly. "I've been trying for the last two hours. I just, I'm not a reader. I've . . . I've never finished a book."

Cath turned to look at him, feeling a sudden guilty grab in her stomach. "Are you trying to tell me you can't read?"

Levi pushed his hair back violently. "Of course I can *read*," he said. "Jesus Christ."

"Well, then, what *are* you trying to tell me? That you don't want to?"

"No. I –" He closed his eyes and took a deep breath through his nose. "– I don't know why I'm trying to tell you anything. I can read. I just can't read *books*."

"So pretend it's a really long street sign and muddle through it."

"Jesus," he said, surprised. Hurt. "What have I ever done to make you be this mean to me?"

"I'm not being mean," Cath said, knowing that she probably was. "I just don't know what you want me to say – that I approve? What you and Reagan do isn't any of my business."

"You think I'm lazy." His eyes were on the ground. "And I'm not."

"Okay."

"It's like I can't focus," he said, turning away from her in the doorway. "Like I read the same paragraph over and over, and I still don't know what it says. Like the words go right through me and I can't hold on to them."

"Okay," she said.

He looked back, just far enough to face her. Levi's eyes were too big in his face when he wasn't smiling. "I'm not a cheater," he said.

Then he walked away, letting the door close behind him.

Cath exhaled. Then inhaled. Her chest was so tight, it hurt both ways. Levi shouldn't get to make her feel this way – he shouldn't even have access to her chest.

Levi wasn't her boyfriend. He wasn't family. She didn't choose him. She was stuck with him because she was stuck with Reagan. He was a roommate-in-law.

The Outsiders was still sitting on her bed.

Cath grabbed it and ran out the door. "Levi!" She ran down the hall. *"Levi!"*

He was standing in front of the elevator with his hands shoved into his coat pockets.

Cath stopped running when she saw him. He turned to look at her. His eyes were still too big.

"You forgot your book." She held it up.

"Thanks," he said, holding out his hand.

Cath ignored it. "Look . . . why don't you come back? Reagan's probably on her way."

"I'm sorry I yelled at you," he said.

"Did you yell at me?"

"I raised my voice."

She rolled her eyes and took a step backwards toward her room. "Come on."

Levi looked in her eyes, and she let him.

"Are you sure?"

"Come on." Cath turned toward her room and waited for him to fall into step beside her. "I'm sorry," she said softly. "I didn't realize we were having a serious conversation until we were."

"I'm just really stressed about this test," he said.

They stopped at her door, and Cath suddenly brought her wrists up to her temples. "Crap." She held her hands on top of her head. "Crap, crap, crap. We're locked out. I don't have my keys."

"I got ya." Levi grinned and pulled out his key ring.

Her jaw dropped. "You have a key to our room?"

"Reagan gave me her spare, for emergencies." He unlocked the door and held it open for her.

"Then why are you always sitting in the hall?"

"That's never an emergency."

Cath walked in, and Levi followed. He was smiling again, but he was still obviously operating at thirty degrees below regular Levi. They might be done fighting, but he was still going to fail his test.

"So you couldn't find the movie?" she asked. "Even online?"

"No. And the movie's no good anyway. Teachers can always tell when you watch the movie." He flopped down at the head of her bed. "Normally, I listen to the audiobook."

"That counts as reading," Cath said, sitting at her desk.

"It does?"

"Of course."

He kicked one of the legs of her chair playfully, then rested his feet there, on the rail. "Well, then, never mind. I guess I *have* read lots of books. . . . This one wasn't available." He unzipped his jacket, and it fell open. He was wearing a green and yellow plaid shirt underneath.

"So, what? Was Reagan going to read it to you?"

"Usually we just go over the highlights. It helps her, too, to review it."

Cath looked down at the paperback. "Well, I've got nothing for you. All I know about *The Outsiders* is 'Stay gold, Ponyboy.'"

Levi sighed and pushed back his hair. Cath shuffled the pages with her thumb. . . . It really was a short book. With tons of dialogue.

She looked up at Levi. The sun was setting behind her, and he was sitting in a wash of orange light.

Cath turned her chair toward the bed, knocking his feet

without warning to the ground. Then she rested her own feet on the bed frame and took off her glasses, tucking them in her hair. " '*When I stepped out into the bright sunlight from the darkness of the movie house—*' "

"Cath," Levi whispered. She felt her chair wobble and knew he was kicking it. "You don't have to do that."

"Obviously," she said. " '*When I stepped out into the bright sunlight—*' "

"Cather."

She cleared her throat, still focused on the book. "Shut up, I owe you one. At least one. And also, I'm trying to read here. . . . *When I stepped out into the bright sunlight from the darkness of the movie house, I had just two things on my mind. . . .*"

When Cath glanced up between paragraphs, Levi was grinning. He bent forward to slide out of his coat, then found a new way to rest his legs on her chair and leaned back against the wall, closing his eyes.

Cath had never read out loud this much before. Fortunately it was a good book, so she sort of forgot after a while that she was reading out loud and that Levi was listening – and the circumstances that got them here. An hour or so passed, maybe even two, before Cath dropped her hands and the book into her lap. The sun had finished setting, and the only light in her room was from her desk lamp.

"You can stop whenever you want," Levi said.

"I don't want to stop." She looked up at him. "I'm just really" – she was blushing, she wasn't sure why – "thirsty."

Levi laughed and sat up. "Oh . . . Yeah. Let me get you something. You want soda? Water? I could be back here in ten with a gingerbread latte."

She was about to tell him not to bother, but then she remembered how good that gingerbread latte was. "Really?"

"Back in ten," he said, already standing and putting on his jacket. He stopped in the doorway, and Cath felt tense, remembering how sad he'd looked the last time he stood there.

Levi smiled.

Cath didn't know what to do, so she sort of nodded and gave him the world's lamest thumbs-up.

When he was gone, she stood up and stretched. Her back and her shoulders popped. She went to the bathroom. Came back. Stretched again. Checked her phone. Then lay down on her bed.

It smelled like Levi. Like coffee grounds. And some sort of warm, spicy thing that might be cologne. Or soap. Or deodorant. Levi sat on her bed so often, it was all familiar. Sometimes he smelled like cigarette smoke, but not tonight. Sometimes like beer.

She'd left the door unlocked, so when he knocked again, Cath just sat up and told him to come in. She'd meant to get up and sit back down at her desk, but Levi was already handing her the drinks and taking off his coat. His face was flushed from the cold, and when his coat touched her, it was so cold, she jumped.

"Five below," he said, taking off his hat and riffling his hair until it stuck up again. "Scoot over."

Cath did, scooting up toward her pillow and leaning against the wall. Levi took his drink and smiled at her. She set the drink carrier on her desk; he'd brought her a big glass of water, too.

"Can I ask you something?" She looked down at her Starbucks cup.

"Of course."

"Why did you take a literature class if you can't finish a book?"

He turned to her – they were sitting shoulder to shoulder. "I need six hours of literature to graduate. That's two classes. I tried to get one out of the way freshman year, but I failed it. I failed . . . a lot that year."

"How do you get through *any* of your classes?" Cath had hours of assigned reading, almost every single night.

"Coping strategies."

"Such as?"

"I record my lectures and listen to them later. Professors usually cover most of what's on the test in class. And I find study groups."

"And you lean on Reagan—"

"Not just Reagan." He grinned. "I'm really good at quickly identifying the smartest girl in every class."

Cath frowned at him. "God, Levi, that's so exploitive."

"How is it exploitive? I don't make them wear miniskirts. I don't call them 'baby.' I just say, 'Hello, smart girl, would you like to talk to me about *Great Expectations*?'"

"They probably think you like them."

"I do like them."

"If it wasn't exploitive, you'd harass smart boys, too—"

"I do, in a pinch. Do you feel exploited, Cather?" He was still grinning at her over his coffee cup.

"No," she said, "I know that you don't like me."

"You don't know anything."

"So, this is old hat for you? Finding a girl to read a whole book to you?"

He shook his head. "No, this is a first."

"Well, *now* I feel exploited," she said, setting her drink down and reaching for the book.

"Thank you," he said.

"Chapter seven—"

"I'm serious." Levi pulled the book down and looked at her. "Thank you."

Cath held his eyes for a few seconds. Then she nodded and pulled back the book.

———

After another twenty pages, Cath was getting sleepy. At some point, Levi had leaned against her, and then she'd leaned back, and it was hard to think about what was happening on that side of her body because she was busy reading. . . . Though there was almost an entire chapter there where her lips and her eyes were moving, but her brain wasn't keeping track of anything but how warm he was. How warm her roommate's boyfriend was.

One of her roommate's boyfriends. Did that matter? If Reagan had three boyfriends, did that mean this was only one-third wrong?

Just leaning against Levi probably wasn't wrong. But leaning against him because he was warm and not-exactly-soft . . . Wrong.

Cath's voice rasped, and he sat up away from her a little bit. "Want to take a break?" he asked.

She nodded, only partly grateful.

Levi stood up and stretched. The tails of his flannel shirt didn't quite lift up over the waist of his jeans. Cath stood up, too, and rubbed her eyes.

"You're tired," he said. "Let's stop."

"We're not stopping now," she said. "We're almost done."

"We've still got another fifty pages—"

"Are you getting bored?"

"*No.* I just feel like it's too much, what you're doing for me. Bordering on exploitive."

"Pfft," Cath said. "I'll be right back. And then we'll finish. We're half done, and I want to know what happens. Nobody's said, 'Stay gold, Ponyboy' yet."

When she came back, Levi was in the hallway, leaning against the door. He must have gone up to the boys' floor to use the bathroom. "This is weird now that I know you have a key," she said.

She let him in, and he dropped down onto the bed again and smiled at her. Cath glanced at her desk chair, then felt his hand on her sleeve. He pulled her down next to him on the bed, and their eyes met for a second. Cath looked away as if they hadn't.

"Look what we sell at Starbucks," he said, holding an energy bar out to her.

Cath took it. "Blueberry Bliss. Wow. This takes me back two whole months."

"Months are different in college," Levi said, "especially freshman year. Too much happens. Every freshman month equals six regular months – they're like dog months."

She unwrapped the protein bar and offered him half. He took it and tapped it against hers. "Cheers."

It was really late. And too dark in the room to be reading this much. Cath's voice was rough now, like someone had run a dull knife across it. Like she was recovering from a cold or a crying jag.

At some point Levi had put his left arm around her and pulled her back against his chest – she'd been fidgeting and rubbing her back on the wall, and Levi just reached behind her and pulled her into him.

Then his hand had fallen back down to the bed and stayed there. Except for when he stretched or moved. When he moved, Levi would bring his hand up to Cath's shoulder to hold her against him while he adjusted.

She could feel his chest rising when he breathed. She could feel his breath on her hair sometimes. When he moved his chin, it bumped into the back of her head. The muscles in Cath's arms and her back and her neck were starting to ache, just from being held so long at attention.

She lost her place in the book and stopped reading for a moment.

Levi's chin bumped into her head. "Take a break," he said in a voice that wasn't a whisper but was just as soft.

She nodded, and he held her left elbow while he reached his right arm across her to get the glass of water. His body curved around her for a second, then settled back again against the wall. He kept his hand on her elbow.

Cath took a drink, then set down the water. She tried not to squirm, but her back was stiff, and she arched it against him.

"You okay?" he asked.

She nodded again. And then she felt him slowly moving. "Here . . ."

Levi slid down the wall onto the bed, resting on his side, then tugged Cath down so she was lying on her back in front of him — his arm beneath her head like a pillow. She relaxed her shoulders and felt warm flannel against the back of her neck.

"Better?" he asked in his superscript voice. He was looking at her face. Giving Cath a chance to say no without having to say it out loud. She didn't speak. Or nod. Or answer. Instead she looked down and shifted slightly toward him onto her side, leaning the book against his chest.

She started reading again, and felt Levi's elbow curve around her shoulder.

Cath didn't have to read very loud when he was this close. Which was good because her voice was almost gone. (*Gone.*) God, Levi was warm, and up close, he smelled so much like himself, it made her tear up. Her eyes were tired. She was tired.

When Johnny – one of the main characters – got hurt, Levi took a sharp breath. By that time, Cath's cheek was on his chest, and she could feel his ribs expanding. She took a deep breath, too – her voice broke a little more, and Levi tightened his grip around her.

She wondered whether there was any blood left in his arm.

She wondered what happened when they got to the end of the story.

She kept reading.

There were too many boys in this book. Too many arms and legs and flushed faces.

She'd expected to laugh when she finally got to the line "Stay gold, Ponyboy," but she didn't, because it meant that Johnny was dead, and she thought that maybe Levi was crying. Maybe Cath was crying, too. Her eyes were tired. She was tired.

"'When I stepped out into the bright sunlight from the darkness of the movie house, I had only two things on my mind: Paul Newman and a ride home. . . .'"

Cath closed the book and let it fall on Levi's chest, not sure what happened next. Not sure she was awake, all things considered.

The moment it fell, he pulled her into him. Onto him. With both arms. Her chest pressed against his, and the paperback slid between their stomachs.

Cath's eyes were half closed, and so were Levi's – and his lips only looked small from afar, she realized, because of their doll-like pucker. They were perfectly big, really, now that she had a good look at them. Perfectly something.

He nudged his nose against hers, and their mouths fell sleepily together, already soft and open.

When Cath's eyes closed, her eyelids stuck. She wanted to open them. She wanted to get a better look at Levi's too-dark eyebrows, she wanted to admire his crazy, vampire hairline – she had a feeling this was never going to happen again and that it might even ruin what was left of her life, so she wanted to open her eyes and bear some witness.

But she was so tired.

And his mouth was so soft.

And nobody had ever kissed Cath like this before. Only Abel had kissed her before, and that was like getting pushed squarely on the mouth and pushing back.

Levi's kisses were all taking. Like he was drawing something out of her with soft little jabs of his chin.

She brought her fingers up to his hair, and she couldn't open her eyes.

Eventually, she couldn't stay awake.

"I'm sorry, Penelope."

"Don't waste my time with sorries, Simon. If we stop to apologize and forgive each other every time we step on each other's toes, we'll never have time to be friends."

—from chapter 4, *Simon Snow and the Second Serpent,*
copyright © 2003 by Gemma T. Leslie

SIXTEEN

Cath didn't wake up when the door swung open.

But she jumped when it slammed closed. That's when she felt Levi sprawled out beneath her, the warm scrape of his chin against her forehead. *Then* she woke up.

Reagan was standing at the end of Cath's bed, staring at them. She was still wearing last night's jeans, and her silvery blue eyeshadow had drifted onto her cheeks.

Cath sat up. And Levi sat up. Groggily. And Cath felt her stomach barreling up into her throat.

Levi reached for Cath's phone and looked at it. "Shit," he said. "I'm two hours late for work." He was up then and putting on his coat. "Fell asleep reading," he said, half to Reagan, half to the floor.

"Reading," Reagan said, looking at Cath.

"Later," Levi said, more to the floor than to either of them.

And then he was gone. And Reagan was still standing at the end of Cath's bed.

Cath's eyes were sticky and sore, and suddenly full of tears. "I'm so sorry," she said, feeling it. Feeling it in her stomach and in every sore muscle between her shoulders. "Oh my God."

"Don't," Reagan said. She was obviously furious.

"I . . . I'm just so sorry."

"*Don't*. Do not apologize."

Cath crossed her legs and hunched over, holding her face. "But I knew he was your boyfriend." Cath was crying now. Even though it would probably just make Reagan more angry.

"He's not my boyfriend," Reagan said, very nearly shouting. "Not anymore. Not . . . for a long time, actually. So just, don't." Reagan inhaled loudly, then let it out. "I just didn't expect this to happen," she said. "And, if it did happen, I didn't expect it to bother me. I just . . . it's Levi. And Levi always likes me best."

He's not her boyfriend? "He still likes you best," Cath said, trying not to whimper.

"Don't be an idiot, Cather." Reagan's voice was serrated. "I mean, I know that you are. About this. But try not to be an idiot right this moment."

"I'm sorry . . . ," Cath said, trying and failing to look up at her roommate. "I still don't know why I did it. I swear I'm not that kind of girl."

Reagan finally turned away. She dropped her bag on the bed and grabbed her towel. "What kind of girl is that, Cath? The girl kind? . . . I'm gonna take a shower. When I come back, I'll be over this."

And when she came back, she was.

Cath had curled up on her bed and let herself cry like she hadn't all Thanksgiving weekend. She found *The Outsiders* wedged between the bed and the wall, and threw it on the floor.

Reagan saw the book when she came back to the room. She was wearing yoga pants and a tight gray hoodie, and square brown glasses instead of contacts.

"Oh, fuck," she said, picking up the book. "I was supposed to help him study." She looked over at Cath. "Were you *actually* just reading?"

"Not just," Cath said, her voice a hiccupy wheeze.

"Stop crying," Reagan said. "I mean it."

Cath closed her eyes and rolled toward the wall.

Reagan sat at the end of her own bed. "He's not my boyfriend," she said solemnly. "And I knew he liked you – he was here constantly. I just didn't know that you liked him back."

"I thought he was here constantly because he was your boyfriend," Cath said. "I didn't *want* to like him back. I tried to be mean to him."

"I thought you were just mean," Reagan said. "I liked that about you."

Cath laughed and rubbed her eyes for the five hundredth time in twelve hours. She felt like she had pink eye.

"I'm over it," Reagan said. "I was just surprised."

"You can't be over it," Cath said, sitting up and leaning against the wall. "Even if I didn't kiss your boyfriend, I *thought* I was kissing your boyfriend. That's how I was going to repay you for all the nice things you've done for me."

"Wow . . . ," Reagan said, "when you put it that way, it is pretty fucked up."

Cath nodded miserably.

"So why'd you do it?"

Cath thought of Levi's warmth against her arm last night. And his ten thousand smiles. And his forty-acre forehead.

She closed her eyes, then pressed the heels of her hands into them. "I just really, really wanted to."

Reagan sighed. "Okay," she said. "Here's the deal. I'm hungry, and I have to finish reading *The Outsiders*. Levi likes you, you like him – I'm over it. It could get weird around here real fast if you start dating my high school boyfriend, but there's no turning back, you know?"

Cath didn't answer. Reagan kept talking.

"If he were still my boyfriend, we'd have to throw down. But he's not. So let's go have lunch, okay?"

Cath looked up at Reagan. And nodded her head.

Cath had already missed her morning classes. Including Fiction-Writing. She thought about Nick, and right at that moment it was like thinking about almost anybody.

Reagan was eating a bowl of Lucky Charms. "Okay," she said, stabbing her spoon at Cath, "now what?"

"Now what, what?" Cath said, her mouth full of grilled cheese.

"Now what with Levi?"

Cath swallowed. "Nothing. I don't know. Do I have to know what?"

"Do you want my help with this?"

Cath looked at Reagan. Even without her makeup and hair, the girl was terrifying. There was just no fear in her. No hesitation. Talking to Reagan was like standing in front of an oncoming train.

"I don't know what *this* is," Cath said. She clenched her fists in her lap and forced herself to keep talking. "I feel like . . . what happened last night was just an aberration. Like it could only have happened in the middle of the night, when he and I were both really tired. Because if it had been daylight, we would have seen how inappropriate it was—"

"I already told you," Reagan said, "he's not my boyfriend."

"It's not just that." Cath turned her face toward the wall of windows, then back at Reagan, earnestly. "It was one thing when I had a crush on him and he was totally unattainable. But I don't think I could actually *be* with someone like Levi. It would be like interspecies dating."

Reagan let her spoon drop sloppily into her cereal. "What's wrong with Levi?"

"*Nothing,*" Cath said. "He's just . . . not like me."

"You mean, smart?"

"Levi's really smart," Cath said defensively.

"I know," Reagan said, just as defensively.

"He's *different*," Cath said. "He's older. He smokes. And he drinks. And he's probably had sex. I mean, he looks like he has."

Reagan raised her eyebrows like Cath was talking crazy. And Cath thought – not for the first time, but for the first time since last night – that Levi had probably had sex *with* Reagan.

"And he likes to be outside," Cath said, just to change the subject. "And he likes animals. We don't have anything in common."

"You're making him sound like he's some rowdy mountain man who, like, smokes cigars and has sex with prostitutes."

Cath laughed, despite herself. "Like a dangerous French fur trapper."

"He's just a guy," Reagan said. "Of course he's different from you. You're never going to find a guy who's exactly like you – first of all, because that guy never leaves his dorm room. . . ."

"Guys like Levi don't date girls like me."

"Again – the girl kind?"

"Guys like Levi date girls like you."

"And what does *that* mean?" Reagan asked, tilting her head.

"Normal," Cath said. "Pretty."

Reagan rolled her eyes.

"No," Cath said, "seriously. Look at you. You've got your shit together, you're not scared of anything. I'm scared of *everything*. And I'm crazy. Like maybe you think I'm a little crazy, but I only ever let people see the tip of my crazy iceberg. Underneath this veneer of *slightly* crazy and socially inept, I'm a complete disaster."

Reagan rolled her eyes again. Cath made a mental note to stop rolling her eyes at people.

"What would we do together?" Cath asked. "He'd want to go to the bar, and I'd want to stay home and write fanfiction."

"I'm not going to talk you into this," Reagan said, "especially if you're going to be stupid. But I will say this: You're being stupid. He already likes you. He even likes your creepy fanfiction, he won't stop talking about it. Levi's just a guy. A really, really good – maybe even the *best* – guy, and nobody's saying you have to marry him. So stop making everything so hard, Cath. You kissed him, right? The only question is, do you want to kiss him again?"

Cath clenched her fists until her fingernails bit into her palms.

Reagan started stacking the empty dishes on her tray.

"Why did you break up?" Cath blurted.

"I kept cheating on him," Reagan said flatly. "I'm a pretty good friend, but I'm a shitty girlfriend."

Cath picked up her tray and followed Reagan to the trash.

She didn't see Levi that night. He worked Wednesday nights. That's when Cath realized that she knew Levi's work schedule.

But he texted her about a party Thursday at his house. *"party? thursday? my house?"*

Cath didn't text him back – she tried to. She kept starting messages and deleting them. She almost sent back just a smiley-face emoticon.

Reagan got home from work late that night and went straight to bed. Cath was at her desk, writing. "Levi killed our *Outsiders* quiz," Reagan said, stifling a yawn.

Cath smiled down at her laptop. "Did you talk about me?"

"No. I didn't think you'd want me to. I told you, I'm a pretty good friend."

"Yeah, but you're more Levi's friend than mine."

"Bros before hos," Reagan said.

Before she left the room the next morning, Reagan asked Cath if she wanted to go to Levi's party.

"I don't think so," Cath said. "I have class Friday morning at eight thirty."

"Who registers for a class that meets Friday morning at eight thirty?"

Cath shrugged.

She didn't want to go to Levi's party. Even though she liked *him,* she didn't like parties. And she didn't want the first time she saw him after what had happened to be at a party. With party people. With any people.

Cath was pretty sure she was the only person in Pound Hall tonight. She tried to tell herself that it was kind of cool to have a twelve-story building to herself. Like being trapped in the library overnight.

This is why I can't be with Levi. Because I'm the kind of girl who fantasizes about being trapped in a library overnight – and Levi can't even read.

Cath immediately felt bad for thinking that. Levi could read. (Sort of.)

She'd always thought that either people could read or they couldn't. Not this in-between thing that Levi had, where his brain could catch the words but couldn't hold on to them. Like reading was one of those rip-off claw games they had at the bowling alley.

But Levi clearly wasn't dumb. He remembered everything. He could quote extensively from the Simon Snow movies, and he knew everything there was to know about bison and piping plovers. . . . *And why was she even arguing this point with herself?*

It's not like she was going to send Abel Levi's ACT scores.

She should have texted him back. (Levi, not Abel.)

But that would have been engaging in this situation. Like moving a chess piece. Or kicking off from the ground on a teeter-totter. Better to leave Levi up in the air for a day or two than to end up stuck there by herself. . . .

The fact that she was thinking about whatever this was in terms of playground equipment showed that she wasn't ready for it. For *him*. Levi was an adult. He had a truck. And facial hair. And he'd slept with Reagan; she'd practically admitted it.

Cath didn't want to look at a guy and picture the people he'd slept with. . . .

Which had never been an issue with Abel. Nothing was ever an issue with Abel. *Because,* she could hear Wren screaming, *you didn't like him!*

Cath liked Levi. A lot. She liked looking at him. She liked listening to him – though sometimes she hated listening to him talk to other people. She hated the way he passed out smiles to everyone he met like it didn't cost him anything, like he'd never run out. He made everything look so easy. . . .

Even standing. You didn't realize how much work everyone else put into holding themselves upright until you saw Levi leaning against a wall. He looked like he was leaning on something even when he wasn't. He made standing look like vertical lying down.

Thinking about Levi's lazy hips and loose shoulders just dragged Cath's memory back to her bed.

She'd spent the night with a boy. *Slept* with him. And never mind that that's all they'd done, because it was still a huge deal. She wished she could talk to Wren about this. . . .

Fuck Wren.

No . . . *Damn* her. *Never mind* her. All Wren did lately was complicate Cath's world.

Cath had slept with a boy.

With a guy.

And it was awesome. Warm. And tangly. What would have

happened if they'd woken up any other way? Without Reagan barging in. Would Levi have kissed her again? Or would he still have rushed off with nothing more than a "later"?

Later . . .

Cath stared at her laptop. She'd been working on the same paragraph for two hours. It was a love scene (a pretty mild one), and she kept losing track of where Baz and Simon's hands were supposed to be. It was confusing sometimes with all the *he*s and the *him*s, and she'd been staring at this paragraph for so long, she was starting to feel like she'd written every sentence before. Maybe she had.

She shut the laptop and stood up. It was almost ten o'clock. What time did parties end? (What time did they start?) Not that it mattered, at this point. Cath didn't have any way to get to Levi's house.

She walked over and stood in front of the full-length mirror that was mounted on their door.

Cath looked like exactly who she was – an eighteen-year-old nerd who knew eff-all about boys or parties.

Skinny jeans. Unskinny hips. A faded pink T-shirt that said, THE MAGIC WORD IS *PLEASE*. A pink-and-brown argyle cardigan. Her hair was pulled up into a floppy half bun on top of her head.

Cath pulled the rubber band out of her hair and took off her glasses; she had to step closer to the mirror to see herself clearly.

She lifted her chin up and forced her forehead to relax. "I'm the Cool One," she told herself. "Somebody give me some tequila because I'll totally drink it. And there's no way you're going to find me later having a panic attack in your parents' bathroom. Who wants to French-kiss?"

This is why she couldn't be with Levi. She still called it "French-kissing," and he just went around putting his tongue in people's mouths.

Cath still didn't look like the Cool One. She didn't look like Wren.

She pushed her shoulders back, let her chest stick out. There was nothing wrong with her breasts (that she knew of). They were big enough that nobody ever called her flat-chested. She wished they were a little bigger; then they'd balance out her hips. Then Cath wouldn't have to check "pear-shaped" on those "how to dress for your body type" guides. Those guides try to convince you that it's okay to be any shape, but when your body type is a synonym for FUBAR, it's hard to believe it.

Cath pretended she was Wren; she pretended she didn't care. She pushed her shoulders back and lifted her chin and told her eyes to say, *Have you met me yet? I'm the Pretty One, too.*

The door flew open and the doorknob caught Cath in the ribs.

"Shit," she said, falling halfway onto her bed, halfway onto the floor. Her arms were over her head – she'd managed to protect her face.

"Shit," Reagan said. She was standing over Cath. "Are you okay?"

Cath brought a hand to her side and finished sliding onto the floor. "Jesus," she moaned.

"Cath? *Shit.*"

Cath sat up slowly. Nothing seemed broken.

"Why were you standing right in front of the door?" Reagan demanded.

"Maybe I was on my way out," Cath said. "Jesus. Why do you have to kick the door open every single time you come home?"

"My hands are always full." Reagan set down her backpack and her duffel bag and offered Cath a hand. Cath ignored it and pulled herself up using the bed. "If you *know* I always kick the door open," Reagan said, "you should know not to stand there."

"I thought you were at the party. . . ." Cath put her glasses back on. "Is this how you say you're sorry?"

"Sorry," Reagan said. Like it cost her all her tips. "I had to work. I'm going to the party now."

"Oh. "

Reagan kicked one of her shoes into her closet. "Are you coming with?"

She didn't look at Cath. If she had, Cath might have said something other than what she did — "Sure."

Reagan stopped mid-kick and looked up. "Oh? Okay . . . Well. I'm just going to change."

"Okay," Cath said.

"All right . . ." Reagan grabbed her toothbrush and makeup bag and glanced back at Cath, smiling in approval.

Cath looked at the ceiling. "Just change."

As soon as Reagan left, Cath jumped up, wincing and feeling her side again, and opened her closet. Baz glared at her from the back side of her closet door.

"Don't just stand there," she mumbled to the cutout. "Help me."

When she and Wren divided up their clothes, Wren had taken anything that said "party at a boy's place" or "leaving the house." Cath had taken everything that said "up all night writing" or "it's okay to spill tea on this." She'd accidentally grabbed a pair of Wren's jeans at Thanksgiving, so she put those on. She found a white T-shirt that didn't have anything on it — anything Simon anyway; there was a weird stain she'd have to hide with a sweater. She dug out her least pilled-up black cardigan.

Cath had makeup somewhere . . . in one of her drawers. She found mascara, an eyeliner pencil, and a crusty-looking bottle of foundation, then went to stand in front of Reagan's makeup mirror.

When Reagan came back, gently opening the door, her face

looked fresh, and her red hair was flat and smooth. Reagan looked kind of like Adele, Cath thought. If Adele had a harder, somewhat sharper twin sister. (Doppelgänger.)

"Look at you," Reagan said. "You look . . . slightly nicer than usual."

Cath groaned, feeling too helpless to snark back.

Reagan laughed. "You look fine. Your hair looks good. It's like Kristen Stewart's when she's got extensions. Shake it out."

Cath shook her head like she was emphatically disagreeing with something.

Reagan sighed and took Cath's shoulders, pulling her head down and shaking her hair out at the roots. Cath's glasses fell off.

"If you're not going to blow it out," Reagan said, "you may as well look like you've just been fucked."

"Jesus," Cath said, pulling her head back. "Don't be gross." She bent over to pick up her glasses.

"Do you need those?" Reagan asked.

"Yes" – Cath put them on – "I need them to keep me from becoming the girl in *She's All That*."

"It doesn't matter," Reagan said. "He already likes you. I think he's into the nerdy schoolgirl thing. He talks about you like you're something he found in a natural history museum."

This confirmed everything Cath had ever feared about Levi wanting to buy a ticket to her freak show. "That's not a good thing," she said.

"It is if it's Levi," Reagan said. "He loves that stuff. When he gets really sad, he likes to walk around Morrill Hall."

That was the museum on campus. There were wildlife dioramas and the world's largest mammoth fossil. "He does?" *God that's cute.*

Reagan rolled her eyes. "Come on."

———

It was almost eleven when they got to Levi's house — but not exactly dark, because of all the snow. "Will anybody still be here?" Cath asked Reagan when they got out of the car.

"Levi will still be here. He lives here."

The house was exactly as Cath had imagined it. It was in an old neighborhood with big white Victorian houses. Every house had a huge porch and way too many mailboxes next to the door. Parking was ridiculous. They had to park four blocks away, and Cath was glad she wasn't wearing pointy, high-heeled boots like Reagan's.

By the time they got to the door, Cath's stomach had realized what was happening. It twisted painfully, and she could feel her breath coming and going too soon.

She couldn't believe she was doing this. *Boy. Party. Strangers. Beer. Strangers. Party. Boy. Eye contact.*

Reagan glanced over at her. "Don't be a spaz," she said sternly.

Cath nodded, looking down at the worn-smooth welcome mat.

"I'm not going to abandon you in there," Reagan said, "even if I want to."

Cath nodded again, and Reagan opened the door.

It was immediately warmer and brighter inside — and exactly *not* how Cath had imagined it.

Cath had pictured bare walls and the sort of furniture that sat out on curbs for a week before anybody decided to take it.

But Levi's house was actually nice. Simple, but nice. There were a few paintings hanging on the walls, and houseplants everywhere — ferns and spider plants and a jade tree so big, it looked like an actual tree.

There was music playing — sleepy, electronic music — but not too loud. And somebody was burning incense.

There were plenty of people still there — all older than Cath, at least as old as Levi — and they were mostly just talking. Two guys standing next to the stereo were sort of dancing, sort of just being silly, and they didn't seem to care that they were the only ones.

Cath stood as close as she could to Reagan's back and tried not to be obvious about looking for Levi. (Inside her head, Cath was standing on tiptoe with her hand over her eyes, scanning the horizon for ships.)

Everybody there knew Reagan. Somebody handed them each a beer, and Cath took hers but didn't open it. It was Levi's roommate. One of them. Almost everybody Cath met in the next few minutes was one of Levi's roommates. She looked right through them.

Maybe Levi was in the bathroom.

Maybe he'd already gone to bed. Maybe Cath could climb into his bed like Goldilocks, and if he woke up, she'd just say "later" and run away. Goldilocks plus Cinderella.

Reagan had finished half a beer before she asked somebody, "Where's Levi?"

The person, a guy with a beard and black Ray-Ban frames, looked around the living room. "Kitchen, maybe?"

Reagan nodded like she didn't care. *Because she doesn't really,* Cath thought.

"Come on," she said to Cath. "Let's go find him." And then, when they'd walked away from everyone else: "Be cool."

The house had three big front rooms that were all connected – living room, dining room, and sunroom – and the kitchen was in the back, through a narrow doorway. Cath stuck close behind Reagan, so Reagan saw Levi before Cath was even through the door. "Shit," Cath heard her whisper.

Cath stepped into the kitchen.

Levi was leaning back against the sink. (Levi. Always leaning.) He had a bottle of beer in one hand, the same hand he was pressing into a girl's back.

The girl looked older than Cath. Even with her eyes closed. Levi's other hand was tangled in her long, blond hair, and he was kissing her with his mouth smiling and open. He made it look so easy.

Cath looked down immediately and walked out of the kitchen, walked straight through the house to the front door. She knew Reagan was right behind her because she could hear her muttering. "Shit, shit, shit."

"But I don't understand," Simon stammered, "what *is* the Insidious Humdrum? Is he a man?"

"Perhaps." The Mage wiped the grit from his eyes and swept his wand out in front of them. *"Olly olly oxen free,"* he whispered. Simon braced himself, but nothing happened.

"Perhaps he's a man," the Mage said, recovering his wry smile. "Perhaps he's something else, something less, I should think."

"Is he a magician? Like us?"

"No," the Mage said severely. "Of that we can be certain. He – if indeed he is a *he* – is the enemy of magic. He destroys magic; some think he eats it. He wipes the world clean of magic, wherever he can. . . .

"You're too young to hear this, Simon. Eleven is too young. But it isn't fair to keep it from you any longer. The Insidious Humdrum is the greatest threat the World of Mages has ever faced. He's powerful, he's pervasive. Fighting him is like fighting off sleep when you're long past the edge of exhaustion.

"But fight him we *must*. You were recruited to Watford because we believe the Humdrum has taken a special interest in you. We want to protect you; I vow to do so with my life. But you must learn, Simon, as soon as possible, how best to protect yourself."

—from chapter 23, *Simon Snow and the Mage's Heir,*
copyright © 2001 by Gemma T. Leslie

SEVENTEEN

They didn't talk in the car. And Cath didn't cry. She was grateful for that. She already felt like such a fool. . . .

Because she was one.

What had she been thinking – that Levi really liked her? How could she have believed that, especially after she'd spent the last two days explaining to herself all the reasons he never would.

Maybe she'd thought it was possible because Reagan thought it was possible, and Reagan wasn't anybody's fool. . . .

When they got back to the dorms, Reagan stopped Cath from getting out of the car. "Wait."

Cath sat, holding the passenger door open.

"I'm sorry," Reagan said. "I really didn't expect that to happen."

"I just want to pretend that it didn't," Cath said, feeling tears burning again in her eyes. "I don't want to talk about this – and, I mean, I know he's your best friend, but I really don't want you to talk to him about tonight. . . . Or about me. Ever. I already feel like such an ass."

"Sure," Reagan said, "whatever you want."

"I want to pretend this didn't happen."

"Okay."

———

Reagan was good at not talking about things.

She didn't mention Levi for the rest of the weekend. He called Cath Saturday morning, but she didn't pick up. A few seconds later, Reagan's phone rang.

"Don't ignore him on my account," Cath said. "It never happened."

"Hey . . . ," Reagan said into the phone. "Yeah . . . All right . . . Just call me when you're downstairs. Cath is trying to study."

A half hour later, Reagan's phone rang again, and she got up to leave. "See ya," she said.

Cath nodded. "Later."

Levi tried calling Cath again that weekend. Twice. And once he sent her a text that said, *"so they found the 5th hare, now what? will trade gingerbread lattes and pumkin bread for this information."*

The fact that he misspelled "pumpkin" made Cath wince.

If she hadn't gone to the party – if she hadn't seen Levi in action – she would have thought this text was him asking her out on a date.

She knew she'd have to see him again. He was still Reagan's best friend, the two of them still studied together. . . .

Reagan would probably keep him away completely if Cath wanted that, but Cath didn't want Levi to ask questions. So Cath stayed away instead. She started going to the library after dinner and hanging out in Nick's stacks. Nick generally wasn't there; nobody was. Cath brought her laptop and tried to work on her final project, her ten-thousand-word short story, for Fiction-Writing. She'd started it – she'd started it half a dozen times – but she still didn't have anything she wanted to finish.

Usually she ended up working on *Carry On, Simon*. Cath was on a streak, posting long chapters almost every night. Switching from her Fiction-Writing homework to Simon and Baz was like realizing she'd been driving in the wrong gear. She could actually feel the muscles in her forearms loosen. Her typing got faster; her breathing got easier. She'd catch herself nodding her head as she wrote, almost like she was keeping time with the words as they rushed out of her.

When the library closed, Cath would dial 911 on her phone, then run back to the dorm as fast as she could with her finger on Call.

It was more than a week before she saw Levi again. She came home from class late one afternoon, and he was sitting on Reagan's bed while Reagan typed.

"Cather," he said, grinning, pulling his earphones out of his head. He was listening to a lecture; she knew that now. Reagan said he listened to them all the time, and that he even saved the ones he really liked.

"Hey," he said. "I owe you a beverage. Your choice, hot or fermented. I rocked that *Outsiders* quiz. Did Reagan tell you? I got an A."

"That's great," Cath said, trying not to let her face show how much she wanted to kiss and kill him.

She'd thought Reagan had to work tonight. That was the only reason Cath had come home. But she didn't have to stay here. She was going to meet Nick at the library later anyway. . . .

Cath pretended to get something she needed out of her desk. A pack of gum.

"Okay," she said, "I'm taking off."

"But you just got here," Levi said. "Don't you want to stay and talk about the symbolism of Johnny's relationship with Ponyboy? And the struggle between Sodapop and Darry? Hey, do you think there's such a thing as *Outsiders* fanfiction?"

"I've gotta go," Cath said, trying to say it to Reagan. "Meeting somebody."

"Who are you meeting?" Levi asked.

"Nick. My writing partner."

"Oh. Right. Do you want me to walk you home later?"

"Nick'll probably walk me home," she said.

"Oh." Levi brought his eyebrows together, but still smiled. "Cool. Later."

She couldn't get away from him fast enough. She got to the library and wrote a thousand words of *Carry On* before Nick showed up.

"Shut that thing down," Nick said. "You're corrupting my creative centers with static."

"That's what she said," Cath said, closing her laptop.

Nick looked dubious.

"It was sort of a metaphysical 'that's what she said.'"

"Ah." He set down his backpack and pulled out their notebook. "You working on your final project?"

"Indirectly," Cath said.

"What does that mean?"

"Have you ever heard sculptors say that they don't actually sculpt an object; they sculpt away everything that *isn't* the object?"

"No." He sat down.

"Well, I'm writing everything that *isn't* my final project, so that when I actually sit down to write it, that's all that will be left in my mind."

"Clever girl," he said, pushing the open notebook toward her. She flipped through it. Nick had filled five pages, front and back, since they'd last met.

"What about you?" she asked.

"I don't know," he said. "I might turn in a story I worked on this summer."

"Isn't that cheating?"

"I don't think so. It's more like being really ahead of schedule. . . . All I can think about right now is *this* story." He nudged the notebook toward Cath again. "I want you to read what I did."

This story. Their story. Nick kept trying to call it an anti-love story. "But it's not anti-love," she'd argued.

"It's anti- everything you usually find in a love story. Gooey eyes and 'you complete me.' "

" 'You complete me' is a great line," Cath said. "You wish you came up with 'you complete me.' "

Cath didn't tell him that she'd been writing love stories – rewriting the same love story – every day for the last five years. That she'd written love stories with and without the goo, love-at-first-sight stories, love-before-first-sight stories, love-to-hate-you stories. . . .

She didn't tell Nick that writing love stories was her thing. Her one true thing. And that his anti-love story read like somebody's very first fanfic – Mary Sue to the tenth power. That the main character was obviously Nick and that the girl was obviously Winona Ryder plus Natalie Portman plus Selena Gomez.

Instead Cath fixed it. She rewrote his dialogue. She reined in the quirk.

"Why'd you cross that out?" Nick said tonight, leaning over her left shoulder. He smelled good. *(Breaking news: Boys smell good.)* "I liked that part," he said.

"Our character just stopped her car in a parking lot to wish on a dandelion."

"It's refreshing," Nick said. "It's romantic."

Cath shook her head. Her ponytail brushed Nick's neck. "It makes her seem like a douche."

"You have something against dandelions?"

"I have something against twenty-two-year-old women wishing on dandelions. Stopping the car to wish on dandelions.

Also, the car? *No.* No to vintage Volvos."

"It's a character detail."

"It's a cliché. I swear to God, every surviving Volvo produced between 1970 and 1985 is being driven by quirky fictional girls."

Nick pouted down at the paper. "You're crossing out everything."

"I'm not crossing out everything."

"What are you leaving?" He leaned over more and watched her write.

"The rhythm," Cath said. "The rhythm is good."

"Yeah?" He smiled.

"Yeah. It reads like a waltz."

"Make you jealous?" He smiled some more. His eyeteeth were crooked, but not bad enough to get braces.

"Definitely," Cath said. "I could never write a waltz."

Sometimes, when they talked like this, she was sure they were flirting. But when the notebook closed, the light always went off in Nick's eyes. At midnight, he'd rush off to wherever he always rushed off to, probably to wrap a beer around a blond girl's waist. To kiss her with his twisted eyeteeth showing.

Cath kept working on the scene; a whole new conversation took shape in the margin. When she looked up, Nick was still smiling at her.

"What?" she asked.

"Nothing," he said, laughing.

"What?"

"Nothing. Just . . . It's crazy that this works. Between you and me. That we can actually write together. It's like . . . thinking together."

"It's nice," Cath said, meaning it.

"You wouldn't think we'd be on the same wavelength, you know? We're so different."

"We're not *that* different."

"Totally different," he said. "Look at us."

"We're both English majors," Cath said. "We're both white. We live in Nebraska. We listen to the same music, we watch the same TV shows, we even have the same pair of Chuck Taylors—"

"Yeah. But it's like John Lennon writing with . . . Taylor Swift instead of Paul McCartney."

"Get over yourself," Cath said. "You're not half as pretty as Taylor Swift."

"You know what I mean." Nick poked her in the arm with the end of his pen.

"It's nice," she said, looking up at him, still not sure if they were flirting – pretty sure she didn't want them to be. "Writing is lonely."

There wasn't time for Cath to write a page of her own in the notebook. She and Nick spent the rest of their night in the stacks, revamping his section. The Volvo became a rusty Neon, and the dandelion detail blew away completely.

At eleven forty-five, they packed up. When they got to the library's front steps, Nick was already checking his phone. "Hey," Cath said, "do you feel like walking past Pound Hall on your way to your car? We could walk together."

He didn't look up from his phone. "Better not. I need to get home. See you in class, though."

"Yeah," Cath said, "see ya." She got out her phone and started dialing 911 before he'd disappeared into the shadows.

"Dad? It's Cath. I was just calling to say hi. I was thinking about coming home this weekend. Give me a call."

———

"Dad, I'm calling you at work now. It's Thursday. I think I'm gonna come home tomorrow. Call me back, okay? Or e-mail me? Love you."

_____

"Hey, honey, it's your dad. Don't come home this weekend. I'm going to be gone all weekend at the Gravioli shoot. In Tulsa. I mean, come home if you want to. Throw a big party. Like Tom Cruise in . . . God, what is that movie? Not *Top Gun* – *Risky Business*! Have a big party. Invite a bunch of people over to watch *Risky Business*. I don't have any booze, but there's still some green bean casserole left. I love you, Cath. Are you still fighting with your sister? Don't."

Love Library was busier than normal that weekend; it was the week before finals, and everybody seemed to be digging in. Cath had to roam deeper and deeper into the library to find an empty study carrel. She thought of Levi and his theory that the library invented new rooms the more that you visited. Tonight she walked by a half-sized door in a stairwell. The sign said SOUTH STACKS, and Cath would swear she'd never seen it before.

She opened the door, and there was an immediate step down into a normal-sized hallway. Cath ended up in another siloish room, the mirror image of Nick's; the wind was even blowing in the opposite direction.

She found an empty cubicle and set down her bag, taking off her coat. A girl sitting on the other side of the gray partition was watching her.

The girl sat up a little, so that Cath could see she was smiling. She looked quickly around the room, then leaned forward, holding on to the cubicle wall. "I don't mean to bother you, but I love your shirt."

Cath glanced down. She was wearing her *KEEP CALM AND CARRY ON* shirt from Etsy, the one with Baz and Simon's faces.

"Oh," Cath said, "thanks."

"It's always so cool to meet somebody else who reads fanfiction in real life. . . ."

Cath must have looked surprised. "Oh my God," the girl said, "do you even know what I'm talking about?"

"Yeah," Cath said. "Of course. I mean, I think so. *Carry On, Simon*?"

"Yes!" The girl laughed quietly and looked around the room again. "That was almost embarrassing. I mean, it's like having a secret life sometimes. People think it's so weird. . . . Fanfiction. Slash. You know."

Cath nodded. "Do you read a lot of fic?"

"Not as much anymore," the girl said. "I was an addict in high school." Her blond hair was pulled back in a ponytail, and she was wearing a sweatshirt that read VERDIGRE FOOTBALL — FIGHT, HAWKS, FIGHT! She didn't *look* like a creepy shut-in. . . . "What about you?" she asked.

"I still read a lot . . . ," Cath said.

"Magicath is my absolute favorite," the girl interrupted, like she couldn't hold it back. "I'm obsessed with *Carry On*. Have you been keeping up?"

"Yeah."

"She's been posting *so much* lately. Every time there's a new chapter, I have to stop everything to read it. And then read it again. My roommate thinks I'm crazy."

"Mine, too."

"But it's just *so good*. Nobody writes Simon and Baz like Magicath. I'm in love with her Baz. Like, *in love*. And I used to be a major Simon/Agatha shipper."

Cath wrinkled her nose. *"No."*

"I know, I was young."

"If Agatha actually cared about either of them," Cath said, "she'd pick one."

"I know, right? When Simon broke it off with her in *Carry On* – *such* a good scene."

"You didn't think it was too long?"

"No," the girl said, "did you?"

"I wasn't sure."

"I never think the chapters are too long. I just want more and more and more." The girl waved her hands in front of her mouth like she was Cookie Monster eating cookies. "I'm telling you, I'm obsessed with *Carry On*. I feel like something *big* is about to happen soon."

"Me, too," Cath said. "I think the Mage might turn on Simon."

"No! You think?"

"I've just got a feeling about it."

"It killed me how long it took Simon and Baz to get together. And now I'm dying for them to have a big love scene. That's my only complaint about *Carry On* – not enough Simon/Baz action."

"She almost never writes love scenes," Cath said, feeling her cheeks pink.

"Yeah, but when she does, they're hot."

"You think?"

"Um," the girl laughed. *"Yes."*

"This is why people think we're crazy perverts," Cath said.

The girl just giggled some more. "I know. Sometimes I forget that there's still a real book coming out – like, it's hard for me to imagine that the story is going to end any other way than the way Magicath writes it."

"Sometimes . . . ," Cath said, "when I'm reading canon, I forget that Simon and Baz aren't in love."

"Right? I love Gemma T. Leslie, I always will – I feel like she was this major force in my childhood – and I know that Magicath wouldn't exist without GTL. But now, I think I love

Magicath more. Like she might be my favorite author. And she's never even written a book. . . ."

Cath's jaw was hanging slightly open, and she was shaking her head. "That's *crazy*."

"*I know,*" the girl said, "but I think it's true. . . . Oh my God, I'm sorry. I'm talking your ear off. I just never get to talk about this stuff in real life. Except to my boyfriend. He knows what a freak I am about it."

"Don't apologize," Cath said. "This was cool."

The girl sat down, and so did Cath. She opened up her laptop and thought for a minute about Professor Piper, then opened up the latest chapter of *Carry On*. Something big was about to happen soon.

"Dad, it's Cath. Are you back from Tulsa? Just checking in. Call me."

———

"Dad? It's Cath. Call me."

———

"Hey, Cath, it's your dad. I'm back. I'm fine. Don't worry about me. Worry about school. No, scratch that, don't worry at all. Try not worrying, Cath – it's an amazing way to be. Like flying. Love you, honey, tell your sister hi."

———

"Dad? I know you don't want me to worry. But I would worry less if you called me back. And not at three A.M."

"Ten days . . . ," Professor Piper said.

Instead of sitting in her usual spot on her desk, she was striking a pose at the windows. It was snowing outside – it had already snowed so much this year, and it was only early December – and the professor cut a dramatic figure against the icy glass.

"I'd like to believe that you're all finished with your short stories," she said, turning her blue eyes on them. "That you're just tweaking and tinkering now, tugging every last loose thread –"

She walked back toward their desks and smiled at a few of them one by one. Cath felt a thrill when their eyes met.

"– but I'm a writer, too," the professor said. "I know what it's like to be distracted. To seek out distractions. To exhaust yourself doing every other little thing rather than face a blank page." She smiled at one of the boys. "A blank screen . . .

"So if you haven't finished – or if you haven't started – I understand, I do. But I implore you . . . *start now*. Lock yourself away from the world. Turn off the Internet, barricade the door. Write as if your life depended on it.

"Write as if your *future* depended on it.

"Because I can promise you this one small thing. . . ." She let her eyes rest on another one of her favorites and smiled. "If you're planning to take my advanced course next semester, you won't get in unless you get a B in this class. And this short story is half your final grade.

"This class is for *writers*," she said. "For people who are willing to set aside their fears and move past distractions.

"I love you all – I *do* – but if you're going to waste your time, I'm not going to waste mine." She stopped at Nick's desk and smiled at him. "Okay?" she said only to him.

Nick nodded. Cath looked down at her desk.

She hadn't washed her sheets, but there wasn't any Levi left in them.

Cath pushed her face into her pillow as nonchalantly as she

could, even though there was no one else in the room to judge her for it.

Her pillowcase smelled like a dirty pillowcase. And a little bit like Tostitos.

Cath closed her eyes and imagined Levi lying next to her, his legs touching and crossing hers. She remembered the way her throat had rasped that night and the way he'd put his arm around her, like he wanted to hold her up, like he wanted to make everything easy for her.

She remembered his flannel shirt. And his needy, pink mouth. And how she hadn't spent nearly enough time with her fingers in the back of his hair.

And then she was crying and her nose was running. She wiped it on her pillow because, at this point, what did it matter?

Simon ran as fast as he could. Faster. Casting spells on his feet and legs, casting spells on the branches and stones in his path.

He could already be too late – at first he thought he was, when he saw Agatha lying in a heap on the forest floor. . . . But it was a trembling heap. Agatha may be frightened, but she was still whole.

Baz was kneeling over her and trembling just as hard. His hair hung forward in a way he normally wouldn't allow, and his pale skin glowed oddly in the moonlight, like the inside of a shell. Simon wondered for a moment why Agatha wasn't trying to escape. She must be dazed, he thought. Vampires could do that, couldn't they?

"Go. Away," Baz hissed.

"Baz . . . ," Simon said, holding his hand out.

"Don't look at me."

Simon avoided Baz's eyes, but he didn't look away. "I'm not afraid of you," Simon said.

"You should be. I could kill you both. Her first, then you, before you'd even realized I was doing it. I'm so fast, Simon. . . ." His voice broke on the last two words.

"I know. . . ."

"And so strong . . ."

"I know."

"And so *thirsty*."

Simon's voice was almost a whisper. "I know."

Baz's shoulders shook. Agatha started to sit up – she must be recovering. Simon looked at her gravely and shook his head. He took another step toward them. He was close now. In Baz's reach.

"I'm not afraid of you, Baz."

"Why *not?*" Baz whined. It was an animal whine. Wounded.

"Because I know you. And I know you wouldn't hurt me." Simon held out his hand and gently pushed back the errant lock of black hair. Baz's head tilted up with the touch, his fangs popped and gleaming. "You're so *strong,* Baz."

Baz reached for him then, clutching Simon around the waist and pressing his face into his stomach.

Agatha slid out from between them and ran toward the fortress. Simon held Baz by the back of his neck and curved his body over him. "I know," Simon said. "I know everything."

—from *Carry On, Simon,* posted February 2011
by FanFixx.net author *Magicath*

EIGHTEEN

"Do you just hang out here now?" Nick pushed his library cart to her table.

"Just trying to write," Cath said, closing her laptop before he started peeking at her screen.

"Working on your final project?" He slipped into the chair beside her and tried to open the computer. She laid her arm on top of it. "Have you settled on a direction yet?" he asked.

"Yep," Cath said. "Lots of them."

He frowned for a second, then shook his head. "I'm not worried about you. You can write ten thousand words in your sleep."

She practically could. She'd written ten thousand words of *Carry On* in one night before. Her wrists had really hurt the next day. . . . "What about you?" she asked. "Done?"

"Almost. Well . . . I have an idea." He smiled at her. It was one of those smiles that made her think he might be flirting.

Smiling is confusing, she thought. *This is why I don't do it.*

"I think I'm going to turn in my anti-love story." He raised his Muppet eyebrows and stretched his top lip across his teeth.

Cath felt her mouth hanging open and closed it. "The story? Like . . . the story we've been working on?"

"Yeah," Nick said excitedly, raising his eyebrows high again. "I mean, at first I thought it was too frivolous. A short story is supposed to be about something. But it's like you always say, it's about two people falling in love – what could be bigger than that? And we've workshopped it enough, I think it's ready." He pushed his elbow into hers and tapped his front teeth with the tip of his tongue. He was watching her eyes. "So what do you think? It's a good idea, right?"

Cath snapped her mouth shut again. "It's . . . it's just that . . ." She looked down at the table, where the notebook usually sat. "We worked on it together."

"Cath . . . ," he said. Like he was disappointed in her. "What are you trying to say?"

"Well, you're calling it *your* story."

"*You* call it that," he said, cutting her off. "You're always saying that you feel more like an editor than a cowriter."

"I was teasing you."

"Are you teasing me now? I can't tell."

She glanced up at his face. He looked impatient. And let down. Like Cath was letting him down.

"Can we just be honest?" he asked. He didn't wait for her to answer. "This story was my idea. I started it. I'm the only one who works on it outside the library. I appreciate all of your help – you're a genius editor, and you've got tons of potential – but do you really think it's *your* story?"

"*No,*" Cath said. "Of course not." She felt her voice shrink into a whine. "But we were writing together. Like Lennon–McCartney—"

"John Lennon and Paul McCartney have been quoted multiple times saying they wrote their songs separately, then showed them to each other. Do you really think John Lennon wrote half of 'Yesterday'? Do you think Paul McCartney wrote 'Revolution'? Don't be naïve."

Cath clenched her fists in her lap.

"Look," Nick said, smiling like he was forcing himself to do it. "I really appreciate everything you've done. You really get me, as an artist, like nobody else ever has. You're my best sounding board. And I want us to keep showing each other our stuff. I don't want to feel like, if I offer you a suggestion, it belongs to me. Or vice versa."

She shook her head. "That's not . . ." She didn't know what to say, so she pulled her laptop toward her and started wrapping the cord around it. The one Abel had given her. (It really was a good gift.)

"Cath . . . don't. You're freaking me out here. Are you actually mad about this? Do you really think I'm stealing from you?"

She shook her head again. And put her computer in her bag.

"Are you angry?" he asked.

"No," she whispered. They were still in a library, after all. "I'm just . . ." *Just.*

"I thought you'd be happy for me," he said. "You're the only one who knows how hard I've worked on this. You know how I've poured myself into this story."

"I know," she said. That part was true. Nick had cared about the story; Cath hadn't. She'd cared about the writing. About the magic third thing that lived between them when they were working together. She would have met Nick at the library to write obituaries. Or shampoo packaging. "I'm just . . . ," she said. "I need to work on my story now. It's almost finals week."

"Can't you work here?"

"I don't want to waterboard you with my typing noises," she murmured.

"Do you want to get together one more time before we turn in our stories, just to proof them?"

"Sure," she said, not meaning it.

Cath waited until she got to the stairs to start running, and ran all the way home by herself through the trees and the darkness.

On Wednesday afternoon, after her Biology final, Cath sat in front of her computer. She wasn't going to leave the room or get on the Internet until she finished her Fiction-Writing project.

She wasn't going to stop typing until she had a first draft. Even if that meant typing things like, *I don't know what the fuck I'm typing right now, blah, blah, blah.*

She still hadn't settled on a plot or characters. . . .

She spent an hour writing a conversation between a man and his wife. And then she realized there was no rising or falling action; the man and his wife were just arguing about Brussels sprouts, and the Brussels sprouts weren't a metaphor for anything deeper.

Then she started a story about a couple's breakup, from the perspective of their dog.

And then she started a story where a dog intentionally destroys a marriage. And then she stopped because she wasn't all that interested in dogs. Or married people.

She thought about typing up everything she remembered writing from Nick's anti-love story. That would get Professor Piper's attention.

She thought about taking one of her Simon/Baz stories and just changing the names. (She probably could have gotten away with that if Professor Piper wasn't already on to her.)

Maybe she could take a Simon/Baz story and change all the material details. Simon is a lawyer, and Baz is a spy. Simon is a cop, and Baz owns a bakery. Simon likes Brussels sprouts, and Baz is a dog.

Cath wanted, desperately, to escape to the Internet. Just to check her e-mail or something. But she wouldn't let herself open a browser window, not even to check whether the *b* in "Brussels" should be capitalized.

Instead, she shoved away from her desk and went to the bathroom. She walked slowly down the hall, trolling for distractions, but there was no one milling around trying to be friendly. Cath went back to her room and lay on her bed. She'd stayed up too late the night before studying for Biology, and it was easy to close her eyes.

It was almost a nice change of pace to be stewing about Nick instead of Levi. Had she actually liked him? (Nick, that is. She'd definitely liked Levi.) Or had she just liked everything he represented? Smart, talented, handsome. World War I handsome.

Now just thinking about Nick made her feel so ashamed. She'd been taken. Grifted. Had he planned to steal the story all along? Or was he just desperate? Like Cath was desperate.

Nick and his stupid story.

It really was his story. It was nothing Cath ever would have written on her own. Stupid, quirky girl character. Stupid, pretentious boy character. No dragons.

It was Nick's story. He'd just tricked her into writing it. He was an unreliable narrator, if ever she'd met one.

Cath wanted to work on her own story now. Not the one for class. *Carry On*.

Carry On was *Cath's* story. Thousands of people were reading it. Thousands of people wanted her to finish.

This story she was supposed to be writing for class? Only one person cared if she finished it. And that one person wasn't even Cath.

She fell asleep with her shoes on, lying on her stomach.

When she woke up, it was dark, and she hated that. It was disorienting to fall asleep in the light and wake up in the dark, instead of the other way around. Her head ached, and there was a circle of drool on her pillow. That only happened when she slept during the day.

Cath sat up, miserably, and realized her phone was ringing. She didn't recognize the number.

"Hello?"

"Cather?" It was a man's voice. Gentle.

"Yes, who is this?"

"Hey, Cather, it's Kelly. Kelly from your dad's work."

Kelly was her dad's creative director. The panda bear guy. "Fucking Kelly," her dad called him. As in, "Fucking Kelly is making us start over on the Kilpatrick's campaign." Or, "And then fucking Kelly got it in his head that the robot should be dancing."

Kelly was the reason her dad still had a job. Every time Kelly switched agencies, he talked Cath's dad into following him.

Kelly chalked up all her dad's extreme behavior to "the creative mind." "Your dad's a genius," he'd told the twins at one Christmas party. "His brain was specifically designed to make ads. He's a precision instrument."

Kelly had a soft, wheedling voice – like he was trying to talk you into something or sell you something, every time he opened his mouth. "Have you girls tried the cocktail shrimp here? The cocktail shrimp are *amazing*."

Hearing Kelly's soft-sell voice now sent an unpleasant chill scrabbling up Cath's spine.

"Hi," she said.

"Hey, Cather. I'm sorry to call you at school. It's finals week, right? My Connor tells me it's finals week."

"Yeah," she said.

"Look, I got your number from your dad's phone, and I just wanted to tell you that he's perfectly okay, he's going to be fine. But he's spending tonight – maybe the next day or two – here at the hospital. Here at St. Richard's Hospital—"

"What happened?"

"Nothing happened, he's okay. I mean it. He just needs to get his balance back."

"Why? I mean, what happened? Why did you take him there – did you take him there?"

"Yeah, I did. I brought him here myself. It wasn't that anything happened. It's just that he was really caught up in work, which you know, we all are. It's a fine line sometimes for all of us . . . but your dad didn't want to leave his office. It had been a few days since he'd left his office. . . ."

How many days? she wondered. And was he eating? Was he going to the bathroom? Had he shoved his desk up against the door? Had he thrown a stack of ideas out the seventh-floor window? Had he stood in the hallway and shouted, *You're all limp-dicked sellouts! Every one of you! And especially you, Kelly, you fucking brainless hack!* Did they have to carry him out? Was it during the day? Did everyone watch?

"He's at St. Richard's?" she asked.

"Yep, they're just checking things out. Helping him get some sleep. I think that's really going to help."

"I'm coming," she said. "Tell him I'm coming. Did he hurt himself?"

"No, Cather – he's not hurt. He's just sleeping. I think he's going to be fine. It's just been a rough couple of months."

Months. "I'm coming, okay?"

"Sure," Kelly said. "I'm probably going to head home soon. But this is my cell number. You call me if you need anything, okay?"

"Thank you."

"I mean it. Anything at all. You know how I feel about your dad, he's my lucky penny. I'd do anything for the guy."

"Thank you."

She hung up before Kelly did. She couldn't stand any more.

Then she immediately called Wren. Wren sounded surprised when she answered the phone. Cath cut to the chase – "Dad's at St. Richard's."

"What? Why?"

"He lost it at work."

"Is he okay?"

"I don't know. Kelly said he wouldn't leave his office."

Wren sighed. "Fucking Kelly?"

"Yeah."

"Dad's going to be mortified."

"I know," Cath said. "I'm going up there as soon as I can figure out a ride."

"Did Kelly tell you to come?"

"What do you mean?"

"I mean, it's finals week, and you know that Dad is probably tranqed into oblivion right now. We should call tomorrow and see how he's doing."

"Wren, he's in the hospital."

"St. Richard's isn't exactly a hospital."

"You don't think we should go?"

"I think we should finish our finals," Wren said. "By the time we're done, he'll be just coming out of the haze, and we can be there for him."

"I'm going," Cath said. "I'm gonna see if Grandma will come get me."

"Grandma's in Chicago."

"Oh. Right."

"If you really have to do this, I know that Mom would drive you. If it's that important to you."

"*No*. Are you kidding me?"

"Fine. Whatever. Will you call me when you get to the hospital?"

Cath wanted to say something mean, like, "I'd hate to interrupt your studies during finals week." But instead she said, "Yes."

She called Reagan next. Reagan had a car; Reagan would understand. . . .

Reagan didn't answer.

Cath crawled onto her bed and cried for a few minutes.

For her dad. For his humiliation and his weakness. And for herself — because she hadn't been there to keep this from happening, and because even something *this* shitty couldn't bring her and Wren together. Why was Wren being so cool about this? Just because it had happened before didn't mean it wasn't serious. It didn't mean he didn't need them.

Then she cried over the fact that she hadn't made more friends with cars. . . .

And then she called Levi.

He answered right away. "Cath?"

"Hey, Levi. Um, how are you?"

"Fine. I'm just . . . working."

"Do you usually answer your phone at work?"

"No."

"Oh. Well, um, later when you get off, is there any chance you could drive me to Omaha? I know it's a big hassle, and I'll give you gas money. It's just, sort of, a family emergency."

"I'll come get you now. Give me fifteen."

"No. Levi, it can wait, if you're at work."

"Is it a family emergency?"

"Yeah," she said quietly.

"See you in fifteen."

There was no way Snow would see him here, up on the balcony. Snow was too busy trying to learn his steps for the ball. Too busy stamping all over Agatha's silk boots. She looked lovely today – all golden white hair and creamy pink skin. *That girl is opaque,* Baz thought. *Like milk. Like white glass.*

Simon took a bad step forward, and she lost her balance. He caught her with a strong arm around her waist.

Don't they just shine together? Weren't they every shade of white and gold?

"He'll never give her up, you know."

Baz wanted to whip around at the voice, but he caught himself. Didn't even turn his head. "Hello, Penelope."

"You're wasting your time," she said, and damned if she didn't sound tired. "He thinks she's his destiny – he can't help himself."

"I know," Baz said, turning into the shadows. "Neither can I."

—from "Tyrannus Basilton, Son of Pitch," posted December 2009
by FanFixx.net authors *Magicath* and *Wrenegade*

NINETEEN

Levi didn't ask any questions, and Cath didn't feel like explaining.

She told him that her dad was in the hospital, but she didn't tell him why. She thanked him a lot. She pushed a twenty-dollar bill into his ashtray and told him she'd give him more as soon as she got cash.

She tried not to look at him — because every time she did, she imagined him kissing someone, either her or that other girl, and both memories were equally painful.

She waited for him to turn on the Levi, to needle her with questions and charming observations, but he left her alone. After about fifteen minutes, he asked whether she'd mind if he listened to a lecture — he had a big final the next day.

"Go ahead," Cath said.

Levi set a digital recorder on the dashboard. They listened to a deep-voiced professor talk about sustainable ranching practices for the next forty minutes.

When they got into town, Cath gave Levi directions; he'd only been to Omaha a few times. When they turned into the hospital parking lot, Cath was sure he'd read the sign — ST. RICHARD'S CENTER FOR MENTAL AND BEHAVIORAL HEALTH.

"You can just drop me," she said. "I really appreciate this."

Levi turned off the Range Management lecture. "I'd feel a lot better if I saw you in."

Cath didn't argue. She walked in ahead of him and went straight to the registration desk. She was half-conscious of Levi folding himself into a lobby chair behind her.

The man at the desk wasn't any good. "Avery," he said. "Avery . . . Arthur." He clicked his tongue. "Doesn't look like he's authorized for visitors."

Could Cath talk to a doctor? Or a nurse? The guy wasn't sure about that. Was her dad awake? He couldn't tell her, federal privacy regulations and all.

"Well, I'm just going to sit over there," Cath said. "So maybe you could tell somebody that I'm waiting, and that I'd like to see my dad."

The guy – he was a big guy, more like a muscled-up orderly than a receptionist or a nurse – told her she was welcome to sit all she wanted. She wondered if this guy had been here when they'd brought her dad in. Did they have to restrain him? Was he screaming? Was he spitting? She wanted everyone here, starting with this guy, to know that her dad was a person, not just a crazy person. That he had people who cared about him and who would notice if he was roughed up or given the wrong medicine. Cath huffed down into a chair where the no-good orderly could see her.

Ten minutes of silence passed before Levi said, "No luck?"

"Same old luck." She glanced over at him, but not at his face. "Look, I'm probably here for the long haul. You should head back."

Levi leaned forward on his knees, scrubbing at the back of his hair, like he was thinking about it. "I'm not going to leave you alone in a hospital waiting room," he said finally.

"But all I can do now is wait," she said. "So this is the perfect place for me."

He shrugged and sat back, still rubbing his neck. "I may as

well see you through. You might need a ride later."

"Okay," Cath said, then forced herself to keep going. "Thank you . . . This isn't going to be a regular thing, you know. I promise not to call you the next time one of my relatives gets drunk or goes crazy."

Levi took off his green jacket and laid it on the seat next to him. He was wearing a black sweater and black jeans, and he was holding his digital recorder. He pushed it into his pocket. "I wonder if there's coffee around here," he said.

St. Richard's wasn't a regular hospital. Nothing but the waiting room was open to the public, and the waiting room was more like a hallway with chairs. There wasn't even a TV hanging in the corner tuned to Fox News.

Levi stood up and moseyed over to the orderly's window. He leaned forward on the counter and started to make conversation.

Cath felt a surge of irritation and got out her phone to text Wren. *"at st richard's, waiting to see dad."* She thought about calling their grandma, but decided to wait until she had more information.

When she looked up from the phone, Levi was being buzzed through the main doors. He glanced back at her just before they closed behind him, and smiled. It had been so long since Levi smiled at her – Cath's heart leapt up into her sinuses. It made her eyes water. . . .

He was gone a long time.

Maybe he was getting a tour, she thought. He'd probably come back with a pitcher of beer, lipstick all over his face, and Fiesta Bowl tickets.

Cath didn't have anything to distract herself with except her phone – but the battery was low, so she shoved it into her bag and tried not to think about it.

Eventually she heard a buzz, and Levi walked back through

the doors, holding two disposable coffee cups and balancing two boxed sandwiches on his forearms.

"Turkey or ham?" he asked.

"Why are you always feeding me?"

"Well, I work in food service and my major is basically *grazing*. . . ."

"Turkey," she said, feeling grateful, but still not feeling like she could look Levi in the eye. (She knew what that was like. His eyes were warm and baby blue. They made you feel like he liked you better than other people.) She took a coffee cup. "How did you get back there?"

"I just asked about coffee," he said.

Cath unwrapped the sandwich and started tearing off bite-sized pieces. She pinched them flat before pushing them into her mouth. Her mom used to tell her not to mutilate her food. Her dad never said anything; his table manners were much worse.

"You can, you know," Levi said, unwrapping his sandwich.

"Can what?"

"Call me the next time somebody goes crazy or gets arrested . . . I was glad you called me tonight. I thought you were mad at me."

Cath smashed another chunk of sandwich. Mustard oozed out the sides. "Are you the guy who everybody calls when they need help?"

"Am I Superman?" She could hear him smiling.

"You know what I mean. Are you the guy all your friends call when they need help? Because they know you'll say yes?"

"I don't know . . . ," he said. "I'm the guy everybody calls when they need help moving. I think it's the truck."

"When I called you tonight," she said to her shoes, "I knew that you'd give me a ride. If you could."

"Good," he said. "You were right."

"I think I might be exploiting you."

He laughed. "You can't exploit me against my will. . . ."

Cath took a sip of the coffee. It tasted nothing like a gingerbread latte.

"Are you worried about your dad?" Levi asked.

"Yeah," she said. "And no. I mean" – she glanced over at him quickly – "this isn't the first time. This just happens. . . . Usually it doesn't get this bad. Usually we're there for him."

Levi held his sandwich by one corner and took a bite from the other. "Are you too worried about your dad to talk about why you're mad at me?" His mouth was full.

"It's not important," she muttered.

"It is to me." He swallowed. "You leave the room every time I walk in." Cath didn't say anything, so he kept talking. . . . "Is it because of what happened?"

She didn't know how to answer that question. She didn't want to. She looked up at the wall across from her, up where there'd be a TV if this place wasn't such a prison.

She felt Levi lean toward her. "Because I'm sorry about that," he said. "I didn't mean to make you feel uncomfortable."

Cath pinched the top of her nose, wishing she knew where her tear ducts were, so she could hold them closed. "You're sorry?"

"I'm sorry I upset you," he said. "I think maybe I was reading you wrong, and I'm sorry about that."

Her brain tried to come up with something mean to say about Levi and reading. "You didn't read me wrong," she said, shaking her head. Just for a second, she felt more angry than pathetic. "I went to your party."

"What party?"

She turned her head to face him – even though she'd started to cry, and her glasses were fogging up, and she hadn't officially brushed her hair since yesterday morning. "The party," she said. "At your house. That Thursday night. I came with Reagan."

"Why didn't I see you?"

"You were in the kitchen . . . preoccupied."

Levi's smile faded, and he sat back slowly. Cath set her sandwich down on the chair next to her and clenched her hands in her lap.

"Oh, Cath . . . ," Levi said. "I'm sorry."

"Don't apologize. You both seemed pretty happy about it."

"You didn't say you were coming."

She looked over. "So if you'd known I was coming, you wouldn't have been making out with somebody else in the kitchen?"

For once Levi didn't have anything to say. He set his sandwich down, too, and pushed both hands through his wispy blond hair. His hair was made of finer stuff than Cath's. Silk. Down. Blown-out dandelion seeds.

"Cath . . . ," he said. "I'm so sorry."

She wasn't quite sure what he was apologizing for. He looked up at her, from the top of his eyes, looking genuinely sorry – and sorry for her. "It was just a kiss," he said, pleating his forehead.

"Which one?" she asked.

Levi pushed his hands to the back of his head, and his bangs fell loose. "*Both* of them."

Cath took a deep, shaky breath and let it break out through her nose. "Right," she said. "That is, um . . . good information to have."

"I didn't think—"

"*Levi*." She cut him off and looked him straight in the eye, trying to look stern despite her tears. "I can't thank you enough for bringing me here. But I couldn't mean this more: I'd like it if you left now. I don't just kiss people. Kisses aren't . . . *just* with me. That's why I've been avoiding you. That's why I'd like to avoid you now. Okay?"

"Cath—"

The door buzzed, and a nurse stepped through it, wearing

flowered scrubs. She smiled at Levi. "You guys want to come back now?"

Cath stood up and grabbed her bag. She looked at Levi. "Please." And then she followed the nurse.

Levi was gone when Cath came back to the lobby.

She took a cab to her dad's office to get his car. It was full of fast-food wrappers and crumpled-up ideas. When she got home, she did the dishes and texted Wren.

Cath didn't feel like calling. She didn't feel like saying, *Hey, you were right. He's all drugged up and probably won't come out of it for a few days, and there's no real reason for you to come home – unless you just can't stand the idea of him going through this alone. But he won't be alone, because I'll be here.*

Her dad hadn't done laundry for a while. The steps to the basement were covered with dirty clothes, like he'd just been throwing stuff down there for a few weeks.

She started a load of laundry.

She threw out pizza boxes with desiccated slices of pizza.

There was a poem painted on the bathroom mirror with toothpaste – maybe it was a poem, maybe it was just words. It was lovely, so Cath took a photo with her phone before she wiped it clean.

Any *one* of these things would have tipped them off if they'd been at home.

They looked out for him.

They'd find him sitting in his car in the middle of the night, filling page after page with ideas that didn't quite make sense, and they'd lead him back inside.

They'd see him skip dinner; they'd count the cups of coffee. They'd notice the zeal in his voice.

And they'd try to rein him back in.

Usually it worked. Seeing that they were scared terrified their dad. He'd go to bed and sleep for fifteen hours. He'd make an appointment with his counselor. He'd try the meds again, even if they all knew it wouldn't stick.

"I can't think when I'm on them," he'd told Cath one night. She was sixteen, and she'd come downstairs to check the front door and found it unlocked – and then she'd inadvertently locked him out. Her dad had been sitting outside on the steps, and it scared her half to death when he rang the doorbell.

"They slow your brain down," he said, clutching an orange bottle of pills. "They iron out all the wrinkles. . . . Maybe all the bad stuff happens in the wrinkles, but all the good stuff does, too. . . .

"They break your brain like a horse, so it takes all your orders. I need a brain that can break *away*, you know? I need to think. If I can't *think*, who am I?"

It wasn't so bad when he got lots of sleep. When he ate the eggs they made him for breakfast. When he didn't work straight through three weekends in a row.

A little manic was okay. A little manic made him happy and productive and charismatic. Clients would eat awesome straight out of his hands.

She and Wren had gotten good at watching him. At noticing when a little manic slid into a lot. When charismatic gave way to crazed. When the twinkle in his eyes turned into a burnt-out flash.

Cath stayed up until three o'clock that morning, cleaning up his messes. If she and Wren had been here, they would have seen this coming. They would have stopped it.

———

The next day, Cath took her laptop to St. Richard's with her. She had thirty-one hours to write her short story. She could e-mail it to Professor Piper; that would be okay.

Wren finally texted her back. *"are you here? psych final tomorrow. right?"*

They had the same pychology professor but were in different classes.

"i'll have to miss it," Cath typed.

"NOT ACCEPTABLE," Wren replied.

"NOT LEAVING DAD ALONE," Cath texted back.

"email the professor, maybe he'll let you make it up."

"ok."

"email him. and i'll talk to him."

"ok." Cath couldn't bring herself to say thanks. Wren should be missing that final, too.

Her dad woke up around noon and ate mashed potatoes with yellow gravy. She could tell he was angry – angry that he was there and angry that he was too groggy for any of his anger to rise to the top.

There was a TV in his room, and Cath found a *Gilmore Girls* rerun. Their dad always used to watch *Gilmore Girls* with them; he had a crush on Sookie. Cath's computer kept falling asleep in her lap, so she finally set it down, and leaned on his bed to watch TV.

"Where's Wren?" he asked during a commercial break.

"School."

"Shouldn't you be there, too?"

"Christmas break starts tomorrow."

He nodded. His eyes looked dull and distant. Every time he blinked, it seemed like maybe he wasn't going to manage to open them again.

A nurse came in at two in the afternoon with more meds. Then came a doctor who asked Cath to wait in the hall. The doctor smiled at her when he left the room. "We'll get there," he said in a cheerful, comforting voice. "We had to bring him down pretty fast."

Cath sat next to her dad's bed and watched TV until visiting hours were over.

There was no more cleaning to do, and Cath felt uneasy being in the house by herself. She tried sleeping on the couch, but it felt too close to the outside and too close to her dad's empty room – so she went up to her room and crawled into her own bed. When that didn't work, she climbed into Wren's bed, taking her laptop with her.

Their dad had stayed at St. Richard's three times before. The first time was the summer after their mom left. They'd called their grandma when he wouldn't get out of bed, and for a while, she'd moved in with them. She filled the freezer with frozen lasagna before she moved out.

The second time was in sixth grade. He was standing over the sink, laughing, and telling them that they didn't have to go to school anymore. Life was an education, he said. He'd cut himself shaving, and there were tiny pieces of toilet paper stuck with blood to his chin. Cath and Wren had gone to stay with their aunt Lynn in Chicago.

The third time was in high school. They were sixteen, and their grandma came to stay, but not until the second night. That first night they'd spent in Wren's bed, Wren holding Cath's wrists, Cath crying.

"I'm like him," she'd whispered.

"You're not," Wren said.

"I am. I'm crazy like him." She was already having panic attacks. She was already hiding at parties. In seventh grade, she'd been late to class for the first two weeks because she couldn't stand being in the halls with everyone else during passing periods. "It's probably going to get worse in a few years. That's when it usually kicks in."

"You're not," Wren said.

"But what if I am?"

"Decide not to be."

"That's not how it works," Cath argued.

"Nobody knows how it works."

"What if I don't even see it coming?"

"*I'll* see it coming."

Cath tried to stop crying, but she'd been crying so long, the crying had taken over, making her breathe in harsh sniffs and jerks.

"If it tries to take you," Wren said, "I won't let go."

A few months later, Cath gave that line to Simon in a scene about Baz's bloodlust. Wren was still writing with Cath back then, and when she got to the line, she snorted.

"I'm here for you if you go manic," Wren said. "But you're on your own if you become a vampire."

"What good are you anyway?" Cath said. Their dad was home by then. And better. And Cath didn't feel, for the moment, like her DNA was a trap ready to snap closed on her.

"Apparently, I'm good for something," Wren said. "You keep stealing all my best lines."

Cath thought about texting Wren Friday night before she fell asleep, but she couldn't think of anything to say.

The Humdrum wasn't a man at all, or a monster. It was a boy.

Simon stepped closer, perhaps foolishly, wanting to see its face. . . . He felt the Humdrum's power whipping around him like dry air, like hot sand, an aching fatigue in the very marrow of Simon's bones.

The Humdrum – the boy – wore faded denims and a grotty T-shirt, and it probably took Simon far too long to recognize the child as himself. His years-ago self.

"Stop it," Simon shouted. "Show yourself, you coward. Show yourself!"

The boy just laughed.

—from chapter 23, *Simon Snow and the Seventh Oak,*

copyright © 2010 by Gemma T. Leslie

TWENTY

Her dad and Wren came home on the same day. Saturday.

Her dad was already talking about going back to work – even though his meds were still off, and he still seemed alternately drunk or half-asleep. Cath wondered if he'd stay on them through the weekend.

Maybe it would be okay if he went off his meds. She and Wren were both home now to watch out for him.

With everything that had happened, Cath wasn't quite sure whether she and Wren were on speaking terms. She decided that they were; it made life easier. But they weren't on sharing terms – she still hadn't told Wren anything about Levi. Or about Nick, for that matter. And she didn't want Wren to start talking about her adventures with their mom. Cath was sure Wren had some mother–daughter Christmas plans.

At first, all Wren wanted to talk about was school. She felt good about her finals, did Cath? And she'd already bought her books for next semester. What classes was Cath taking? Did they have any together?

Cath mostly listened.

"Do you think we should call Grandma?" Wren asked.

"About what?"

"About Dad."

"Let's wait and see how he does."

All their friends from high school were home for Christmas. Wren kept trying to get Cath to go out.

"You go," Cath would say. "I'll stay with Dad."

"I can't go without you. That would be weird."

It *would* seem weird to their high school friends to see Wren without Cath. Their college friends would think it was weird if they showed up anywhere together.

"Somebody should stay with Dad," Cath said.

"Go, Cath," their dad said after a few days of this. "I'm not going to lose control sitting here watching *Iron Chef*."

Sometimes Cath went.

Sometimes she stayed home and waited up for Wren.

Sometimes Wren didn't come home at all.

"I don't want you to see me shit-faced," Wren explained when she rolled in one morning. "You make me uncomfortable."

"Oh, *I* make *you* uncomfortable," Cath said. "That's priceless."

Their dad went back to work after a week. The next week he started jogging before work, and that's how Cath knew he was off his meds. Exercise was his most effective self-medication — it was what he always did when he was trying to take control.

She started coming downstairs every morning when she heard the coffeemaker beeping. To check on him, to see him off. "It's way too cold to jog outside," she tried to argue one morning.

Her dad handed her his coffee — decaf — while he laced up his shoes. "It feels good. Come with me."

He could tell she was trying to look in his eyes, to take his mental temperature, so he took her chin and let her. "I'm fine," he said gently. "Back on the horse, Cath."

"What's the horse?" she sighed, watching him pull on a South High hoodie. "Jogging? Working too much?"

"Living," he said, a little too loud. "Life is the horse."

Cath would make him breakfast while he ran – and after he ate and left for work, she'd fall back to sleep on the couch. After a few days of this, it already felt like a routine. Routines were good for her dad, but he needed help sticking to them.

Cath would usually wake up again when Wren came downstairs or came home.

This morning, Wren walked into the house and immediately headed into the kitchen. She came back into the living room with a cold cup of coffee, licking a fork. "Did you make omelettes?"

Cath rubbed her eyes and nodded. "We had leftovers from Los Portales, so I threw them in." She sat up. "That's decaf."

"He's drinking decaf? That's good, right?"

"Yeah . . ."

"Make me an omelette, Cath. You know I suck at it."

"What will you give me?" Cath asked.

Wren laughed. It's what they used to say to each other. *What will you give me?* "What do you want?" Wren asked. "Do you have any chapters you need betaed?"

It was Cath's turn to say something clever, but she didn't know what to say. Because she knew that Wren didn't mean it, about betaing her fic, and because it was pathetic how much Cath wished that she did. What if they spent the rest of Christmas break like that? Crowded around a laptop, writing the beginning of the end of *Carry On, Simon* together.

"Nah," Cath said finally. "I've got a doctoral student in Rhode Island editing all my stuff. She's a machine." Cath stood up and headed for the kitchen. "I'll make you an omelette; I think we've got some canned chili."

Wren followed. She jumped up onto the counter next to the stove and watched Cath get the milk and eggs from the refrigerator. Cath could crack them one-handed.

Eggs were her thing. Breakfasts, really. She'd learned to make omelettes in junior high, watching YouTube videos. She could do poached eggs, too, and sunny side up. And scrambled, obviously.

Wren was better at dinners. She'd gone through a phase in junior high when everything she made started with French onion soup mix. Meat loaf. Beef Stroganoff. Onion burgers. "All we need is soup mix," she'd announced. "We can throw all these other spices away."

"You girls don't have to cook," their dad would say.

But it was either cook or hope that he remembered to pick up Happy Meals on the way home from work. (There was still a toy box upstairs packed with hundreds of plastic Happy Meal toys.) Besides, if Cath made breakfast and Wren made dinner, that was at least two meals their dad wouldn't eat at a gas station.

"QuikTrip isn't a gas station," he'd say. "It's an everything-you-really-need station. And their bathrooms are immaculate."

Wren leaned over the pan and watched the eggs start to bubble. Cath pushed her back, away from the fire.

"This is the part I always mess up," Wren said. "Either I burn it on the outside or it's still raw in the middle."

"You're too impatient," Cath said.

"No, I'm too *hungry*." Wren picked up the can opener and spun it around her finger. "Do you think we should call Grandma?"

"Well, tomorrow's Christmas Eve," Cath said, "so we *should* probably call Grandma."

"You know what I mean. . . ."

"He seems like he's doing okay."

"Yeah . . ." Wren cranked open the can of chili and handed it to Cath. "But he's still fragile. Any little thing could throw him off. What'll happen when we go back to school? When you're not here to make breakfast? He needs somebody to look out for him."

Cath watched the eggs. She was biding her time. "We still have to go shopping for Christmas dinner. Do you want turkey? Or we could do lasagna – in Grandma's honor. Maybe lasagna tomorrow and turkey on Christmas—"

"I won't be here tomorrow night." Wren cleared her throat. "That's when . . . Laura's family celebrates Christmas."

Cath nodded and folded the omelette in half.

"You could come, you know," Wren said.

Cath snorted. When she glanced up again, Wren looked upset.

"What?" Cath said. "I'm not arguing with you. I assumed you were doing something with her this week."

Wren clenched her jaw so tight, her cheeks pulsed. "I can't believe you're making me do this alone."

Cath held up the spatula between them. "*Making* you? I'm not making you do anything. I can't believe you're even doing this when you know how much I hate it."

Wren shoved off the counter, shaking her head. "Oh, you hate everything. You hate *change*. If I didn't drag you along behind me, you'd never get anywhere."

"Well, you're not dragging me anywhere tomorrow," Cath said, turning away from the stove. "Or anywhere, from now on. You are hereby released of all responsibility, re: dragging me along."

Wren folded her arms and tilted her head. The Sanctimonious One. "That's not what I meant, Cath. I meant . . . We should be doing this together."

"Why this? You're the one who keeps reminding me that we're two separate people, that we don't have to do all the same things all the time. So, fine. You can go have a relationship with the parent who abandoned us, and I'll stay here and take care of the one who picked up the pieces."

"Jesus Christ" – Wren threw her hands in the air, palms out – "could you stop being so melodramatic? For just five minutes? Please?"

"*No.*" Cath slashed the air with her spatula. "This isn't

melodrama. This is actual drama. She left us. In the most dramatic way possible. On *September eleventh*."

"*After* September eleventh—"

"*Details*. She left us. She broke Dad's heart and maybe his brain, and she left us."

Wren's voice dropped. "She feels terrible about it, Cath."

"Good!" Cath shouted. "So do I!" She took a step closer to her sister. "I'm probably going to be crazy for the rest of my life, thanks to her. I'm going to keep making fucked-up decisions and doing weird things that I don't even realize are weird. People are going to feel sorry for me, and I won't ever have any normal relationships – and it's always going to be because I didn't have a mother. *Always*. That's the ultimate kind of broken. The kind of damage you never recover from. I *hope* she feels terrible. I hope she never forgives herself."

"Don't say that." Wren's face was red, and there were tears in her eyes. "I'm not broken."

There weren't any tears in Cath's eyes. "Cracks in your foundation." She shrugged.

"Fuck that."

"Do you think I absorbed all the impact? That when Mom left, it hit my side of the car? Fuck *that,* Wren. She left you, too."

"But it didn't break me. Nothing can break me unless I let it."

"Do you think Dad *let* it? Do you think he chose to fall apart when she left?"

"Yes!" Wren was shouting now. "And I think he keeps choosing. I think you both do. You'd rather be broken than move on."

That did it. Now they were both crying, both shouting. *Nobody wins until nobody wins,* Cath thought. She turned back to the stove; the eggs were starting to smoke. "Dad's sick, Wren," she said as calmly as she could manage. She scraped the omelette out of the pan and dropped it onto a plate. "And your omelette's burnt. And

I'd rather be broken than wasted." She set the plate on the counter. "You can tell Laura to go fuck herself. Like, to infinity and beyond. She doesn't get to move on with me. Ever."

Cath walked away before Wren could. She went upstairs and worked on *Carry On*.

There was always a Simon Snow marathon on TV on Christmas Eve. Cath and Wren always watched it, and their dad always made microwave popcorn.

They'd gone to Jacobo's the night before for popcorn and other Christmas supplies. "If they don't have it at the *supermercado*," their dad had said happily, "you don't really need it." That's how they ended up making lasagna with spaghetti noodles, and buying tamales instead of a turkey.

With the movies on, it was easy for Cath not to talk to Wren about anything important – but hard not to talk about the movies themselves.

"Baz's hair is sick," Wren said during *Simon Snow and the Selkies Four*. All the actors had longer hair in this movie. Baz's black hair was swept up into a slick pompadour that started at his knifepoint widow's peak.

"I know," Cath said, "Simon keeps trying to punch him just so he can touch it."

"Right? The last time Simon swung at Baz, I thought he was gonna brush away an eyelash."

"Make a wish," Cath said in her best Simon voice, *"you handsome bastard."*

Their dad watched *Simon Snow and the Fifth Blade* with them, with a notebook on his lap. "I've lived with you two for too long," he said, sketching a big bowl of Gravioli. "I went to see the new *X-Men* movie with Kelly, and I was convinced the whole time that Professor X and Magneto were in love."

"Well, obviously," Wren said.

"Sometimes I think you're obsessed with Basilton," Agatha said onscreen, her eyes wide and concerned.

"He's up to something," Simon said. *"I know it."*

"That girl is worse than Liza Minnelli," their dad said.

An hour into the movie, just before Simon caught Baz rendezvousing with Agatha in the Veiled Forest, Wren got a text and got up from the couch. Cath decided to use the bathroom, just in case the doorbell was about to ring. *Laura wouldn't do that, right? She wouldn't come to the door.*

Cath stood in the bathroom near the door and heard her dad telling Wren to have a good time.

"I'll tell Mom you said hi," Wren said to him.

"That's probably not necessary," he said, cheerfully enough. *Go, Dad*, Cath thought.

After Wren was gone, neither of them talked about her.

They watched one more Simon movie and ate giant pieces of spaghetti-sagna, and her dad realized for the first time that they didn't have a Christmas tree.

"How did we forget the tree?" he asked, looking at the spot by the window seat where they usually put it.

"There was a lot going on," Cath said.

"Why couldn't Santa get out of bed on Christmas?" her dad asked, like he was setting up a joke.

"I don't know, why?"

"Because he's North bi-Polar."

"No," Cath said, "because the bipolar bears were really bringing him down."

"Because Rudolph's nose just seemed too bright."

"Because the chimneys make him Claus-trophobic."

"Because —" Her dad laughed. "— the highs and lows were

too much for him? On the sled, get it?"

"That's terrible," Cath said, laughing. Her dad's eyes looked bright, but not too bright. She waited for him to go to bed before she went upstairs.

Wren still wasn't home. Cath tried to write, but closed her laptop after fifteen minutes of staring at a blank screen. She crawled under her blankets and tried not to think about Wren, tried not to picture her in Laura's new house, with Laura's new family.

Cath tried not to think of anything at all.

When she cleared her head, she was surprised to find Levi there underneath all the clutter. Levi in gods' country. Probably having the merriest Christmas of them all. Merry. That was Levi 365 days a year. (On leap years, 366. Levi probably loved leap years. Another day, another girl to kiss.)

It was a little easier to think about him now that Cath knew she'd never have him, that she'd probably never see him again.

She fell asleep thinking about his dirty-blond hair and his overabundant forehead and everything else that she wasn't quite ready to forget.

"Since there isn't a tree," their dad said, "I put your presents under this photo of us standing *next* to a Christmas tree in 2005. Do you know that we don't even have any houseplants? There's nothing alive in this house but us."

Cath looked down at the small heap of gifts and laughed. They were drinking eggnog and eating two-day-old *pan dulce*, sweet bread with powdery pink icing. The *pan dulce* came from Abel's bakery. They'd stopped there after the *supermercado*. Cath had stayed in the car; she figured it wasn't worth the awkwardness. It'd been months since she stopped returning Abel's occasional texts, and at least a month since he'd stopped sending them.

"Abel's grandma hates my hair," Wren said when she got back into the car. "*¡Qué pena! ¡Qué lástima! ¡Niño!*"

"Did you get the *tres leches* cake?" Cath asked.

"They were out."

"*Qué lástima.*"

Normally, Cath would have a present from Abel and one from his family under the tree. The pile of presents this year was especially thin. Mostly envelopes.

Cath gave Wren a pair of Ecuadorian mittens that she'd bought outside of the Union. "It's alpaca," she said. "Warmer than wool. And hypoallergenic."

"Thanks," Wren said, smoothing out the mittens in her lap.

"So I want my gloves back," Cath said.

Wren gave Cath two T-shirts she'd bought online. They were cute and would probably be flattering, but this was the first time in ten years that Wren hadn't given her something to do with Simon Snow. It made Cath feel tearful suddenly, and defensive. "Thanks," she said, folding the shirts back up. "These are really cool."

iTunes gift certificates from their dad.

Bookstore gift certificates from their grandma.

Aunt Lynn had sent them underwear and socks, just to be funny.

After their dad opened his gifts (everybody gave him clothes), there was still a small, silver box under the Christmas tree photo. Cath reached for it. There was a fancy tag hanging by a burgundy ribbon – *Cather,* it said in showy, black script. For a second Cath thought it was from Levi. ("Cather," she could hear him say, everything about his voice smiling.)

She untied the ribbon and opened the box. There was a necklace inside. An emerald, her birthstone. She looked up at Wren and saw a matching pendant hanging from her neck.

Cath dropped the box and stood up, moving quickly, clumsily toward the stairs.

"Cath," Wren called after her, "let me explain—"

Cath shook her head and ran the rest of the way to her room.

Cath tried to picture her mom.

The person who had given her this necklace. Wren said she was remarried now and lived in a big house in the suburbs. She had stepkids, too. Grown ones.

In Cath's head, Laura was still young.

Too young, everyone always said, *to have two big girls*. That always made their mom smile.

When they were little and their mom and dad would fight, Wren and Cath worried their parents were going to get divorced and split them up, just like in *The Parent Trap*. "I'll go with Dad," Wren would say. "He needs more help."

Cath would think about living alone with her dad, spacey and wild, or alone with her mom, chilly and impatient. "No," she said, "I'll go with Dad. He likes me more than Mom does."

"He likes both of us more than Mom does," Wren argued.

"Those can't be yours," people would say, "you're too young to have such grown-up girls."

"I feel too young," their mom would reply.

"Then we'll both stay with Dad," Cath said.

"That's not how divorce works, dummy."

When their mom left without either of them, in a way it was a relief. If Cath had to choose between everyone, she'd choose Wren.

———

Their bedroom door didn't have a lock, so Cath sat against it. But nobody came up the stairs.

She sat on her hands and cried like a little kid.

Too much crying, she thought. *Too many kinds.* She was tired of being the one who cried.

"You're the most powerful magician in a hundred ages." The Humdrum's face, Simon's own boyhood face, looked dull and tired. Nothing glinted in its blue eyes. . . . "Do you think that much power comes without sacrifice? Did you think you could become *you* without leaving something, without leaving *me,* behind?"

—from chapter 23, *Simon Snow and the Seventh Oak,*
copyright © 2010 by Gemma T. Leslie

TWENTY-ONE

Their dad got up to jog every morning. Cath woke up when she heard his coffeemaker beep. She'd get up and make him breakfast, then fall back to sleep on the couch until Wren woke up. They'd pass on the staircase without a word.

Sometimes Wren went out. Cath never went with her.

Sometimes Wren didn't come home. Cath never waited up.

Cath had a lot of nights alone with her dad, but she kept putting off talking to him, *really* talking to him; she didn't want to be the thing that made him lose his balance. But she was running out of time. . . . He was supposed to drive them back to school in three days. Wren was even agitating to go back a day early, on Saturday, so they could "settle in." (Which was code for "go to lots of frat parties.")

On Thursday night, Cath made huevos rancheros, and her dad washed the dishes after dinner. He was telling her about a new pitch. Gravioli was going so well, his agency was getting a shot at a sister brand, Frankenbeans. Cath sat on a barstool and listened.

"So I was thinking, maybe this time I just let Kelly pitch his terrible ideas first. Cartoon beans with Frankenstein hair. 'Monstrously delicious,' whatever. These people always reject the first thing they hear—"

"Dad, I need to talk to you about something."

He peeked over his shoulder. "I thought you'd already googled all that period and birds-and-bees stuff."

"Dad . . ."

He turned around, suddenly concerned. "Are you pregnant? Are you gay? I'd rather you were gay than pregnant. Unless you're pregnant. Then we'll deal. Whatever it is, we'll deal. Are you pregnant?"

"No," Cath said.

"Okay . . ." He leaned back against the sink and began tapping wet fingers against the counter.

"I'm not gay either."

"What does that leave?"

"Um . . . school, I guess."

"You're having problems in school? I don't believe that. Are you sure you're not pregnant?"

"I'm not really having problems. . . ." Cath said. "I've just decided that I'm not going back."

Her dad looked at her like he was still waiting for her to give a real answer.

"I'm not going back for second semester," she said.

"Because?"

"Because I don't want to. Because I don't like it."

He wiped his hands on his jeans. "You don't *like* it?"

"I don't belong there."

He shrugged. "Well, you don't have to stay there forever."

"No," she said. "I mean, UNL is a bad fit for me. I didn't choose it, Wren did. And it's fine for Wren, she's happy, but it's bad for me. I just . . . it's like every day there is still the first day."

"But Wren is there—"

Cath shook her head. "She doesn't need me." *Not like you do,* Cath just stopped herself from saying.

"What will you do?"

"I'll live here. Go to school here."

"At UNO?"

"Yeah."

"Have you registered?"

Cath hadn't thought that part through yet. "I will. . . ."

"You should stick out the year," he said. "You'll lose your scholarship."

"No," Cath said, "I don't care about that."

"Well, I do."

"That's not what I meant. I can get loans. I'll get a job, too."

"And a car?"

"I guess. . . ."

Her dad took off his glasses and started cleaning them with his shirt. "You should stick out the year. We'll look at it again in the spring."

"*No*," she said. "I just . . ." She rubbed the neck of her T-shirt into her sternum. "I can't go back there. I hate it. And it's pointless. And I can do so much more good here."

He sighed. "I wondered if that's what this was about." He put his glasses back on. "Cath, you're not moving back home to take care of me."

"That's not the main reason — but it wouldn't be a bad thing. You do better when you're not alone."

"I agree. And I've already talked to your grandmother. It was too much, too soon when you guys both moved out at once. Grandma's going to check in with me a few times a week. We're going to eat dinner together. I might even stay with her for a while if things start to look rough again."

"So *you* can move back home, but I can't? I'm only eighteen."

"Exactly. You're only eighteen. You're not going to throw your life away to take care of me."

"I'm not throwing my life away." *Such as it is,* she thought. "I'm trying to think for myself for the first time. I followed Wren to

Lincoln, and she doesn't even want me there. Nobody wants me there."

"Tell me about it," he said. "Tell me why you're so unhappy."

"It's just . . . *everything*. There are too many people. And I don't fit in. I don't know how to *be*. Nothing that I'm good at is the sort of thing that matters there. Being smart doesn't matter – and being good with words. And when those things *do* matter, it's only because people want something from me. Not because they want *me*."

The sympathy in his face was painful. "This doesn't sound like a decision, Cath. This sounds like giving up."

"So what? I mean –" Her hands flew up, then fell in her lap. "– so *what*? It's not like I get a medal for sticking it out. It's just school. Who cares where I do it?"

"You think it would be easier if you lived here."

"*Yes.*"

"That's a crappy way to make decisions."

"Says who? Winston Churchill?"

"What's wrong with Winston Churchill?" her dad said, sounding mad for the first time since they'd started talking. Good thing she hadn't said Franklin Roosevelt. Her dad was nuts about the Allied Forces.

"Nothing. *Nothing*. Just . . . isn't giving up allowed sometimes? Isn't it okay to say, 'This really hurts, so I'm going to stop trying'?"

"It sets a dangerous precedent."

"For avoiding pain?"

"For avoiding life."

Cath rolled her eyes. "Ah. The horse again.'

"You and your sister and the eye-rolling . . . I always thought you'd grow out of that." He reached out and took her hand. She started to pull away, but he held tight.

"Cath. Look at me." She looked up at him reluctantly. His hair was sticking up. And his round, wire-rimmed glasses were crooked on his nose. "There is so much that I'm sorry for, and so much that scares me—"

They both heard the front door open.

Cath waited a second, then pulled her hand away and slipped upstairs.

"Dad told me," Wren whispered that night from her bed.

Cath picked up her pillow and left the room. She slept downstairs on the couch. But she didn't really sleep, because the front door was right there, and she kept imagining someone breaking in.

Her dad tried to talk to her again the next morning. He was sitting on the couch in his running clothes when she woke up.

Cath wasn't used to him fighting her like this. Fighting either of them ever, about anything. Even back in junior high, when she and Wren used to stay up too late on school nights, hanging out in the Simon Snow forums – the most their dad would ever say was, "Won't you guys be tired tomorrow?"

And since they'd come home for break, he hadn't even *mentioned* the fact that Wren was staying out all night.

"I don't want to talk anymore," Cath said when she woke up and saw him sitting there. She rolled away from him and hugged her pillow.

"Good," he said. "Don't talk. Listen. I've been thinking about you staying home next semester. . . ."

"Yeah?" Cath turned her head toward him.

"Yeah." He found her knee under the blanket and squeezed it. "I know that I'm part of the reason you want to move home. I know that you worry about me, and that I give you lots of reasons to worry about me. . . ."

She wanted to look away, but his eyes were unshakable sometimes, just like Wren's.

"Cath, if you're really worried about me, I'm begging you, go back to school. Because if you drop out because of me, if you lose your scholarship, if you set yourself back – *because of me* – I won't be able to live with myself."

She pushed her face back into the couch.

After a few minutes, the coffeemaker beeped, and she felt him stand up.

When she heard the front door close, she got up to make breakfast.

She was upstairs, writing, when Wren came up that afternoon to start packing.

Cath didn't have much to pack or not to pack. All she'd really brought home with her was her computer. For the last few weeks she'd been wearing clothes that she and Wren hadn't liked well enough to take to college with them.

"You look ridiculous," Wren said.

"What?"

"That shirt." It was a Hello Kitty shirt from eighth or ninth grade. Hello Kitty dressed as a superhero. It said SUPER CAT on the back, and Wren had added an H with fabric paint. The shirt was cropped too short to begin with, and it didn't really fit anymore. Cath pulled it down self-consciously.

"Cath!" her dad shouted from downstairs. "Phone."

Cath picked up her cell phone and looked at it.

"He must mean the house phone," Wren said.

"Who calls the house phone?"

"Probably 2005. I think it wants its shirt back."

"Ha-bloody-ha," Cath muttered, heading downstairs.

Her dad just shrugged when he handed her the phone.

"Hello?" Cath said.

"Do we want a couch?" someone asked.

"Who is this?"

"It's Reagan. Who else would it be? Who else would need to get your permission before they brought home a couch?"

"How'd you get this number?"

"It's on our housing paperwork. I don't know why I don't have your cell, I guess I usually don't have to look very far to find you."

"I think you're the first person to call our house phone in years. I didn't even remember where it was."

"That's fascinating, Cath. Do we want a couch?"

"Why would we want a couch?"

"I don't know. Because my mom is insisting that we need one."

"Who would sit on it?"

"Exactly. It might have been useful last semester to keep Levi from shedding all over our beds, but that's not even an issue anymore. And if we have a couch, we'll literally have to climb over it to get to the door. *She's saying no, Mom.*"

"Why isn't Levi an issue anymore?"

"Because. It's your room. It's stupid for you to be hiding in the library all the time. And he and I only have one class together next semester anyway."

"It doesn't matter—," Cath said.

Reagan cut her off: "Don't be stupid. It does matter. I feel really shitty about what happened. I mean, it's not my fault you kissed him and that he kissed that idiot blonde, but I shouldn't have encouraged you. It won't happen again, ever, with anyone. I'm fucking done with encouragement."

"It's okay," Cath said.

"I know that it's okay. I'm just saying, that's the way it's gonna be. So no to the couch, right? My mom is standing right here, and I don't think she'll leave me alone until she hears you say no."

"No," Cath said. Then raised her voice: *"No to the couch."*

"Fuck, Cath, my eardrum . . . *Mom, you're pushing me to swear with this stupid furniture.* . . . All right, I'll see you tomorrow. I'll probably have an ugly lamp with me and maybe a rug. She's pathological."

Cath's dad was standing in the kitchen watching her. Her dad, who actually was pathological.

"Who was that?" he asked.

"My roommate."

"She sounds like Kathleen Turner."

"Yeah. She's something." Cath pulled her shirt down and turned away.

"Taco truck?" he asked. "For dinner?"

"Sure."

"Why don't you change – you can ride with me."

"Sure."

SPRING SEMESTER, 2012

Fried tomatoes at breakfast. Every lump in his bed. Being able to do magic without worrying whether anyone was watching. Agatha, of course. And Penelope. Getting to see the Mage – not often, but still. Simon's uniform. His school tie. The football pitch, even when it was muddy. Fencing. Raisin scones every Sunday with real clotted cream . . .

What *didn't* Simon miss about Watford?

—from chapter 1, *Simon Snow and the Selkies Four,*

copyright © 2007 by Gemma T. Leslie

TWENTY-TWO

"There are already four light fixtures in here," Reagan said. "What are we supposed to do with a lamp?"

The lamp was black and shaped like the Eiffel Tower.

"Just leave it in the hall," Cath said. "Maybe somebody'll take it."

"She'll just ask where it is the next time she's here. . . . She's insane." Reagan shoved the lamp into the back of her closet and kicked it. "What brand of crazy is your mom?"

Cath's gut pitched reliably. "I don't know. She left when I was eight."

"Fuck," Reagan said, "that *is* crazy. Are you hungry?"

"Yeah," Cath said.

"They're doing a back-to-school luau downstairs. They roast a pig on a spit. It's disgusting."

Cath grabbed her ID and followed Reagan to the dining hall.

In the end, Cath hadn't decided to come back.

She'd just decided to pack up her laptop.

And then she'd decided to ride along with Wren and her dad to Lincoln.

And then, after they dropped Wren off outside Schramm Hall,

her dad asked if Cath wanted to go to her own dorm, and Cath decided that she did. If nothing else, she could get her stuff.

And then they just sat there in the fire lane, and Cath felt wave after wave of anxiety pound against her. If she stayed, she'd see Levi again. She'd have to deal with the Psych final she'd missed. She'd have to register for classes, and who even knew what would still be available. *And she'd see Levi again.* And everything about that that would feel good – his smiling face, his long lines – would also feel like getting shot in the stomach.

Cath didn't really decide to get out of the car.

She just looked over at her dad in the driver's seat, tapping his two middle fingers on the steering wheel; and as scared as she was to leave him, Cath couldn't bear to think about letting him down.

"One more semester," she said. She was crying; that's how bad it felt to say this.

His chin jerked up. "Yeah?"

"I'll try."

"Me, too," he said.

"Promise?"

"Yeah. Cath, yeah. I promise. . . . Do you want me to come up with you?"

"No. That'll just make it worse."

He laughed.

"What?"

"Nothing. I just flashed back to your first day of kindergarten. You cried. And your mom cried. It felt like we were never gonna see you guys again."

"Where was Wren?"

"God, I don't know, probably anointing her first boyfriend."

"Mom cried?"

Her dad looked sad again and smiled ruefully. "Yeah . . ."

"I really hate her," Cath said, shaking her head, trying to

imagine what kind of mother cried on the first day of kindergarten, then walked out in the middle of third grade.

Her dad nodded. "Yeah . . ."

"Answer your phone," Cath said.

"I will."

"Somebody else got Ugg boots for Christmas," Reagan said, watching the dinner line empty into the dining room. "If we had whiskey, this is when we'd take a shot."

"I find Ugg boots really comforting," Cath said.

"Why? Because they're warm?"

"No. Because they remind me that we live in a place where you can still get away with, even get excited about, Ugg boots. In fashionable places, you have to pretend that you're over them, or that you've always hated them. But in Nebraska, you can still be happy about new Ugg boots. That's nice. There's no end of the innocence."

"You're such a weirdo . . . ," Reagan said. "I kinda missed you."

"I just don't want to," Simon said.

"Don't want to what?" Baz asked. He was sitting on his desk, eating an apple. He left the apple in his teeth and started tying his green and purple school tie. Simon still had to use a mirror for that. Even after seven years.

"Anything," Simon said, pressing his head back into his pillow. "I don't want to *do* anything. I don't even want to start this day because then I'll just be expected to finish it."

Baz finished his half-Windsor and took a bite out of the apple. "Now, now, Snow, that doesn't sound like 'the most powerful magician in a hundred ages' talking."

"That's such crap," Simon said. "Who even started calling me that?"

"Probably the Mage. He won't shut up about you. 'The one who was prophesied,' 'the hero we've been waiting for,' et cetera."

"I don't want to be a hero."

"Liar." Baz's eyes were cool grey and serious.

"Today," Simon said, chastened. "I don't want to be a hero today."

Baz looked at his apple core, then tossed it onto Simon's desk. "Are you trying to talk me into skipping Politickal Science?"

"Yes."

"Done," Baz said. "Now, get up."

Simon grinned and leapt out of bed.

—from *Carry On, Simon,* posted January 2012
by FanFixx.net author *Magicath*

TWENTY-THREE

"What does 'inc' mean?" Cath asked.

Reagan looked up from her bed. She was making flash cards (Reagan liked flash cards), and there was a cigarette hanging from her mouth, unlit. She was trying to quit smoking. "Ask that question again so it makes sense."

"*I-n-c,*" Cath said. "I got my grades back, but instead of an A or a B, it says, 'inc.'"

"Incomplete," Reagan said. "It means they're holding your grade."

"Who is?"

"I don't know, your professor."

"Why?"

"*I don't know.* It's usually, like, a special thing, like when you get extra time to make something up."

Cath stared at her grade report. She'd made up her Psychology final the first week back, so she was expecting to see the A there. (Her grade was so high in Psychology, she practically didn't need to take the final.) But Fiction-Writing was a different story. Without turning in a final project, the best that Cath had expected was a C – and a D was far more likely.

Cath was okay with that, she'd made peace with that D. It was the price she'd decided to pay for last semester. For Nick. And Levi. For plagiarism. It was the price for learning that she didn't want to write books about decline and desolation in rural America, or about anything else.

Cath was ready to take her D and move on.

Inc.

"What am I supposed to do?" she asked Reagan.

"Fuck, Cath. I don't know. Talk to your professor. You're giving me lung cancer."

This was Cath's third time back in Andrews Hall since she got her grades back.

The first two times, she'd walked in one end of the building and walked straight through to the door on the other side.

This time was already better. This time, she'd stopped to use the bathroom.

She'd walked into the building just as four o'clock classes were getting out, a flash flood of girls with cool hair and boys who looked like Nick. Cath ducked into the bathroom, and now she was sitting in a wooden stall, waiting for the coast to clear. Somebody had taken the time to carve most of "Stairway to Heaven" into the stall door; it was a serious amount of carving. *English majors*.

Cath didn't have any English classes this semester, and she was thinking about changing her major. Or maybe she'd just change her concentration from Creative Writing to Renaissance Lit; that would be useful in the real world, a head full of sonnets and Christ imagery. *If you study something that nobody cares about, does that mean everyone will leave you alone?*

She opened the stall door slowly, flushing the toilet for appearances, then ran water in one of the sinks (hot in one faucet, cold in the other) and rinsed her face. She could do this. She just had to find the department office, then ask where Professor Piper's personal office was. Professor Piper probably wouldn't even be there.

The hallway was nearly empty now. Cath found the stairs and followed the signs pointing to the main office. Down the hall, around the corner. Maybe if she just walked by the main office, that would be enough progress for the day. She walked slowly, touching each wooden door.

"Cath?"

Even though it was a woman's voice, Cath's first panicky thought was *Nick*.

"Cath!"

She turned toward the voice – and saw Professor Piper in the office across the hall, standing up behind her desk. The professor motioned for Cath to come forward. Cath did.

"I've been wondering about you," Professor Piper said, smiling warmly. "You just disappeared. Come in, come talk to me."

She motioned for Cath to sit down, so Cath did. (Apparently, Professor Piper could control Cath with simple hand gestures. Like the Dog Whisperer.)

The professor came around to the front of her desk and hopped onto it. Her signature move. "What happened to you? Where did you go?"

"I . . . didn't go anywhere," Cath said. She was thinking about going right now. This was too much progress; she hadn't planned for this eventuality – for actually accomplishing what she came here to do.

"But you never turned in your story," Professor Piper said. "Did something happen?"

Cath took a deepish breath and tried to sound steady. "Sort of. My dad was in the hospital. But that's not really why – I'd already decided not to write it."

The professor looked surprised. She held on to the lip of her desk and leaned forward. "But, Cath, *why*? I was so eager to see what you'd do."

"I just . . . ," Cath started again: "I realized that I'm not cut out for fiction-writing."

Professor Piper blinked and pulled her head back. "What are you talking about? You're exactly cut out for it. You're a Butterick pattern, Cath – this is what you were meant to do."

It was Cath's turn to blink. "No. I . . . I kept trying. To start the story. I . . . look, I know how you feel about fanfiction, but that's what I want to write. That's where my passion is. And I'm really good at it."

"I'm sure you are," Professor Piper said. "You're a natural storyteller. But that doesn't explain why you didn't finish your final project."

"Once I realized that it wasn't right for me, I couldn't bring myself to do it anymore. I just wanted to move on."

Professor Piper regarded Cath thoughtfully, tapping the edge of the desk. *This is what it looks like when a sane person taps her fingers.*

"Why do you keep saying that it wasn't right for you?" the professor asked. "Your work last semester was excellent. It was *all* right. You're one of my most promising students."

"But I don't want to write my own fiction," Cath said, as emphatically as she could. "I don't want to write my own characters or my own worlds – I don't care about them." She clenched her fists in her lap. "I care about Simon Snow. And I know he's not mine, but that doesn't matter to me. I'd rather pour myself into a world I love and understand than try to make something up out of nothing."

The professor leaned forward. "But there's nothing more profound than creating something out of nothing." Her lovely face turned fierce. "Think about it, Cath. That's what makes a god – or a mother. There's nothing more intoxicating than creating something from nothing. Creating something from yourself."

Cath hadn't expected Professor Piper to be happy about her decision, but she hadn't expected this either. She didn't think the professor would push back.

"It just feels like nothing to me," Cath said.

"You'd rather take – or borrow – someone else's creation?"

"I *know* Simon and Baz. I know how they think, what they feel. When I'm writing them, I get lost in them completely, and I'm happy. When I'm writing my own stuff, it's like swimming upstream. Or . . . falling down a cliff and grabbing at branches, trying to invent the branches as I fall."

"*Yes,*" the professor said, reaching out and grasping the air in front of Cath, like she was catching a fly. "That's how it's supposed to feel."

Cath shook her head. There were tears in her eyes. "Well, I hate it."

"Do you hate it? Or are you just afraid."

Cath sighed and decided to wipe her eyes on her sweater. Another type of adult would hand her a box of Kleenex about now. Professor Piper just kept pushing.

"You got special permission to be in my class. You must have wanted to write. And your work was delightful – didn't you enjoy it?"

"Nothing I wrote compared to Simon."

"Good gracious, Cath, are you really comparing yourself to the most successful author of the modern age?"

"*Yes,*" Cath said. "Because, when I'm writing Gemma T. Leslie's characters, sometimes, in some ways, I *am* better than her. I know how crazy that sounds – but I also know that it's true. I'm not a god. I could never create the World of Mages; but I'm really, really good at manipulating that world. I can do more with her characters than I could ever do with my own. My characters are just . . . sketches compared to hers."

"But you can't do anything with fanfiction. It's stillborn."

"I can let people read it. Lots of people *do* read it."

"You can't make a living that way. You can't make a career."

"How many people make a career out of writing anyway?" Cath snapped. She felt like everything inside her was snapping. Her nerves. Her temper. Her esophagus. "I'll write because I love it, the way other people knit or . . . or scrapbook. And I'll find some other way to make money."

Professor Piper leaned back again and folded her arms. "I'm not going to talk to you any more about the fanfiction."

"Good."

"But I'm not done talking to you."

Cath took another deep breath.

"*I'm* afraid," Professor Piper said, "afraid that you're never going to discover what you're truly capable of. That you won't get to see – that I won't get to see – any of the wonder that's inside of you. You're right, nothing you turned in last semester compared to *Simon Snow and the Mage's Heir*. But there was so much potential. Your characters quiver, Cath, like they're trying to evolve right off the page."

Cath rolled her eyes and wiped her nose on her shoulder.

"Can I ask you something?" the professor asked.

"I'm pretty sure you will anyway."

The older woman smiled. "Did you help Nick Manter on his final project?"

Cath looked up at the corner of the ceiling and quickly licked her bottom lip. She felt a new wave of tears rushing through her head. Damn. She'd had a solid month now of no crying.

She nodded.

"I thought so," the professor said gently. "I could hear you. In some of the best parts."

Cath held every muscle still.

"Nick's my teaching assistant, he was just here, actually, and he's in my Advanced Fiction-Writing class. His style has . . . shifted quite a bit."

Cath looked at the door.

"Cath," the professor pressed.

"Yes?" Cath still couldn't look at her.

"What if I made you a deal?"

Cath waited.

"I haven't turned in your grade yet; I was hoping you'd come see me. And I don't have to turn it in — I could give you the rest of this semester to finish your short story. You were headed toward a solid A in my class, maybe even an A-plus."

Cath thought about her grade point average. And her scholarship. And the fact that she was going to have to get perfect grades this semester if she wanted to keep it. She didn't have any room for error. "You could do that?"

"I can do whatever I want with my students' grades. I'm the god of this small thing."

Cath felt her fingernails in her palms. "Can I think about it?"

"Sure." Professor Piper's tone was air-light. "If you decide to do this, I'd like you to meet with me regularly, throughout the semester, just to talk about your progress. It will be like independent study."

"Okay. I'll think about it. I'll, um — thank you."

Cath picked up her bag and stood up. She was immediately standing too close to the professor, so she looked down and moved quickly toward the door. She didn't look up again until she was back in her dormitory, stepping out of the elevator.

"This is Art."

"That's how you answer the phone?"

"Hey, Cath."

"No hello?"

"I don't like hello. It makes me sound like I have dementia, like I've never heard a phone ring before and I don't know what's supposed to happen next. *Hello?*"

"How are you feeling, Dad?"

"Good."

"*How* good?"

"I'm leaving work every day at five. I'm eating dinner with Grandma. Just this morning, Kelly told me that I seemed 'impressively grounded.'"

"That *is* impressive."

"He'd just told me that we couldn't use Frankenstein in our Frankenbeans pitch, because nobody cares about Frankenstein anymore. Kids want zombies."

"But they're not called *Zombie*beans."

"They will be if fucking Kelly has his way. We're pitching 'Zombeanie Weenies.'"

"Wow, how did you stay grounded through all that?"

"I was fantasizing about eating his brain."

"I'm still impressed, Dad. Hey – I think I'm gonna come home next weekend."

"If you want . . . I don't want you to *worry* about me, Cath. I do better when I know you're happy."

"Well, I'm happy when I'm not worried about you. We have a symbiotic relationship."

"Speaking of . . . how's your sister?"

Her dad was wrong about worrying. Cath *liked* to worry. It made her feel proactive, even when she was totally helpless.

Like with Levi.

Cath couldn't control whether she saw Levi on campus. But she could worry about it, and as long as she was worrying about it, it probably wasn't going to happen. Like some sort of anxiety vaccine. Like watching a pot to make sure it never boiled.

She wore comforting grooves in her head, worrying about seeing Levi, then telling herself all the reasons it wasn't going to happen:

First, because Reagan had promised to keep him away.

And second, because Levi didn't have any business on City Campus. Cath told herself that Levi spent all his time either studying buffalo on East Campus, or working at Starbucks, or making out in his kitchen with pretty girls. There was no reason for their paths ever to cross.

Still . . . she froze every time she saw blond hair and a green Carhartt jacket – or every time she wished she did.

She froze *now*.

Because there he was, right where he wasn't supposed to be, sitting outside her door. Proof positive that she hadn't been worrying enough.

Levi saw Cath, too, and sprang to his feet. He wasn't smiling. (Thank God. She wasn't up for any of his smiles.)

Cath stepped warily forward. "Reagan's in class," she said when she was still a few doors away.

"I know," he said. "That's why I'm here."

Cath shook her head. It could have meant "no" or it could have meant "I don't understand" – both were true. She stopped walking. Her stomach hurt so bad, she wanted to bend over.

"I just need to tell you something," Levi said quickly.

"I really don't want you to come in," she said.

"That's fine. I can tell you out here."

Cath crossed her arms over her stomach and nodded.

Levi nodded back. He pushed his hands into his coat pockets.

"I was wrong," he said.

She nodded. Because *duh*. And because she didn't know what he wanted from her.

He pushed his hands deeper into his coat. "Cath," he said earnestly, "it wasn't just a kiss."

"Okay." Cath looked past him to her door. She took a step closer then, toward the door, holding her key up like they were done here.

Levi stepped out of her way. Confused, but still polite.

Cath put her key in the door, then held on to the handle, hanging her head forward. She could hear him breathing and fidgeting behind her. *Levi*.

"Which one?" she asked.

"What?"

"Which kiss?" Her voice was weak and thin. Wet paper.

"The first one," Levi said after a few seconds.

"But the second one was? It was just a kiss?"

Levi's voice got closer: "I don't want to talk about the second one."

"Too bad."

"Then yes," he said. "It was just a – it was nothing."

"What about the third one?"

"Is that a trick question?"

Cath shrugged.

"Cath . . . I'm trying to tell you something here."

She turned around and immediately regretted it. Levi's hair was tousled, most of it pushed back, bits of it falling over his forehead. And he wasn't smiling, so his blue eyes were taking over his whole long face.

"What are you trying to tell me?"

"That it wasn't *just* a kiss, Cather. There was no just."

"No just?"

"No."

"So?" Her voice sounded much cooler than she felt. Inside, her internal organs were grinding themselves into nervous pulp. Her intestines were gone. Her kidneys were disintegrating. Her stomach was wringing itself out, yanking on her trachea.

"So . . . *aahhggch,*" Levi said, frustrated, running both hands through his hair. "So I'm sorry. I don't know why I said that at the hospital. I mean, I know why I said it, but I was wrong. Really wrong. And I wish I could go back to that morning, when I woke up here, and have a stern talk with myself, so that the rest of this crap wouldn't have happened."

"I wonder . . . ," she said, "if there was such a thing as time machines, would anyone ever use them to go to the future?"

"Cather."

"What."

"What are you thinking?"

What was she thinking? She wasn't thinking. She was wondering if she could live without her kidneys. She was holding herself up on two feet. "I still don't know what all this means," she said.

"It means . . . I really like you." His hand was in his hair again. Just the one. Holding it back. "Like, *really* like you. And I want that kiss to have been the start of something. Not the end."

Cath looked at Levi's face. His eyebrows were pulled down in the middle, bunching up the skin above his nose. His cheeks, for once, were absolutely smooth. And his lips were at their most doll-like, not even a quirk of a smile.

"It *felt* like the start of something," he said. He put his hands in his pockets and swayed forward a little bit. Like he wanted to bump into her. Cath backed up flat against the door.

She nodded. "Okay."

"Okay?"

"Okay." She turned around and unlocked the door. "You can come in. I'm not sure yet about all the other stuff."

"Okay," Levi said. She heard the very beginning of a smile in his voice – a fetal smile – and it very nearly killed her.

"I don't trust you," Simon said, grasping Basil's forearm.

"Well, I don't trust you," Basil spat at him. Actually spat at him, bits of wet landing on Simon's cheeks.

"Why do you need to trust *me*?" Simon asked. "I'm the one hanging off a cliff!"

Basil looked down at him distastefully, his arm shaking from Simon's weight. He swung his other arm down and Simon grabbed at it.

"Douglas J. Henning," Basil cursed breathlessly, his body inching forward. "Knowing you, you'll bring the both of us down just to spite me."

—from *Carry On, Simon,* posted November 2010
by FanFixx.net author *Magicath*

TWENTY-FOUR

Levi sat on her bed.

Cath tried to pretend that he wasn't watching while she took off her coat and threaded her scarf out from under her hair. She felt weird taking her snow boots off in front of him, so she left them on.

She sat on her chair.

"How'd you do in YA Lit?" she asked.

Levi just looked at her for a few seconds. "I got a B-minus."

"That's good, right?"

"It's great. . . ."

She nodded.

"How's your dad?" he asked.

"Better," she said. "It's complicated."

"How's your sister?"

"I don't know, we're not really talking."

He nodded.

"I'm not very good at this," Cath said, looking down at her lap.

"What?"

"Whatever this is. Boy–girl stuff."

Levi laughed, lightly.

"What?" she asked.

"You're a lot better at boy–boy, aren't you?"

"Ha."

They were both quiet again. Levi eventually broke the silence. She was pretty sure he could be counted on in every silence-breaking scenario. "Cath?"

"Yeah?"

"Is this—? Are you giving me another chance?"

"I don't know," she said, watching her hands clench and unclench in her lap.

"Do you want to?"

"What do you mean?" She let her eyes stumble up to his face. His cheeks were pale, and he was chewing on his bottom lip.

"I mean . . . are you rooting for me?"

Cath shook her head, and this time it just meant that she was confused. "What do you mean?"

"I mean . . ." Levi leaned forward, hands still fisted in his pockets. "I mean, I spent four months trying to kiss you and the last six weeks trying to figure out how I managed to fuck everything up. All I want now is to make it right, to make you see how sorry I am and why you should give me another chance. And I just want to know – are you rooting for me? Are you hoping I pull this off?"

Cath's eyes settled on his, tentatively, like they'd fly away if he moved.

She nodded her head.

The right side of his mouth pulled up.

"I'm rooting for you," she whispered. She wasn't even sure he could hear her from the bed.

Levi's smile broke free and devoured his whole face. It started to devour her face, too. Cath had to look away.

———

That's how she ended up with hundred-watt Levi. Sitting on her bed and grinning like everything was going to be just fine.

She felt like telling him to slow down – that it wasn't fine. She hadn't forgiven him yet, and even though she was probably going to, she still didn't trust him. She didn't trust anyone, and that was a problem. *That was a fundamental problem*.

"You should take off your coat," Cath said instead.

Levi unzipped his jacket and shouldered out of it, setting it on her bed. He was wearing a sweater she'd never seen before. An olive green cardigan with pockets and leather buttons. She wondered if it was a Christmas present.

"C'mere," he said.

Cath shook her head. "I'm not ready for 'c'mere.'"

Levi reached out, and she went still – but he was just reaching toward her desk, for her laptop. He picked it up and held it. "I'm not gonna do anything," he said. "Just come here."

"Is that your best line? 'I'm not gonna do anything'?"

"I know that sounded stupid," he said, "but you make me nervous. *Please*." The ultimate magic word. Cath was already standing up. She kicked off her boots and sat twelve inches away from him on the bed. If she made Levi nervous, he made her catatonic.

He set the computer in her lap.

When she looked up to his eyes, he was smiling. Nervously.

"Cather," he said, "read me some fanfiction."

"What? Why?"

"Because. I don't know where else to start. And it makes things easier. It makes . . . *you* easier." Cath raised her eyebrows, and he shook his head, agitating his hair with one hand. "That sounded stupid, too."

Cath opened her laptop and turned it on.

This was crazy. They should be talking. She should be asking questions, he should be apologizing – and then *she* should be apologizing and telling him what a bad idea it was for them even to be talking.

"I don't remember where we left off," she said.

"Simon had just touched Baz's hand, and it was cold."

"How can you possibly remember that?"

"All of my reading brain cells go to remembering things instead."

Cath opened up the Word doc and scrolled through it. " 'Baz's hand was cold and limp,' " she read out loud. " 'When Simon looked closer, he realized that the other boy was asleep. . . .' " Cath looked up again. "This is weird," she said. "Isn't this weird?"

Levi had turned sideways to face her. His arms were folded, and his shoulder was pushed into the wall. He smiled at her and shrugged.

Cath shook her head again, wasn't sure what she meant by it, then looked down at the computer and started to read.

Simon was tired, too. He wondered if there was an enchantment in the nursery that made you sleepy. He thought about all the little babies, the toddlers – about Baz – waking up to a room full of vampires. And then Simon fell asleep.

When he woke up, Baz was sitting with his back to the fire, staring up at the rabbit.

"I decided not to kill you in your sleep," Baz said without looking down. "Happy Christmas."

Simon rubbed his eyes and sat up. "Thanks?"

"Have you tried any spells?"

"On what?"

"The hares."

"The letter didn't say to spell them. It just said to find them."

"Yes," Baz said impatiently. They must not have slept long – Baz still looked tired. "But presumably the sender knows you're a magician and assumes you might actually *consider* using magic from time to time."

"What kind of spells?" Simon asked, glancing up at the sleeping rabbit.

"I don't know." Baz waved his white-tipped wand in the air. *"Presto chango."*

"A changing spell? What are you trying to do?"

"I'm experimenting."

"Didn't you say I should do more research before barreling forward into danger?"

"That was before I'd stared at this damnable rabbit for half the night." Baz flicked his wand. *"Before and after."*

"Before and after only works on living things," Simon said.

"Experimenting. *Cock-a-doodle-doo."* Nothing happened.

"Why didn't you stay asleep?" Simon asked. "You look like you haven't slept since first year. You're pale as a ghost."

"Ghosts aren't pale, they're translucent. And pardon me if I don't feel like snuggling up with you in the room where my mother was murdered."

Simon grimaced and cast his eyes down. "Sorry," he said. "I hadn't thought of that."

"Stop the bleeding presses," Baz said, and waved his wand at the rabbit again. *"Please."*

Baz gulped. Simon thought he might be crying, and turned away to give him some space.

"Snow . . . are you absolutely sure there was nothing more in that letter?"

Simon heard a heavy rustling above them. He looked up to see the giant, luminous animal stirring in its sleep. Baz was stumbling to his feet. Simon stood, too, and stepped back, taking Baz's arm. "Careful," Baz hissed, jerking away from Simon and away from the fireplace behind them.

"Vampire," Levi said smugly. "Flammable." Levi's eyes were closed now and his head was tipped against the wall. Cath looked at him for a moment. He opened an eye and nudged her leg with his knee. She hadn't thought she was sitting that close.

Above them, the rabbit seemed to take on dimension and heft. It stretched its back legs against the sky and twitched its nose. Its ears quivered to attention.

"Are we supposed to catch it?" Baz asked. "Talk to it? Sing it a nice, magical song?"

"I don't *know*," Simon said. "I was awaiting further instructions."

The rabbit opened one boulder-sized, pink eye.

"Here's an instruction – do you have your sword?"

"Yes," Simon said.

"Unsheathe it."

"But it's the Moon Rabbit . . . ," Simon argued. "It's famous."

The rabbit turned its head from the ceiling (on closer inspection, its eyes were more red than pink) and opened its mouth – to yawn, Simon hoped – revealing incisors like fangs, like long white knives.

"Sword, Snow. Now." Baz was already holding his wand in the air like he was about to start conducting a symphony. He really was grandiose sometimes.

Simon held his right hand over his hip and whispered the incantation the Mage had taught him. "In justice. In courage. In defense of the weak. In the face of the mighty. Through magic and wisdom and good."

He felt the hilt materialize in his hand. It wouldn't always come, the Mage had warned him; the blade had a mind of its own. If Simon called it in the wrong situation, even in ignorance, the Sword of Mages wouldn't answer.

The hare reached with its forepaw almost timidly toward the

floor of the nursery – then fell from the ceiling in a graceful lump, like a pet rabbit shuffling off a sofa.

"Don't strike," Simon said. "We still don't know its intentions. . . . *What are your intentions?*" he shouted. It was a magic rabbit – perhaps it could talk.

The rabbit cocked its head, as if in answer, and shrieked at the empty spot in the sky.

"We're not here to hurt you," Simon said. "Just . . . calm down."

"Crowley, Snow, are you going to ask it to heel next?"

"Well, we've got to do *something*."

"I think we should run."

The rabbit was crouching between them and the door. Simon reached for his wand with his left hand. "Calm down. *Please!*" he shouted, trying the powerful word again. The rabbit sent a stream of angry spittle in his direction.

"Yes, all right," Simon said to Baz, "we run. On the count of three."

Baz had already made a break for the door. The rabbit screeched at him but wouldn't turn its back on Simon. It swiped at Simon's legs with a deadly-looking claw.

He managed to jump clear, but the hare immediately aimed at him from the other direction. When it cuffed him on the head, Simon wondered if Baz would even bother to bring back help. It probably wouldn't matter; no one would ever get here in time. Simon swung his sword at the rabbit, slicing it, and it pulled back its paw as if it'd caught a thorn there. Then the beast rose up onto its haunches, practically howling.

Simon scrambled to his feet . . . and saw ball after ball of fire catch in the rabbit's white fur.

"You filthy, bloody rodent!" Baz was shouting. "You're supposed to be a protector. A good-luck charm. Not a fucking monster. To think I used to make cakes for you and burn incense. . . . I take back the cakes!"

"You tell him," Simon said.

"Shut *up*, Snow. You've got a wand and a sword, and you choose to wag your useless tongue at me?"

Simon swung his sword again at the rabbit. In a fight, he always favored his sword over his wand.

In between balls of fire magic, Baz was trying paralyzing spells and painful curses. Nothing but the fire seemed to make a difference.

The sword was working – Simon could hurt the rabbit – but not enough. He may as well have been scratching at it with an embroidery needle.

"I think it's immune to magic!" Baz yelled, just as the rabbit charged toward him.

Simon ran up the hare's back and tried to sink his sword through the dense fur at its scruff. The blade slid along its hide without piercing it.

Baz charged, too, casting his wand aside and leaping onto the rabbit's chest. The animal thrashed, and Simon grabbed its neck and held on. He caught glimpses of Baz through the frenzy of fur and fang. The rabbit was swinging at Baz with its teeth, and Baz was holding on to a long ear – bashing at its nose with his arm. Then Baz's head disappeared into the rabbit's fur. The next time Simon saw a flash of him, the other boy's face was painted red with blood.

"Baz!" Simon lost his grip, and the rabbit threw him across the room. He landed on the ring of futons and tried to roll with the impact. When he picked himself up again, he saw that the rabbit was flailing around on its back, all four paws tearing at the air. Baz lay across its stomach like he was hugging a giant stuffed animal – the white fur around his head a bloody mess.

"No," Simon whispered. "Baz. No!" He ran toward the rabbit, holding his sword with both hands over his head, then plunged it with all his strength into one red eye. The rabbit collapsed, utterly limp, a paw falling into the fire.

"Baz," Simon croaked, tugging at the other boy's arm. He expected Baz to be limp, too, but he wouldn't budge. Simon tried again, digging his fingers into Baz's slim shoulder. Baz reached back and pushed him off. Simon fell to the ground, confused.

That's when he noticed that Baz was pressing his face into the rabbit's neck. Nursing at it. There were gashes along the hare's throat and ear, much deeper than anything Simon had accomplished with his sword. Baz hiked his knees up the rabbit's chest and pushed its giant maw to the side, craning his head deeper into the gore at its neck.

"Baz . . . ," Simon whispered, slowly finding his feet. For a moment – for a few moments – he just watched.

Finally Baz seemed . . . finished.

He dropped down off the rabbit and stood there, with his back to Simon. Simon watched as Baz reached for the Mage's Sword and slid it bloodily from the beast's eye.

Baz turned then, pulling his shoulders back and lifting his chin in the air. His face, his whole front – his school tie and his white shirt – were slick with blood. It dripped from his nose and his chin, and was already puddling under the hand that held the sword. So much blood. As wet as if he'd just stepped out of the bath.

Baz tossed the sword, and it fell at Simon's feet. Then he rubbed his sleeve across his mouth and eyes. It just moved the blood around, not away.

Simon didn't know what to say. How to respond to . . . this. All this bloody information.

He picked up the sword and wiped it clean on his cloak. "You all right?"

Baz licked his lips – like they were dry, Simon thought – and nodded his head.

"Good," Simon said. And realized that he meant it.

Cath stopped reading. Levi's eyes were open. He was watching her. His mouth was closed, but not tight – and he looked almost excited.

"Is that the end?" he asked.

She held on to the laptop. "Is this why you like me?"

"Why?"

"Because I read to you?"

"Do I like you because you know how to read?"

"You know what I mean."

His smile widened, so she could just see his teeth. It was strange to look at him like this. Up close. Like she was allowed to.

"Partly," he said.

Cath looked anxiously over his shoulder. "Is Reagan going to mind, you think?"

"I don't think so. We haven't been together since high school."

"How long did you date?"

"Three years."

"Were you in love?"

He pushed back his hair, abashed but not ashamed. "Desperately."

"Oh." Cath shifted away.

Levi tilted his head to catch her eyes. "It was a small town, there were eleven people in our high school class – there was nobody else in a two-hundred-mile radius that either of us would have even considered dating."

"What happened?"

"We came here. We realized that we weren't the only two datable people on the planet."

"She said she cheated on you."

Levi's eyes fell, but he didn't completely stop smiling. "Also that."

"How old are you?"

"Twenty-one."

Cath nodded. "You seem older."

"It's the hair," he said, still smiling.

"I love your hair," she blurted out.

He raised an eyebrow. Just the one.

Cath shook her head, embarrassed, closing her eyes, closing the laptop.

Levi let his head fall slowly toward her so that his bangs hung forward and brushed her ear. She pulled her head away, knowing she was blushing.

"I like your hair, too," he said. "I think, anyway. . . . It's always roped up and tied down."

"This is crazy," Cath said, scooting away.

"What?"

"This. You and me. This conversation."

"Why?"

"Well, I don't even know how it happened."

"I don't think anything's happened quite yet. . . ."

"We don't have anything in common," she said. She felt like she was brimming with objections, and they were just now starting to spill out. "You don't even know me. You're old and you smoke – and you have a job. You have experience."

"I don't really smoke unless someone else is smoking. . . ."

"That counts."

"But it doesn't matter. Nothing you just said matters, Cath. And most of it isn't even true. We have lots of stuff in common. We talk all the time – we used to. And it just made me want to talk to you more. That's a really good sign."

"What do we have in common?"

"We like each other," he said. "What more is there? Also, compared to the rest of the world, we have everything in common. If aliens came down to earth, they probably wouldn't even be able to tell us apart."

This was too much like what she'd said to Nick. . . .

"You do like me . . . ," Levi said, "right?"

"I wouldn't have kissed you if I didn't like you," Cath said.

"You might have—"

"No," she said firmly. "I wouldn't have. And I wouldn't have stayed up all night reading to you. . . ."

Levi smiled so that she could see his canine teeth. And then his bicuspids. It was wrong. He shouldn't be smiling.

"Why did you tell me it was just a kiss?" she asked, waiting for her voice to break. "I don't even care about that other girl. I mean, I do, but not as much. Why was your first instinct to tell me that what happened between you and me *didn't matter*? And why should I believe you now when you say that it did? Why should I believe anything you say?"

Levi got it now. That he shouldn't be smiling. He looked down at his lap and turned, settling his back against the wall. "I guess I panicked. . . ."

Cath waited. Levi pushed his hand into the front of his hair and made a fist. (Maybe that's why he was losing it prematurely. Constant handling.)

"I panicked," he said again. "I thought that if you knew how much kissing you meant to me . . . it would seem even worse that I kissed another girl."

Cath let that sink in. "That's terrible reasoning," she said.

"I wasn't reasoning." He turned back to her, a little too quickly. "I was panicking. Honestly? I'd forgotten all about that girl."

"Because you kiss so many girls at parties?"

"*No*. I mean . . . Ahhgh." He looked away. "*Sometimes,* but *no*.

I only kissed that girl because you weren't there. Because you didn't return my texts. Because I was back to thinking you didn't like me. I was confused, and a little drunk, and here was *this girl* who obviously *did* like me. . . . She probably left five minutes after you did. And five minutes after that, I was staring at my phone, trying to come up with an excuse to call you."

"Why didn't you just tell me all that at the hospital?"

"Because I felt like such an asshole. And I'm not used to being the asshole – I'm usually Dudley Do-Right, you know?"

"No."

"I'm usually the good guy. That was the whole plan for winning you over—"

"There was a plan?"

"There was . . ." He thunked the back of his head against the wall, and his hands fell to his lap. "It was more of a hope. That you'd see that I was a decent guy."

"I saw that."

"Right. And then you saw me kissing somebody else."

Cath wanted him to stop talking, she'd heard enough. "The thing is, Levi . . ." Saying his name out loud finished the destruction inside of her. Something, maybe Cath's spleen, gave up the ghost. She leaned forward and pulled on the sleeve of his sweater, squeezing a few inches into her fist.

"I know you're a decent guy," she said. "And I want to forgive you; it's not like you cheated on me – I mean, it's only kind of like that. But even if I do forgive you . . ." She pulled on his new sweater, stretching it. "I don't think I'm any good at this. Boy–girl. Person–person. I don't trust anybody. Not anybody. And the more that I care about someone, the more sure I am they're going to get tired of me and take off."

Levi's face clouded over. Not grimly, she thought – thoughtfully. In thoughtful clouds.

"That's crazy," he said.

"I know," Cath agreed, feeling almost relieved. "*Exactly*. I'm crazy."

He reached his fingers back and hooked them inside the cuff of her sweater. "But you still want to give me a chance, right? Not just me, this? Us?"

"Yeah," Cath said, like she was giving in.

"Good." He tugged on her sleeve and smiled down at their not-quite-touching hands. "It's okay if you're crazy," he said softly.

"You don't even know—"

"I don't have to know," he said. "I'm rooting for you."

He was going to text her the next day. They were going to go out when he got off work.

On a date.

Levi didn't call it a date, but that's what it would have to be, right? He liked her, and they were going out. He was coming to get her.

She wished she could call Wren. *I have a date. And not with an end table. Not with someone who has anything in common with furniture. He kissed me. And I think he might do it again if I let him.*

She didn't call Wren. She studied. Then stayed up as late as she could writing Baz and Simon – "*'The Insidious Humdrum,' Baz groused. 'If I ever become a supervillain, help me come up with a name that doesn't sound like an ice cream sundae.'*" – and wishing that Reagan would come home.

Cath was mostly asleep when the door opened.

Reagan shuffled around in the dark. She was good at coming and going without turning on any lights. She almost never woke Cath up.

"Hey," Cath rasped.

"Go back to sleep," Reagan whispered.

"Hey. Tonight . . . Levi came over. I think we might have a date. Is that okay?"

The shuffling stopped. "Yeah," Reagan said, practically in her normal voice. "Is it okay with you?"

"I think so," Cath said.

"Okay." Reagan's closet door opened, and she kicked her boots off with two heavy thumps. A drawer opened and closed, and then she was climbing into bed. "So fucking weird . . . ," she murmured.

"I know," Cath said, staring up into the darkness. "I'm sorry."

"Stop apologizing. Good for you. Good for Levi. Better for you, I think."

"What does that mean?"

"It means that Levi is a great guy. And that he always falls for girls who are a complete pain in the ass."

Cath rolled over and pulled her comforter up tight. "Better for me," she agreed.

"You're finally going on a date with Agatha?" Penelope's voice was soft, despite the surprise in her face. Neither of them wanted Sir Bleakly to hear – he was prone to giving ridiculous detentions; they could end up dusting the catacombs for hours or proofreading confiscated love notes.

"After dinner," Simon whispered back. "We're going to look for the sixth hare in the Veiled Forest."

"Does Agatha know it's a date? Because that just sounds like 'Another Tuesday Night with Simon.'"

"I think so." Simon tried not to turn and frown at Penelope, even though he wanted to. "She said she'd wear her new dress. . . ."

"Another Tuesday Night with Agatha," Penelope said.

"You don't think she likes me?"

"Oh, Simon, I never said that. She'd have to be an idiot not to like you."

Simon grinned.

"So I guess what I'm saying," Penelope said, going back to her homework, "is we'll just have to see."

—from chapter 17, *Simon Snow and the Six White Hares,*
copyright © 2009 by Gemma T. Leslie

TWENTY-FIVE

Reagan was sitting at Cath's desk when Cath woke up.

"Are you awake?"

"Have you been watching me sleep?"

"Yes, Bella. Are you awake?"

"No."

"Well, wake up. We need to set some ground rules."

Cath sat up, rubbing the gunk out of her eyes. "What is wrong with you? If I woke you up like this, you'd murder me."

"That's because I've got all the hand in our relationship. Wake up, we need to talk about Levi."

"Okay . . ." Cath couldn't help but smile a little, just hearing his name. Levi. She had a date with Levi.

"So you guys made up?"

"Yeah."

"Did you sleep with him?"

"Holy crap, Reagan. *No*."

"Good," Reagan said. She was sitting on Cath's chair with one leg tucked under the other, wearing an intramural-football T-shirt and black yoga pants. "I don't want to know when you sleep with him. That's the first ground rule."

"I'm not gonna sleep with him."

"See, that's exactly the kind of thing I don't want to know —

wait, what do you mean, you're not gonna sleep with him?"

Cath pressed both palms into her eyes. "I mean, not in the immediate future. We just talked."

"Yeah, but you've been hanging out with him all year—"

"Things you pressure me to do: one, underage drinking; two, prescription drug abuse; three, premarital sex."

"Oh my God, Cath, 'premarital sex'? Are you kidding me?"

"Where are you going with this?"

"Levi was my boyfriend."

"I know."

"All through high school."

"I know, I know." Cath was hiding her eyes again. "Don't paint me a picture."

"I lost my virginity with him."

"*Achhhh*. Stop. Seriously."

"This is exactly what the ground rules are for," Reagan said. "Levi is one of my best friends, and I'm your only friend, and I don't want this to get weird."

"Too late," Cath said. "And you're not my only friend."

"I know —" Reagan rolled her eyes and waved a hand in the air. "— you've got the *whole* Internet."

"What are the ground rules?"

Reagan held up a finger. Her nails were long and pink.

"One. Nobody talks to me about sex."

"*Done.*"

"Two, no lovey-dovey stuff in front of me."

"Done and done. I'm telling you, there is no lovey-dovey stuff."

"Three, shut up, nobody talks to me about their relationship."

Cath nodded. "Fine."

"Four . . ."

"You've really been thinking about this, haven't you?"

"I came up with the ground rules the first time you guys

kissed. Four, Levi is my friend, and you can't be jealous of that."

Cath looked at Reagan. At her red hair and her full lips and her totally out-sticking breasts. "I feel like it's too soon to agree to that," she said.

"No," Reagan said, "we've got to get this out of the way. You can't be jealous. And in return, I won't flex my best-friend muscles just to remind myself, and Levi, that he loved me first."

"Oh my God" – Cath clutched her comforter in disbelief – "would you actually do that?"

"I might," Reagan said, leaning forward, her face as shocked as Cath's. "In a moment of weakness. You've got to understand, I've been Levi's favorite girl practically my whole life. He hasn't dated anyone else, not seriously, since we broke up."

"God," Cath said, "I really hate this."

Reagan nodded, and it was like a dozen I-told-you-sos.

"Why did you let this happen?" Cath asked. "Why'd you let him hang out here so much?"

"Because I could tell that he liked you." Reagan sounded almost angry about it. "And I really do want him to be happy."

"You guys haven't . . . relapsed, have you? Since you broke up?"

"No . . ." Reagan looked away. "When we broke up freshman year, it was pretty awful. We only started hanging out again at the end of last year. I knew he was having trouble in his classes, and I wanted to help. . . ."

"Okay," Cath said, deciding to take this seriously. "What are the rules again? No talking about sex, no PDA, no talking about relationship stuff—"

"No being jealous."

"No being *unnecessarily* jealous, is that fair?"

Reagan pursed her lips. "All right, but be rational if this comes up. No being unnecessarily jealous."

"And no being a horrible, narcissistic bitch who gets off on her ex-boyfriend's affection."

"Agreed," Reagan said, holding out her hand.

"Do we really have to shake on this?"

"Yes."

"Levi and I might not even be anything, you know. We haven't even gone on a date. "

Reagan smiled tightly. "I don't think so. I've got a good/bad feeling about this. Shake."

Cath reached out and shook her hand.

"Now, get up," Reagan said. "I'm hungry."

As soon as Reagan left for work that afternoon, Cath jumped up from her desk and started going through her closet to figure out what to wear. Probably a T-shirt with a cardigan and jeans. There was nothing in Cath's closet that wasn't a T-shirt, a cardigan, or jeans. She laid her options out on the bed. Then she went looking for something she'd bought at a flea market last year – a little green knit collar that fastened with an antique pink button.

She wondered where Levi would take her.

Her first date with Abel had been to a movie. Wren and some of their other friends had come, too. After that, going out with Abel usually just meant hanging out at the bakery or studying up in Cath's room. Swim meets during swim season. Math contests. Those probably weren't dates, come to think of it. She wasn't going to tell Levi that her last date had been at a math contest.

Cath looked at the clothes she'd laid out and wished that Wren were here to help. She wished that she'd talked to Wren about Levi before they'd started fighting. . . . Which would have been last year, before Cath had even met him.

What would Wren say if she were here? *Pretend that he likes you more than you like him. It's like buying a car – you have to be willing to walk away.*

No . . . that was the kind of advice Wren gave herself. What would she say to Cath? *Stop frowning. We're prettier when we smile. Are you sure you don't want to do a shot?*

God, thinking about Wren was just making Cath feel worse. Now she felt nervous *and* sad. And lonely.

It was a relief when Reagan kicked in the door and started talking about dinner.

"Wear your hair down," Reagan said, tearing a piece of pizza in half. "You have good hair."

"That comment is definitely against the ground rules," Cath said, taking a bite of cottage cheese. "Number three, I think."

"I know." Reagan shook her head. "But you're so helpless sometimes. It's like watching a kitten with its head trapped in a Kleenex box."

Cath rolled her eyes. "I don't want to feel like I have to look different for him all of a sudden. It'll seem lame."

"It's lame to want to look nice on a date? Levi is shaving right now, I promise you."

Cath winced. "Stop. No insider Levi information."

"That's insider *guy* information. That's how dates work."

"He already knows what I look like," Cath said. "There's no point in being tricky about it now."

"How is doing your hair – and maybe putting on some lip gloss – being tricky?"

"It's like I'm trying to distract him with something shiny." Cath circled her spoon hand in front of her face, accidentally flicking cottage cheese on her sweater. "He already knows about all this. This is what I look like." She tried to scrape the cottage cheese off without rubbing it in.

Reagan leaned across the table and grabbed the clip out of Cath's hair. It slumped over her ears and into her eyes.

"There," Reagan said. "Now *that's* what you look like. *Presto chango*."

"Oh my God," Cath said, grabbing her clip out of Reagan's hand and immediately twisting her hair back up. "Was that a Simon Snow reference?"

Now Reagan rolled *her* eyes. "Like you're the only one who's read Simon Snow. Like it isn't a global phenomenon."

Cath started giggling.

Reagan scowled at her. "What are you eating anyway? Are those peaches in your cottage cheese?"

"Isn't it disgusting?" Cath said. "You kinda get used to it."

When they turned down the hallway, they could see Levi sitting against their door. In no circumstances would Cath ever run squealing down the hall into his arms. But she did her version of that – she smiled tensely and looked away.

"Hey," Levi said, sliding up the door to his feet.

"Hey," Reagan said.

Levi ruffled the top of his hair sheepishly, like he wasn't sure which one of them to smile at. "You ready?" he asked Cath while Reagan opened the door.

Cath nodded. "Just . . . my coat." She found her coat and slipped it on.

"Scarf," Levi said. So she grabbed it.

"See you later," she said to Reagan.

"Probably not," Reagan said, shaking her hair out in front of her mirror.

Cath felt herself blushing. She didn't look over at Levi again until they were standing together in front of the elevator. (*Condition: smiling, stable.*) When it opened, he put his hand on her back and she practically jumped in.

"What's the plan?" she asked.

He grinned. "My plan is to do things that make you want to hang out with me again tomorrow. What's your plan?"

"I'm going to try not to make an ass of myself."

He grinned. "So we're all set."

She smiled back at him. In his general direction.

"I thought I'd show you East Campus," Levi said.

"At night? In February?"

The elevator doors opened, and he waited for her to step out. "I got a great deal on an off-season tour. Besides, it's not *that* cold out tonight."

Levi led the way outside and started walking away from the parking lot.

"Don't we have to drive?" Cath asked.

"I thought we'd take the shuttle."

"There's a shuttle?"

He shook his head. "City folk."

The shuttle was a bus, and it rolled up almost immediately. "After you," Levi said.

Inside, the bus was lit up brighter than daylight and nearly empty. Cath chose a seat and sat down sideways with one knee up, so that there wasn't room to sit down right next to her. Levi didn't seem to mind. He swung sideways into the seat in front of her and rested his arm on the back.

"You have very nice manners," she said.

"My mother would be thrilled to hear that." He smiled.

"So you have a mother."

He laughed. "Yes."

"And a father?"

"And four sisters."

"Older or younger?"

"Older. Younger."

"You're in the middle?"

"Smack-dab. What about you? Are you the older or younger twin?"

She shrugged. "It was a C-section. But Wren was bigger. She was stealing my juice or something. I had to stay in the hospital for three weeks after she went home."

Cath didn't tell him that sometimes she felt like Wren was still taking more than her fair share of life, like she was siphoning vitality off Cath – or like she was born with a bigger supply.

Cath didn't tell him that, because it was dark and depressing. And because, for the moment, she wouldn't trade places with Wren, even if it meant getting the better umbilical cord.

"Does that mean she's more dominant?" Levi asked.

"Not necessarily. I mean, I guess she *is*. About most things. My dad says we used to share the bossiness when we were kids. Like I'd decide what we were gonna wear, and she'd decide what we were playing."

"Did you dress alike?"

"When we were little. We liked to."

"I've helped deliver twins before," he said. "Calves. It almost killed the cow."

Cath's eyes got big. "How did that happen?"

"Sometimes when a bull meets a cow, they decide to spend more time together—"

"How did you end up being there for the delivery?"

"It happens a lot on a ranch. Not twins, but births."

"You worked on a ranch?"

He raised an eyebrow, like he wasn't sure whether she was serious. "I *live* on a ranch."

"Oh," Cath said. "I didn't know people lived on ranches. I thought it was like a factory or a business, someplace where you go to work."

"You're sure you're from Nebraska?"

"I'm starting to feel like Omaha doesn't count. . . ."

"Well" – he smiled – "I live on a ranch."

"Like on a farm?"

"Sort of. Farms are for crops. Ranches are for grazing livestock."

"Oh. That sounds . . . are there just cows wandering around?"

"Yeah." He laughed, then shook his head. "No. There are cattle in designated areas. They need a lot of space."

"Is that what you want to do when you're done with school? Work on a ranch?"

Something passed over Levi's face. His smile faded a bit, and he scrunched his eyebrows together. "It's . . . not that simple. My mom shares the ranch with my uncles, and nobody really knows what's going to happen to it when they all retire. There are twelve cousins, so we can't just split it. Unless we sell it. Which . . . nobody really wants. Um . . ." He shook his head again quickly and smiled back up at her. "I'd like to work on a ranch or with ranchers – helping them be better at what they do."

"Range management."

"And you try to pretend like you're not paying attention – hey, this is our stop."

"Already?"

"East Campus is only two miles from your dorm; it's shameful that you've never been here."

Cath followed him off the bus. He stopped to thank the driver by name.

"Did you know that guy?" she asked when the bus pulled away.

Levi shrugged. "He was wearing a name tag. Okay –" He

stepped directly in front of her and spread a long arm out toward a parking lot. He was smiling like a game show host. "— Cather Avery, as a student of the Agricultural College, a member of the agricultural community, and a citizen of Lincoln, Nebraska, I would like to welcome you to East Campus."

"I like it," Cath said, looking around. "It's dark. There are trees."

"You can park your snark at the gate, Omaha."

"Who would have thought that being from Omaha would make me citified?"

"On your right is the East Campus Union. That's where we keep our bowling alley."

"Another bowling alley—"

"Don't get excited, there's no bowling on the agenda tonight."

Cath followed Levi along a winding sidewalk path and smiled politely at all the buildings when he pointed to them. He kept touching her back to get her attention or to make sure she was facing the right direction. She didn't tell him that East Campus (in February, at night) looked a lot like City Campus.

"If we were here during the day," he said, "we'd stop at the Dairy Store and have some ice cream."

"Too bad," she said. "It's the perfect freezing night for it."

"Are you cold?" He stopped in front of her and frowned. "Is that how your mother taught you to put on a scarf?"

Her scarf was hanging around her collar. He pulled it snugly against her neck and wrapped it, tucking in the ends. Cath hoped her coat hid the embarrassingly shaky breath she'd taken.

Levi moved his hands up to the side of her head and gently pinched the top of her ears. "Not too bad," he said, rubbing them. "*Are* you cold?" He raised an eyebrow. "Do you want to go in?"

She shook her head. "No. I want to see East Campus."

He grinned again. "As well you should. We haven't even gotten to the Tractor Museum. It's closed, of course."

"Of course."

"But still worth seeing."

"Of course."

After a half hour or so, they stopped to use the bathroom in the Dental College. People were spread out on blue couches in the lounge, studying. Levi bought a cup of hot chocolate from the coffee machine for them to share. Cath had a weird thing about sharing drinks, but she decided it would be stupid to say anything. She'd already kissed him.

When they stepped outside again, the night seemed quieter. Darker.

"I saved the best for last," Levi said softly.

"What's that?"

"Patience. This way . . ."

They walked together along another curving sidewalk until he stopped her with a hand on her shoulder. "Here we are," he said, pointing down an unshoveled path. "The Gardens."

Cath tried to look appreciative. You wouldn't know there was a path here at all if it weren't for one set of footprints in the melting snow. All she could see were the footprints, some dead bushes, and a few weedy patches of mud.

"It's breathtaking," she laughed.

"I knew you'd like it. Play your cards right, and I'll bring you back during the high season."

They walked slowly, occasionally stopping to look at educational plaques that were sticking out through the snow. Levi would lean over, clear one off with his sleeve, and read out loud what plants were supposed to be growing there.

"So what we're really missing out on," Cath said as they bent together over a sign, "is a variety of native grasses."

"And wildflowers," Levi said. "We're also missing the wildflowers."

She stepped away from him, and he took her hand. "Wait," he said. "I think there might be an evergreen over there—"

Cath looked up.

"False alarm," he said, squeezing her hand.

She shivered.

"Are you cold?"

She shook her head.

He squeezed her hand again. "Good."

They didn't talk about any more of the flowers they were missing as they finished their loop through the Gardens. Cath was glad she wasn't wearing gloves; Levi's palm was smooth, almost slick, against her own.

They walked over a pedestrian bridge, and she felt her arm pull. He'd stopped to lean against the trusses.

"Hey. Cath. Can I ask you something?"

She stopped and looked back at him. He took her other hand and pulled her closer — not against him or anything, just closer — fingers crossing like they were about to play London Bridge.

Levi was a black-and-white photograph in the dark. All pale skin, gray eyes, streaky hair . . .

"Do you really think I just go around kissing people all the time?" he asked.

"Sort of," Cath said. She tried to ignore the fact that she could feel every single one of his fingers. "Up until about a month ago, I thought you were kissing Reagan all the time."

"How could you think that? She's seeing, like, five other guys."

"I thought you were one of them."

"But I was always flirting with *you*." He pushed Cath's hands forward for emphasis.

"You flirt with *everything*." She could tell that her eyes were popping – her eyeballs actually felt cold around the edges. "You flirt with old people and babies and everybody in between."

"Oh, I do not. . . ." He tucked his chin into his neck indignantly.

"You do so," she said, pushing his hands back. "That night at the bowling alley? You flirted with every human being in the building. I'm surprised the shoe guy didn't give you his number."

"I was just being nice."

"You're *extra* nice. With *every*one. You go out of your way to make everyone feel special."

"Well, what's wrong with that?"

"How is anyone supposed to know that they *are* special? How was I supposed to know you weren't just being nice?"

"You can't see that I'm different with you?"

"I thought I could. For like twelve hours. And then . . . For all I know, yeah, you do go around kissing people. Just to be nice. Because you have this weird thing where you get off on making people feel special."

Levi winced, his chin almost flat against his neck. "I've been hanging around your room, and inviting you to parties, and just trying to be there whenever you might need anything for *four months*. And you didn't even notice."

"I thought you were dating my roommate!" she said. "And I repeat, you're nice to everybody. You give away nice like it doesn't cost you anything."

Levi laughed. "It *doesn't* cost me anything. It's not like smiling at strangers exhausts my overall supply."

"Well, it does mine."

"I'm not you. Making people happy makes me feel good. If anything, it gives me more energy for the people I care about."

Cath had been trying to maintain eye contact through all this, like a grown-up human being, but it was getting to be too much – she let her eyes skitter down to the snow. "If you smile at everyone," she said, "how am I supposed to feel when you smile at me?"

He pulled their hands toward him, up, so they were practically over his shoulders. "How *do* you feel when I smile at you?" he asked – and then he did smile at her, just a little.

Not like myself, Cath thought.

She gripped his hands tightly, for balance, then stood on tiptoe, leaning her chin over his shoulder and brushing her head gently against his cheek. It was smooth, and Levi smelled heavy there, like perfume and mint.

"Like an idiot," she said softly. "And like I never want it to stop."

They sat next to each other on the shuttle, looking down at their hands because it was too bright on the bus to look at each other's faces. Levi didn't talk, and Cath didn't worry about why not.

When they got back to her room, they both knew it was empty, and they both had keys.

Levi unwrapped her scarf and pulled her forward by the tails, briefly pressing his face into the top of her head.

"Tomorrow and tomorrow and tomorrow," he said.

He meant it.

He came to see her the next day. And the next. And after a week or so, Cath just expected Levi to insinuate himself into her day somehow. And to act like it had always been that way.

He never said, *Can I see you tomorrow?* Or, *Will I see you tomorrow?* It was always *When?* and *Where?*

They met in the Union between classes. She met him at

Starbucks on his breaks. He waited in the hallway for her or for Reagan to let him in.

They'd kept it from being weird so far between the three of them. Cath would sit at her desk, and Levi would sit on her bed and tell them both stories and tease them. Sometimes the intimacy and affection in his voice were too much for Cath. Sometimes she felt like he was talking to them like her dad talked to her and Wren. Like they were both *his girls*.

Cath tried to shake it off. She tried to meet him other places if Reagan was in the room.

But when they were alone in the room without Reagan, they didn't act much differently. Cath still sat at her desk. And Levi still sat on her bed with his feet on her chair, talking circles around her. Lazy, comforting circles.

He liked to talk about her dad and Wren. He thought the twin thing was fascinating.

He liked to talk about Simon Snow, too. He'd seen all the movies two or three times. Levi saw lots of movies – he liked anything with fantasy or adventure. Superheroes. Hobbits. Wizards. If only he were a better reader, Cath thought, he could have been a proper nerd.

Well . . . maybe.

To really be a nerd, she'd decided, you had to prefer fictional worlds to the real one. Cath would move into the World of Mages in a heartbeat. She'd felt almost despondent last year when she realized that, even if she discovered a magical wormhole into Simon's world, she was too old now to go to the Watford School of Magicks.

Wren had been bummed, too, when Cath pointed it out. They were lying in bed on the morning of their eighteenth birthday.

"Cath, wake up, let's go buy some cigarettes."

"Can't," Cath said. "I'm going to watch an R-rated movie – in the theater. And then I'm gonna go get drafted."

"Oh! Let's skip class and go see *Five Hundred Days of Summer*."

"You know what this means, don't you?" Cath looked up at the giant map of Watford they'd taped to the ceiling. Their dad had paid one of the designers at work to draw it for them one year for Christmas. "It means we're too old for Watford."

Wren sat back against her headboard and looked up. "Oh. You're right."

"It's not that I ever thought it was real," Cath said after a minute, "even when we were kids, but still—"

"But still . . ." Wren sighed. "Now I'm too sad to start smoking."

Wren was an actual nerd. Despite her fancy hair and her handsome boyfriends. If Cath had found that wormhole, that rabbit hole, that doorway in the back of the closet, Wren would have gone through with her.

Wren might still go through with her, even in their current state of estrangement. (That would be another good thing about finding a magic portal. She'd have an excuse to call Wren.)

But Levi wasn't a nerd; he liked real life too much. For Levi, Simon Snow was just a story. And he loved stories.

Cath had fallen behind on *Carry On, Simon* since this thing with Levi started – which on the one hand, was perfectly okay; she wasn't such a nerd that she'd rather make up love scenes with boys than be in one.

On the other hand . . . *Simon Snow and the Eighth Dance* was coming out in less than three months, and Cath had to finish *Carry On* by then. She had to. *The Eighth Dance* was the very end of the Simon Snow saga – it was going to settle everything – and Cath had to settle it her way first. Before Gemma T. Leslie closed the curtains.

Cath could study when Levi was in the room (he needed to study, too – he sat on her bed and listened to his lectures; sometimes he played solitaire at the same time), but she couldn't write with him there. She couldn't get lost in the World of Mages. She was too lost in Levi.

Levi was five-foot-eleven. She'd thought he was taller.

He was born on a ranch. Literally. His mom's labor came on so fast that she sat down on the stairs and caught him herself. His dad cut the cord. ("I'm telling you," Levi said, "it's not that different from calving.")

He lived with five other guys. He drove a truck because he thought everybody should drive a truck — that driving around in a car was like living with your hands tied behind your back. "What if you need to haul something?"

"I can't think of a single time my family has needed a truck," Cath said.

"That's because you've got car blinders on. You don't even allow yourself to see outsized opportunities."

"Like what?"

"Free firewood."

"We don't have a fireplace."

"Antlers," he said.

Cath snorted.

"Antique couches."

"Antique couches?"

"Cather, someday, when I get you up to my room, I will entertain you on my beautiful antique couch."

When he talked about the ranch or his family or his truck, Levi's voice slowed down, almost like he had an accent. A drawl. A drag on his vowel sounds. She couldn't tell if it was for show or not.

"When I get you up to my room" had become a joke between them.

They didn't *have* to meet at the Union or wait for Reagan to leave them alone in Cath's room. They could hang out at Levi's house anytime.

But, so far, Cath hadn't let that happen. Levi lived in a *house,* like an adult. Cath lived in a dorm, like a young adult – like someone who was still on adulthood probation.

She could handle Levi here, in this room, where nothing was grown-up yet. Where there was a twin bed and posters of Simon Snow on the wall. Where Reagan could walk in at any minute.

Levi must feel like somebody'd pulled a bait-and-switch on him. Back when they were nothing to each other – back when she thought he belonged to somebody else – Cath had crawled into bed with him and fallen asleep mouth to mouth. Now that they were seeing each other (not really dating, but everyday seeing each other), they only sometimes held hands. And when they did, Cath sort of pretended that they weren't – she just didn't acknowledge it. And she never touched him first.

She *wanted* to.

God, she wanted to tackle him and roll around in him like a cat in a field of daisies.

Which is exactly why she didn't. Because she was Little Red Riding Hood. She was a virgin and an idiot. And Levi could make her breathless in the elevator, just resting his hand – through her coat – on the small of her back.

This was something she might talk to Wren about, if she still had a Wren.

Wren would tell her not to be stupid – that boys wanted to touch you so badly, they didn't care if you were good at it.

But Levi wasn't a boy. He wasn't panting to get up somebody's shirt for the first time. Levi had been up shirts; he probably just took them off.

The thought made Cath shiver. And then she thought of Reagan, and it turned into more of a shudder.

Cath wasn't planning to be a virgin forever. But she'd planned to do all this stuff with somebody like Abel. Somebody who was, if anything, more pathetic and inexperienced than she was. Somebody who didn't make her feel so out of control.

If she thought about it objectively, Abel might actually be better looking than Levi in some ways. Abel was a swimmer. He had broad shoulders and thick arms. And he had hair like Frankie Avalon. (According to Cath's grandma.)

Levi was thin and weedy, and his hair – well, his *hair* – but everything about him made Cath feel loose and immoral.

He had this thing where he bit his bottom lip and raised an eyebrow when he was trying to decide whether to laugh at something. . . . *Madness.*

Then, if he decided to laugh, his shoulders would start shaking and his eyebrows would pull up in the middle – Levi's eyebrows were pornographic. If Cath were making this decision just on eyebrows, she would have been "up to his room" a long time ago.

If she were being rational about this, there was a lot on the touching continuum between holding hands and eyebrow-driven sex. . . . But she wasn't being rational. And Levi made Cath feel like her whole body was a slippery slope.

She sat at her desk. He sat on her bed and kicked her chair.

"Hey," he said. "I was thinking that this weekend, we should go on a real date. We could go out to dinner, see a movie. . . ." He was smiling, so Cath smiled back. And then she stopped.

"I can't."

"Why not? You already have a date? Every night this weekend?"

"Sort of. I'm going home. I've been going home more this semester, to check on my dad."

Levi's smile dimmed, but he nodded, like he understood. "How're you getting home?"

"This girl down the hall. Erin. She goes home every weekend

to see her boyfriend – which is probably a good idea, because she's boring and awful, and he's bound to meet somebody better if she doesn't keep an eye on him."

"I'll drive you home."

"On your white horse?"

"In my red truck."

Cath rolled her eyes. "No. You'd have to make two round trips. It'd take a thousand dollars in gas."

"I don't care. I want to meet your dad. And I'll get to hang out with you for a few hours in the truck – in a nonemergency situation."

"It's okay. I can ride with Erin. She's not that bad."

"You don't want me to meet your dad?"

"I haven't even thought about you meeting my dad."

"You haven't?" He sounded wounded. (Mildly wounded. Like, hangnail-wounded – but still.)

"Have you thought about introducing me to your parents?" she asked.

"Yeah," he said. "I figured you'd go with me to my sister's wedding."

"When is it?"

"May."

"We've only been dating for three and a half weeks, right?"

"That's six months in freshman time."

"You're not a freshman."

"Cather . . ." Levi hooked his feet on her chair and pulled it closer to the bed. "I really like you."

Cath took a deep breath. "I really like you, too."

He grinned and raised a hand-drawn eyebrow. "Can I drive you to Omaha?"

Cath nodded.

"That does it," Simon said, charging forward, climbing right over the long dinner table. Penelope grabbed the tail of his cape, and he nearly landed face-first on a bench. He recovered quickly – "Let *go*, Penny" – and ran hard at Basil, both fists raised and ready.

Basil didn't move. *"Good fences make good neighbors,"* he whispered, just barely tipping his wand.

Simon's fist slammed into a solid barrier just inches from the other boy's unflinching jaw. He pulled his hand back, yelping, still stumbling against the spell.

This made Dev and Niall and all the rest of Basil's cronies cackle like drunk hyenas. But Basil himself stayed still. When he spoke, it was so softly, only Simon could hear him. "Is that how you're going to do it, Snow? Is that how you're going to best your Humdrum?" He dropped the spell with a twitch of his wand, just as Simon regained his balance. *"Pathetic,"* Basil said, and walked away.

—from chapter 4, *Simon Snow and the Five Blades*,
copyright © 2008 by Gemma T. Leslie

TWENTY-SIX

Professor Piper held out her arms when Cath walked in. "Cath, you're *back*. I wish I could say that I knew you would be, but I wasn't sure – I was hoping."

Cath was back.

She'd come to tell Professor Piper that she'd made up her mind. Again. She wasn't going to write this story. She had enough to write right now and enough to worry about. This project was leftover crappiness from first semester. Just thinking about it made Cath's mouth taste like failure (like plagiarism and stupid Nick stealing her best lines); Cath wanted to put it behind her.

But once she was standing in Professor Piper's office, and Professor Piper was Blue Fairy-smiling at her, Cath couldn't say it out loud.

This is so obviously about me needing a mother figure, she thought, disgusted with herself. *I wonder if I'm going to get swoony around middle-aged women until I am one.*

"It was really kind of you to offer me a second chance," Cath said, following the professor's gesture to sit down. This was when she was supposed to say, *But I'm going to have to say no.*

Instead she said, "I guess I'd be an idiot not to take it."

Professor Piper beamed at her. She leaned forward with an elbow on the desktop, resting her cheek against her fist like she was posing for a senior picture. "So," she said, "do you have an idea in mind for your story?"

"No." Cath squeezed her fists shut and rubbed them into her thighs. "Every time I've tried to come up with something, I just feel . . . empty."

Professor Piper nodded. "You said something last time that I've been thinking about – you said that you didn't want to build your own world."

Cath looked up. "Yes. Exactly. I don't have brave new worlds inside of me begging to get out. I don't want to start from nothing like that."

"But Cath – most writers *don't*. Most of us aren't Gemma T. Leslie." She waved a hand around the office. "We write about the worlds we already know. I've written four books, and they all take place within a hundred and twenty miles of my hometown. Most of them are about things that happened in my real life."

"But you write historical novels—"

The professor nodded. "I take something that happened to me in 1983, and I make it happen to somebody else in 1943. I pick my life apart that way, try to understand it better by writing straight through it."

"So everything in your books is true?"

The professor tilted her head and hummed. "Mmmm . . . yes. And no. Everything starts with a little truth, then I spin my webs around it – sometimes I spin completely away from it. But the point is, I don't start with nothing."

"I've never written anything that isn't magical," Cath said.

"You still can, if that's what you want. But you don't have to start at the molecular level, with some sort of Big Bang in your head."

Cath pressed her nails into her palms.

"Maybe for this story," Professor Piper said delicately, "you could start with something real. With one day from your life. Something that confused or intrigued you, something you want to explore. Start there and see what happens. You can keep it true, or you can let it turn into something else – you can add magic – but give yourself a starting point."

Cath nodded, more because she was ready to leave than because she'd processed everything the professor was saying.

"I want to meet again," Professor Piper said. "In a few weeks. Let's get back together and talk about where you are."

Cath agreed and hurried toward the door, hoping she wouldn't seem rude. *A few weeks. Sure. Like a few weeks will fix the hole in my head.* She pushed her way through a mob of gaudy English majors, then escaped out into the snow.

Levi wouldn't put her laundry hamper down.

"I can carry it," Cath said. Her head was still in Professor Piper's office, and she wasn't in the mood for . . . well, for Levi. For the constant good-natured game of him. If Levi were a dog, he'd be a golden retriever. If he were a game, he'd be Ping-Pong, incessant and bouncing and light. Cath didn't feel like playing.

"I've got this," he said. "You get the door."

"No, seriously," she said. "I can carry it."

Levi was all smiles and fond glances. "Sweetheart, get the door. I've got this."

Cath pressed her fingertips into her temples. "Did you just call me 'sweetheart'?"

He grinned. "It just came out. It felt good."

"Sweetheart?"

"Would you prefer 'honey'? That reminds me of my mom. . . . What about 'baby'? No. 'Loveboat'? 'Kitten'? 'Rubber duck'?" He paused. "You know what? I'm sticking with 'sweetheart.' "

"I don't even know where to start," Cath said.

"Start with the door."

"Levi. I can carry my own gross, dirty laundry."

"Cath. I'm not going to let you."

"There's no *let*ting. It's my laundry."

"Possession is nine-tenths of the law."

"I don't need you to carry things for me. I have two functioning arms."

"That's not the point," he said. "What kind of creep would I be if I let my girl carry something heavy while I walked along, swinging my arms?"

Your girl? "The kind that respects my wishes," she said. "And my strength, and my . . . *arms*."

Levi grinned some more. Because he wasn't taking her seriously. "I have a lot of respect for your arms. I like how they're attached to the rest of you."

"You're making me feel fragile and limp. Give me the laundry." She reached for it.

He stepped back. "Cather. I know you're capable of carrying this. But I'm not capable of letting you. I literally couldn't walk next to you empty-handed. It's nothing personal; I'd do this for anyone with two X chromosomes."

"Even *worse*."

"Why? Why is that worse? That I'm respectful to women."

"It's not respectful, it's undermining. Respect our strength."

"I do." His hair fell in his eyes, and he tried to blow it away. "Being chivalrous is respectful. Women have been oppressed and persecuted since the beginning of time. If I can make their lives easier with my superior upper-body strength, I'm going to. At every opportunity."

"Superior."

"Yes. Superior. Do you want to arm wrestle?"

"I don't need superior upper-body strength to carry my own dirty laundry." She put her fingers on the handles, trying to push his aside.

"You're deliberately missing the point," he said.

"No, that's you."

"Your face is flushed, did you know that?"

"Well," she said. "I'm frustrated."

"Don't make me angry-kiss you."

"Give me the laundry."

"Tempers rising, faces flushed . . . This is how it happens."

That made Cath laugh. And that was irritating, too. She used most of her inferior upper-body strength to shove the hamper into his chest.

Levi pushed it back gently, but didn't let go. "Let's fight about this the next time I try to do something nice for you, okay?"

She looked up at his eyes. The way he looked back at her made her feel wide open, like every thought must be closed-captioned on her face. She let go of the hamper and picked up her laptop bag, opening the door.

"Finally," he said. "My triceps are killing me."

This was the coldest, snowiest winter Cath could remember. It was the middle of March already, technically spring, but it still felt like January. Cath put on her snow boots every morning without thinking about it.

She'd gotten so used to the snow, to being a pedestrian in the snow, that she hadn't even thought to check the weather today – she hadn't thought about road conditions and visibility or the fact that maybe this wasn't the best afternoon for Levi to drive her home.

She was thinking about it now.

It felt like they were the only car on the interstate. They

couldn't see the sun; they couldn't see the road. Every ten minutes or so, red taillights would emerge out of the static ahead of them, and Levi would ease onto the brakes.

He'd stopped talking almost an hour ago. His mouth was straight, and he was squinting at the windshield like he needed glasses.

"We should go back," Cath whispered.

"Yeah . . . ," he said, rubbing his mouth with the back of his hand, then clenching a fist around the gearshift. "But I think it might be easier now to keep going. It's worse behind us. I thought we'd beat it to Omaha."

There was a metallic ringing as a car passed them on the left.

"What's that noise?" she asked.

"Tire chains." Levi didn't sound scared. But he was being so awfully quiet.

"I'm sorry," she said. "I wasn't thinking about the weather."

"My fault," he said, sparing a second to smile at her. "I didn't want to let you down. Think I'll feel worse if I actually kill you. . . ."

"That would not be chivalrous."

Levi smiled again. She reached out to the gearshift and touched his hand, running her fingers along his, then pulling them away.

They were quiet again for a few minutes – maybe not that long. It was hard to judge time with everything so tense and gray.

"What are you thinking about?" Levi asked.

"Nothing."

"Not nothing. You've seemed thinky and weird ever since I got to your room. Is this about me meeting your dad?"

"No," Cath said quickly. "I kind of forgot about that."

More quiet.

"What then?"

"Just . . . something that happened with a professor. I can tell you when we're not in mortal peril."

Levi felt on the seat for her hand, so she gave it to him. He clutched it. "You're not in mortal peril." He moved his hand back to the gearshift. "Maybe . . . stranded-in-a-ditch-for-a-few-hours peril. Tell me. I can't really talk right now, but I can listen. I'd like to listen."

Cath turned away from the window and faced him. It was nice to look at Levi when he couldn't look back. She liked his profile. It was very . . . flat. A straight line from his long forehead into his longish nose – his nose veered out a bit at the tip, but not much – and another straight line from his nose to his chin. His chin went soft sometimes when he smiled or when he was feigning surprise, but it never quite mushed away. She was going to kiss him there someday, right at the edge of his jaw where his chin was most vulnerable.

"What happened in class?" he asked.

"After class, I went . . . Well, okay, so you know how last semester, I was taking Fiction-Writing?"

"Yeah."

"Well, I didn't turn in my final project. I was supposed to write a short story, and I didn't."

"What?" His chin tucked back in surprise. "Why?"

"I . . . lots of reasons." This was more complicated than Cath thought. She didn't want to tell Levi how unhappy she'd been last semester – how she hadn't wanted to come back to school, how she hadn't wanted to see him. She didn't want him to think he had that much power over her.

"I didn't want to write it," she said. "I mean, there's more to it than that, but . . . mostly I didn't want to. I had writer's block. And my dad, you know, I didn't come back to school, finals week, after he had his breakdown."

"I didn't know that."

"Well. It's true. So I decided not to finish my final project. But my Fiction-Writing professor didn't turn in my grade. She wants to give me a second chance — she said I could write the story this semester. And I sort of said that I would."

"Wow. That's awesome."

"Yeah . . ."

"It's not awesome?"

"No. It is. Just . . . it was nice to have it behind me. To feel like I was through with that whole idea. Fiction-Writing."

"You write fiction all the time."

"I write *fan*fiction."

"Don't be tricky with me right now. I'm driving through a blizzard." A car materialized ahead of them, and Levi's face tensed.

Cath waited until he relaxed again. "I don't want to make up my own characters, my own world — I don't have that inside of me."

Neither of them spoke. They were moving so slowly. . . . Something caught Cath's eye through Levi's window; a semi truck had jackknifed in the median. She took a stuttering breath, and Levi found her hand again.

"Only fifteen miles," he said.

"Does he need help?"

"There was a State Patrol car."

"I didn't see it."

"I'm so sorry about this," Levi said.

"Stop," she said. "You didn't make it snow."

"Your dad's going to hate me."

She raised his hand to her mouth and kissed his knuckles. His forehead wrinkled, almost like it hurt.

Cath listened to the windshield wipers and watched the front window for whatever was coming next.

"Are you sure?" Levi asked after a few miles. "About the

fiction-writing? Are you sure you don't have that inside you? You're fathomless when it comes to Simon and Baz—"

"They're different. They already exist. I just move them around."

He nodded. "Maybe you're like Frank Sinatra. He didn't write his own songs – but he was a genius interpreter."

"I hate Frank Sinatra."

"Come on, nobody hates Frank Sinatra."

"He treated women like things."

"Okay –" Levi adjusted himself in the seat, shaking his neck out. "– not Frank Sinatra, then . . . Aretha Franklin."

"Blech. Diva."

"Roy Acuff?"

"Who?"

Levi smiled, and it made Cath kiss his fingers again. He gave her a quick, questioning look.

"The point is . . . ," he said softly. Something about the storm made them both talk softly. "There are different kinds of talent. Maybe your talent is in interpretation. Maybe you're a stylist."

"And you think that counts?"

"Tim Burton didn't come up with Batman. Peter Jackson didn't write *Lord of the Rings*."

"In the right light, you are such a nerd."

His smile opened up. The truck hit a slick spot, and he pulled his hand away, but the smile lingered. A coffeepot-shaped water tower slowly moved past his window. They were on the edge of town now; there were more cars here, on the road and in the ditches.

"You still have to write that story," Levi said.

"Why?"

"To bring your grade up. Don't you need to keep your GPA up for your scholarship?"

She'd only just told him about the scholarship a few nights ago. ("I'm dating a genius," he'd said, "and a scholar.")

Of course she wanted to keep her GPA up. "Yeah—"

"So, write the story. It doesn't have to be great. You don't have to be Ernest Hemingway. You're lucky you're getting a second chance."

Cath sighed. "Yeah."

"I don't know where you live," he said. "You're going to have to give me instructions."

"Just be careful," Cath said, leaning in quickly to kiss his smooth cheek.

"You can't shave your head. You'll look mental."

"I look worse than mental with this hair. I look evil."

"There's no such thing as evil hair," Simon giggled. They were lying on the floor of the library between two rows of shelves. Baz on his back. Simon propped up on one shoulder.

"Look at me," Baz said, pushing his chin-length hair back from his forehead. "Every famous vampire has a widow's peak like this. I'm a cliché. It's like I went to the barber and asked for 'a Dracula.'"

Simon was laughing so hard, he nearly fell forward onto Baz. Baz shoved him up with his free hand.

"I mean, honestly," Baz said, still holding back his hair, trying to keep a straight face. "It's like an arrow on my face. *This way to the vampire.*"

Simon swatted Baz's hand away and kissed the point of his hairline as gently as he could. "I like your hair," Simon said against Baz's forehead. "Really, really."

—from *Carry On, Simon,* posted March 2012
by FanFixx.net author *Magicath*

TWENTY-SEVEN

When they pulled crunchily into Cath's driveway, Cath exhaled, completely, for the first time in two hours.

Levi leaned back and let his head fall against the seat. He opened and closed his hands, stretching his fingers. "Let's never do that again," he said.

Cath unbuckled her seat belt and slid toward him, pushing her arms around his shoulders. Levi smiled so wide, she wished it hadn't taken an adrenaline rush for her to feel like she could hug him like this. His arms moved around her waist, and she held him tightly, her face in his coat.

Levi's mouth was close to her ear. "You shouldn't reward me for endangering your life, you know. Think of the precedent you're setting."

Cath held him even tighter. He was good. He was good, and she didn't want to lose him. Not that she felt like she was going to lose him on the interstate. Just, in general. In general, she didn't want to lose him.

"I wouldn't have thought twice of driving through this back home," he said quietly, "by myself. But I shouldn't have done this with you. I'm sorry."

She shook her head.

The street was silent, and the cab of the truck was dark gray and white-bright, and after a few minutes, Levi's hand trailed up her back and down again.

"Cather," he whispered, "I really like you. . . ."

When they got out of the truck, the windshield was covered with snow. Levi carried her laundry. Cath let him. He was nervous about meeting her dad, and she was nervous about her dad, period. She'd talked to him every day since Christmas break, and she'd been home to visit – he seemed like he was doing fine, but you never knew with him. . . .

When Cath opened the door, he was right there in the living room. There were papers everywhere, onionskin taped to the curtains and walls, all his ideas sorted into buckets. And her dad was sitting on the coffee table, chewing on the end of a Sharpie.

"Cath," he said, smiling. "Hey . . . is it Cath time already?" He looked at the windows, then down at his wrist; he wasn't wearing a watch. Then he saw Levi and stopped. He took his glasses off his head and put them on, standing.

"Dad, this is Levi. He gave me a ride." That hadn't come out right. Cath tried again: "He's, um . . . Levi."

Levi held out his hand. "Mr. Avery, nice to meet you." He was drawling. Maybe his accent was a nervous tic.

"It's nice to meet you," her dad said. And then – "Levi."

"I'm really sorry about taking Cather out in this weather," Levi said. "I didn't realize how bad it was."

Nothing registered on her dad's face. He looked toward the windows. "Is it messy out? I guess I haven't been paying attention. . . ."

Levi's face went nearly blank. He smiled politely.

Her dad looked at Cath and remembered that he was going to

hug her. "Are you hungry?" he said. "Is it dinnertime? I've been in a Franken-fog all day."

"Did you guys get the Frankenbeans account?" she asked.

"Still pitching. Eternally pitching. So, Levi," he said, "are you staying for dinner?"

"Oh," Levi said. "Thank you, sir, but I better get back while there's still some light."

Cath wheeled around. "Are you kidding me? You're not driving back to Lincoln in this."

"I'll be fine," he said. "Four-wheel drive. Snow tires. Cell phone."

"No," Cath said harshly. "Don't be an idiot. We're lucky that we got here okay – you're not going back."

Levi bit his lips and raised his eyebrows helplessly.

Her dad walked past them to the door. "Jesus," he said from the porch. "She's right, Levi – I'm just going to keep saying your name until I remember it, is that okay?"

"Yes, sir."

Cath pulled on Levi's sleeve. "You're staying, all right?"

He licked his bottom lip nervously. She wasn't used to seeing him nervous. "Yes, ma'am," he whispered.

"Okay," her dad said, walking back into the living room, "dinner . . ." He still looked like he was in a Franken-fog.

"I got it," Cath said. "You keep working. You look like you're on to something."

He smiled at her gratefully. "Thanks, honey. Just give me another half hour to sort through this." He turned back to his concepts. "Levi, take off your coat."

Cath started taking off her boots and hung her coat on a hook. She pulled on Levi's sleeve again. "Take off your coat."

He did.

"Come on," she said, walking into the kitchen. Everything

seemed in order. She glanced into her dad's room and into the bathroom. No toothpaste poetry.

"I'm sorry," Levi said when they got into the kitchen.

"Shut up," she said. "You're making me nervous."

"I should go."

"Not as nervous as I'd be if you were driving home in a blizzard. Jesus. Sit down. It's okay, okay?"

He smiled a Levi smile — "Okay" — and sat down on one of the stools.

"It's weird to see you here," she said. "Like, worlds colliding."

Levi ran his fingers through his hair, shaking out a bit of snow. "Your dad seems unfazed."

"He's used to guys being around."

Levi cocked an eyebrow. "Really?"

"My sister . . . ," Cath said, feeling her cheeks warm.

She opened the refrigerator. Her grandmother had obviously been here. All her dad's crusty condiment bottles were gone, and there were Tupperware containers labeled with grease pencil. Plus fresh milk and eggs and yogurt. She opened the freezer. . . . Healthy Choice meals, probably the same Healthy Choice meals as the last time Cath was home.

She looked over at Levi. "How do you feel about eggs?"

"Awesome." He smiled. "I feel awesome about eggs."

One of the Tupperware containers had Italian sausage with red peppers. Cath emptied it into a pan and decided to make poached eggs. Just to show off. There was bread for toast. And butter. This wouldn't be half bad.

"Can I help you?" Levi asked.

"No. I've got this." She glanced over her shoulder at him, then smiled back down at the stove. "Let me do something for you for once."

"Okay . . . ," he said. "What's your dad doing in there?"

She told him. She told him about Fucking Kelly and Gravioli –
and the time they'd gone to the Grand Canyon on a family
vacation, and their dad had sat in the rental car with a notebook
and a Sharpie.

Her dad had worked on a lot of agricultural clients over the
years, this being Nebraska, and Levi actually recognized a line
he'd written for a fertilizer: *Bigger yields, brighter fields – trust next
year to Spurt.*

"Your dad's a Mad Man," he said.

Cath laughed, and Levi looked sheepish. "That's not what I
meant."

They ate at the dining room table, and by the middle of dinner,
Cath felt like maybe she didn't have to be so nervous. Levi had
relaxed into a slightly more polite version of his usual everyone-
must-love-me self, and her dad just seemed happy that Cath was
home.

Her eggs were *perfect*.

The only sour note was when her dad asked about Wren. Cath
shrugged and changed the subject. He didn't seem to notice. He
was a little twitchy and tappy tonight, a little distant, but Cath
decided he was just lost in work. His color was good, and he told
her he'd been jogging every morning. Every once in a while, he
seemed to surface enough to give Levi an appraising look.

After dinner, Levi insisted on clearing the table and doing the
dishes. As soon as he was in the kitchen, her dad leaned over. "Is
that your boyfriend in there?" Cath rolled her eyes, but she
nodded.

"For how long?"

"A month," Cath said. "Sort of. Longer. I don't know."

"How old is he?"

"Twenty-one."

"He looks older. . . ."

"It's the hair."

Her dad nodded. "He seems nice."

"He's the nicest," Cath said as sincerely as she could, wanting him to believe her. "He's a good guy, I swear."

"I didn't know you'd broken up with Abel."

Once the dishes were done – Cath dried – she and Levi were going to watch a movie, but her dad winced when she started moving his papers off the couch.

"Do you guys mind watching TV upstairs? I promise, Cath, I'm all yours tomorrow. I just—"

"Sure," she said. "Not too late, okay?"

He smiled, but he was already turning back to his notebook.

Cath looked at Levi and motioned her head toward the stairs. She felt him on the steps behind her, her stomach tightening all the way. When they got to the top, Levi touched the back of her arm, and she stepped away from him into her bedroom.

It looked like a kid's room now that she was imagining it through his eyes. It was big, a half story, with a slanted roof, deep-pink carpet, and two matching, cream-colored canopy beds.

Every inch of the walls and ceiling was covered with posters and pictures; she and Wren never really took things down as they got older. They just put new things up. Shabby Simon Snow chic.

When Cath looked up at Levi, his eyes were sparkling, and he was biting his bottom lip. She pushed him and he burst into laughter.

"This is the cutest thing I've ever seen," he said.

She sighed. "Okay . . ."

"No, seriously. I feel like this room should be preserved so that people of the future know what it was like to be a teenage girl in the twenty-first century."

"I get it—"

"Oh God," Levi said, still giggling. "I can't take it—" He started walking back down the stairs, and then, after a second, he walked back up and re-burst into laughter.

"*Okay,*" Cath said, walking over to her bed and sitting down against the headboard. Her comforter was pink and green plaid. She had Simon Snow pillowcases. There was a Sanrio mobile hanging over her head like a dream-catcher.

Levi strolled over to her bed and sat down in the middle. "You look so blindingly cute right now, I feel like I need to make a pinhole in a piece of paper just to look at you."

She rolled her eyes, and Levi swung his feet up, pushing them through hers so their legs crossed at the shins. "I still can't believe your dad sent me up to your room the first time he met me. All he knows about me is that I took you out into a blizzard."

"He's just like that," Cath said. "He's never kept us on much of a leash."

"Never? Not even when you were kids?"

"Uh-uh." She shook her head. "He trusts us. Plus, you saw him – his mind wanders."

"Well, when you meet my parents, don't expect my mom to let us out of her sight."

"I'll bet Reagan loved that."

Levi's eyes widened. "There is no love lost between my mom and Reagan, believe me. Reagan's older sister got pregnant her senior year, and my mom was pretty sure it ran in families. She had her whole prayer circle working on us. When she found out we broke up, she actually raised her hands to heaven."

Cath smiled uncomfortably and pulled a pillow into her lap, picking at the fabric.

"Does it bother you when I talk about Reagan?" he asked.

"I'm the one who brought her up."

"Does it?"

"A little," Cath said. "Tell me more about your mom."

"I finally get you up to a room, and now we're talking about my ex-girlfriend and my mom."

Cath smiled down at the pillow.

"Well . . . ," he said. "My mom grew up on a ranch. She quilts. She's active in her church."

"What kind?"

"Baptist."

"What's her name?"

"Marlisse," he said. "What's your mom's name?"

"Laura."

"What's she like?"

Cath raised her eyebrows and shrugged. "She was an artist. I mean, maybe she still is. She and my dad met at an ad agency right out of college."

He knocked one of his knees against hers. "And . . ."

Cath sighed. "And she didn't want to get married or get pregnant or anything like that. They weren't even dating seriously, she was trying to get a job in Minneapolis or Chicago. . . . But she got pregnant – I think it ran in her family, too, there were *generations* of pregnancies – so they got married." Cath looked up at him. "And it was a disaster. She didn't want one baby, so two was a nasty surprise."

"How do you know all that? Did your dad tell you?"

"*She* told us. She thought we should know who she really was and how she'd ended up in such a lamentable situation, I guess so that we wouldn't make the same mistakes."

"What did she expect you to learn?"

"I don't know," Cath said. "Stay away from men? Maybe just 'use a condom.' Or 'stay away from men who don't know how to work a condom.'"

"You're making me appreciate the prayer circle."

Cath laughed for half a breath.

"When did she leave?" he asked. He already knew that her mom had left. Cath had told him once in a way that let him know she didn't want to elaborate. But now . . .

"When we were eight," she said.

"Did you see it coming?"

"No." Cath looked up at him. "I don't think anyone would ever see that coming. I mean, when you're a kid, you don't expect your mom to leave, no matter what, you know? Even if you think she doesn't like you."

"I'm sure she liked you."

"She left," Cath said, "and she never came back. Who does that?"

"I don't know . . . someone who's missing a piece."

Cath felt tears in her eyes, and tried to blink them away.

"Do you miss her?" Levi asked.

"No," Cath said quietly, "I couldn't care less about her. I miss *Wren.*"

Levi pulled his legs back and leaned forward, crawling up Cath's bed until he was sitting next to her. He put his arm around her shoulder and pulled her into his chest. "Okay?"

She nodded and leaned into him hesitantly, like she wasn't sure how she'd fit. He traced circles on her shoulder with his thumb.

"You know," he said, "I keep wanting to say that it's like Simon Snow threw up in here . . . but it's more like someone else ate Simon Snow – like somebody went to an all-you-care-to-eat Simon Snow buffet – and *then* threw up in here."

Cath laughed. "I like it."

"Never said I didn't like it."

As long as they were talking, it was easy. And Levi was always talking.

He told her about 4-H.

"What do the *H*'s stand for?"

"Head, heart, hands, health. They don't have 4-H in South Omaha?"

"They do, but it stands for hard, hip-hop and Homey-don't-play-that."

"Well, I'm sorry to hear that. You missed out on a lot of competitive rabbit breeding."

"You raised rabbits?"

"Prize-winning rabbits," he said. "And one year, a sow."

"It's like you grew up on a different planet."

"Head, heart, hands, health . . . that's really nice, don't you think?"

"Are there photos of you somewhere with rabbits?"

"And blue ribbons," he said.

"I might have to make a pinhole camera just to look at them."

"Are you kidding? I was so cute, you'll have to wear special glasses. Oh, hey, I just remembered the 4-H pledge – 'I pledge my head to clearer thinking, my heart to greater loyalty, my hands to larger service, and my health to better living, for my club, my community, my country and my world.' "

Cath closed her eyes. "Where are those glasses?"

Then he told her about the state fair – more rabbits, more sows, plus a year of serious brownie-making – and he showed her photos of his four blond sisters on his phone.

Cath couldn't keep track of their names. They were all from the Bible. "Old Testament," Levi said. He had one sister Cath's age and one who was still in high school.

"Doesn't this creep you out?"

"What?"

"Dating someone as young as your little sister?"

"Dating my little sister would creep me out—"

"I'm still a teenager."

He shrugged. "You're legal."

She shoved him.

"Cath, I'm only two and a half years older than you."

"College years," she said. "That's like a decade."

He rolled his eyes.

"My dad thought you were thirty."

He pulled back his chin. "He did *not*. . . . Did he really?"

She giggled. "No."

Levi saw that she had Simon Snow *Scene It?* and insisted that they play. Cath thought she'd cream him, but his memory was insane, and all the questions were about the movies, not the books.

"Too bad for you that there aren't any questions about homosexual subtext," Levi said. "I want you to make me a blue ribbon when I win this."

At midnight, Cath started thinking about her dad downstairs and how he should really be getting some sleep.

"Are you tired?" she asked Levi.

"Do I get my own tent bed?"

"It's called a canopy, and no. You get your own couch. If I tell my dad you're tired, it'll force him to stop working."

Levi nodded.

"Do you need pajamas or something?"

"I can sleep in my clothes. It's only one night."

She found an extra toothbrush for him, dug out a clean sheet, and grabbed one of her pillows.

When they got downstairs, the papers had multiplied – but her dad gamely cleared off the couch and kissed Cath on the forehead. She made him promise not to keep working in his bedroom – "Don't make me yell at you in front of company." Cath made up the couch, and when Levi got out of the bathroom, his face and the front of his hair damp, she handed him the pillow. He set it on the couch and grinned at her.

"Do you need anything else?" she asked.

He shook his head. Cath took a step backwards and he caught her hand. She ran her fingers along his palm, pulling away.

"Good night," she said.

"Good night, sweetheart."

Cath woke up at three, her head too clear and her heart beating too fast.

She tiptoed down the stairs, but she knew they'd still creak.

She walked through the kitchen, made sure the stove was turned off, that the back door was locked, that everything was okay. . . .

Her dad's door was open; she stood in the doorway until she could hear him breathe. Then she walked as quietly as she could past the couch. The front door was locked. The curtains were drawn. A snowplow was crawling up their street.

When she turned around, Levi had raised himself up on his elbow and was watching her.

He'd taken off his sweater and had on a loose white T-shirt. His hair was wild, and his lips and eyes were thick with sleep.

Head, heart, hands . . .

"What's wrong?" he whispered.

Cath shook her head and hurried back upstairs.

Levi had to leave before breakfast; he had to get to Starbucks. Jim Flowers, her dad's favorite weatherman, said that the roads were much better, but that everybody should "take it slow out there."

Her dad said he'd drive Cath back to school on Sunday, but

Levi looked at the snowed-in Honda and said it was no trouble to come back.

"So . . . ," her dad said. They were standing on the porch, watching Levi's truck turn the corner. "That's your new boyfriend."

She nodded.

"Still dying to move home? Transfer to UNO? Spend your whole life taking care of your mentally unstable father?"

Cath pushed past him into the living room. "Breakfast?"

It was a good weekend. Five thousand words of *Carry On*. Fish tacos with radish and shredded cabbage. Only two more conversations about Wren. And Sunday afternoon brought Levi back, taking her front steps two at a time.

The Humdrum bounced a small red ball in its hand.

Simon had carried that ball everywhere, for at least a year. He'd lost it when he came to Watford – he hadn't needed it anymore.

"You're lying," Simon said. "You're not me. You're no part of me."

"I'm what's left of you," the Humdrum said. And Simon would swear his own voice was never so high and so sweet.

—from chapter 23, *Simon Snow and the Seventh Oak,*

copyright © 2010 by *Gemma T. Leslie*

TWENTY-EIGHT

"Geez, Cather, if you need a break, just tell me."

Levi was lying on her dorm-room bed, and he'd just told her that he was going home for a few days for his sister's birthday party – and instead of saying *I'll miss you* or even *Have fun,* Cath had said, "Oh, that's perfect."

"I didn't mean it like that," she apologized. "It's just, my dad's going to Tulsa this weekend, so he doesn't need me. And if you're going home, you won't need me, and that means I have all weekend to write; I'm so far behind on *Carry On.* . . ."

So far behind. And so out of rhythm.

If she didn't work on her fic, at least a little bit, every day, Cath lost the thread of it, the momentum. She ended up writing long, go-nowhere conversations – or scenes where Baz and Simon memorized the planes in each other's faces. (These scenes were weirdly popular with commenters, but they didn't help the story along.)

"I'll still *need* you," Levi said, teasing.

There followed a long go-nowhere conversation during which she tried to memorize the planes of his face. (It was harder than you'd think; they were constantly shifting.) She'd almost kissed him then. . . .

She'd almost kissed him again this afternoon, when he'd stopped by her dormitory to say good bye on his way out of town.

Cath had stood on the sidewalk, and Levi had leaned out of the cab of his truck, and it would have been so easy to just meet him halfway. It would have been safe, too, because he was trapped in the truck and also leaving the city. So no cascade effect. No one-thing-leads-to-another. No *another*.

If Cath had kissed him – if she'd let Levi know that he could kiss her – she wouldn't still be living off that half-asleep kiss from November. . . .

It had been six hours since Levi left for Arnold, and Cath had already written two thousand words of Simon. She'd made so much progress tonight, she was thinking about taking a break tomorrow to start her Fiction-Writing assignment – maybe she'd even finish it. It would be awesome to tell Levi she was done when he came home on Sunday.

Cath was leaning back in her chair, stretching her arms, when the door flew open and Reagan barged in. (Cath didn't even jump.)

"Well, look who we have here," Reagan said. "All by her lonesome. Shouldn't you be off bonding somewhere with the pride of Arnold?"

"He went home for his sister's birthday."

"I know." Reagan walked over to her closet and stood there, deliberating. "He tried to get me to ride with him. That boy's allergic to solitude."

"He tried to get me to go with him, too," Cath said.

"Where would you have stayed?"

"He hadn't worked that out."

"Ha," Reagan said, loosening her Olive Garden necktie. "I'd go back to Arnold for that. To see you meet Marlisse."

"Is she really that bad?"

"Probably not anymore. I broke her in for you—" Reagan lifted her white button-down shirt over her head and reached for a black sweater. Her bra was bright purple.

This. This was exactly the sort of thing that crawled into Cath's head and kept her from kissing Levi. Getting to see his ex-girlfriend's Technicolor lingerie. Knowing exactly who it was who broke him in. If only Cath didn't *like* Reagan so much . . .

Reagan crossed over to Cath's side of the room, leaning over and sticking the top of her head in Cath's face. "Does my hair smell like garlic bread?"

Cath took a cautious breath. "Not unpleasantly."

"Damn," Reagan said, standing back up. "I don't have time to wash it." She shook her hair out in front of the mirror on the door, then picked up her purse. "Okay," she said, "unless something goes incredibly wrong, you should have the room to yourself to-night. Don't do anything I wouldn't do."

"I haven't so far," Cath said dryly.

Reagan snorted and walked out.

Cath frowned at the door. *Don't be jealous.* There was already a rule about this, but Cath should make another one, just for herself: *Don't compare yourself to Reagan. It's like comparing apples and . . . grapefruits.*

When her phone rang a few minutes later, Cath shook off the last of her green feelings and smiled. Levi was supposed to call her before he went to bed. She picked up the phone and was about to answer when she saw Wren's name on the screen. WREN.

She and Wren hadn't talked – they hadn't even texted – since Christmas break. Almost three months ago. Why would Wren be calling her now? Maybe it was a mistake. Maybe it was just another wrong *C*.

Cath held the phone in her palm and stared at it, like she was waiting for an explanation.

The phone stopped ringing. Cath watched. It started again.

WREN.

Cath pushed Accept and held the phone up to her ear. "Hello?"

"Hello?" It wasn't Wren's voice. "Cather?"

"Yes?"

"Thank God. It's . . . your mom."

Your mom. Cath pulled her ear away.

"Cather?"

"Yes," Cath said faintly.

"I'm at the hospital with Wren."

Your mom. Cather.

Wren.

"Why? Is she okay?"

"She's had too much to drink. Someone – honestly, I don't really know anything – someone dropped her off. I thought maybe *you'd* know."

"No," Cath said, "I don't. I'm coming. You're at the hospital?"

"St. Elizabeth's. I called your dad already – he's flying back."

"Right," Cath said. "I'm coming."

"Okay," Laura said. *Your mom.* "Good."

Cath nodded, still holding the phone away from her ear, then let it drop to her lap and pressed End.

Reagan came back for her. Cath had tried to call Levi first – not because she thought he could help, he was four hours away – but she wanted to touch base. (The "tag" kind of base. The kind that means safe.) Levi didn't pick up, so she sent him a bare-bones text, *"wren's in the hospital,"* then called her dad. He didn't pick up either.

Reagan knew where St. Elizabeth's was and dropped Cath off at the front door. "Do you need company?"

"No," Cath said, hoping that Reagan would see right through her. Reagan didn't. She drove away, and Cath stood for a moment in the revolving door, feeling like she couldn't push through.

The hospital was mostly locked up for the night. The reception desk was empty, and the main elevators were turned off. Cath eventually made her way to the emergency room. A clerk there told her that Wren was already upstairs, and sent Cath down another empty hallway. Eventually she was stepping out of an elevator onto the sixth floor, not sure whom she was looking for.

When she tried to picture Laura, all Cath could remember was what her mother looked like in family photos. Long brown hair, big brown eyes. Silver rings. Faded jeans. In a simple yellow sundress on her wedding day, already starting to show.

That woman wasn't here.

The waiting room was empty except for a blond woman sitting in the corner, her fists clenched in her lap. She looked up when Cath walked into the room.

"Cather?"

It took a few seconds for the lines and colors to resolve into a face Cath thought she might recognize. In those seconds, a part of Cath ran to the blond stranger, wrapped her arms around her thighs, and pressed her face into her stomach. Part of Cath screamed. As loud as she could. And part of her set the whole world on fire just to watch it burn.

The woman stood up and stepped toward Cath.

Cath stood still.

Laura walked past her to the nurses' station and said something quietly.

"You're the sister?" the nurse asked, looking up.

Cath nodded.

"We just need you to answer a few questions."

Cath did her best. She didn't know what Wren had been drinking. She didn't know where she'd been or whom she was with.

All the other questions felt like things Cath shouldn't answer in front of a stranger – in front of Laura, who was just standing there, watching Cath's face like she was taking notes. Cath looked at her, helplessly, defensively, and Laura walked back to the corner. *Was Wren a regular drinker?* Yes. *Did she often drink to drunkenness?* Yes. *Did she black out?* Yes. *Did she use any other drugs?* I don't know. *Was she on any medication?* Birth control. *Do you have an insurance card?* Yes.

"Can I see her?" Cath asked.

"Not yet," the nurse answered.

"Is she okay?"

"I'm not her nurse. But the doctor just briefed your mom."

Cath looked back at Laura, at her mom, at this upset blond woman with tired eyes and really expensive jeans. Cath went to sit across from her, steadying herself. This wasn't a reunion; this wasn't anything. Cath was here for Wren.

"Is she okay?"

Her mom looked up. "I think so. She hasn't woken up yet. Someone dropped her off at the emergency room a few hours ago, then left. I guess she wasn't breathing . . . enough. I don't really know how it works. They're giving her fluids. It's just time now. Waiting."

Laura's hair was cut into a long bob that hung like two sharp wings under her chin. She was wearing a stiff, white shirt and too many rings on her fingers.

"Why did they call you?" Cath asked. Maybe it was a rude thing to ask; she didn't care.

"Oh," Laura said. She reached into a cream-colored Coach bag and pulled out Wren's phone, holding it across the aisle.

Cath took it.

"They looked in her contacts," Laura said. "They said they always call the mom first."

The mom, Cath thought.

Cath dialed her dad's number. It went straight to voice mail. She stood up and walked a few chairs away, for two feet of privacy. "Dad, it's Cath. I'm at the hospital. I haven't seen Wren yet. I'll call you when I know more."

"I talked to him earlier," Laura said. "He's in Tulsa."

"I know," Cath said, looking down at the phone. "Why didn't *he* call me?"

"I . . . I said I would. He had to call the airline."

Cath sat back down, not right across from Laura anymore. She didn't have anything more to say to her, and there was nothing she wanted to hear.

"You —" Laura cleared her throat. She was starting every sentence like she didn't have the breath to finish it. "— you still look so much alike."

Cath jerked her head up to look at her.

It was like looking at nobody at all.

And then it was like looking at the person you expected to see comforting you when you woke up from a nightmare.

Whenever Levi had asked about her mother, Cath always said she didn't remember much. And that had always been true.

But now it wasn't. Now, just sitting this close to Laura unlocked some secret, half-sized door in Cath's brain. And she could see her mom, in perfect focus, sitting on the other side of their dining room table. She was laughing at something that Wren had said – so Wren kept saying it, and their mom kept laughing. She laughed through her nose. Her hair was dark, and she tucked Sharpies into her ponytail, and she could draw anything. A flower. A seahorse. A unicorn. And when she was irritated, she snapped at them. Snapped her fingers. Snap, snap, snap, while she was talking on the phone. Stern eyebrows, bared teeth. "*Shhh.*" She was in the bedroom with their dad, shouting. She was at the zoo, helping Wren chase a peacock. She was rolling out dough for gingerbread cookies. She was on the phone, snapping. She was in the bedroom, yelling. She was standing on the porch, pushing Cath's hair behind her ears again and again, stroking her cheek with a long, flat thumb, and making promises she wasn't going to keep.

"We're twins," Cath said. Because it was the stupidest thing she could think to say. Because that's what "you still look so much alike" deserved when your mom was the one saying it.

Cath took out her phone and texted Levi. *"at the hospital now, still haven't seen wren. alcohol poisoning. my mom's here. i'll call you tomorrow."* And then she texted, *"i'm glad that you're out there somewhere reading this, eventually reading this, it makes me feel better."* Her battery indicator turned red.

Laura got out her phone, too. (Why was Cath calling her that? When she was a kid, Cath hadn't even known their mom's name. Their dad called her "honey" – strained and tense and careful – "honey" – and their mom called him "Art.") Laura was texting someone, probably her husband, and for some reason it pissed Cath off. That she was texting someone right now. That she was flaunting her new life.

Cath folded her arms and watched the nurses' station. When she felt the tears coming on, she told herself that they were for Wren, and surely some of them were.

They waited.

And waited.

But not together.

Laura got up to use the bathroom once. She walked like Wren, hips swaying, flicking her hair away from her face. "Would you like some coffee?" she asked.

"No, thank you," Cath said.

While Laura was gone, Cath tried to call her dad again. If he answered the phone, she was pretty sure she'd cry some more, she might even call him "Daddy." He didn't answer.

Laura brought back a bottle of water and set it on the table next to Cath. Cath didn't open it.

The nurses ignored them. Laura flipped through a magazine. When a doctor walked out to the waiting room, they both stood up.

"Mrs. Avery?" he said, looking at Cath's mother.

"How is she?" Laura said, which Cath thought was a deft response.

"I think she's going to be fine," the doctor said. "Her breathing is good. Her oxygen is good. She's sucking up those fluids – and she roused a bit to talk to me a few minutes ago. I think this is just going to be a scare. . . . Sometimes a scare can be valuable."

"Can I see her?" Cath asked.

The doctor looked over at Cath. She could almost hear him think *twins*. "Yeah," he said. "That should be fine. We're just running another test. I'll have the nurse come out for you when we're done."

Cath nodded and folded her arms again around her stomach.

"Thank you," Laura said.

Cath went back to her chair to wait. But Laura stood there by the nurses' station. After a minute, she walked back to her chair and picked up her Coach bag, tucking a used Kleenex into a pocket and nervously smoothing out the leather straps.

"Well," she said. "I think I'm going to head home."

"What?" Cath's head snapped up.

"I should go," Laura said. "Your dad will be here soon."

"But – you can't."

Laura slid her handbag up over her arm.

"You heard the doctor," Cath said. "We're going to be able to see her in a few minutes."

"You go see her," Laura said. "You should go."

"You should come, too."

"Is that what you really want?" Laura's voice was sharp, and part of Cath shrank back.

"It's what Wren would want."

"Don't be so sure," Laura said, sounding tired again, pinching the bridge of her nose. "Look . . . I shouldn't be here. It was a fluke that they called me. You're here now, your dad's on his way—"

"You don't just leave somebody alone in the hospital," Cath said. It came out aflame.

"Wren's not alone," Laura said sternly. "She has you."

Cath jerked to her feet and swayed there. *Not Wren,* she thought. *I didn't mean Wren.*

Laura wrenched her handbag straps higher. "Cather—"

"You can't leave like this—"

"It's the right thing to do," Laura said, lowering her voice.

"In what alternate universe?" Cath felt the rage burst up her throat like a cork popping. "What sort of a mother leaves the hospital without seeing her kid? What sort of a mother *leaves*? Wren is unconscious – and if you think that has nothing to do with you, you are skimming the surface of reality – and I'm right here, and you haven't even seen me for ten years, and now you're leaving? Now?"

"Don't make this about *me*," Laura hissed. "You obviously don't want me here."

"I'm making it about *me*," Cath said. "It's not my job to want you or not want you. It's not my job to earn you."

"Cather" – Laura's mouth and fists were tight – "I've reached out to you. I've tried."

"You're *my mother*," Cath said. Her fists were even tighter. "Try harder."

"This isn't the time or the place for this," Laura said softly, steadily, tugging on her handbag. "I'll talk to Wren later. I'd love to talk to you later, too. I'd love to *talk* to you, Cather — but I don't belong here right now."

Cath shook her head. "Now is all you get," she spat out, wishing she could make more sense. Wishing for more words, or better ones. "Now is all you ever get."

Laura lifted her chin and flicked her hair away from her face. She wasn't listening anymore. She was the Cool One. "I don't belong here," she said again. "I won't intrude like this."

And then she walked away. Shoulders back, hips swaying.

He'd have to tell the Mage what he saw.

I've finally seen the Humdrum, sir. I know what we're fighting –
me.

"What's left of you," the monster had said.

What is *left of me?* Simon wondered. *A ghost? A hole? An echo?*
An angry little boy with nervous hands?

—from chapter 24, *Simon Snow and the Seventh Oak,*

copyright © 2010 by Gemma T. Leslie

TWENTY-NINE

It was another hour before the nurse came back. Cath drank her bottled water. She wiped her face in her shirt. She thought about how much nicer this waiting room was than the one at St. Richard's. She tried to mess with her phone, but it was dead.

When the nurse came out, Cath stood up. "Are you here for Wren Avery?"

Cath nodded.

"You can come back now. Do you want to wait for your mom?"

Cath shook her head.

Wren was in a room by herself. It was dark, and her eyes were closed. Cath couldn't tell if she was sleeping.

"Do I need to watch for anything?" Cath asked the nurse.

"No, she's just resting now."

"Our dad will be here soon," Cath said.

"Okay. We'll send him back."

Cath sat down slowly, quietly, in the chair by Wren's bed. Wren looked pale. She had a dark spot, maybe a bruise, on her cheek. Her hair was longer than it had been at Christmas, hanging over her eyes and curling at her neck. Cath pushed it back.

"I'm awake, you know," Wren whispered.

"Are you still drunk?"

"A little. Muzzy."

Cath tucked Wren's hair back again in a soothing gesture. Soothing for Cath, anyway. "What happened?"

"Don't remember."

"Who brought you in?"

Wren shrugged. There was an IV in her arm and something taped to her index finger. Up close, she smelled like puke. And like Wren – like Tide and Marc Jacobs Lola.

"Are you okay?"

"Muzzy," she said. "Sick."

"Dad's coming."

Wren groaned.

Cath folded her arms on the edge of the mattress and laid her head down, exhaling. "I'm glad they brought you in," she said, "whoever it was who brought you in. I'm . . . sorry."

That I wasn't there, that you didn't want me there, that I wouldn't have known how to stop you anyway.

Now that she was with Wren and Wren was okay, Cath realized how exhausted she was. She shoved her glasses into her coat pocket and laid her head back down. She was just drifting off – or maybe she'd just drifted off – when she heard Wren whimper. Cath lifted her head. Wren was crying. Her eyes were closed, and tears were running down into her hair. Cath could almost feel the tickle. "What's wrong?"

Wren shook her head. Cath wiped Wren's tears away with her fingers, and wiped her fingers on her shirt.

"Should I get the nurse?"

Wren shook her head again and started shifting in the bed. "Here," she said, making room.

"Are you sure?" Cath asked. "I don't want to be the reason you choke on your own vomit."

"None left," Wren whispered.

Cath kicked off her boots and climbed up over the railing, lying down in the space Wren had cleared for her. She put her arm carefully under Wren's neck. "Here," Cath said.

Wren curled against her with her head on Cath's shoulder. Cath tried to untangle the tubes around Wren's arm, then held her hand tightly. It was sticky.

Wren's shoulders were still shaking.

"It's okay," Cath said. "It's okay."

Cath tried not to fall asleep until Wren did, but it was dark, and she was tired, and everything was blurry.

"Oh, God," she heard their dad say. "Oh, Wren. Baby."

Cath opened her eyes, and her dad was leaning over them both, kissing both of their foreheads. Cath sat up carefully.

Wren's eyes were crusty and puffy, but open.

Their dad stood back and put his hand on Wren's cheek. "Jesus Christ," he said, shaking his head. "Kid."

He was wearing gray dress pants and a light blue shirt, untucked. His tie, orange with white starbursts, was stuffed into and hanging out of his pocket. Presentation clothes, Cath thought.

She checked his eyes out of habit. They were tired and shining, but clear.

Cath felt overwhelmed then, all of a sudden, and even though this wasn't her show, she leaned forward and hugged him, pressing her face into his stale shirt until she could hear his heart beating. His arm came up, warm, around her. "Okay," he said roughly. Cath felt Wren take her hand. "Okay," their dad said again. "We're okay now."

———

Wren didn't have to stay in the hospital. "You can sleep and drink water at home," the doctor said.

Real home. Omaha. "You're coming back with me," their dad said, and Wren didn't argue.

"I'm coming, too," Cath said, and he nodded.

A nurse took out Wren's IV, and Cath helped her to the bathroom, patting her back while she dry-heaved over the sink. Then Cath helped her wash her face and change into her clothes — jeans and a tank top.

"Where's your coat?" their dad asked. Wren just shrugged. Cath took off her cardigan and handed it to her.

"It smells like sweat," Wren said.

"It'll be the best-smelling part of you," Cath answered.

Then they had to wait for Wren's paperwork. The nurse asked if she'd like to speak to an addictions specialist. Wren said no. Their dad just frowned.

"Have you eaten anything?" Cath asked him.

He yawned. "We'll drive though someplace."

"I'm driving," Cath said.

Their dad had tried to get a flight out of Tulsa the night before, but there weren't any until this afternoon, so he'd ended up renting a car — "Kelly gave me the agency Visa" — and driving for seven hours.

The nurse came back with discharge papers and told Wren that she'd have to leave the hospital in a wheelchair. "It's policy."

Wren complained, but their dad just stood behind the wheelchair and said, "Do you want to argue or do you want to go home?"

When the nurse buzzed them out into the waiting room, Cath felt her stomach jump and realized that she was half-expecting to see Laura still sitting out there. *Fat chance*, Cath thought.

The doors opened, and Wren made a sobby little gasping noise.

For a second Cath thought maybe Laura *was* still there. Or maybe Wren was trying to throw up again.

There was a guy sitting in the waiting room with his head in his hands. He heard Wren's gasp and looked up, then stood up, and Wren was out of the wheelchair, shuffling toward him. He took her in his arms and pushed his face down into her pukey hair.

It was the big guy from Muggsy's. The guy who threw punches. Cath couldn't remember his name. Javier. Julio . . .

"Who's that?" her dad asked.

"Jandro," Cath said.

"Ah," he said, watching them hug. "Jandro."

"Yeah . . ." Cath hoped that it wasn't Jandro who dropped Wren off at the emergency room, then left her alone. She hoped that he didn't know anything about that bruise on her cheek.

"Hey," someone said, and Cath stepped aside, realizing she was standing in the middle of the hallway. "Hey," he said again.

She looked up – and into Levi's smiling face.

"Hey," she said, and it almost came out with an exclamation point. "What are you doing here?"

"I got your text – I texted you back."

"My phone's dead." Cath looked up at Levi's crinkle-cut eyes and relieved smile, trying to take him all in.

He was holding two cups of coffee and had a banana shoved into the pocket of his flannel shirt. "Mr. Avery?" he said, holding out a cup of coffee. "This was for Jandro, but it looks like he's covered."

Her dad took the coffee. "Thanks. Levi."

"Levi," Cath repeated, and she knew she was close to crying. "You didn't have to come."

He made a loose fist and chucked her gently on the bottom of her chin, taking a half step toward her. "Yeah, I did."

Cath tried not to smile – but ended up smiling so wide, her ears almost popped.

"They wouldn't let me back," he said. "Or Jandro. Only immediate family."

Cath nodded.

"Is your sister okay?"

"Yeah. Hungover. Embarrassed . . . We're going back to Omaha now, all three of us."

"Are *you* okay?"

"Yeah. *Yeah*." She reached for his hand and squeezed it. "Thank you," she said.

"You didn't even know I was here."

"I know now, and I'll apply these feelings backwards. Thank you. . . . Did you miss your sister's birthday party?"

"No, it's tomorrow after church. I'll take a nap and head back that way – unless you need anything."

"Nope."

"Are you hungry?"

Cath laughed. "Are you about to offer me a banana?"

"I'm about to offer you *half* a banana," Levi said, letting go of her hand. He gave her the coffee and took the banana out of his pocket, peeling it. Cath glanced over at Wren. She was introducing their dad to Jandro. Wren looked like hell, but Jandro was looking at her like she was the Lady of the Lake. Levi handed Cath half a banana, and she took it. "Cheers," he said, tapping his hand against hers.

Cath ate the banana and held on to his gaze. "I'd give you the moon right now," she said.

Levi's eyes flashed happily, and he hitched up an eyebrow. "Yeah, but would you slay it for me?"

———

Cath drove home. They drove through McDonald's first, and her dad ordered two Filet-O-Fish sandwiches and said that neither of them could nag him about it.

Wren grimaced. "I don't even care if it's bad for your cholesterol. It's the smell that's making me sick."

"Maybe you shouldn't have drunk yourself into a bilious stupor," their dad said. And that's when Cath realized that he wasn't going to pretend that nothing was wrong. That he wasn't just going to let Wren go about her business.

Cath smashed her cheeseburger against the steering wheel and was the only person on the interstate observing the speed limit.

When they got home, Wren went straight in to take a shower.

Her dad stood in the living room, looking lost. "You go next," Cath told him. "I'm not that gross."

"We have to talk about all this," he said. "Tonight. I mean, not you. You don't. Wren and I have to talk. I should have talked to her at Christmas, but there was so much else going on—"

"I'm sorry."

"Don't, Cath."

"It's my fault, too. I hid it from you."

He took off his glasses and rubbed his forehead. "Not that well. I saw what she was doing. . . . I thought she'd, I don't know, self-correct. That she'd get it out of her system."

His necktie had worked its way almost completely out of his pocket. "You should sleep," Cath said. "Take a shower, then sleep."

Wren walked out of the bathroom wearing their dad's robe and smiled feebly at them. Cath patted her dad's arm, then followed Wren upstairs. When Cath got up to their room, Wren was standing at her dresser, impatiently riffling through a mostly empty drawer. "We don't have any pajamas."

"Calm down, Junie B. Jones," Cath said, walking over to her own dresser. "Here." She handed Wren a T-shirt and a pair of shorts left over from high school gym.

Wren changed and climbed into her bed. Cath crawled on top of the comforter beside her.

"You smell like puke," Wren said.

"Yours," Cath said. "How are you feeling?"

"Tired." Wren closed her eyes.

Cath tapped softly on Wren's forehead. "Was that your boyfriend?"

"Yes," Wren whispered. "Alejandro."

"Alejandro," Cath said, breathing the *j* and rolling the *r*. "Have you been dating since last semester?"

"Yes."

"Were you out with him last night?"

Wren shook her head. Tears were starting to pool between her eyelashes.

"Who'd you go out with?"

"Courtney."

"How'd you bruise your face?"

"I don't remember."

"But it wasn't Alejandro."

Wren's eyes flew open. "God, Cath. *No.*" She squeezed her eyes shut again and flinched. "He's probably going to break up with me. He hates it when I get drunk. He says it's unbecoming."

"He didn't look like he was going to break up with you this morning."

Wren took a deep, shuddering breath. "I can't think about it right now."

"Don't," Cath said. "Sleep."

Wren slept. Cath went downstairs. Her dad was already asleep. He'd skipped the shower.

Cath felt inexplicably peaceful. The last thing Levi had said to her, when they'd parted in the hospital lobby, was, "Plug in your phone." So Cath did. Then she started some laundry.

"We can't be friends," Baz said, passing Simon the ball.

"Why not?" Simon asked, kicking the ball up and bouncing it on his knee.

"Because we're already enemies."

"It's not like we have to stay that way. There isn't a rule."

"There is a rule," Baz said. "I made it myself. *Don't be friends with Snow. He already has too many.*" He shouldered Simon out of the way and caught the ball on his own knee.

"You're infuriating," Simon said.

"Good. I'm fulfilling my role as your nemesis."

"You're not my nemesis. The Humdrum is."

"Hmmm," Baz said, letting the ball drop and kicking it back to Simon. "We'll see. The story's not over yet."

—from "Baz, You Like It," posted September 2008
by FanFixx.net authors *Magicath* and *Wrenegade*

THIRTY

"We don't need to talk about this," Wren said.

"You were just hospitalized for alcohol poisoning," their dad said. "We're talking about it."

Cath set a stack of foil-wrapped burritos on the table between them, then sat down at the head of the table.

"There's nothing to say," Wren insisted. She still looked terrible. There were circles under her eyes, and her skin was waxy and yellow. "You're just going to say that I shouldn't drink that much, and then I'm going to say that you're right—"

"No," their dad interrupted, "I'm going to say that you shouldn't drink at all."

"Well, that's not very realistic."

He smacked his fist on the table. "Why the hell not?"

Wren sat back in her chair and took a second to recover. He'd never cursed at either of them. "Everybody drinks," she said calmly. The Only Rational One.

"Your sister doesn't."

Wren rolled her eyes. "Forgive me, but I'm not going to spend my college years sitting soberly in my dorm room, writing about gay magicians."

"Objection," Cath said, reaching for a burrito.

"Sustained," their dad said. "Your sister has a four-point-oh,

Wren. And a very polite boyfriend. She's doing just fine with her college years."

Wren's head whipped around. "You have a boyfriend?"

"You haven't met Levi?" Their dad sounded surprised – and sad. "Are you guys even talking?"

"You stole your roommate's boyfriend?" Wren's eyes were big.

"It's a long story," Cath said.

Wren kept staring at her. "Have you kissed him?"

"*Wren,*" their dad said. "I'm serious about this."

"What do you want me to say? I drank too much."

"You're out of control," he said.

"I'm fine. I'm just eighteen."

"Exactly," he said. "You're coming back home."

Cath almost spit out her carnitas.

"I am not," Wren said.

"You are."

"You can't make me," she said, managing to sound at least twelve.

"I can, actually." He was tapping his fingers so hard on the table, it looked painful. "I'm your father. I'm pulling rank. I should have done this a long time ago, but better late than never, I guess – *I'm your father.*"

"Dad," Cath whispered.

"No," he said, staring at Wren. "I am not letting this happen to you. I'm not taking a call like that again. I'm not spending every weekend from now on, wondering where you are and who you're with, and whether you're even sober enough to know when you've landed in the gutter."

Cath had seen her dad this mad before – heard him rant, watched him wave his arms around, cursing, steam pouring out of his ears – but it was never about them. It was never *at* them.

"This was a warning," he said, stabbing his finger at Wren,

nearly shouting. "This was your canary in the goddamn coal mine. And you're trying to ignore it. What kind of father would I be if I sent you back to that school, knowing you hadn't learned your lesson?"

"I'm eighteen!" Wren shouted. Cath thought this was probably a bad strategy.

"I don't care!" he shouted back. "You're still my daughter."

"It's the middle of the semester. I'll fail all my classes."

"You weren't worried about school or your future when you were poisoning yourself with tequila."

She cocked her head. "How did you know I was drinking tequila?"

"Christ, Wren," he sighed bitterly. "You smelled like a margarita blender."

"You kinda still do," Cath muttered.

Wren planted her elbows on the table and hid her face in her hands. "Everybody drinks," she said stubbornly.

Their dad pushed his chair back. "If that's all you have to say for yourself, then all I have to say is — *you're coming home*."

He got up and went into his room, slamming the door.

Wren let her head and her hands fall to the table.

Cath scooted her chair closer. "Do you want some aspirin?"

Wren was quiet for a few seconds. "Why aren't you mad at me?"

"Why should I be mad at you?" Cath asked.

"You've been mad at me since November. Since *July*."

"Well, I'm done now. Does your head hurt?"

"You're done?" Wren turned her head toward Cath, her cheek lying on the table.

"You scared me last night," Cath said. "And I decided that I never want to drift that far away from you again. What if you'd died? And I hadn't talked to you for three months?"

"I wasn't going to die." Wren rolled her eyes again.

"Dad's right," Cath said. "You sound like a moron."

Wren looked down, rubbing her face in her wrist. "I'm not going to stop drinking."

Why not? Cath wanted to ask. Instead she said, "Just pause, then. For the rest of the year. Just to show him that you can."

"I can't believe you have a boyfriend," Wren whispered, "and I didn't even know about it." Her shoulders started to shake. She was crying again. Cath had never seen Wren cry this much.

"Hey . . . ," Cath said, "it's okay."

"I wasn't going to *die*," Wren said.

"Okay."

"I just . . . I've really missed you. . . ."

"Are you still drunk?" Cath asked.

"I don't think so."

Cath leaned over, on the edge of her chair, and tugged at Wren's hair. "It's okay. I miss you, too. Not all this drunk stuff, but you."

"I've been a jerk to you," Wren whispered into the table.

"I was a jerk back."

"That's true," Wren said, "but . . . God, will you forgive me?"

"No," Cath said.

Wren looked up pathetically.

"I don't have to forgive you," Cath said. "It's not like that with you. You're just *in* with me. Always. No matter what happens."

Wren lifted her head and wiped her eyes with the back of her thumbs. "Yeah?"

Cath nodded her head. "Yeah."

Their dad went for a run.

Wren ate a burrito and went back to bed.

Cath finally read all her texts from Levi.

"turning round rite now .. be there by 3"

"cather .. i really care about you. seemed like maybe a good time to tell you that. hour a way now."

"in the waiting room, not family, cant come back, handros here to. here .. ok? if you need me"

"back in arnold. gorgous day. did you know arnold has loess canyons and sand hills? the biological diversaty would make you weep Cather Avery. call me sweetheart. and by that i mean that you should call me .. not that you should call me sweetheart tho you can if you want. call me call me call me."

Cath did. Levi was having dinner with his family. "You okay?" he asked.

"Yeah," she said, "it's just tense. My dad's mad at Wren, but he doesn't really know how to be mad at either of us – and Wren is acting like a huge brat. I don't think she knows how to be wrong."

"I wish I could talk more," Levi said, "but my mom's weird about phone calls during family time. I'll call you tomorrow from the road, okay?"

"Only if the road is straight and flat, and there's no other traffic."

"Will you be back tomorrow?" he asked.

"I don't know."

"I miss you."

"That's stupid," she said. "I saw you this morning."

"It's not the time," Levi said, and she could hear that he was smiling. "It's the distance."

A few minutes later he texted her: *"IDEA .. if your bored and you miss me you should write some dirty fan fiction about us. you can read it to me later. great idea right?"*

Cath smiled down at the phone stupidly.

She tried to imagine what it would be like to move back home now, to leave Levi behind. She couldn't even think about what it was going to be like this summer without him.

Their dad wouldn't really do this. Make Wren drop out of school. That would be crazy. . . .

But their dad *was* crazy. And maybe he was right: Wren was out of control. She was the worst kind of out of control – the kind that thinks it's just fine, thanks.

Cath liked the idea of Wren here. Wren and her dad, all in one place, where Cath could take care of them. If only Cath could break off a piece of herself and leave it here to keep watch.

The front door opened and her dad huffed in from his run, still breathing hard, dropping his keys and his phone on the table. "Hey," he said to Cath, taking off his glasses to wipe his face, then putting them back on.

"Hey," she said. "I put your burrito in the oven."

He nodded and walked past her into the kitchen. Cath followed.

"Are you coming to plead her case?" he asked.

"No."

"She could have died, Cath."

"I know. And . . . I think it's been bad for a long time. I think she's just been lucky."

"As far as we know," her dad said.

"I just . . . *dropping out of school*?"

"Do you have a better idea?"

Cath shook her head. "Maybe she should talk to a counselor or something."

Her dad made a face like Cath had thrown something wet at him. "God, Cath, how would you feel if somebody forced you to talk to a counselor?"

Somebody has, she thought. "I'd hate it," she said.

"Yeah . . ." He had the burrito out of the oven and onto a plate, and he was pouring himself a glass of milk. He looked tired still and completely miserable.

"I love you," she said.

He looked up, holding the carton of milk over the glass. Some of the strain disappeared from his forehead. "I love you, too," he said, like it was a question.

"It just seemed like a good time to tell you," she said.

Her dad nodded, his eyes full of some dense feeling.

"Can I borrow your laptop?" she asked.

"Yeah. Of course. It's in—"

"I know. Thanks." Cath went to the living room and picked up her dad's silver laptop. She'd lusted over this thing, but he always said she didn't need an eighteen-hundred-dollar word processor.

When Cath got upstairs, Wren was on the phone, crying. She got up off her bed and walked into the closet, sitting on the floor and closing the door behind her. This wasn't strange behavior, except for the crying – it's what they always did when they needed privacy. They had a big closet.

Cath opened her FanFixx account and paged idly through the comments. There were too many to respond to individually, so she posted a general, *"Hey, everybody, thanks – too busy writing to write back!"* then opened up the draft of her most recent chapter. . . .

She'd left off with Baz kneeling at his mother's gravestone. He was trying to explain to her why he was turning against his father, why he was turning his back on the house of Pitch to fight by Simon's side.

"It's not just for him," Baz said, *running his long fingers over his mother's name. "It's for Watford. It's for the World of Mages."*

After a while, Wren came out of the closet and crawled onto Cath's bed. Cath scooted over and kept typing.

After another while, Wren got under the covers and fell asleep.

And after that, a while later, their dad peeked up over the top of the stairs. He looked at Cath and mouthed, *Good night*. Cath nodded.

She wrote a thousand words.

She wrote five hundred more.

The room was dark, and Cath wasn't sure how long Wren had been awake or how long she'd been reading over Cath's elbow.

"Is the Mage really going to betray Simon, or is it a red herring?" Wren was whispering, even though there was nobody to wake up.

"I think he really is," Cath said.

"That chapter where he had Simon burn the dragon eggs made me cry for three days."

Cath stopped typing. "You read that?"

"Of course I did. Have you seen your hits lately? They're through the roof. Nobody's bailing on *Carry On* now."

"I thought you had," Cath said. "A long time ago."

"Well, you were wrong." Wren propped her head up on her hand. "Add that to the towering stack of important things you're wrong about."

"I think the Mage is going to kill Baz." Cath hadn't told anyone else that yet, not even her beta.

Wren sat up, her face actually aghast. "Cath," she whispered, "no . . ."

"Did Alejandro break up with you?"

Wren shook her head. "No . . . he's just upset. *Cath*. You can't kill Baz."

Cath couldn't think of what to say.

Wren took the laptop and slid it mostly into her own lap. "Jesus Christ, consider this an intervention. . . ."

When Cath woke up the next morning, Sunday, she was alone in the bedroom. She could smell coffee. And food.

She went downstairs and found her dad sitting at the table with a notebook. She handed him his laptop. "Ah. Good," he said. "Wren said we had to wait for you."

"For what?"

"For my verdict. I'm about to go all King Solomon on your asses."

"Who's King Solomon?"

"It was your mother who wanted to raise you without religion."

"She also thought you should raise us without a mother."

"Solid point, my dear. Wren? Come on. Your sister's awake."

Wren walked into the dining room, holding a saucepan and a trivet. "You were asleep," she said, setting it on the table, "so I made breakfast."

"Oh, Christ," their dad said. "Is that Gravioli?"

"No," Wren said, "it's new *Cheese* Gravioli."

"Sit down," he said. "We're talking." He was in running clothes again. He looked tense and nervous.

Wren sat down. She was acting playful, but she was nervous, too – Cath could tell by the way she was squeezing her fists. Cath wanted to reach out and unclench them.

"Okay," their dad said, pushing the Gravioli away, so that it wasn't right between them on the table. "Here are my terms. You can go back to school." Wren and Cath both exhaled. "But you don't drink. At all. Not in moderation, not with your boyfriend, not at parties – never. You see a counselor every week, starting this week, and you start attending AA meetings."

"Dad," Wren said. "I'm not an alcoholic."

"Good. It's not contagious. You're going to meetings."

"I'll go with you," Cath offered.

"I'm not done," their dad said.

"What more do you want?" Wren whined. "Blood tests?"

"You come home every weekend."

"*Dad.*"

"Or you can just move home. It's your choice, really."

"I have a life," Wren said. "In Lincoln."

"Don't talk to me about your life, kid. You've shown complete disregard for your life."

Wren's hands were tight fists, lumps of coal, in her lap. Cath kicked her ankle. Wren's head dropped. "Fine," she said. *"Fine."*

"Good," their dad said, then took a deep breath and held on to it for a second. "I'll drive you back later, if you think you're ready." He stood up and looked at the Gravioli. "I'm not eating that."

Cath pulled the pan closer and picked up a spoon. "I'll eat it." She took a bite. The noodly parts dissolved immediately in her mouth. "I like how soft it is," she said. "I like how I don't have to use my teeth."

Wren watched Cath for a few seconds, then took the spoon and scooped up a bite. "It tastes like regular Gravioli—"

Cath took it back. "But cheesier."

"It's three comfort foods in one," Wren said.

"They're like pizza pillows."

"They're like wet Cheetos."

"That's terrible," Cath said. "We can't use that."

"I'm starting to feel like you don't want me around."

"I've *never* wanted you around," Simon said, trying to push past his roommate.

"Point." Baz moved to block the door. "That *was* true. Until you decided that you *always* wanted me around – that life is just a hollow shell of itself unless you know my heart is beating somewhere in the very local vicinity."

"Have I decided that?"

"Maybe it was me who decided. Never mind. Same difference."

Simon took a deep, obviously unnerved, breath.

"Snow. Are you unnerved?"

"Slightly."

"Aleister almighty, I never thought I'd see the day."

—from *Carry On, Simon,* posted February 2012
by FanFixx.net author *Magicath*

THIRTY-ONE

Alejandro was waiting for them when they got to Schramm Hall. He shook hands with Cath formally. "Frat boy manners," Wren said, "they all have them." Jandro was in a fraternity on East Campus, she said, called FarmHouse. "That's actually its name."

Most of the FarmHouse guys were Ag majors from outstate Nebraska. Jandro was from Scottsbluff, which was practically Wyoming. "I didn't even know there were Mexicans out there," Wren said, "but he claims there's this huge community."

Jandro didn't say much besides, "It's nice to finally meet you, Cath. Wren talks about you all the time. When you post your Simon Snow stories, I'm not allowed to talk to her until she's finished." He looked like most of Wren's boyfriends – short hair, clean-cut, built to play football – but Cath couldn't remember Wren looking at any of them the way she looked at Alejandro. Like she'd been converted.

It was ten o'clock by the time Levi got back from Arnold.

Cath had already showered and put on pajamas. She felt like the weekend had been two years long, not two days. *Freshman days,* she could hear Levi say.

He called to tell her he was back. Knowing they were in the

same city again made the missing him flare up inside her. In her stomach. Why were people always going on and on about the heart? Almost everything Levi happened in Cath's stomach.

"Can I stop by?" he asked. Like he wanted it. "Say good night?"

"Reagan's here," Cath said. "She's in the shower. I think she's going to bed."

"Can you come down?"

"Where would we go?" Cath asked.

"We could sit in my truck—"

"It's freezing out."

"We could run the heater."

"The heater doesn't work."

"We could run the heater."

"The heater doesn't work."

He hesitated – "We could go to my house."

"Aren't your roommates home?" It was like she had a list of arguments, and she was going through them one by one – and she wasn't even sure why anymore.

"It doesn't matter," Levi pushed. "I have my own room. Plus, they want to meet you."

"I think I met most of them at the party."

Levi groaned. "How many ground rules did Reagan give us?"

"I don't know. Five, maybe? Six?"

"Okay, here's seven: No more talking about that godforsaken party unless it's absolutely relevant."

Cath smiled. "But what will I have left to needle you with?"

"I'm sure you'll come up with something."

"I won't," she said. "You're incessantly good to me."

"Come home with me, Cath." She could hear him smiling. "It's early, and I don't want to say good night."

"I never want to say good night, but we still manage."

"Wait, you don't?"

"No," she whispered.

"Come home with me," he whispered back.

"To your den of iniquity?"

"Yes, that's what everyone calls my room."

"Gah," Cath said. "I've told you. It's just too much . . . your house. Your room. We'll walk in, and all that will be in there is a bed. And I'll throw up from nerves."

"And desire?"

"Mostly nerves," she said.

"Why is this such a big deal? All *your* room has in it is a bed."

"*Two* beds," she said, "and *two* desks. And the constant threat of my roommate walking in."

"Which is why we should go to my house. Nobody will ever walk in on us."

"That's what makes me nervous."

Levi *hmmm*ed. Like he was thinking. "What if I promise not to touch you?"

Cath laughed. "Now I have zero incentive to come."

"What if I promise to let you touch me first?"

"Are you kidding? I'm the untrustworthy person in this relationship. I'm all hands."

"I've seen no evidence of that, Cather."

"In my *head*, I'm all hands."

"I want to live in your head."

Cath covered her face with her hand, as if he could see her. They didn't usually flirt quite like this. Quite so frankly. Maybe the phone brought it out in her. Maybe it was this weekend. Everything this weekend.

"Hey, Cath . . ." Levi's voice was so soft. "What exactly are we waiting for?"

"What do you mean?"

"Did you take an abstinence pledge?"

She laughed, but still managed to sound affronted. *"No."*

"Is it –" He exhaled quickly, like he was forcing something out." – is it still about trust? Me earning your trust?"

Cath's voice dropped to almost nothing. "God, Levi. No. I trust you."

"I'm not even talking about sex," he said. "I mean . . . not just sex. We can take that off the table completely if it will make you feel better."

"Completely?"

"Until further discussion. If you knew that I wasn't pushing for that, if that wasn't even on the horizon, do you think you could relax and just . . . let me touch you?"

"What kind of touching?" she asked.

"Do you want me to show you on a doll?"

Cath laughed.

"Touching," he said. "I want to touch you. Hold you. I want to sit right next to you, even when there are other options."

She took a deep breath. She felt like she owed it to him to keep talking. To at least reciprocate this conversation. "I want to touch you, too."

"Yeah?"

"Yeah," she said.

"What kind of touching?" he asked.

"Did you already give the operator your credit card number?"

Levi laughed. "Come home with me, Cath. I miss you. And I don't want to say good night."

The door swung open, and Reagan came back into the room wearing a T-shirt and yoga pants, a towel wrapped around her hair.

"Yeah, okay," Cath said. "When you will get here?"

He was obviously grinning. "I'm already downstairs."

Cath put on brown cable-knit leggings and a plaid shirtdress that she'd taken from Wren's dorm room. Plus knit wristlet thingies that made her think of gauntlets, like she was some sort of knight in pink, crocheted armor. Levi's teasing her about her sweater predilection had just made it more extreme.

"Going out?" Reagan asked.

"Levi just got back."

"Should I wait up for you?" she leered.

"Yes," Cath said. "You should. It will give you time to think about what a shameless ground-rule breaker you are."

Cath felt silly waiting for the elevator. Girls were walking by in their pajamas, and Cath was dressed to go out.

When she stepped out into the lobby, Levi was there, leaning against a column and talking to somebody, some girl he must know from somewhere. . . . When he saw Cath, his smile widened and he pushed off the column with his shoulder, immediately waving good-bye to the girl.

"Hey," he said, kissing the top of Cath's head. "Your hair's wet."

"That's what happens when you wash it."

He pulled up her hood. She took his hand before he could reach for hers, and he rewarded her with an especially toothy grin.

When they walked out of the building, she knew in her heart, in her stomach, that she wasn't coming back until morning.

At first Cath thought there was another party going on at Levi's house. There was music playing, and there were people in almost every room.

But they were all just his roommates — and his roommates' friends and girlfriends and, in one case maybe, boyfriend.

Levi introduced her to them all. "This is Cather." "This is my girlfriend, Cather." "Everyone? Cather." She smiled tensely and knew that she wouldn't remember any of their names.

Then Levi led her up a staircase that couldn't have been original to the house – the landings were strange and cramped, and the hallways shot out at irregular intervals. Levi pointed out everyone's rooms. He pointed out the bathrooms. Cath counted three floors, and Levi kept climbing. When the staircase got so narrow they couldn't walk side by side anymore, he led the way.

The stairs turned one more time and ended at a single doorway. Levi stopped there and turned, awkwardly, holding on to the handrails on both sides of the hall.

"Cather." He grinned. "I have officially gotten you up to my room."

"Who knew it was at the end of a labyrinth?"

He opened the door behind him, then took both her hands, pulling her up and in.

The room was small, with narrow dormer windows pushing out of it on two sides. There was no overhead light, so Levi turned on a lamp next to the queen-sized bed. It really was just a room with a bed – and a shiny turquoise love seat that was at least fifty years old.

She looked up and around. "We're at the very top of the house, aren't we?"

"Servants' quarters," he said. "I was the only one willing to climb all these stairs."

"How'd you get this couch up here?"

"Talked Tommy into helping me. It was terrible. I don't know how anyone ever got this mattress up around all those corners. It's been here since the beginning of time."

Cath shifted nervously, and the floor creaked beneath her. Levi's bed was unmade, an old-looking quilt thrown over it, the pillows in disarray. He straightened the quilt and picked a pillow up off the floor.

The room felt closer to the outdoors than to the rest of the house. Exposed. Cath could hear wind whistling in the window frames. "I'll bet it gets cold up here—"

"And hot in the summer," he said. "Are you thirsty? I could make tea. I should have asked while we were still downstairs."

"I'm fine," she said.

Where Levi was standing, his hair brushed against the ceiling. "Do you mind if I change? I helped water the horses before I left. Got kind of muddy."

Cath tried to smile. "Sure, go ahead."

There were drawers built into a wall. Levi knelt over one, then ducked out of the room – the doorway was at least an inch too short for him – and Cath sat down carefully on the love seat. The fabric was cool beneath her. She ran her palm along it, some kind of slick cotton with nubby swirls and flowers.

This room was worse than she thought.

Dark. Remote. Practically in the trees. Practically enchanted.

A calculus test would feel intimate in here.

She took off her coat and set it on his bed, then tugged off her soggy boots and pulled her legs up onto the love seat. If she held her breath, she could hear Bon Iver quietly blaring at least two floors below.

Levi was back before Cath was ready for him. (Which was bound to happen.) He looked like he'd washed his face, and he was wearing jeans and a baby blue flannel shirt. It was a nice color on him. It made his face tan and his hair yellow and his mouth pink. He sat down on the couch next to her – she knew he would. There was no room in this room for personal space.

He picked Cath's hand up off the couch and held it loosely in both of his, looking down at it, then running his fingertips along the back, up and down her fingers.

She took a deep breath. "How did you end up living here?"

"I worked with Tommy at Starbucks. One of his old roommates graduated and moved out, I was living in a house with three deadbeats, and I didn't mind the stairs. . . . Tommy's dad bought this house as a real estate investment. He's lived here since he was a sophomore."

"What is he now?"

"Law student."

Cath nodded. The more that Levi touched her hand, the more that it tickled. She stretched out her fingers and took a soft breath.

"Feel nice?" he asked, looking up at her with his eyes without lifting his head. She nodded again. If he kept touching her, she wouldn't be able to do even that; she'd have to blink once for yes, twice for no.

"So what happened this weekend?" he asked. "How is everybody?"

Cath shook her head. "Crazy. Fine. I — I think Wren and I are okay again. I think we made up."

His lips twitched up on one side. "Yeah?"

"Yeah."

"That's great." You could tell that he really thought so.

"*Yeah*," Cath said. "It is. I feel—"

Levi brought one leg up between them and bumped her thigh with his knee. She practically jumped back over the arm of the couch.

He made a frustrated noise that was half laugh, half sigh, and wrinkled his nose. "Are you really that nervous?"

"I guess so," she said. "I'm sorry."

"Do you know why? I mean, what's making you nervous? I meant what I said earlier about the table, and what's on and off of it."

"There is no table in here," Cath said. "There's just a bed."

He pulled her hand into his chest. "Is that what you're scared of?"

"I don't know what I'm scared of. . . ." That was a lie. A giant one. She was scared that he'd start touching her, and then that they wouldn't stop. She was scared that she wasn't ready to be that person yet. The person who doesn't stop. "I'm sorry," she said. Levi looked down at their hands, and he looked so disappointed and confused – and it was such a piss-poor way to treat him. Dishonestly. Distantly. After he'd put himself out there for her again and again.

"This weekend . . . ," Cath said, and she tried to scoot closer. She knelt on the couch cushion next to him. "Thank you."

Levi smiled again and lifted his eyes, just his eyes, up to her.

"I don't think I can tell you how much it meant to me," she said. "That you were there at the hospital. That you came." He squeezed her hand. Cath pressed on: "I don't think I can tell you how much you mean to me," she said. "Levi."

He lifted his whole face. His eyes were hopeful now. Wary.

"C'mere," he said, tugging on her hand.

"I'm not sure I know how."

He clenched his jaw. "I have an idea."

"I can't read you fanfiction," she said, teasing. "I don't have my computer."

"Don't you have your phone?"

She tilted her head. "Was that really your idea? Fanfiction?"

"Yeah," he said, rubbing the palm of her hand. "It always relaxes you."

"I thought you'd been asking me to read to you because you liked the story—"

"I *do* like the story. And I like the way it relaxes you. You never finished reading me the rabbit one, you know. And you've never read me anything from *Carry On*."

Cath looked over at her coat. Her phone was in her pocket. "I feel like I'm failing you," she said. "I was supposed to come over here and do stuff with you, not read lame fanfiction."

Levi bit his lip and stifled a laugh. "*Do stuff.* Is that the street name for it? Come on, Cath, I want to know what happens. They just killed the rabbit, and Simon had finally figured out that Baz was a vampire."

"Are you sure about this?"

Levi smiled, still looking overly cautious, and nodded.

Cath leaned off the couch and found her phone. She wasn't used to googling her own stories, but when she typed in "Magicath" and "The Fifth Hare," her story came right up.

While she looked for their place, Levi gently put his hands on her waist and pulled her back against him. "Okay?" he asked.

She nodded. "Have I read this part, '*Simon didn't know what to say. How to respond to . . . this. All this bloody information*'?"

"Yeah, I think so."

"Did we get to the part where the rabbit caught fire?"

"What? No."

"Okay," Cath said. "I think I've got it." She leaned back against Levi's chest and felt his chin in her hair. *This is fine,* she told herself. *I've been just here before.* She propped her glasses in her hair and cleared her throat.

Simon didn't know what to say. How to respond to . . . this. All this bloody information.

He picked up the sword and wiped it clean on his cloak. "You all right?"

Baz licked his bloody lips – like they were dry, Simon thought – and nodded his head.

"Good," Simon said, and realized that he meant it.

Then a plume of flame shot up behind Baz, throwing his face into shadow.

He whipped around and backed away from the rabbit. Its paw was well and truly on fire now, and the flames were already crawling up the beast's chest.

"My wand . . . ," Baz said, looking around him on the floor. "Quick, cast an extinguishing spell, Snow."

"I . . . I don't know any," Simon said.

Baz reached for Simon's wand hand, and wrapped his own bloody fingers around Simon's. *"Make a wish!"* he shouted, flicking the wand in a half circle.

The fire sputtered out, and the nursery fell dark.

Baz let go of Simon's hand and started hunting around on the floor for his wand. Simon stepped closer to the gruesome corpse. "Now what?" he asked it.

As if in answer, the rabbit began to shimmer, then fade – and then it was gone, leaving nothing behind but the smell of pennies and burnt hair.

And something else . . .

Baz conjured one of his blue balls of light. "Ah," he said, picking up his wand. "Filthy bugger was lying on it."

"Look," Simon said, pointing to another shadow on the floor. "I think it's a key." He stooped to pick it up – an old-fashioned key with fanged white rabbit's teeth on its blade.

Baz stepped closer to look. He was dripping with blood; the smell of gore was overwhelming.

"Do you think this is what I was meant to find?" Simon asked.

"Well," Baz said thoughtfully, "keys do seem more useful than giant, murderous rabbits. . . . How many more of these do you have to fight?"

"Five. But I can't do it alone. This one would have murdered me if—"

"We have to clean up this mess," Baz said, looking down at

the stains on the thick-piled rug.

"We'll have to tell the Mage when he comes back," Simon said. "There's too much damage here to handle ourselves."

Baz was silent.

"Come on," Simon said, "we can at least get ourselves cleaned up now."

The boys' showers were as empty as the rest of the school. They chose stalls at opposite ends. . . .

"What's wrong?" Levi asked.

Cath had stopped reading.

"I feel weird reading this mushy gay stuff out loud – your roommates are here. Is one of them gay? I don't think I can read this with actual gay people in the house."

Levi giggled. "Micah? Trust me, it's okay. He watches straight stuff in front of me all the time. He's obsessed with *Titanic*."

"That's different."

"Cath, it's okay. Nobody can hear you. . . . Wait, is this really a shower scene? Like, *a shower scene*?"

"No," Cath said. "Geez."

Levi moved his arms around her waist until he was holding her properly. Then he pushed his mouth into her hair. "Read to me, sweetheart."

Simon finished first and put on fresh jeans. When he looked back at Baz's stall, the water was still running pink at the other boy's ankles.

Vampire, Simon thought, allowing himself to think the word for the first time, watching the water run.

It should have filled him with hate and revulsion – the thought of Baz usually filled him with those things. But all Simon could feel right now was relief. Baz had helped him find the rabbit, helped him fight it, had kept both of them alive.

Simon was relieved. And grateful.

He shoved his singed and stained clothes into the trash, then went back to their room. It was a long time before Baz joined him. When he did, he looked better than Simon had seen him look all year. Baz's cheeks and lips were flushed dark pink, and his grey eyes had come out of their shadows.

"Hungry?" Simon asked.

Baz started laughing.

The sun hadn't quite broken the horizon yet, and no one was about in the kitchens. Simon found bread and cheese and apples, and tossed them onto a platter. It seemed strange to sit alone in the empty dining hall, so he and Baz sat on the kitchen flagstones instead, leaning back against a wall of cabinets.

"Let's get this over with," Baz said, biting into a green apple, obviously trying to seem casual. "Are you going to tell the Mage about me?"

"He already thinks you're a nasty git," Simon said.

"Yes," Baz said quietly, "but this is worse, and you know it. You know what he'll have to do."

Turn Baz over to the Coven.

It would mean certain imprisonment, perhaps death. Simon had been trying for six years to get Baz expelled, but he'd never wanted to see him staked.

Still . . . Baz was a vampire – a *vampire*, damn it. A monster. And he was already Simon's enemy.

"A *monster*," Levi repeated. He raised one hand to unclip Cath's hair. Her glasses were stuck there and fell sideways onto her arm. Levi picked them up and tossed them onto his bed. "Your hair's still wet," he said, shaking it out with one hand.

Simon looked at Baz and tried again to summon the proper amount of horror. All he could manage was some weary dismay. "When did it happen?" he asked.

"I already told you," Baz said. "We've just left the scene of the crime."

"You were bitten in the nursery? As a child? Why didn't anyone notice?"

"My mother was dead. My father swooped in and swept me back to the estate. I think he might have suspected. . . . We've never talked about it."

"Didn't he notice when you started drinking people's blood?"

"I *don't*," Baz snapped imperiously. "And besides, the . . . thirst doesn't manifest itself right away. It comes on during adolescence."

"Like acne?"

"Speak for yourself, Snow."

"When did it come on for you?"

"This summer," Baz said, looking down.

"And you haven't—"

"*No.*"

"Why not?"

Baz turned on him. "Are you kidding me? Vampires murdered my mother. And if I'm found out, I'll lose everything. . . . My wand. My family. Possibly my life. I'm a *magician*. I'm not —" He gestured toward his throat and his face. "*– this.*"

Simon wondered if he and Baz had ever been so close, had ever allowed each other to sit this close, in all their years of living together. Baz's shoulder was nearly touching his own, and Simon could see every tiny bump and shadow on Baz's admittedly very clear skin. Every line of his lips, every flare of blue in his grey eyes.

"How are you staying alive?" Simon asked.

"I manage, thanks."

"Not well," Simon said. "You look like hell."

Baz smirked. "Again, thank you, Snow. You're a comfort."

"I don't mean now," Simon said. "You look great now." Baz raised one eyebrow and lowered the other. "But lately . . . ," Simon pressed on, "you just seem like you're fading away. Have you been . . . *drinking* . . . anything?"

"I do what I can," Baz said, dropping his apple core onto the plate. "You don't want to know the details."

"I do," Simon argued. "Look, as your roommate, I have a vested interest in you not wandering around in a bloodlust."

Levi's hand was still in Cath's hair. She felt him lift it up, felt his mouth on the back of her neck. His other arm pulled her tight against him. Cath concentrated on her phone. It had been so long since she'd written this story, she couldn't quite remember how it ended.

"I'd *never* bite you," Baz said, locking on to Simon's eyes.

"That's good," Simon said. "I'm glad you still plan to kill me the old-fashioned way – but you have to admit that this is hard on you."

"Of course it's hard on me." He threw a hand in the air in what Simon recognized as a very Baz-like gesture. "I've got the thirst of the ancients, and I'm surrounded by useless bags of blood all day."

"And all night," Simon said softly.

Baz shook his head and looked away again. "I said I'd never hurt you," he muttered.

"Then let me help." Simon moved just an inch, so their shoulders were touching. Even through his T-shirt and through Baz's cotton button-down, he could feel that Baz wasn't freezing anymore. He was warm. He seemed healthy again.

"Why do you want to help?" Baz asked, turning back to Simon, who was close enough now to feel the soft heat of Baz's breath on his chin. "You'd keep a secret from your mentor to help your enemy?"

"You're not my enemy," Simon said. "You're just . . . a really bad roommate."

Levi laughed, and Cath felt it on her neck.

Baz laughed, and Simon felt it on his eyelashes.

"You hate me," Baz argued. "You've hated me from the moment we met."

"I don't hate *this*," Simon said. "What you're doing – denying your most powerful urges, just to protect other people. It's more heroic than anything I've ever done."

"They're not my *most* powerful urges," Baz said under his breath.

"Do you know," Simon said, "that half the time we're together, you're talking to yourself?"

"Ah, Snow, I didn't think you noticed."

"I *notice*," Simon said, feeling six years of irritation and anger – and twelve hours of exhaustion – coming to a dizzy peak between his ears. He shook his head, and he must have leaned forward because it was enough to bump his nose and chin against Baz's. . . . "Let me *help* you," Simon said.

Baz held his head perfectly still. Then he nodded, gently thudding his forehead against Simon's.

"I *notice*," Simon said, letting his mouth drift forward. He thought of everything that had passed over the other boy's lips. Blood and bile and curses.

But Baz's mouth was soft now, and he tasted of apples.

And Simon didn't care for the moment that he was changing everything.

Cath closed her eyes and felt Levi's chin track the back of her collar.

"Keep reading," he whispered.

"I can't," she said, "it's over."

"It's over?" He pulled his face away. "But what happens? Do they fight the other rabbits now? Are they together? Does Simon break up with Agatha?"

"That's up to you. It doesn't say."

"But *you* could say. You wrote it."

"I wrote it two years ago," Cath said. "I don't know what I was thinking then. Especially about that last paragraph. It's pretty weak."

"I liked the whole thing," Levi said. "I liked 'the thirst of the ancients.'"

"Yeah, that was an okay line. . . ."

"Read something else," he whispered, kissing the skin below her ear.

Cath took a deep breath. "What?"

"Anything. More fanfiction, the soybean report . . . You're like a tiger who loves Brahms – as long as you're reading, you let me touch you."

He was right: As long as she was reading, it was almost like he was touching someone else. Which was kind of messed up, now that she thought about it. . . .

Cath let her phone drop to the floor.

She slowly turned toward Levi, feeling her waist twist in his arms, looking up as far as his chin and shaking her head. "No," she said. "*No.* I don't want to be distracted. I want to touch you back."

Levi's chest rose steeply, just as she set both hands on his flannel shirt.

His eyes were wide. "Okay . . ."

Cath focused on her fingertips. Feeling the flannel, feeling it slide against the T-shirt he wore underneath – feeling Levi underneath that, the ridges of muscle and bone. His heart beat in the palm of Cath's hand, right there, like her fingers could close around it. . . .

"I really like you," Levi whispered.

She nodded and spread out her fingers. "I really like you, too."

"Say it again," he said.

She laughed. There should be a word for a laugh that ends as soon as it starts. A laugh that's more a syllable of surprise and acknowledgment than it is anything else. Cath laughed like that, then hung her head forward, pushing her hands into his chest. "I really like you, Levi."

She felt his hands on her waist and his mouth in her hair.

"Keep saying it," he said.

Cath smiled. "I like you," she said, touching her nose to his chin.

"I would've shaved if I'd known I was going to see you tonight."

His chin moved when he talked. "I like you like this," she said, letting it scrape her nose and her cheek. "I like you."

He lifted a hand to the back of her neck and held her there. "Cath . . ."

She swallowed and set her lips on his chin. "Levi."

Right about then, Cath realized just how close she was to the edge of Levi's jaw – and remembered what she'd promised herself to do there. She closed her eyes and kissed him below his chin, behind his jaw, where he was soft and almost chubby, like a baby. He arched his neck, and it was even better than she'd hoped.

"I like you," she said. "So much. I like you here."

Cath brought her hands up to his neck. God, he was warm — skin so warm and thick, a heavier ply than her own. She slid her fingers into his hair, cradling the back of his head.

His hands mimicked hers, pulling her face up to his. "Cath, if I kiss you now, are you going to leap away from me?"

"No."

"Are you going to panic?

She shook her head. "Probably no."

He bit the side of his bottom lip, and smiled. His bowed lips didn't quite reach the corners.

"I like you," she whispered.

He pulled her forward.

Right. There was *this*. Kissing Levi.

So much better when she was awake and her mouth wasn't muddy from reading out loud all night. She nodded and nodded and kissed him back.

When Baz and Simon kissed, Cath always made a big deal out of the moment when one of them opened his mouth. But when you're actually kissing someone, it's hard to keep your mouth closed. Cath's mouth was open before Levi even got there. It was open now.

Levi's mouth was open, too, and he kept pulling back a little like he was going to say something; then his chin would jut forward again, back into hers.

God, his chin. She wanted to make an honest woman of his chin. She wanted to lock it down.

The next time Levi pulled back, Cath went back to kissing his chin, pressing her face up under his jaw. "I just like you so much here."

"I just like you so much," he said, his head falling back against the couch. "Even more than that, you know?"

"And here," she said, pushing her nose up against his ear. Levi's earlobes were attached to his head. Which made Cath think of Punnett squares. And Mendel. And made her try to pull his earlobe away with her teeth. "You're really good here," she said. He brought his shoulders up, like it tickled.

"C'mere, c'mere," he said, pulling at her waist. She was sitting just beside him, and he seemed to want her in his lap.

"I'm heavy," she said.

"Good."

Cath always knew that she'd make a spectacle of herself if she ever got Levi alone, and that's just what she was doing. She was mauling his ear. She wanted to feel it on every part of her face.

It was okay . . . , she could imagine him telling Reagan or one of his eighteen roommates tomorrow. *She wouldn't stop licking my ear – I think she might have an ear fetish. And you don't even want to know what she did to my chin.*

Levi was still holding her waist, too tight, like he was getting ready for a figure-skating lift. "Cath . . . ," he said, and swallowed. The knot in his throat dipped, and she tried to catch it with her mouth.

"Here, too," she said. Her voice sounded pained. He was too lovely, too good, too much. "So much here. Really . . . your whole head. I like your whole head."

Levi laughed, and she tried to kiss everything that moved. His throat, his lips, his cheeks, the corner of his eyes.

Baz would never kiss Simon this chaotically.

Simon would never crush his nose against Baz's widow's peak the way Cath was about to.

She gave in to Levi's hands and climbed onto his lap, her knees on either side of his hips. He craned his neck to gaze up at her, and Cath held his face by his temples. "Here, here, here," she said, kissing his forehead, letting herself touch his feather-light hair.

"Oh God, Levi . . . you drive me crazy here."

She smoothed his hair back with her hands and her face, and she kissed the top of his head the way he always kissed her (the only kisses she'd allowed for so many weeks).

Levi's hair didn't smell like shampoo – or freshly mown clover. It smelled like coffee mostly, and like Cath's pillow the week after he spent the night. Her mouth settled on his hairline, where his hair was the lightest and finest; her own hair was nowhere this soft. "Like you," she said, feeling weird and tearful. "Like you so much, Levi."

And then she kissed my receding hairline and cried, she imagined him saying. In her imagination, Levi was Danny Zuko, and his roommates were the rest of the T-Birds. *Tell me more, tell me more.*

His face felt hot in her hands.

"Come *here,*" he said, catching her jaw with one hand, chinning his mouth up to hers.

Right.

There was *this*. Kissing Levi.

This and this and *this*.

"You're not all hands . . . ," he whispered later. He was tucked back into the corner of the love seat, and she was resting on top of him. She'd spent hours on top of him. Curled over him like a vampire. Even exhausted, she couldn't stop rubbing her numb lips into his flannel chest. "You're all mouth," he said.

"Sorry," Cath said, biting her lips.

"Don't be stupid," he said, pulling her lips free of her teeth with his thumb. "And don't be sorry . . . ever again."

He hitched her up, so her face was above his. Her eyes wandered down to his chin, out of habit. "Look at me," he said.

Cath looked up. At Levi's pastel-colored face. Too lovely, too good.

"I like you here," he said, squeezing her. "With me."

She smiled, and her eyes started to drift downward.

"Cather . . ."

Back up to his eyes.

"You know that I'm falling in love with you, right?"

"You knew all along?"

"Not *all* along," Penelope said. "But *a* long. At least since fifth year, when you insisted we follow Baz around the castle every other day. You made me go to all of his football games."

"To make sure he wasn't cheating," Simon said, out of habit.

"Right," Penelope said. "I was starting to wonder whether *you'd* ever figure it out. You have figured it out, haven't you?"

Simon felt himself smiling and blushing, not for the first time this week. Not for the fiftieth. "Yeah . . ."

—from *Carry On, Simon*, posted March 2011
by FanFixx.net author *Magicath*

THIRTY-TWO

Wren was back, and it felt like someone had turned Cath's world right side up. Like she'd been hanging from the floor all year long, trying not to drop through the ceiling.

Cath could call Wren now whenever she wanted. Without thinking or worrying. They met for lunch and for dinner. They wrapped their schedules around each other's, filling in all the small spaces.

"It's like you got your lost arm back or something," Levi said. "Like you're a happy starfish." The way he was beaming, you'd think he was the one who got his sister back. "That was some bad medicine. Not talking to your mom. Not talking to your sister. That was some Jacob-and-Esau business."

"I'm still not talking to my mom," Cath said.

She *had* talked to Wren about their mom. A lot, actually.

Wren wasn't surprised that Laura hadn't stayed at the hospital. "She doesn't do heavy stuff," Wren said. "I can't believe she even came."

"She probably thought you were dying."

"I wasn't dying.'"

"How do you not do the heavy stuff?" Cath said, indignant. "Being a parent is all heavy stuff."

"She doesn't want to be a parent," Wren said. "She wants me to call her 'Laura.'"

Cath decided to start calling Laura "Mom" again in her head. Then she decided to stop calling Laura anything at all in her head. . . .

Wren still talked to her (She Who Would Not Be Named). She said they texted mostly and that they were friends on Facebook. Wren was okay with that amount of involvement; she seemed to think it was better than nothing and safer than everything.

Cath didn't get it. Her brain just didn't work that way. Her heart didn't.

But she was done fighting with Wren about it.

Now that Cath and Wren were Cath and Wren again, Levi thought they should all be hanging out all the time. The four of them. "Did you know that Jandro's in the Ag School?" he asked. "We've even had classes together."

"Maybe we should go on lots of double dates," Cath said, "and then we can get married on the same day in a double ceremony, in matching dresses, and the four of us will light the unity candle all at the same time."

"Pfft," Levi said, "I'm picking out my own dress."

The four of them *had* all hung out together once or twice, incidentally. When Jandro was coming to get Wren. When Levi was coming to get Cath.

"You don't want to hang out with Wren and me," Cath had tried to tell him. "All we do is listen to rap music and talk about Simon."

There were only six weeks left until *The Eighth Dance* came out, and Wren was more stressed out about it than Cath was. "I just don't know how you're going to wrap everything up," she'd say.

"I've got an outline," Cath kept telling her.

"Yeah, but you've got classes, too. Let me see your outline."

Usually, they huddled over the laptop in Cath's room. It was closer to campus.

"Don't expect me to tell you apart," Reagan said when this became a routine.

"I have short hair," Wren said, "and she wears glasses."

"Stop," Reagan groaned, "don't make me look at you. It's like *The Shining* in here."

Wren cocked her head and squinted. "I can't tell if you're being serious."

"It doesn't matter," Cath said. "Ignore her."

Reagan scowled at Cath. "Are you Zack, or are you Cody?"

Today they were in Wren's room, just to give Reagan a break. They were sitting on Wren's bed, the laptop resting on both their knees. Courtney was there, too, getting ready to go out; she was studying with the Sigma Chis tonight.

"You can't kill Baz," Wren said, pressing the down-arrow key and skimming Cath's *Carry On* outline. They kept coming back to this point; Wren was adamant.

"I never thought I *would* kill Baz," Cath said. "Ever. But it's the ultimate redemption, you know? If he sacrifices himself for Simon, after all their years of fighting, after this one precious year of love . . . it makes everything they've been through together that much sweeter."

"I'll have to kill you if you kill Baz," Wren said. "And I'll be first in a long line."

"I totally think Basil's going to die in the last movie," Courtney said, putting on her jacket. "Simon *has* to kill him – he's a vampire."

"He'll have to die in the last *book* first," Cath said. She still couldn't tell whether Courtney was actually stupid or whether she just couldn't be bothered to think before she talked. Wren shook her head at Cath and rolled her eyes, like, *Don't waste your time with her.*

"Don't work too hard, ladies," Courtney said, waving on her way out. Only Cath waved back.

Something had happened between Wren and Courtney. Cath wasn't sure if it was the emergency room or something else. They were still friends; they still ate lunch together. But even small things seemed to irritate Wren – the way Courtney wore heels with jeans, or the way she thought "boughten" was the past participle of "bought." Cath had tried to ask about it, but Wren always shrugged her off.

"She's wrong," Cath said now. "I don't think GTL could ever kill off Baz."

"And you can't either," Wren said.

"But it makes him the ultimate romantic hero. Think of Tony in *West Side Story* or Jack in *Titanic* – or Jesus."

"That's horseshit," Wren said.

Cath giggled. "*Horse*shit?"

Wren elbowed her. "*Yes*. The ultimate act of heroism shouldn't be death. You're always saying you want to give Baz the stories he deserves. To rescue him from Gemma—"

"I just don't think she realizes his potential as a character," Cath said.

"So you're going to kill him off? Isn't the best revenge supposed to be a life well-lived? The punk-rock way to end *Carry On* would be to let Baz and Simon live happily ever after."

Cath laughed.

"I'm serious," Wren said. "They've been through so much together – not just in your story, but in canon and in all the hundreds of fics we've read about them. . . . Think of your readers. Think about how good it'll feel to leave us with a little hope."

"But I don't want it to be cheesy."

"Happily ever after, or even just *together* ever after, is not cheesy," Wren said. "It's the noblest, like, the most courageous thing two people can shoot for."

Cath studied Wren's face. It was like looking at a lightly warped mirror. *Through a glass, darkly.* "Are you in love?"

Wren blushed and looked down at the laptop. "This isn't about me. It's about Baz and Simon."

"I'm making it about you," Cath said. "Are you in love?"

Wren pulled the computer fully onto her lap and started scrolling back up to the top of Cath's outline. "Yes," she said coolly. "There's nothing wrong with that."

"I didn't say there was." Cath grinned. "You're *in love.*"

"Oh shut up, so are you."

Cath started to argue.

"Give it up," Wren said, pointing at Cath's face. "I've seen you look at Levi. What's that thing you wrote about Simon once, that his eyes followed Baz 'like he was the brightest thing in the room, like he cast everything else into shadow'? That's you. You can't look away from him."

"I . . ." Cath was pretty sure that Levi actually *was* the brightest thing in the room, in any room. Bright and warm and crackling – he was a human campfire. "I really like him."

"Have you slept with him?"

"*No.*" Cath knew what Wren meant, knew she didn't want to hear about Levi's grandmother's quilt and the way they'd slept curled up in each other, like stackable chairs. "Have you? With Jandro?"

Wren laughed. "Duh. So . . . are you going to?"

Cath rubbed her right wrist. Her typing wrist. "Yeah," she said. "I think so."

Wren grabbed Cath's arm, then shoved her away. "Oh. My. God. Will you tell me about it when you do?"

"Duh." Cath pushed her back. "Anyway, I don't feel like it has to happen now, like immediately, but he makes me want to. And he makes me think . . . that it'll be okay. That I don't have to worry about screwing it up."

Wren rolled her eyes. "You're not going to screw it up."

"Well, I'm not going to nail it either, am I? Remember how long it took me to learn how to drive? And I still can't backwards skate—"

"Think of how many beautiful *first times* you've written for Simon and Baz."

"That's totally different," Cath said dismissively. "They don't even have the same parts."

Wren started giggling and then couldn't stop. She hugged the laptop to her chest. "You're more comfortable with *their* parts than —" She couldn't stop giggling. "— your *own* and . . . and you've never even *seen* their parts. . . ."

"I try to write around it." Cath was giggling, too.

"I know," Wren said, "and you do a really good job."

When they were done laughing, Wren punched Cath's arm. "You'll be fine. The first few times you do it, you only get graded on attendance."

"Great," Cath scoffed. "That makes me feel better." She shook her head. "This whole conversation is premature."

Wren smiled, but she looked serious, like she wanted something. "Hey, Cath—"

"What now?"

"Don't kill Baz. I'll even beta for you, if you want. Just . . . don't kill him. Baz deserves a happy ending more than anybody."

"Shhh."

"I just—"

"Hush."

"I worry—"

"Don't."

"But—"

"Simon."

"Baz?"

"Here."

—from *Carry On, Simon,* posted September 2011

by FanFixx.net author *Magicath*

THIRTY-THREE

"Have you started?" Professor Piper asked.

"Yes," Cath lied.

She couldn't help it. She couldn't say no – Professor Piper was liable to abort this whole endeavor. Cath still hadn't shown her any progress . . .

Because Cath hadn't *made* any progress.

There was just too much else going on. Wren. Levi. Baz. Simon. Her dad . . . Actually, Cath wasn't as worried about her dad as she used to be. That was one nice thing about Wren going home every weekend. On the weekends that Wren was stuck at home, she was so bored, she practically live-blogged the whole thing for Cath, sending constant texts and emails. *"dad is making me watch a lewis & clark documentary. it's like he's DRIVING me to drink."* Wren didn't even know about Cath's Fiction-Writing assignment.

Cath had considered telling Professor Piper – again – that she wasn't cut out for fiction-writing, that she was practically fiction-phobic. But once Cath was here, looking up at Professor Piper's hopeful, confident face . . .

She could never get it out. She'd rather endure these excruciating checkups than tell the truth – that she only ever thought about her project when she was sitting in this room.

"That's wonderful," the professor said, leaning forward off her desk to pat Cath's arm, smiling just the way Cath wanted her to. "I'm so relieved. I thought I was going to have to give you another 'blood, toil, tears, and sweat' speech – and I didn't know if I had one in me."

Cath smiled. And thought about what a repugnant creature she was.

"So, tell me about it," the professor said. "May I read what you have so far?"

Cath shook her head too quickly, then kept shaking her head at a more normal pace. "No, I mean, not yet. I just . . . not yet."

"Fair enough." Professor Piper looked suspicious. (Or maybe Cath was just paranoid.) "Can you tell me what you're writing about?"

"Yeah," Cath said. "Of course. I'm writing about . . ." She imagined a big wheel spinning around. Like on *The Price Is Right* or *Wheel of Fortune*. Wherever it landed, that would be it – that's what she'd have to write. "I'm writing about . . ."

Professor Piper smiled. Like she knew Cath was lying, but still really wanted her to pull this off.

"My mom," Cath said. And swallowed.

"Your mom," the professor repeated.

"Yeah. I mean . . . I'm starting there."

The professor's face turned almost playful. "Everyone does."

"The aerie," Cath said, "that's what this is."

Levi was sitting against his headboard, and Cath was in his lap, her knees around his hips. She'd spent a lot of time in his lap lately. She liked to be on top, to feel like she could move away if she wanted to. (She almost never wanted to.) She also spent a lot of time deliberately not thinking about anything else that might be happening in his lap; his lap was abstract territory, as far as Cath was concerned. Unfixed. Unmapped. If she thought about Levi's lap in concrete terms, she ended up crawling off the bed and curling up by herself on the love seat.

"What's an aerie?" he asked.

"An eagle's nest."

"Oh." He nodded. "Right." He ran a hand up through his hair. Cath followed with her own hand, feeling his hair slip silkily through her fingers. He smiled at her like she was someone who'd just ordered a peppermint latte.

"Is everything okay?" she asked.

He nodded and kissed her nose. "Of course." When he smiled again, only his mouth moved.

"What's wrong?" Cath started to move off his lap, but he caught her.

"*Nothing*. Nothing important, I just –" He closed his eyes, like he had a headache. "– I got a test back today. It wasn't good, even for me."

"Oh. Did you study for it?"

"Clearly not enough."

Cath wasn't sure how much Levi studied. He never cracked a book – but he went everywhere with earbuds. He was always listening to a lecture when she came down to his truck. He always pulled them out when she climbed in.

Cath thought back to the way he used to study with Reagan, flash cards spread all over the room, asking question after question. . . .

"It's because of me, isn't it?"

"No." He shook his head.

"Indirectly," she said. "You're not studying with anyone else."

"Cather. Look at me. I've never been this happy in my life."

"You don't seem happy."

"I didn't mean right this minute." He smiled; it was tired, but genuine. Cath wanted to kiss his little pink mouth immobile.

"You need to study," she said, punching his chest.

"Okay."

"With Reagan. With all those girls you exploit."

"Right."

"With me, if you want. I could help you study."

He reached up to her ponytail and started tugging out the rubber band. She let her head fall back.

"You have enough homework," he said. "And thousands of Simon Snow fans hanging on your every word."

Cath looked up at the cracks in the plaster ceiling while he worked the hair tie free. "If it meant being *here,* in *the aerie,* with you," she said, "instead of you being some*where* else with some*one* else, I would gladly make the sacrifice."

He pulled her hair forward; it fell just past her shoulders. "I can't decide if you love me," he said, "or this room."

"Both," Cath said, then thought through his choice of words and blushed.

He smiled, like he'd tricked her. "Okay," he said, playing with her hair. "I'll study more." He lifted his legs up and bounced her forward. "Take off your glasses."

"Why? I thought you liked my glasses."

"I love your glasses. I especially love the moment when you take them off."

"Do you need to study tonight?"

"Nope. I just bombed a test. I got nothing to study for." He bounced her on his legs again.

She rolled her eyes and took off her glasses.

Levi grinned. "What color are your eyes?"

She opened them as wide as she could.

"I can see them," he said. "But I can't decide what color they are. What does it say on your driver's license?"

"Blue."

"They're not blue."

"They are. On the outside."

"And brown in the middle," he said. "And gray on the edge and green in between."

Cath shrugged and looked down at his neck. There was a mole just below his ear, and another one at the bottom of his throat. He was paler now than when she'd first met him; he'd seemed so tan that day, like a little kid who'd been playing outside all summer.

"What are you doing this summer?" she asked.

"Working on the ranch."

"Will I see you?"

"Yes."

"When?"

"We'll make it work." He touched her cheek.

"Not like this . . ."

Levi looked around the room and took her face in his hands. "Not like this," he conceded.

Cath nodded and bent to kiss the spot under his ear. "You're sure you don't need to study?"

"Do you?"

"No," she said. "It's Friday."

Levi had just shaved, so his jaw and neck were something extra. Soft plus minty. She ran a hand down the front of his flannel shirt until her fingers caught at the first button – and decided right then to unbutton it.

Levi inhaled.

She found the next button.

When she'd finished with the third, he pulled away from her and yanked the shirt up over his head. The T-shirt came next. Cath looked down at his chest like she'd never seen anything like it before. Like she'd never been to a public swimming pool.

"You look thinner with your clothes on," she said with surprise, tracing her fingers over his shoulders.

He laughed. "Is that a compliment?"

"It's a . . . I didn't expect you to look so strong."

He tried to kiss her, but she leaned back – she wasn't ready to look away. Levi wasn't noticeably muscular. Not like Jandro. Not even like Abel. But he was firm and nicely shaped, muscles curving around his shoulders, over his arms, across his chest.

Cath wanted to go back and rewrite every scene she'd ever written about Baz or Simon's chests. She'd written them flat and sharp and hard. Levi was all soft motion and breath, curves and warm hollows. Levi's chest was a living thing.

"You're beautiful," she said.

"That's you."

"Don't argue with me. You're beautiful."

Taking off Levi's shirt had been such an inspired idea, Cath was thinking about losing her own. Levi was thinking about it, too. He was playing with the hem, sliding his fingers just underneath it while they kissed. *Kissed.* Cath loved that word. She used it sparingly in her fic, just because it felt so powerful. It felt like kissing to say it. *Well done, English language.*

Levi kissed with his jaw and his bottom lip. She hadn't done this with enough people to know whether that was distinctive, but she felt like it was. He kissed her, and ran his fingers under her hem; and if she just raised her arms now, he'd probably take care of her shirt. She could count on him to pitch in. Cath couldn't remember what she was waiting for, what she was so scared of. . . .

Was she waiting for marriage? At the moment, it was hard to think beyond Levi . . . whom she was nowhere near marrying. That fact only made her want him more. Because if she didn't end up marrying Levi, she wouldn't have lifetime access to his chest and his lips and whatever might be happening in his lap. What if they married other people? She should probably have sex with him *now,* while she still could.

Flawed logic, her brain was shouting. *Miserably flawed.*

How do you even know when you're anywhere near marrying someone? she wondered. *Is that question about time? Or distance?*

Cath's phone chimed.

Levi licked her mouth like he was trying to get the last bit of jam off the back of her throat.

Her phone chimed again.

It probably wasn't important. Wren. Complaining about their dad. Or their dad complaining about Wren. Or one of them being rushed to a hospital . . .

Cath pulled away, catching Levi's hands and trying to catch her breath.

"Let me check," she said. "Wren—"

He nodded and pulled his hands away from her shirt. Cath resisted the urge to slide down his legs like he was a hobby horse. (It would feel good, but she might never recover her dignity.) Instead she climbed drunkenly off him, reaching off the bed for her phone.

He crawled after her, trying to read over her shoulder.

Wren. *"hey, you should come to omaha. jandro's here, we're going dancing later at guaca maya. fun! come!"*

"can't," Cath texted back. *"levi time."*

She threw her phone on the floor, then tried to find her way back to Levi's lap. But he'd already leaned back against the headboard with his knees up. Lap unavailable.

She tried to move his knees out of the way, but he wouldn't let her. He was looking at her like he was still trying to figure out what color her eyes were.

"Is everything okay?" she asked, kneeling in front of him.

"Yeah. Everything okay on your end?" He moved his chin toward her phone.

Cath nodded. "Perfectly."

Levi nodded.

Cath nodded again.

Then she lifted her arms up over her head.

Agatha wrung her fingers in her cape miserably. (But still prettily. Even Agatha's tear-stained face was a thing of beauty.) Simon wanted to tell her it was all right, to forget the whole scene with Baz in the forest. . . . *Agatha standing in the moonlight, holding both of Baz's pale hands in her own . . .*

"Just tell me," Simon said, his voice shaking.

"I don't know what to say," she wept. "There's you. And you're good. And you're right. And then there's him. . . . And he's *different*."

"He's a monster." Simon clenched his square jaw.

Agatha just nodded. "Perhaps."

—from chapter 18, *Simon Snow and the Seventh Oak,*
copyright © 2010 by Gemma T. Leslie

THIRTY-FOUR

They stepped into the elevator, and Cath pressed 9.

"I can't believe we've been arguing for fifteen minutes about whether Simon Snow should reach for his sword or his wand in a lame piece of fanfiction."

And by "I can't believe," Cath meant "I can't believe how happy I am." Wren was coming up to her room, and they were going to work on *Carry On* until Levi was done with work. This was the routine now. Cath liked routines. She felt flushed with serotonin.

Wren shoved her. "It's not lame. It's important."

"Only to me."

"And me. And everyone else who's reading. And besides, you by yourself should be enough. You've been working on this for almost *two years*. This is your life's work."

"God, that's pathetic."

"I meant your life's work so far – and it's extremely impressive. It would be, even if you didn't have thousands of fans. Jandro can't believe how many readers you have. He thinks you should try to monetize it. . . . He doesn't really get the whole fanfiction thing. We tried to watch *The Mage's Heir,* and he fell asleep."

Cath gasped, only partly in jest. "You never told me he was a nonbeliever."

"I wanted you to get to know him first. What about Levi?"

The elevator doors opened, and they got off on Cath's floor. "He loves it," she said. "Simon Snow. Fanfiction, everything. He makes me read my stuff out loud to him."

"Isn't he squicked by the slash?"

"No, he's Zen. Why? Is Jandro?"

"Oh yeah."

"Is he squicked by gay people?"

"No . . . Well, maybe. It's more the idea of straight girls writing about gay boys; he thinks it's deviant."

That made Cath giggle. Then Wren started giggling with her.

"He thinks *I'm* the deviant one," Cath said.

"Shut up." Wren shoved her again.

Cath stopped – there was a boy standing outside her room.

The wrong boy.

"What's up?" Wren stopped, too. "Did you forget something?"

"Cath," Nick said, taking a few steps forward. "Hey. I've been waiting for you."

"Hey," Cath said. "Hey, Nick."

"Hey," he said again.

Cath was still six feet away from her room. She didn't want to come any closer. "What are you doing here?"

Nick's eyebrows were low, and his mouth was open. She could see his tongue sliding along his teeth. "I just wanted to talk to you."

"Is this your library guy?" Wren asked, looking at him like he was a photo on Facebook, not a human being.

"No," Cath said, reacting more to the "your" than to anything else.

Nick glanced at Wren, then decided to ignore her. "Look, Cath—"

"You couldn't just call?" Cath asked.

"I didn't have your cell number. I tried to call your room phone – you're in the student directory – I left a bunch of voice mails."

"We have voice mail?"

The door to her room opened abruptly, and Reagan looked out. "Is this yours?" she asked Cath, nodding at Nick.

"No," Cath said.

"I didn't think so. I told him he had to wait outside."

"You were right," Wren said, not very quietly. "He does look very Old World. . . ."

Reagan and Wren didn't know what happened with Nick, how he'd used Cath. All they knew was that she didn't want to talk about him anymore – and that she refused to go to Love Library. She'd been too embarrassed to tell anyone the details.

Cath didn't feel embarrassed now, now that she was looking right at him. She felt angry. Robbed. She'd written some good stuff with Nick, and now she'd never get it back. If she tried to use any of those lines, any of those jokes, people could say she stole them from him. Like she'd ever steal anything from Nick – except for the paisley scarf he was wearing; she'd always liked that scarf. But Nick could keep his shitty second-person, present-tense. And all his skinny girl characters with nicotine-stained fingers. (Those girls were telling Cath's jokes now; it was infuriating.)

"Look, I just need to talk to you," he said. "It won't take long."

"So talk," Wren said.

"Yeah," Reagan said, leaning against the doorjamb. "Talk."

Nick looked like he was waiting for Cath to bail him out, but she wasn't in the mood. She thought about walking away and leaving him here to deal with Reagan and Wren, who were difficult and unpleasant a lot of the time even if they liked you.

"Go ahead," Cath said. "I'm listening."

"Okay . . ." Nick cleared his throat. "Um. Fine. I came to tell you, to tell Cath" – he looked at her – "that my story was selected for *Prairie Schooner*. That's the university's literary journal," he said to Wren. "It's an incredible honor for an undergraduate."

"Congratulations," Cath said, feeling all used up all over again. Like he was robbing her again, this time at gunpoint.

Nick nodded. "Yeah. Well . . . The faculty adviser, you know, Professor Piper, she, um –" he looked around the hallway, agitated, then gave a little huff – "she knows that you helped me out on my story, and she thought it would be nice if we shared the credit."

"*His* story . . ." Wren looked at Cath.

"Nice?" Cath asked.

"It's a prestigious journal," Nick said. "And it will be a full coauthor credit – we can even do it alphabetically. Your name will come first."

Cath felt someone's hand on her back. "Hey," Levi said, kissing the top of her head. "Got off early. Hey," he said brightly to Nick, holding his arm out and around Cath to shake hands. "I'm Levi."

Nick took his hand, looking confused and hassled. "Nick."

"Nick from the library," Levi said, still cheerful, resting his arm around Cath's shoulders.

Nick looked back at Cath. "So what do you think? Is that cool? Will you tell Professor Piper that it's cool?"

"I don't know," Cath said. "It's just . . ." *Just, just, just.* "After everything, I'm not sure I'm comfortable . . ."

He pressed his navy blue eyes into her. "You've got to say yes, Cath. This is such an opportunity for me. You know how badly I want this."

"Then take it," Cath said quietly. She was trying to pretend that everyone in her whole life wasn't standing right there listening. "You can have it, Nick. You don't have to share it with me."

Nick was pretending, too. "I can't," he said, moving another step closer. "She – Professor Piper – says it runs with both of our names or not at all. Cath. *Please.*"

The hallway had gotten very quiet.

Reagan was looking at Nick like she was already tying him to the railroad tracks.

Wren was looking at him like she was one of the cool girls in his stories. Oozing contempt.

Levi was smiling. Like he'd smiled at those drunk guys at Muggsy's. Before he'd talked Jandro into throwing a punch.

Cath went back to pretending they weren't there. She thought about Nick's story – their story? – about everything she'd poured into it and the chance, now, that she might get something out.

And then she thought about sitting next to Nick in the stacks, trying to get him to let go of the notebook.

Levi squeezed her shoulder.

"I'm sorry," Cath said. "But I don't want any credit. You were right all along. It's your story."

"No," he said, clenching his teeth. "I can't lose this."

"You'll get another opportunity. You're a great writer, Nick," she said, and meant it. "You don't need me."

"*No.* I can't lose this. I already lost my teaching assistantship because of you."

Cath stepped back. Into Levi.

Reagan opened the door wider, and Wren pushed past Nick, pushing Cath into the room. "It was nice to meet you," Levi said, and you'd have to really know Levi to know that he didn't mean it.

Nick held his ground, like he still thought he might talk Cath into helping him.

Reagan kicked the door shut in his face. "Were you really going out with that guy?" she asked before it had quite closed. "Was that your library boyfriend?"

"Writing partner," Cath said, avoiding them all, setting her bag on her desk.

"What a douche," Reagan muttered. "I'm pretty sure my mom has that scarf."

"Did he steal your story?" Wren asked. "The one you were working on together?"

"No. Not exactly." Cath spun around. "It doesn't matter," she said with as much irony as she could. "Okay?"

She looked up at all three faces, all ready to be offended for her, and she realized that it really *didn't* matter. Nick – Nick who couldn't write his own anti-love story without her – was ancient history.

Cath grinned at Levi.

"Are you okay?" he asked, grinning back because he couldn't help it. (Bless him. Bless him to infinity and beyond.)

"I'm great," she said.

Her sister was still sizing Cath up. "Great," Wren said, deciding something. "Okay. Great." Then she turned to Levi and punched his arm. "All right, Lieutenant Starbuck, since you're here, you might as well take me to FarmHouse. And you might as well get us White Chocolate Mochas on the way."

"Might as well leave now," Levi said gamely. "I'm parked in the fire lane."

Cath picked up her bag again.

"And I want you both to know," Levi said, opening the door – Cath peeked out to make sure Nick was gone – "that I know that was a *Battlestar Galactica* reference."

"Yeah, yeah, yeah," Wren said, "you're a first-class geek."

When they got to Jandro's frat house, Levi got out again to help Wren. He only sometimes helped Cath in and out anymore. Usually she was already there before he got a chance. When Wren got out of the truck, Cath reluctantly slid away from the driver's seat and buckled her seat belt.

Levi started the truck and shifted gears without looking at her. He hadn't really looked at her since they'd left her room.

"Are you all right?" she asked.

"Yeah. Just hungry. Are you hungry?" He still didn't look at her.

"Is this about Nick?" she asked. She realized that she was waiting for it to be about Nick.

"No," Levi said. "Should it be? You seemed like you didn't want to talk about him."

"I don't," Cath said.

"Okay. Are you hungry?"

"No. Are you jealous?"

"No." He shook his head, like he was shaking something off; then he turned to her and smiled. "Do you want me to be?" He raised an eyebrow. "I can throw a big tantrum if you like that sort of thing."

"I don't think so," Cath said. "Thanks, though."

"Good. I'm too hungry to rage. Do you mind if we stop somewhere?"

"No," she said. "Or I could make you something if you want. Eggs."

Levi beamed at her. "God, yes. Can I watch?"

Cath smiled. "You're ridiculous."

Levi wanted an omelette. He got the eggs and cheese out of the refrigerator, and Cath found a pan and butter. (This kitchen almost didn't remind Cath of the missing blond girl anymore. That girl had no staying power.)

Cath had just cracked three eggs when Levi tugged on her ponytail. "Hey."

"Yeah?"

"Why doesn't your sister like me?"

"Everyone likes you," Cath said, whisking the eggs with a fork.

"Then how come you only hang out with her when I'm not around?"

Cath glanced back at him. He was leaning against the sink.

"Cheese," she said, nodding at his hands. "Grate." When he just kept looking at her, Cath said, "Maybe I like having you all to myself."

"Maybe . . . ," he said, raking one hand into his hair. "Maybe I embarrass you."

She poured the eggs into the pan and reached for the cheese grater herself. "What am I embarrassed by? Your rangy good looks or your irresistible personality?"

"Alejandro is a Regents Scholar," Levi said softly behind her. "And his family owns half the Sand Hills."

"Wait . . . what?" Cath set everything down and turned back to him. "You really think I'm embarrassed by you?"

Levi smiled gently and shrugged. "I'm not angry, sweetheart."

"No, you're *crazy*. I didn't even know those things about Jandro, and anyway, who cares?" Cath reached up to his chest and clenched her fists in his black sweatshirt. "God. Levi. Look at you . . . you're . . ." She didn't have words for what Levi was. He was a cave painting. He was *The Red Balloon*. She lifted her heels and pulled him forward until his face was so close, she could look at only one of his eyes at a time. "You're *magic*," she said.

Levi's eyes smiled almost shut. She kissed the corner of his mouth, and he moved his face to catch her lips.

When Cath heard the eggs start to snap, she pulled away – but Levi took hold of her waist.

"Why, then?" he asked. "*Doesn't* Wren like me? Do I cramp your style? I can tell you don't want me around when she's there."

Cath pushed against his chest, away, and went back to the stove, quickly grating the cheese over the eggs. "It has nothing to with you."

Levi tried to move into her line of sight, leaning against the counter next to the stove. "How do you figure?"

"It's just . . . nothing, it's weird," she said. "It'd be different if you'd grown up with us, or if you'd met us both at the same time—"

"What would be different?"

Cath shrugged and scraped at the omelette with a wooden spatula. "Then I would know that you had enough information to choose me."

Levi leaned over the stove, trying again to catch her eye.

"Get back," Cath said, "you're going to burn yourself."

He backed up, but only few inches. "Of course I chose you."

"But you didn't know Wren."

"Cath . . ."

She wished there was more to do with omelettes than watch them. "I know you think she's pretty—"

"You know that because I think *you're* pretty."

"You said she was hot."

"When?"

"When you met her." Levi looked confused for a second, one eyebrow arched beautifully. "You called her Superman," Cath said.

"*Cather,*" he said, remembering, "I was trying to get *your* attention. I was trying to say that you were hot without actually saying it."

"Well, it sucked."

"I'm sorry." He reached out for her waist again. She kept looking down at the eggs.

"I know that you like me," she said.

"You know that I love you."

Cath kept staring at the pan. "But she's a lot like me. Some of our best friends couldn't even tell us apart. And then, when they could, it would be because Wren was the better one. Because she talked more or smiled more – or just flat-out looked better."

"I can tell you apart just fine."

"Long hair. Glasses."

"Cath . . . come on, look at me." He pulled at her belt loops, and she flipped the omelette before she let herself turn toward him. "I can tell you apart," he said.

"We sound the same. We kind of talk the same. We have all the same gestures."

"True," he said, nodding, holding her chin up, "but it's almost like that makes your differences more dramatic."

"What do you mean?"

"It means, sometimes your sister will say something, and it will sort of shock me to hear her saying it with your voice."

Cath looked up to his eyes, unsure. They were big and earnest. "Like what?"

"I can't think of anything specific," he said. "It's like . . . she smiles more than you. But she's harder somehow. Closed up."

"I'm the one who never leaves my room."

"I'm not explaining this right. . . . I *like* Wren," he said, "what I know of her. But she's more . . . forceful than you."

"Confident."

"Partly. Maybe. More like – she takes what she wants from a situation."

"There's nothing wrong with that."

"No, I know," Levi said. "But it's not you. You don't push through every moment. You pay attention. You take everything in. I like that about you – I like that better."

Cath closed her eyes and felt tears catch on her cheeks.

"I like your glasses," he said. "I like your Simon Snow T-shirts. I like that you don't smile at everyone, because then, when you smile at me. . . . *Cather*." He kissed her mouth. "Look at me."

She did.

"I choose you over everyone."

Cath took a painful breath and reached up with one hand to touch his chin. "I love you," she said. "Levi."

Levi's face broke open just before he kissed her.

He pulled away again a few seconds later. . . .

"Say it again."

She had to make him another omelette.

"Do you know what the most disappointing thing is about being a magician?"

Penelope shook her head and rolled her eyes, a combination she'd gotten terribly good at over the years. "Don't be silly, Simon. There's nothing disappointing about magic."

"There is," he argued, only partly just to tease her. "I always figured we'd learn a way to fly by now."

"Oh, pish," Penelope said. "Anyone can fly. Anyone with a friend."

She held her ringed hand out to him and grinned – *"Up, up and away!"*

Simon felt the steps drift away from him and laughed his way through a slow somersault. When he was upright again, he leveled his wand at Penelope.

—from chapter 11, *Simon Snow and the Five Blades,*

copyright © 2008 by Gemma T. Leslie

THIRTY-FIVE

"Look at them," Reagan said, shaking her head fondly. "They're all grown up."

Cath turned to the cereal bar and watched two very hungover freshmen fumble with the scoops.

"I can still remember the night they came home with their first My Little Pony tattoos," Reagan said.

"And the morning that we noticed those tattoos were infected," Cath added, drinking her tomato juice. That's something Cath would miss about the dorms. Four different kinds of juice on tap, including tomato – where else could you get tomato juice? Reagan hated watching her drink it. "It's like you're drinking blood," Reagan would say, "if blood had the consistency of gravy."

Reagan was still gazing at the hungover girls. "I wonder how many familiar faces we'll see next year. Every year it's a new batch, and most of them don't come back to the dorms for a second tour."

"Next year," Cath said, "I won't make the mistake of getting so attached."

Reagan snorted. "We need to turn in our housing forms if we want the same room next year."

Cath set down her juice glass. "Wait . . . Are you saying you want to live with me again?"

"Eff yeah, you're never even home. It's like I've finally got a room to myself."

Cath smiled. Then took another long pull of tomato juice. "Well . . . I'll think about it. Do you have any more hot ex-boyfriends?"

Wren was right.

She'd been on Cath to post a chapter of *Carry On, Simon* every single night. "Otherwise you're never going to beat *The Eighth Dance*."

They were going to go to the midnight release party at the Bookworm, back in Omaha. Levi wanted to go, too.

"Are we gonna dress up in costumes?" he'd asked the other night, up in his room.

"We haven't done costumes since junior high." Cath was sitting on the love seat with her laptop. She could write with him in the room now; she was so focused on *Carry On*, she could have written in a room full of circus animals.

"Damn," he said, "I wanted to do costumes."

"Who do you want to go as?"

"The Mage. Or maybe one of the vampires – Count Vidalia. Or Baz. Would that make you wild with desire?"

"I'm already wild with desire."

"She said from across the room."

"Sorry," Cath said, rubbing her eyes. Levi had been needling her all night. Teasing her. Trying to get her to come out of her head and play. "I just need to finish this chapter if I want Wren to read it before she falls asleep."

Cath was so close to the end of *Carry On* that every chapter felt important. If she wrote something stupid now, she wouldn't be able to fix it or rein it in later. There was no room left for filler;

every chapter meant the resolution of a plot line or a character's last big scene. She wanted all of them to get the ending they deserved. Not just Baz and Simon and Agatha and Penelope, but all the other characters, too – Declan the reluctant vampire hunter, Eb the goatherd, Professor Benedict, Coach Mac. . . .

Cath was trying not to pay attention to her hit counts – that just added more pressure – but she knew they were off the chart. In the tens of thousands. She was getting so many comments that Wren had taken to handling them for her, using Cath's profile to thank people and answer basic questions.

Cath was keeping up in her classes, but just barely. All her other assignments felt like the hoops she had to jump through to get to Simon and Baz.

One thing about writing this much . . . her brain never really shifted out of the World of Mages. When she sat down to write, she didn't have to wade back into the story slowly, waiting to get used to the temperature. She was just there, all the time. All day. Real life was something happening in her peripheral vision.

Her laptop snapped shut, and Cath pulled back her fingers just in time. She hadn't even noticed Levi moving over to the love seat. He took her computer and gingerly set it on the floor. "Commercial break."

"Books don't have commercials."

"I'm not much of a book person," he said, pulling her into his lap. "Intermission, then?"

Cath climbed onto him reluctantly, still thinking about the last thing she'd typed, not sure she wanted to leave it behind. "Books don't have intermissions either."

"What do they have?"

"Endings."

His hands were on her hips. "You'll get there," he said, nosing at the collar of her T-shirt. His hair tickled her chin, and it broke the spell in Cath's head. Or cast a new one.

"Okay," she sighed, kissing his head and rocking into his stomach. "Okay. Intermission."

"You've got to give Penelope her own chapter," Wren said. They were walking back to the dorms, sloshing through puddles. Wren had yellow rubber boots, and she kept jumping into puddles, soaking Cath's legs and ankles.

"Where would I put it?" Cath puffed. The snow was melting, but she could still see her breath. "I should have written it two weeks ago. Now it'll seem forced. . . . This is why real authors wait until they've got a whole book before they show anybody; I'd kill to go back to the beginning and rewrite."

"You're a real author," Wren said, splashing. "You're like Dickens. He wrote in installments, too."

"I'm going to destroy those boots."

"Jealous." Wren stepped in another puddle.

"I'm not jealous. They're gross. I bet they make your feet sweat."

"Who cares, nobody can tell."

"I'll be able to tell when you get back to my room and take them off. They're disgusting."

"Hey," Wren said, "I sort of want to talk to you about that."

"What?"

"Your room. Rooms. Roommates . . . I was thinking that next year we could room together. We could live in Pound, if you want; I don't care."

Cath stopped and turned to her sister. Wren kept walking for a second before she noticed and stopped, too.

"You want to be roommates?" Cath asked.

Wren was nervous. She shrugged. "Yeah. If you want to. If you're not still mad about . . . everything."

"I'm not mad," Cath said. She remembered the day last summer when Wren told her she didn't want to live together. Cath had never felt so betrayed. Almost never. "I'm not mad," she said again, this time really meaning it.

Wren's lips quirked up, and she stamped a puddle between them. "Good."

"But I can't," Cath said.

Wren's face fell. "What do you mean?"

"Well, I already told Reagan I'd live with her again."

"But Reagan hates you."

"What? No, she doesn't. Why would you say that?"

"She's so mean to you."

"That's just her way. I think I'm her best girl friend, actually."

"Oh," Wren said. She looked small and wet. Cath wasn't sure what to say. . . .

"You're *my* best friend," Cath said awkwardly. "You know. Built-in. For life."

Wren nodded. "Yeah . . . No, it's okay. I should have thought of that, of you guys living together again." She started walking and Cath followed.

"What about Courtney?"

"She's moving into the Delta Gamma house."

"Oh," Cath said. "I forgot she was a pledge."

"But that's not why I asked you," Wren said, like it was important to say so.

"You should move to Pound. You could live on our floor – I'm serious."

Wren smiled and squared her shoulders, already recovering herself. "Yeah," she said. "Okay. Why not? It's closer to campus."

Cath leapt into the next big puddle, soaking Wren up to her thighs. Wren jumped and screamed, and it was totally worth it. Cath's feet were already soaked.

"Morgan's grace, Simon – slow down." Penelope held an arm out in front of his chest and glanced around the weirdly lit courtyard. "There's more than one way through a flaming gate."

—from chapter 11, *Simon Snow and the Third Gate*,

copyright © 2004 by Gemma T. Leslie

THIRTY-SIX

Cath had been writing for four hours, and when she heard someone knocking at her door, it felt like she was standing at the bottom of a lake, looking up at the sun.

It was Levi.

"Hey," she said, putting on her glasses. "Why didn't you text? I would have come down."

"I did," he said, kissing her forehead. She took her phone out of her pocket. She'd missed two texts and a call. Her ringer was turned off.

"Sorry," she said, shaking her head. "Let me just pack up."

Levi fell onto her bed and watched. Seeing him there, leaning against the wall, brought back so many memories and so much tenderness, she climbed onto the bed and started kissing his face all over.

He grinned and draped his long arms around her. "Do you have much writing to do?"

"Yeah," she said, rubbing her chin into his. " 'Miles to go before I sleep.' "

"Have you shown anything to your professor yet?"

Cath had just started to bite his chin and she pulled away, looking at the teeth marks. "What do you mean?"

"Have you been turning stuff in piece by piece, or are you

waiting until the whole story is done?"

"I'm . . . I've been working on *Carry On.*"

"No, I know," he said, smiling and smoothing his hand over her hair. "But I was wondering about your Fiction-Writing project. I want you to read it to me when you're done."

Cath sat back on the bed. Levi's hands didn't leave her head and her hip. "I'm . . . I'm not doing that," she said.

"You don't want to read it to me? Is it too personal or something?"

"No. I'm not. I'm just . . . I'm not going to do it."

Levi's smile faded. He still didn't understand.

"I'm not writing it," she said. "It was a mistake to say that I would."

His hands tightened on her. "No, it wasn't. What do you mean? You haven't started?"

Cath sat back farther, stepping off the bed and going to pack her laptop. "I was wrong when I told my professor I could do it – I can't. I don't have an idea, and it's just too much. I'm not sure I'm even going to finish *Carry On.*"

"Of course you'll finish."

She looked up at him sharply. "I've only got nine days left."

Levi still seemed confused. And maybe a little hurt. "You've got twelve days left until the end of the semester. And about fourteen before I go back to Arnold, but as far as I can tell, you've got the rest of your life to finish *Carry On.*"

Cath felt her face go hard. "You don't understand," she said. "At all."

"So explain it to me."

"*Simon Snow and the Eighth Dance* comes out in *nine days.*"

Levi shrugged. "So?"

"So I've been working two years toward this."

"Toward finishing *Carry On*?"

"Yes. And I have to finish before the series ends."

"Why? Did Gemma Leslie challenge you to a race?"

Cath jammed the knotted power cord into her bag. "You don't understand."

Levi sighed harshly and ran his fingers through his hair. "You're right. I don't."

Cath's hands were trembling as she pushed them through the arms of her jacket, a thick cable-knit sweater lined with fleece.

"I don't understand how you could throw this class away *twice*," Levi said, frowning and flustered. "I have to fight for every grade I get – I'd kill for a second chance at most of my classes. And you're just walking away from this assignment because you don't feel like it, because you've got this arbitrary deadline, and it's all you can see."

"I don't want to talk about this," she said.

"You don't want to talk at all."

"You're right. I don't have time right now to argue with you."

It was the wrong thing to say. Levi looked up at her, stricken. Cath fumbled for something else to say, but everything in her reach was wrong. "Maybe I should just stay here tonight."

His eyes swept over her, more coolly than she would have thought possible. There were two deep lines between his eyebrows.

"Right," he said, standing up. "See you in nine days."

He was out the door before she could stutter out, "What?"

Cath wasn't trying to pick a nine-day fight; she'd just wanted to escape from tonight – she didn't have time to feel guilty about Fiction-Writing. Even thinking about that stupid story made Cath feel clawed up and open.

She lay down on her bed and started to cry. Her pillow didn't smell like Levi. It didn't smell like either of them.

He didn't understand.

When the last Simon Snow book came out, it was over.

Everything. All these years of imagining and reimagining. Gemma T. Leslie would get the last word, and that would be it; everything Cath had built in the last two years would become alternate universe. Officially noncompliant . . .

The thought made her giggle wetly, pathetically, into her pillow.

As if beating GTL to the punch made any difference.

As if Cath could actually make Baz and Simon live happily ever after just by saying it was so. *Sorry, Gemma, I appreciate what you've done here, but I think we can all agree that it was supposed to end like this.*

It wasn't a race. Gemma T. Leslie didn't even know Cath existed. Thank God.

And yet . . . when Cath closed her eyes, all she could see was Baz and Simon.

All she could hear was them talking in her head. They were hers, the way they'd always been hers. They loved each other because she believed they did. They needed her to fix everything for them. They needed her to carry them through.

Baz and Simon in her head. Levi in her stomach.

Levi somewhere, gone.

In nine days, it would be over. In twelve days, Cath wouldn't be a freshman anymore. And in fourteen . . .

God, she was an idiot.

Was she always going to be this stupid? Her whole miserable life?

Cath cried until it felt pointless, then stumbled off the bed to get a drink of water. When she opened her door, Levi was sitting in the hallway, his legs bent in front of him, hunched forward on his knees. He looked up when she stepped out.

"I'm such an idiot," he said.

Cath fell between his knees and hugged him.

"I can't believe I said that," he said. "I can't even go nine *hours* without seeing you."

"No, you're right," Cath said. "I've been acting crazy. This whole thing is crazy. It isn't even real."

"That's not what I meant — it *is* real. You have to finish."

"Yeah," she said, kissing his chin, trying to remember where she'd left off. "But not today. You were right. There's time. They'll wait for me." She pushed her hands inside his jacket.

He held her by her shoulders. "You do what you have to," he said. "Just let me be there. For the next two weeks, okay?"

She nodded. Fourteen days. With Levi. And then curtains closed on this year.

"Maybe fighting him isn't the answer," Simon said.

"What?" Baz was leaning against a tree, trying to catch his breath. His hair was hanging in slimy tendrils, and his face was smeared with muck and blood. Simon probably looked even worse. "You're not giving up now," Baz said, reaching for Simon's chest and pulling him forward, fiercely, by the buckled straps of his cape. "I won't let you."

"I'm not giving up," Simon said. "I just . . . Maybe fighting isn't the answer. It wasn't the answer with you."

Baz arched an elegant brow. "Are you going to snog the Humdrum – is that your plan? Because he's eleven. And he looks just like you. That's both vain and deviant, Snow, even for you."

Simon managed a laugh and raised a hand to the back of Baz's neck, holding him firmly. "I don't know what I'm going to do. But I'm done fighting, Baz. If we go on like this, there won't be anything left to fight for."

—from *Carry On, Simon,* posted April 2012
by FanFixx.net author *Magicath*

THIRTY-SEVEN

"Cather."

"Mmmm."

"Hey. Wake up."

"No."

"Yes."

"Why?"

"I have to go to work. If we don't leave soon, I'll be late."

Cath opened her eyes. Levi had already showered and put on his gothy Starbucks clothes. He smelled like an actual Irish spring.

"Can I stay?" she asked.

"Here?"

"Yeah."

"You'll be stuck here all day."

"I like here. And anyway, I'm just writing."

He grinned. "Okay – sure. I'll bring back dinner. . . . You write all the words," he said, kissing her forehead. "Give Simon and Baz my best."

She thought she might go back to sleep, but she couldn't. She got up and took a shower (now she smelled like Levi), glad not to see anyone else in the hall. At least one of his roommates was home. She could hear music.

Cath climbed back to Levi's room. It had been warm last night, and they'd fallen asleep with the windows open. But the weather had shifted – it was too cold in here now, especially for someone with wet hair. She grabbed her laptop and crawled under his quilt, doubling it up on top of her; she didn't want to close the windows.

She pressed the Power button and waited for her computer to wake up. Then she opened a Word document and watched the cursor blink at her – she could see her face in the blank screen. Ten thousand words, and none of them had to be good; only one other person would ever read them. It didn't even matter where Cath started, as long she finished. She started typing. . . .

I sat on the back steps.

No . . .

She sat on the back steps.

Every word felt heavy and hurt, like Cath was chipping them one by one out of her stomach.

A plane flew overhead, and that was wrong, all wrong, and her sister knew it, too, because she squeezed her hand like they'd both disappear if she didn't.

This wasn't good, but it was something. Cath could always change it later. That was the beauty in stacking up words – they got cheaper, the more you had of them. It would feel good to come back and cut this when she'd worked her way to something better.

The plane was flying so low, moving so sluggishly through the sky, you'd think it was just choosing the perfect rooftop to land on. They could hear the engine; it sounded closer than the voices shouting inside the house. Her sister reached up like she might touch it. Like she might grab on.

The girl squeezed her sister's other hand, trying to anchor her to the steps. If you leave, *she thought,* I'm going with you.

Sometimes writing is running downhill, your fingers jerking behind you on the keyboard the way your legs do when they can't quite keep up with gravity.

Cath fell and fell, leaving a trail of messy words and bad similes behind her. Sometimes her chin was trembling. Sometimes she wiped her eyes on her sweater.

When she took a break, she was starving, and she had to pee so bad, she barely made it down to the third-floor bathroom. She found a protein bar in Levi's backpack, climbed back into his bed, then kept writing until she heard him running up the stairs.

She closed the laptop before the door opened — and the sight of him smiling made her eyes burn right down to her throat.

"Stop *bouncing*," Wren snapped. "You're making us look like nerds."

"Right," Reagan said. "That's what's making us look like nerds. The bouncing."

Levi smiled down at Cath. "Sorry. The atmosphere is getting to me." He was wearing her red *CARRY ON* T-shirt over a long-sleeved black T-shirt, and for some reason, the sight of Baz and Simon facing off across his chest was disturbingly hot.

"S'okay," she said. The atmosphere was getting to her, too. They'd been waiting in line for more than two hours. The bookstore was playing the Simon Snow movie soundtracks, and there were people everywhere. Cath recognized a few of them from past midnight releases; it was like they were all part of a club that met every couple years.

11:58.

The booksellers started setting out big boxes of books — special boxes, dark blue with gold stars. The manager of the store was wearing a cape and an all-wrong pointed witch's hat. (Nobody at

Watford wore pointy hats.) She stood on a chair and tapped one of the cash registers with a magic wand that looked like something Tinker Bell would carry. Cath rolled her eyes.

"Spare me the theater," Reagan said. "I've got a final tomorrow."

Levi was bouncing again.

The manager rang up the first person in line with great ceremony, and everyone in the store started applauding. The line jerked forward – and a few minutes later, Cath was there at the register, and the clerk was handing her a book that was at least three inches thick. The dust jacket felt like velvet.

Cath stepped away from the register, trying to get out of the way, clutching the book with both hands. There was an illustration of Simon on the front, holding up the Sword of Mages under a sky full of stars.

"Are you okay?" she heard someone – Levi? – ask. "Hey . . . are you crying?"

Cath ran her fingers along the cover, over the raised gold type.

Then someone else ran right into her, pushing the book into Cath's chest. Pushing two books into her chest. Cath looked up just as Wren threw an arm around her.

"They're both crying," Cath heard Reagan say. "I can't even watch."

Cath freed an arm to wrap around her sister. "I can't believe it's really over," she whispered.

Wren held her tight and shook her head. She really was crying, too. "Don't be so melodramatic, Cath," Wren laughed hoarsely. "It's never over. . . . It's *Simon*."

Simon stepped toward the Humdrum. He'd never been this close. The heat and the pull were almost too much for him; he felt like the Humdrum would suck his heart through his chest, his thoughts from his head.

"I created you with my hunger," Simon said. "With my need for magic."

"With your capacity," it said.

Simon shrugged, a Herculean effort in the presence and pressure of the Humdrum.

Simon had spent his whole life, well, the last eight years of it, trying to become more powerful, trying to live up to his destiny – trying to become the sort of magician, maybe the only magician, who could defeat the Insidious Humdrum.

And all he'd ever done was stoke the Humdrum's need.

Simon took the last step forward.

"I'm not hungry anymore."

—from chapter 27, *Simon Snow and the Eighth Dance,*
copyright © 2012 by Gemma T. Leslie

THIRTY-EIGHT

It was her last Friday night in Pound Hall.

There was a boy in her room.

In Cath's bed, taking up way more than his fair share of space, and eating the rest of her peanut butter.

He pulled the spoon out of his mouth. "Did you turn it in?"

"Slid it under her door. I'll e-mail it, too, just in case."

"Are you gonna read it to me?"

"Pfft." Cath got *The Eighth Dance* out of her bag and dropped it onto the bed. "Priorities," she said. "Make room."

Levi scrunched his nose and tried to suck the peanut butter off his teeth.

Cath shoved his shoulder – *"Make room"* – and he grinned, leaning back against her pillow and patting the bed between his bent legs. She climbed between his knees, and he put his arms around her, pulling her in close. She felt his chin on the back of her head.

"Are you getting peanut butter in my hair?"

"It's preventative. When I get gum in your hair later, it won't stick."

She opened the book and tried to find their place. It was massive. They'd been reading for two days, taking breaks between studying and finals, and they still had four hundred pages left. They had one weekend left together, and Cath was going to read until she ran out of air.

"I can't believe I haven't been spoiled yet," she said.

"I was planning to despoil you later," Levi said. "But if you want, we can do that first."

"I had lunch with Wren today, and she almost spoiled me four different times. I don't dare get on the Internet – people are blabbing all over FanFixx."

"I made a sign to wear on my apron that says, DON'T TELL ME WHAT HAPPENS TO SIMON SNOW."

"Maybe I should write that on my forehead," Cath said.

"I could make that part of the despoiling. . . ."

"Do you remember where we left off? I dropped the bookmark."

"Page three nineteen. The Humdrum had turned the merwolves against the school, and they were crawling around, dragging their fins, getting everything wet and gnashing their teeth at little kids, and then Penelope Bunce, the hero of our story, cast a spell that made the clouds rain silver—"

"I think Baz cast that spell."

"Yeah, but Penelope watched. She was instrumental."

"Page three nineteen," Cath said. "Are you ready?"

Levi jostled her around, kissed her neck a few times, then bit it, pinched Cath between his knees and squeezed her middle. "Ready."

Cath imagined his eyes closing – then cleared her throat.

The silver bounced like mercury off Simon's skin, but it was drawn sickly into the merwolf's fur. Steely grey lines appeared in the beast's yellow eyes, and it went limp, sloshing to the ground.

Simon caught his breath and looked around the lawn. All the merwolves had collapsed, and Penelope was herding the younger kids back into the relative safety of the fortress.

Basil strode across the lawn toward Simon, brushing the silver from his black cloak. He wasn't even bothering to hide his fangs; Simon could see them from here.

Simon adjusted his grip on the Sword of Mages and held it up in warning.

Baz stopped in front of him and sighed. "Give it a rest, Snow."

Simon held the sword higher.

"Do you really think I want to fight you?" Baz asked. "Now?"

"Why should today be any different from every other day of our lives?"

"Because today we're at war. And we're losing. *You're* losing . . . for once. And it isn't nearly as satisfying as I always thought it would be."

Simon wanted to argue – to say that he wasn't losing, that he couldn't afford to lose this fight – but he didn't have the heart for it. He was afraid, terrified, that Baz was right. "What do you want, Baz?" he asked wearily, letting the sword fall to his side.

"I want to help you."

Simon laughed and wiped his face on his sleeve. It left streaks of blood and silver. "Really? You'll excuse me, I hope, if I don't take you at your word, given the last eight years of you trying to kill me, et cetera."

"Don't you think I would have killed you by now if I really wanted to?" Baz raised a dark eyebrow. "I'm not that ineffectual, you know. I mostly just wanted to make you miserable . . . and to steal your girlfriend."

Simon's fingers tensed on the hilt of his sword. Baz took a step closer.

"Snow, if you lose this, we all lose. I may want a world without you – and a world without your tyrant of a father. But I don't want a world without magic. If the Humdrum wins . . ."

Simon studied Baz's pale, grave face and his smoldering grey eyes. There were times when Simon thought he knew those eyes better than his own –

Levi giggled.

"Shhh," Cath said. "I can't believe this is happening. . . ."

– times when he thought he could read his enemy's face better than anyone else's. Better even than Agatha's.

"Let me help you," Baz said. There was something Simon didn't recognize in his voice. Sincerity, maybe. Vulnerability.

Simon made up his mind quickly. (The only way he ever did.) He nodded once and sheathed the Sword of Mages. Then he wiped his hand on his jeans and held it out before him.

Baz locked on to Simon's gaze as ferociously as ever, and Simon wondered whether there was too much animosity – too much history – between them ever to breach. Too much to set aside or get over.

All the curses.

All the spells.

All the times they'd fallen to the ground, fists and wands swinging, grabbing at each other's throats . . .

And then Baz took his hand.

The two magicians, young men now, shook hands and shared a moment that held nothing more – for what *could* be more? – than understanding.

"What about Agatha?" Simon asked when the moment had passed, when their hands dropped again to their sides.

Baz grinned and started walking up the steep hill to the castle.

"Don't be a fool, Snow. I'm never giving up on Agatha."

The problem with playing hide-and-seek with your sister is that sometimes she gets bored and stops looking for you.

And there you are – under the couch, in the closet, wedged behind the lilac tree – and you don't want to give up, because maybe she's just biding her time. But maybe she's wandered off. . . .

Maybe she's downstairs watching TV and eating the rest of the Pringles.

You wait. You wait until you forget that you're waiting, until you forget that there's anything to you beyond stillness and quiet; an ant crawls over your knee, and you don't flinch. And it doesn't matter now whether she's coming for you – the hiding is enough. (You win when no one finds you, even if they're not looking.)

When you break from behind the tree, it's because you want to. It's the first breath after a long dive. Branches snap under your feet, and the world is hotter and brighter. *Ready or not, here I come.*

Here I come, ready or not.

—from "Left" by Cather Avery, winner of the
Underclassmen Prize, *Prairie Schooner,* Fall 2012

FANGIRL FAQ WITH RAINBOW ROWELL

Cath spends most of us the book working on an epic piece of fanfiction, *Carry On, Simon* – does she ever finish? And does she kill Baz?

Yes. She absolutely finishes – and then immediately starts a new Simon/Baz fic.

And no! She doesn't kill Baz! No one is allowed to kill Baz on my watch. BAZ IS FOREVER.

When I was writing *Fangirl,* I never even considered that Cath might walk away from fandom or fanfiction. The question for me was whether she would expand her world. Would she make room for new people? Would she try writing something completely original? Would she find the courage to take a few risks?

I think Cath's fanfiction epiphany is that she doesn't *have* to choose. She doesn't have to give up *Carry On* to write original stories. She doesn't have to let go of her family to make room for Levi and Reagan.

So you don't see her growing out of fandom, like Wren did?

No, I don't. (And even Wren hasn't really grown out of fandom.) But I do see Cath *growing*.

That's what your first year of university is all about – finding a way to reconcile your life as a child with your future as an adult. It's not like you drop everything and everybody you love and replace them; but your relationships and priorities change. They have to.

Levi is the first person Cath meets at school. (She thinks he's her roommate!) Levi is such a specific character, he definitely didn't come from the Romantic Hero Factory — did you base him on someone you know?

Not exactly. I almost never take people I know and drop them into my books. But I will steal certain qualities.

With Levi, it was his sunniness and affability. I've had friends who couldn't help but try to charm every single person they met — man, woman and child. And whenever I was with those friends, both guys, I would react by getting crabby and misanthropic, just to balance them out. When Cath tells Levi to put his charm away before it gets all over everything — that's something I've said to a friend before.

Also, like Levi, a number of people in my life have reading issues.

When I worked in advertising, my creative partner was one of the smartest, most artistic people I've ever met — and a great writer. But he would never read my stuff.

Our job was to brainstorm advertising campaigns together. We'd both come up with ideas and write headlines, then I'd write the copy — and he wouldn't read it. Sometimes he'd ask me to read my copy to him, which I found vaguely insulting. *"Read it yourself, it's not that long!"*

I think I was unkind to him for a long time, even after he explained to me that he couldn't stay focused on more than a few sentences of printed words at a time . . . I'm such a reader, it didn't seem possible to me that someone who was so eloquent and who could write beautiful headlines and commercials wouldn't be able to read a few pages of copy.

The more we worked together, the more I realized he was telling the truth. It opened my mind to how different we all are. I think I grew up equating bookishness with intelligence – thinking that words and stories always took the same path into (and out of) people's brains.

Now I know that's so wrong!

This is one of the reasons I never judge or tease people about bad spelling – or things like confusing "your" and "you're." It's thoughts and ideas that are important. I hate to think that people might be afraid to say something beautiful just because they're worried about apostrophes.

Does Levi have a last name? Did we miss it?

He does! Well, he does now. After the book came out in the U.S., so many people asked about his last name that I gave him one.

All the characters in the book who have last names are named after buildings on the University of Nebraska-Lincoln campus. (Cather, Avery, Abel, Piper, Manter.)

Because Levi is ambassador of East Campus, I named him after a building there – Levi *Stewart*, inspired by Stewart Seed Laboratory.

You said you don't usually base characters on real people – does that include yourself? Do you see yourself in Cath?

Well, there's a lot of me in Cath. I was terrified to leave home for college. I had decided not to, actually, then a friend from high school said she'd be my roommate. Cath's social anxiety, her fear of change, her desire to escape into fiction – those are all mine.

And of all my characters, Cath is closest to who I am as a writer. We both love to write dialogue. We both worry that we won't have anything new to say. And we both crave collaboration.

Are you a fangirl like Cath?

Maybe not just like Cath. But yeah, definitely, I'd call myself a fangirl. I've always had extreme feelings about pop culture. If I like something, I probably love it — and if I love it, I can't get enough.

And I've always used the things I love to identify myself. Like, "I love The Beatles. This is an important part of who I am."

The first thing I was obsessively fannish about was *Star Wars*. I lived inside the *Star Wars* universe during grade school. My friend and I used to make up adventures. She'd get to be Princess Leia — because she had dark hair and her own toy lightsaber. And I'd be her cousin — the lesser Princess Leah.

As I got older it was the *X-Men*, *Beauty and the Beast*, *Alice in Wonderland*, Wham!, *Star Wars* again, *Dawson's Creek*, *Harry Potter*, *Sherlock* . . .

I sort of missed the beginning of Internet fandom because it happened when I was having my kids. But I feel like I'm making up for lost time now.

This book was definitely inspired by the time I spent as an adult reading Harry Potter fanfiction. I kept thinking about how different my teen years would have been if I'd had access to fanfiction and to the community of fandom.

Would you mind if people wrote *Fangirl* fanfiction? Or do you side with Cath's Professor Piper, who calls it stealing?

Oh, people *do* write *Fangirl* fanfiction, and I think it's great. It's mind-blowing, actually, to think that I've made something that's inspired people to tell their own stories or make their own art.

I don't read the fanfiction because I'm not quite done with these characters, and I don't want to pollute my headcanon. But I love looking at the fan art. I have fan art up all over my office. It's one of the most exciting things that's happened to me as an author – to see other people bring my characters to life. (You can check out fan art on my Pinterest or Tumblr profiles. I'm "rainbowrowell.")

BONUS SNOW!

" Other students went home for the summer. Simon just went to Lancashire.

He'd spend the summer in whatever care home he was assigned to. It was too much to hope for a room to himself, but he took some solace in the fact that even the worst of the summer orphans, castoffs and ne'er-do-wells were better roommates than Baz. At least they didn't hate Simon *personally*.

He only had to get through another few summers like this. After fifth year, students could stay at Watford all summer long if they liked. Maybe the Mage would make an exception for Simon after fourth year. *Imagine — three months at Watford without Baz.*

Simon got on the bus that would take him to the train that would dump him off at another bus headed for his summer assignment.

He looked back once at the wide green lawns and weathered fortress behind him . . .

The Watford School of Magicks was the only place he'd ever thought of as home. **"**

—Chapter 21, *Simon Snow and the Second Serpent,* copyright Gemma T. Leslie, 2003

" Watford was best in September.

When the days were long, and the football pitch was green.

If Simon had time between classes or before dinner, he'd dump his books at the side of the pitch and join the game that never seemed to end, not until the first snow, anyway.

Penelope would sit at the sidelines and read while he played. It was a shame that Penelope didn't like football. She was such a good mate in every other way, smart and funny and brave as a dragon.

She'd make a great boy . . . if she wasn't such a girl. **"**

—Chapter 6, *Simon Snow and the Third Gate*, copyright Gemma T. Leslie, 2004

"" "Do you know, that when we were kids, they'd sing us songs about you?"

"They did not," Simon said, throwing an apple at Baz.

Baz caught it and took a bite. "They did," he said with his mouth full. *"Comes, he comes, the Mage's Heir, with blade of fire and golden hair."*

Baz had a steady, warm singing voice.

"How did they know I was coming?" Simon muttered. "*I* didn't even know I was coming."

> *"Comes, he comes, the Mage's Heir,*
> *And should evil meet him there,*
> *The blood will flow, the world will know,*
> *Our just and handsome,*
> *Blue-eyed, winsome,*
> *Lovely, blushing Mage's Heir."*

"You made that last part up," Simon said, feeling his cheeks burn.

Baz laughed and took another bite. "I made that last part up." **""**

—from *Carry On, Simon,* **posted June 2011 by FanFixx.net author** *Magicath*

ACKNOWLEDGMENTS

Thank you, thank you, thank you to everyone who was good to me while I wrote this book — but especially to:

Bethany, who is an excellent, tireless beta and a marvellous friend — and who just goes around making life and the Internet better.

Forest, who talks about these characters like they're real people; and Jade, who never gets tired of them.

My editor, Sara, who is fucking awesome.

And everyone at St. Martin's Press who's worked so hard to help my books find readers — and to help readers find my books.

Thank you to Christopher, who is ten pounds of agent in a five-pound sack.

To Rosey and Laddie, who make me happy.

And to Kai, who tells me to write all the words.

Also: I decided to write this book after reading a lot (I mean, *a lot*) of fanfiction. Reading fic was a transformative experience for me — it changed the way I think about writing and storytelling, and helped me more deeply understand my own intense relationships with fictional worlds and characters. So thank *you* for writing it.

MYKINDABOOK.COM

LOVE BOOKS?
JOIN MYKINDABOOK.COM
YOUR KINDA BOOK CLUB

READ BOOK EXTRACTS

RECOMMENDED READS

BE A PART OF THE MKB CREW

WIN STUFF

BUILD A PROFILE

GET CREATIVE

CHAT TO OTHER READERS

CHAT TO AUTHORS